Palm Beach
Busybodies

Donna Drejza

For all of my lucky angels.

To
Sherri,
With many Thanks,
Donna Dreyya

Introduction

This book is a work of fiction. The names, characters, places and incidents either are the product of the author's imagination or are used fictitiously. Any resemblance to actual persons, living or dead, events or locales is entirely coincidental.

If I have mentioned an actual person, place or thing, then it means I recommend it with my whole heart. Plus, I have no idea how to reach the people who make Veuve Clicquot, or how to call the beloved Phil Collins.

My style may be different from others, with more details and sensory inputs. I loved writing and "researching" the book. Many a night was spent alone writing, but I never felt lonely because I was surrounded by my book characters. It is my intention for readers to get into the scenes and live the book: Drink the wine, eat the oysters, play the songs, watch the movies, and kiss the man.

I hope you enjoy the adventure with all of your senses. Like life, there is no need to race to the end of this vacation in your head. The sequel will pick up where we left off in Nantucket.

Acknowledgements

Mom, Dad, Mike, Terri and Jeff; editor, Elizabeth A. White, C. Edward Marr, Chris Henderson, James Larman, Hans Young, Michael Fox Jones, Dr. Sherman, Richard Waryn, Wayne Cowan, Betty Reisenfeld, David Aldo, Jay Pearson, Phil Leverrier, James Weiner, Angela Casey, M. Bailey, Robert Stone, Mel Cabot, Jennifer Off, Ursula, Stella, Maura Walsh and Reno; the PB police, fire and Rescue; the town and county of Palm Beach. And especially, my secret angels.

1

April 20, 2014

Just as I spy the topless Russian's personnel file, curiosity gets the better of me. This does not fall into the category of snooping I think as I slide the manila folder to the edge of the desk. Then suddenly curiosity's helper, gravity, talks the file off the ledge to the floor where it scatters—face side up.

I'm wondering about the blonde who has a rack for luring my men away. Rats! She's only 33. Well, it's just a matter of time before she turns 39, and resorts to snooping. I wouldn't be surprised if her job description says, "Employee shall be tasked with lounging about in bikini bottom whilst swilling wine." She "works" on the yacht captained by my boyfriend, Graham. He left me alone at the ball last night, and I can only conclude she had something to do with it. Oh well, maybe I can be her apprentice and learn some of her tricks.

As I sip the black syrup that was my lab experiment with the espresso machine, I am reminded of the coffee that Eva Gabor used to make on that 1960's TV show. I loved the way she just threw the dirty dishes out the "vindow" and think that is what I should do now. My real estate clients are coming to view the place in a few hours and it's still a mess from the party. Somehow, I never made it home last night, so here I am spraying Fantastic in a white evening gown and yellow rubber gloves. A lovely pairing for a Realtor at 9 a.m. When I find my phone, I come to a rude awakening: it's 10:54. Oh No! The power went off during the party and the stove clock must be wrong. When will I learn that stove clocks are in another dimension of time.

Suddenly, there is a knock on the door. I look up to see an entire limb of the Aggarwal family tree cheerfully waving at me. I decide that cheerfulness and punctuality are overrated traits in the morning. There is no way to hide or change my clothes, as the house is an architecturally inspired fishbowl. Not that I want to hide—I really need this sale—so I let them in.

As I trail along, my assistant Ursula leads the gaggle-o-Aggarwals, from room to room. When she develops a keen interest in the ancient one's sari she has to be demoted to her previous role as my dog. Taking over, I guide them through the estate with the precision of an aimless ant. Suddenly, the ancient one halts at the top of the stairs. I think she's having some sort of stroke, then a smile cracks on her face and she gives a big thumb up. This is real estate code for: Yay! A $27 million sale! I love the Aggarwals—so swift and cheerful.

Not wanting to waste a precious minute, I suggest we take the sleek elevator to the main floor; I do a little happy dance as we wait, until I realize they can see my reflection in the chrome elevator. When the door opens, there is a chorus of screams and Aggar-wails—like they practiced on the way over. I look into the elevator and think this can't be good. There is a dead body.

3 months earlier - Washington DC

As I wait for the ever tardy Kevin, I embark on one of my favorite pastimes: painting still lifes. I usually do cakes and naked men, but neither of them happen to be lying around, so I settle on painting a butterscotch Krimpet. To get in a painterly mood, I pour a glass of my beloved Ferrari-Carano Fume Blanc and play a Phil Collins record. I find there is nothing more comforting than the timeless furry voice of Phil Collins, played on an old scratchy record player.

After a few burnt umber brush strokes, I notice my wine glass is empty again. Hmm. Must quit drinking, I vow as I venture for a new bottle. Right then, my pug steals a kiss with her aardvarkesque tongue—then she steals my wine. Right in front of me!

I have had dogs before—many without drinking problems—but Ursula is one of those bad pugs you read about. Indeed, the former owners declared her "The Worst Dog in the World." Usually in these cases an owner "accidentally" leaves the front door open, or deposits the dog untethered outside the grocery store hoping some poor sap will wander by. As with all great plans, things can go awry. The major hitch of this plan: the dog can return—with a vengeance. Come to find out, the previous owners actually drove Ursula to the dog pound then smartly moved away. Of course, there was no disclosure of this by the dog pound people when I stumbled in that day. No, the hoodwinkers somehow left that out. They practically made me adopt her, offering to throw in a water dish if I took her right then and there. A purebred with a free water dish? I should have known it was all too good to be true.

Ursula now has tail cancer, a particularly difficult type to operate on notwithstanding the curliness of a pug tail. The worst part is that I have just enough money to pay my rent, but not enough for the operation.

My best friend Kevin is now here. He doesn't knock like normal people. No, his entrance is more of an appearance on the scene through a sliding swerve. He's wearing his signature royal blue bathrobe and because he had to pass through public to get here, he's wearing pants. While my other gay friends are more subtle, Kevin saves onlookers the trouble of having to fire up their gaydar. He plays a caterer in the melodrama that is his life, but always gets fired because his creations are somehow phallic – or melt into phallic shapes.

When I tell him of my latest dilemma he says to simply borrow the money from my fiancé, Larry. "That way, you don't have to pay it back."

I hadn't really thought of that, but it seems to me like a bad way to start a happy marriage.

Kevin unwittingly nibbles on the Krimpet as he makes painterly brush strokes to enhance the painting. "Kevin, you just bit my model!"

"So, that's what that was," he says innocently.

Right then the phone rings; it's Larry. Kevin answers for me and after a few 'ah ha's' informs me that Larry is cancelling our dinner tonight. This bit of information leads Kevin to conclude that Larry is cheating on me. While I process this thought, Kevin is busy planning a stake out. The next thing I know we are in the back of my previously owned Mercedes parked in front of Larry's house. We are dressed as spies, or so I am told by Kevin, who is up on the latest in spywear. I'm wearing a trench coat over a night gown; Kevin has added a beret to his ensemble; Ursula has a stocking over her head like a Dr. Seuss character gone bad.

We have jelly donuts, which Kevin says are required for a proper stake out, but apparently a pug can't eat with a stocking on. This explains why you don't see pugs robbing banks very often.

Kevin pops up like a periscope, "Look, there's a strawberry blonde going into his house." Kevin always puts everything in food terms; he describes me as a chocolate brunette. I say that could be his sister as he drags me out of the car. Now we are sitting on a stone retaining wall overlooking Larry's pool with a good view into his living room window. He is pouring his sister a glass of champagne in the good crystal. Our spy pet has insisted on coming along, but may be pulled off mission due to her constant licking to get donut powder off her mossy face. Then she moves on to Kevin's face, and he pushes her away, causing her to land in the pool. Thank goodness Larry has loud music playing to drown out our espionage-ineptitude.

Peering through the windows we see Larry full frontal, now French kissing the woman. I am starting to think that is probably not his sister. Either way, this is not good. Kevin points out that now Larry is unbuttoning her blouse. I can't look anymore. Like a sports announcer, Kevin says, "now she's taking off his pants." I look up to see Larry wearing the David Beckham boxer briefs I bought him—only so I could keep the box. One glance and all can see that Larry has a full Beckham going. I take my coat off and jump into the pool to save my pollywog pug. I am quietly trying to catch Ursula but she must think it's some sort of game and maintains an out of reach distance from me.

Kevin soon decides that this spectator sport requires a beer. He opens the pool fridge, which causes a chain reaction of tumbling beers, sore toes and screaming. Larry halts his kissing and disrobing and comes out—with the Beck safely retired. Shirley Bassey's maroon velvet voice singing, "If you go away" escapes from the opened doors. Larry looks back to see if I noticed anything amiss, like a strawberry blonde pulling his pants down.

Yelling at him, I punctuate each syllable with a whack on the head with the only thing I can find: a styrofoam swim noodle. He says it's not what it looks like. *Oh yeah?*

I grab my baby pug and make a run for the moving vehicle that is my car with Kevin as mad getaway driver. When I look back I realize I've left behind my rain coat, that and what I thought was my future.

First, I'm shocked— a *whoa!* moment. Then it's like a slow deadness coming over me, like when a steamroller backs over a new birthday bicycle. There it lies, still shiny, but no longer so new and now very flat. Like my heart.

2

After a few weeks of eating, drinking and shopping, I'm starting to get over Larry. This tri-fecta therapy is quite a lot of fun. I highly recommend it, especially if one has available credit on their Visa card.

Eventually, I find the bright side of not marrying Larry—despite Kevin's comment that it was probably my last hope of marriage as I'm pushing 40. Kevin makes it sound so old, until I remind him that he's the exact same age. "Never mind," he says as he dances around like Auntie Mame. "You live in color and Larry lives in black and white." It does occur to me that I would have eventually become Larry. My still life and real life would have been painted in Mars black & Zinc white. While I would not have to worry about money—I would have lost all joy of spending. I would have become an organized person. I would have lost the messy little me.

It was just a matter of time before I'd run out of money again, what with paying for Ursula's operation and paying off the Visa bill. Thankfully, I have a miracle real estate deal and will soon have $7,447 in the bank. I am grateful for this last deal as mortgage rates have just sky rocketed, and the real estate market is now dead.

To cheer myself up, Kevin suggests I move away. He says somewhere fancy; somewhere he would like to visit. "Say, who is your mother's friend in Palm Beach—the animal water aerobics instructor?"

Well, that narrows it down a bit. "Irene," I answer.

"Yes. Maybe you can work for her."

"Are you crazy? I'm not teaching poodles to swim! Besides, she was sued and forced to close down."

"What happened?"

"Ginger, the Chihuahua, got sucked up by the pool scrubber."

"Chihuahuas filing lawsuits; what's this world coming to?"

I look at Kevin and hope he's not serious.

Then he says, "What's she doing now? Irene I mean."

"What can you do after that? She's in real estate now."

"Perfect. Do you still have a Florida real estate license from when you stalked that tanned guy throughout his 64 hour class?"

"It wasn't stalking, it was a board requirement."

I hesitantly say yes, knowing I'm halfway to Palm Beach. I call Irene, and she says I can stay with her, but I can't bring my dog. Then she says she knows of a little cottage by the sea I could rent for a few months. It is one of the three stooges, she says. In the background, I hear the David Aldo song, "Life is Calling." It's a sign! For what I am not sure, but I'm game.

Kevin, who claims to have a master's degree in packing, takes over. He puts all my worldly belongings in storage and loads *his stuff* in my car. He announces that he's moving there with me. He says he needs to leave town and I can only deduce that he has accidently poisoned another client.

We stop at my Mother's house in South Carolina, making me glad I have a geographically desirable mother. We had planned to stay a few days, but –somebody—ate an entire box of cookies and threw up on Mom's white sofa.

"Why Mother, I think it was Mr. Abercrombie," I say, trying to frame her cat. The next morning we notice our suitcases lined up by the car. In the passenger seat, we find my dog, all ready to go, with her water dish taped to her head like a sailor about to go on leave. We take this as a not so subtle hint by Mom and her cat that it is time for us to go.

After a few miles of smarting from the inhospitable gesture, I conclude an early start is an auspicious beginning to our new lives. Besides, we have to stop every few miles for various fire hydrant, petrol and girl cookie breaks. I come to learn that a woman and two fugitives do not make for swift travels.

After about 20 more hours, we arrive in ritzy Palm Beach. I kind of know my way around from that time I stayed with Irene; plus, she told me how to get to our new street. Here's how she gives directions: "Go over my bridge and take a left by that place where we saw that fat girl drop her ice cream sandwich and then pick it up and lick it. Remember?" Oddly, I find her instructions useful. But, I don't think Irene will be getting a job at OnStar any time soon.

It's a beautiful, starry night as we turn off Royal Poinciana Street. What a perfect location. It looks like we can walk to about seven restaurants and The Breaker's hotel, depending on how high our heels are. It would be easier to find our street if there were useful things like, say, street signs; instead we are told to take a right when we see sleeping cats.

"Look, there's a whole pack of cats!"

"Are you referring to this clowder of cats?" Kevin says in a now annoying faux English accent.

The cats aren't moving, so I have to get out of the car to shoo them away. This is no simple task as we have roped the doors shut with our inept roof packing. We find our street to be an adorable little lane, cutting through a dark jungle of palm trees, leading to the sea.

How lucky are we to live this close to the water? I'll bring my easel down every morning and paint lovely seascapes. Or maybe a still life of a lifeguard.

Instead of reveling in the majesty of the ocean, Kevin exclaims, "Oh no! Stop!" like we're about to drive off the edge of the planet.

It's a one-way street and someone is behind us, so we have to go all the way around two blocks to find our street again. We drive very slowly this time so we don't miss our house. Whoa. No wonder we keep passing it; it's only a car-length wide. Plus it's covered by foliage, which will be handy if we ever need to join any sort of witness protection program.

The house is a tiny, pink, two-story Key West style cottage. Kevin says the key should be under the mat. It's not, but the kitchen window is open so Kevin climbs in without hesitation. He gives me a detailed description through the opened window. "Oh how cute. It's like being on a boat. There's teak on the walls and a captain's wheel. Oh, look at this bathroom, or should I say head?"

"Kevin, will you just open the door for me?"

I enter a narrow living room with a tropical nautical theme full of wicker and ropes, like someone was expecting pirates and monkeys to live here.

"Emma, look at this darling kitchen."

I swing the wooden door open and see a kitchen so small you can't open the dishwasher and stand in the kitchen at the same time.

"This must be Curly," Kevin sighs.

"I'll settle on Larry then."

"You must sign a one year lease," Kevin says in a moment of practicality, "if you don't, the rent will go up from $1800 to the seasonal rate of $3600."

We climb the stairs. Fortunately, the second floor is cantilevered out and is actually quite large, with huge French doors on all four sides and a raised princess platform bed. It feels like it was decorated for the Pirate's Parisian paramour.

"Emma, let's go see Larry, it must be the one over there."

We trek a total of three feet to the next house on the street, which is painted a darling blue with a little white picket fence. The thoughtful landlord left a key under the mat this time. We turn the lights on and discover it's a much larger house, with a more Bermuda feel. We run upstairs and find two real bedrooms, making me think we could have shared a house to save money. Well, I suppose any savings would be consumed by therapy and legal fees. Like Goldilocks, I try out the beds to see which is the softest, while Kevin plays bear.

He returns with a cold beer and starts chugging it. "It doesn't look like anyone got around to cleaning the place, but they did stock the fridge with necessities like beer and Bacardi."

Knowing how this party will pan out, I suggest we unload the car first, then go to Publix for extravagances like food.

Fortunately, it doesn't take long to move in. Kevin pulls the car right up front and we have a conga line of boxes and chafing dishes straight into the front door. We decide to leave Ursula at our new abode, making a note to buy scissors to remove her "sailor hat" so we can pour dog food in it.

Kevin and I walk the few blocks to the Publix grocery store because we don't want to lose our good parking space. Yay, Publix sells wine. We pick out a few bottles of our favorite Ferrari-Carano Fume Blanc to go with our celebratory Coquilles St. Jacques. While we're waiting in line at the fish counter, I hear a dog barking under a woman's caftan. The caftan is festooned with lily pads and gigantic frogs, so I know this can only be one person—Irene.

She turns her gray head and smacks me with gobs of coral lipstick. "Emma! You must have hauled ass. I thought you weren't due here for a few days."

"Mom thought we should be getting on our journey."

Irene laughs. "Don't tell me, Ursula broke something."

"I see Ursula's reputation has preceded her," Kevin chimes in.

It's not unusual to run into Irene on the tiny island of Palm Beach; it has a standing population in the Mayberry category, before it triples with tourists in season. Plus, Irene lives near the Publix and has been known to eat food. She owns a house in Boca, some thirty minutes south of here, but had to move out due to a flood and subsequent insect infestation. The insurance company put her up at the swanky Flagmore Condo, where she remains an oblivious outcast. Pets are not permitted, so the ever-crafty Irene developed an elaborate scheme to register her cross-dressing dog, Dr. Phil, as a service dog. It was just a matter of time before the lemmings in the building claimed their dogs were also "service pets," and now the condo is over run. They fall for it at the Flagmore, but are not keen on it at the grocery store, which is why she has a dog under her caftan. Which is why she wears caftans. Which is why I adore Irene.

On the way back I muse about what a fortuitous encounter this was. Mostly because Irene invited me to lunch tomorrow at the Flagmore Beach Club restaurant. Not Kevin, just me.

When we arrive home, Kevin uses the handy key under the mat to open my door. He walks in and instantly screams. I ignore this, as Kevin has been known to scream at the sighting of an ant. But then I hear another scream, this one in a lower pitch.

3

We've been here a total of forty-five minutes and we've already been broken into. And the burglar is holding my dog hostage. Well, actually he's rubbing her belly. The Latin-looking burglar yells something very Ricky Ricardo at Kevin and points to our pile of stuff. He's wearing nothing but a bath towel. Odd for a burglar.

Kevin grabs Ursula to use as his guard dog. "What are you doing here?"

The young dark Latin guy tightens his towel. "I live here!"

I calmly try to explain that we just leased Larry and Curly as of the first of January.

I hear the words, "This is Moe," coming through his coconut-white teeth.

Kevin makes an "egad" look with his mouth and apologizes. "Oh, our mistake."

I introduce myself. "Hi, I'm Emma, and this is Kevin. We are so sorry we moved in on you."

The chiseled brown statute points with each name. "I'm Ernesto and this is Moe. Larry is the pink house over there, and Curly is the yellow one out back."

Ursula seems to like this new Ernesto person—perhaps it's because he has removed her hat and has filled it with pet food. She's licking his knees and he's desperately trying to keep the towel from falling to the floor.

"It won't take long to get your stuff out," Ernesto says.

13

I can tell that Kevin is hoping Ernesto's towel will fall off; Ernesto must sense this too and runs upstairs to put on pants. We use his car as part of our moving assembly line of boxes and pots. "It's been nice to meet you and help you move, but I'm just getting ready to go out," Ernesto finally says.

"Come on, Kevin," I say, dragging him by the hand.

"I'm a dog walker so let me know if you need me," Ernesto calls from behind us.

I nudge Kevin. "That's odd. His seasonal rent has to be close to $5000 a month, he drives a BMW convertible...and he's a dog walker?"

Kevin looks him over. "He must be very good."

Out back is a small tropical garden with a stone patio, palm trees and, more importantly, a barbeque grill. Kevin and I debate which of our two houses gets the patio, then decide we'll share it. We climb through a mini jungle and see it—the tiny, golden Curly. There is an old screen door, which is open, so we embark on our tour. It doesn't take long as the house has no living room, only a metal contraption for a kitchen, and a bath on the main floor. Kevin crawls up the tiny, corkscrew spiral staircase which is covered with leopard print carpeting and finds a little Ernest Hemingway room with a bed that, like Papa himself, monopolizes the space. Kevin looks around. "I'll take this one, but let's just do month-to-month; I'm not living in this shoe box for a year."

I'm secretly relieved that I get Larry, despite the name. Kevin, Ursula and I relax on our shared terrace and enjoy our first dinner of sautéed scallops and asparagus. With a furtive cock of his head, Kevin discovers he can see right into Ernesto's bedroom. When I catch Kevin peering in, he justifies it with, "I thought he said he was going out. I was just making sure it wasn't an intruder." Kevin is always ready with an excuse.

The next day I linger in bed until after eleven. It's a rare morning that Kevin isn't pestering me with on-the-spot diagnoses of suspicious moles, which is how he likes to begin our day. I rifle through my closet of black dresses. As I tend to spill on my clothes, Kevin suggested I always wear black until they come up with something darker. Now, he says I should just go Lilly.

It seems the famous Palm Beacher, Lilly Pulitzer, invented her print dresses specifically to hide juice stains. Juice stains? I'll find prints that hide wine stains, and make it my new look.

For now, I compromise on a size-6 black dress, as my size-4 motivational dress doesn't fit, likely due to the bulk of sporting bikini bottoms for substitute underpants. Somehow the box holding all my underpants has failed to turn up and Kevin thinks it might have fallen off the roof of the car somewhere south of the Georgia border.

Today I am to meet Irene at her private lunch club on the ocean. Her directions for this locale are: "Head for the Frankie Avalon looking building, then hang a left when you see a man with a walker. I just drove by twenty minutes ago and he should still be trying to cross."

The Flagmore Lunch Club looks like a fake movie set for a restaurant that was decorated by a committee of Muffys—who compromised on the color coral. I worry I won't be able to see Irene, as she will blend in with the wallpaper. Besides the busboy and the new wives, I'm the only one here who is under seventy years old. Thankfully, Irene jumps up to wave me over. She's wearing a dress with leapfrogs on it. Irene is one of those "frog people." When I hug her, I notice they are not "leaping" but copulating frogs.

"Oh, Emma, I'm so excited. I just got a new listing for $27 million. I've got a plan and it involves you." Normally such an ominous comment would inspire me to consider a timely exit out the ladies room window to an idling sedan, but I'm intrigued so I stay.

"I need to have surgery this month. So I'm going to need someone to help me with the listing, and I don't want any of those dragon ladies from my office to get involved."

Her cell phone suddenly plays a loud "Hokey Pokey" ring; she answers it, jokingly putting her left foot in and putting her left foot out. Then she winks at me and mouths, "It's her."

That's not enough of a clue, so I sit and wait, wondering whom it could be. I'm dying of thirst, so I make flagrant efforts to catch the attention of the drum majorette who is posing as our waitress. When I finally attract her attention, she seems miffed by my request for water.

"Sorry you can't make it, Bunny. No prob." Irene snaps her phone shut. "She just cancelled. I'll bet it's some sort of Botox tragedy. I'm no Fan-o-Bunny; did you know she got me fired from my Santa job last year?"

I apparently missed this news flash. "They let women be Santas?"

"At Petco they do. Dogs don't care. Not so sure about cats."

I try to picture this scenario and wonder what she did to get fired, but am afraid to ask. Then a devilish smile takes over Irene's face. "The good news is we get to deal with her husband. He's a doll."

She goes on about how he's been in this horrible marriage for ten years, adding a "poor dear" every time she says his name. Just as Irene is about to fill me in on the dollish husband, the waitress feels it's time to detail today's specials. My head is reeling as I wonder how the waitress can possibly remember baked oysters from the seas off Prince Edward Island with a beurre blanc shallot and 1989 Pouilly-Fuissé reduction, yet she forgets to bring our waters! Irene quickly deflates the waitress's enthusiasm when she asks for her signature lunch, a BLT.

After waiting what seems like weeks for our sandwiches, Irene stands up and loudly harkens the manager over to our table. The sweaty man apologizes, saying they are short of help because a waiter just quit at the last minute to go on a gay cruise. This naturally makes me think of Kevin, who would do the same. I tell the manager about my friend, leaving out the gay and quitter parts, and he hands me his card and says to send Kevin over. Perfect.

When I return to my new home, I look out back to see that Kevin is finally up. Well, for him "up" is a relative term, meaning he is awake but still in his bathrobe and still horizontal. It appears he has found some sort of South Seas inspired hammock, hitching a neighbor's tree to the local telephone pole. Okay, so now we are living Green Acres *and* Gilligan's Island. In keeping with the theme, he's drinking out of a plastic coconut. My dog is in character too, with a matching plastic coconut—on her head.

"Look at all the stuff I got at Green's pharmacy." He points to the hammock area enthusiastically. "This is going to be my veranda. That, of course, is my tropical kitchen," he says, pointing to the grill. "And that is my alfresco bath," he says, pointing to the outdoor shower. He tilts his chin to his house. "I should have taken Larry; I can't possibly live in Curly for another minute."

I say it's only been one day. He says he'll just live out here all winter. I look up to see Ernesto in his bedroom window, wearing nothing but a towel—evidently his favorite uniform. Moe is larger and set back a few feet from Larry, giving us a side view into Ernesto's house.

I tell Kevin my exciting news. "You'll never believe this; Irene is getting a $27 million listing and needs someone to help her with it."

Kevin hands me my very own coconut cup. "So, are you going to share the commission with me?"

"Umm, no. You don't have a real estate license. Besides, I have good news for you. They're looking for a waiter at the private beach club for the Flagmore residents."

Kevin takes a gulp of his exotic libation. "Are you kidding? I wouldn't be caught dead being a waiter at my age."

Shaking my head, I explain. "Everyone there is about a hundred; they'll think you're twenty."

A coy smile suddenly emerges on Kevin's face. "Well, I suppose it would be a good place to make contacts. You say it's right on the beach?"

I tell him that during breaks he can work on his tan, but really want to say freckle collection. For a moment, I debate whether I should mention the leopard print polyester shirt he'll have to wear; then I think not, as I hand him the manager's card.

Kevin studies the card. "Ok, but I'm telling him up front that I'm not working evenings or weekends or national four-day holidays."

The next day I oversleep until ten because my alarm clock fails to wake me. My alarm clock has a black face and wakes me with a wet pink tongue. I look and see Ursula asleep on my carefully laid out listing appointment dress. Oh well, I'll just spray it with Febreze and pretend it's cashmere. When I walk in to the swanky offices of Bevington & Rickard Real Estate, I am met with aghast stares. At first I think they can detect my absence of undergarments, but then I realize the problem—no one wears black in Palm Beach. And no one wears Pugmere. Fortunately, I am out-frumped by Irene, who is wearing a wrinkled muumuu accessorized with her favorite bracelet—a roll of duct tape.

"Hi, honey. I thought we'd have a little lunch after I show you around."

In the polished dark wood offices, I am introduced to a series of old ladies and dapper men. After we leave, Irene says, "Those are the dragon ladies."

We walk to the Flagmore Beach Club. I start to think it's the only restaurant in town, but then I realize the club might have a minimum monthly food and beverage requirement. Irene is very practical. She was once caught putting buffet foods into Ziploc bags and defended herself with, "It says all you can eat right there on the big sign. Doesn't say when."

As we are seated, she pulls me aside, points out a woman and mouths the name, "Pudge Lichtenfelder." I look up, but only see a really thin woman; so thin, one can see her sternum and the "pulleys" that make her arms move. "Who are you talking about?"

Irene does a full-fledged point to the thin blonde woman.

"That string bean is named Pudge?"

"She weighed 13 pounds at birth so they stopped feeding her."

This Pudge person makes a simulated smile at Irene; just enough to show she still has facial movement. Once we are seated, Irene gulps her iced tea and fills me in from the corner of her mouth. "Pudge is the only person who is more of a gold-digger than Bunny."

Despite my confusion, Irene continues. "Pudge used to date Richard, then Bunny stole Richard out from under Pudge's bobbed nose." While I try to imagine this Bunny person, Irene goes on. "Richard Weinstein was a famous heart surgeon, but he had some malpractice suit over a lost belly button. He retired and now he's the biggest philanthropist in town."

Distracted by the menu, I ask, "And Bunny doesn't mind?"

"Mind? She's got it made. She never has to work again. She spends all her time at the spa paying people to touch her."

I look out at the ocean. "I love living here. Maybe I'll skip real estate and be one of these society wives."

"Well, it's not too late for you. But all the rich guys I know want young and beautiful." Studying Irene's face, I notice a hound-dog like drooping about the eyes, nose and mouth...but without the slobber. She says she's sixty-nine, but Kevin thinks it's because she

19

likes saying the number. She and my seventy-five-year-old mother went to kindergarten together, so unless Mom was a juvenile delinquent, the sixty-nine doesn't add up. I ponder the thought of Mom being held back in kindergarten for an extra six years, and then becoming a gang leader to Irene, a duct-taping toddler.

The Pudge person walks over, clacking her size 9aaa Ferragamo shoes. Her whole face comes to a point near her chin and her gigantic eyes seem to be on the sides of her head, like an insect. Irene makes the introduction using her pointer finger. "Pudge, Emma Budnjk. Emma Budnjk, Pudge. Emma's going to work with me at Bevington & Rickard Real Estate. Oh Emma, that reminds me; you gotta pay $2100 for board dues. Keeps the riffraff out."

"Then how am I getting in?" I ask, worried.

"What is that perfume you're wearing?" Pudge manages to ask me without moving her face.

Before I can make up something, Irene blurts out, "It smells like Febreze."

Pudge's pointed face creates a semblance of a smile. "Oh, this will be fun. Welcome, Emma, but good luck getting any listings in Palm Beach. Everyone has a real estate license, including me." I know not to say anything about the Weinstein listing, but Irene feels the need to kick me under the table.

As Pudge fades away in her Chanel suit, I look around at all the thin society wives; they probably wear all that jewelry to keep from blowing away. Now that I'm going to be a society wife, I've got to be thin. Irene orders a cheeseburger. I order a salad with no dressing.

"Honey, the burgers are great, and you get these cute little individual bottles of catsup you can put in your purse."

"It's too late," I say. "I've already ordered and the waitress is gone."

20

Irene jumps up, oblivious to the genteel diners, and hollers across the dining room, "Make it two burgers!" before plopping back down. "Plan on having a fun winter, but don't plan on making any money."

"But I really need to. I've only had one sale this year."

"Well, hopefully we'll sell the Weinstein listing. I'll take you there tomorrow while Bunny is away."

4

The next day, I walk the few blocks to Irene's place at the Flagmore Condominium. On my walk, I see the magic of this little Alice-in-Wonderland town: the trees are shaped like squares and gumdrops. The enchantment is lost, however, in the constant buzz of tree trimmers. When I reach the parking garage under the building, it's like a car dealership for Rolls Royces and Bentleys. Irene clomps over to her dirty, white Chevy Impala.

We wind down Ocean Drive, which divides the sparkling ocean from the huge hedge-lined estates. Suddenly, Irene puts on the breaks at one of the tall hedges and we wait for a gate to open. Inside is an imposing Asian-modern estate with green tinted glass. Once inside the motor court, we see an Asian man, who has just pulled in front of us in a tank-like Maybach. He hops down from the car and runs over on his short little legs. I say hello to Dr. Weinstein and he giggles.

"No. I Ping." He promptly takes Irene's car and starts hosing it down.

Irene, who can simultaneously walk, talk and apply lipstick says, "I never have to go to the scary $4 drive-through carwash again. Last time, I thought I was going to be decapitated."

"So that's the valet?"

"He's the cook, valet...you name it. He came with the house when they bought it."

We can see into the whole glass house, but must wait for the massive, black Asian-style front door to open. Behind it is a distinguished older gentleman with a regal manner. Attempting poise, I say, "Hi, Dr. Weinstein."

Irene laughs. "No, that's Trevor, the butler. Doesn't he remind you of Christopher Plummer?"

Trevor-the-butler has a huge smile on his face. "Thank you, my dear," he says in the Queen's English to Irene. "I loved him in *Daisy Clover*."

For me, the smile contracts and I get a formal, "Ms. Budnjk, I presume? Please come in."

I look around the huge glass foyer, filled with bamboo and a dramatic curved staircase surrounding a fountain. "Wow. It looks like a bank—like the Bank of Japan."

"I think I'll be the one writing up the brochure," Irene says.

Trevor escorts us to a library with a modern all-white motif and a baby grand piano. As we wait, I hear the water fountain, which always makes me have to go to the bathroom. After excusing myself, I wander around glass corridors and find myself back at the library, except now Irene is gone and the room is dark. Must be on an energy saving timer. Deciding to wait here for now, I round the corner and plop down on the white leather sofa.

"Ow!" a low voice moans. Lying beneath me on the sofa is a man—I just sat on his face.

"I'm so sorry," I say, jumping up.

"Ouch!"

"I didn't see you there," I say, backing away. My heart is pounding. The man gets up from the sofa and opens the drapes. The afternoon light beams on his tanned fifty-ish face, revealing crystal, candy-blue eyes. The pain must be subsiding, because he begins to laugh. Not a sudden laugh, but a gradual indication of amusement. I guess I'm out of trouble, but my heart continues to beat rapidly, except now it's more like a humming bird frequency.

23

He exhales. "May I help you, Miss?"

Judging by his worker clothes, I guess he's some sort of gardener. "I'm Emma. I'm here to look at the house with Irene."

"Oh, the brokers. I thought you were coming tomorrow. Where is ol' Irene?"

I survey the white library, filled with books and modern artwork. "She was just sitting here a minute ago."

The man folds his blanket neatly. "She was?"

"Yes. We were about to have tea, but I was sitting by the fountain and, well, fountains always make me have to go the bathroom. Then I got lost."

"I still get lost," the man says sheepishly.

"I won't tell anyone you were sleeping on the job."

The man guides me to an identical library on the other side of the house, where Irene sits on an identical white sofa. Irene introduces me to the man. "This is Dr. Weinstein."

He smiles. "Please call me Richard. Dr. Weinstein makes me sound old."

Forgetting to update, I automatically respond, "Ok, Dr. Weinstein."

I study his wavy gray hair and short wiry form, realizing he looks like a Dr. Weinstein. Have to remember to call him Richard, so he doesn't feel old.

In the full light, I look into his eyes and feel like I've met him somewhere before. While he gives us a guided tour, I find it hard to pay attention to the house. I am lost in his voice—and his handsome face. He explains that a famous Chinese architect designed the house, which is in an "H" shape with a central bar that has the entry and fountain, and "Y" shaped staircase leading to each side. He tells us the sides were identical, but his wife removed her kitchen, as she never eats, and added an elevator. I guess not eating makes her weak.

"My wife has one wing and I have the other," Richard explains. He then winks at me and adds, "That, my dear, is the secret to a successful marriage." He pauses. "Not that ours is."

"Is Mrs. Weinstein here?"

"No. She's gone to drop off clothes for charity. Every year she donates my favorite things just to annoy me."

Trevor, who is rolling by with a tray of tea, comes to a screeching halt. Ping tries to run past but is blocked by the cart. Trevor says he needs to run out for a moment. Richard shakes his head. "Don't worry, you and Ping are different sizes." Then we see Ping fly out the front door.

"Whenever we donate our clothes, they're snapped up pretty quickly, so the staff likes to get there first," Richard explains.

"Why don't you just give them the clothes?" I naively ask.

"Then Bunny wouldn't get the write-off," Irene replies.

"Sir, has she taken your pale blue Brioni jacket?" Trevor asks.

Richard gets a little smile. "No, I hurried and hid it in your closet."

Trevor bows. "Splendid. I've got my tailor waiting to take down the sleeves."

Richard guides us to the Shangri-Laesque pool, where we can see the makings of a purple and orange sunset over the Intracoastal. There's a pool house with staff quarters by the pool.

Richard looks at his watch. "Ladies, it's nearly five o'clock; why don't we have drinks out by the pool?" He says to Trevor, who has been following us with a heavy tray of tea, "It's too hot for tea; how about some of our best champagne for the ladies?"

"Can I have some too?" Irene jokes.

"Ladies drink champagne," Trevor says. "For you, my darling, I shall serve a fresh grasshopper."

Richard and Irene laugh, while I secretly wonder about this Trevor butler person. Soon he returns with a minty green drink in a gigantic martini glass. As Irene gleefully licks the chocolate edge, Trevor skillfully opens a bottle of Cristal champagne and pours everyone else a glass, then sits down and pours himself one. The withered Trevor looks up. "What are you looking at? Ping drinks this all the time. Besides, I haven't seen Irene in days."

"Will we be having hors d'oeuvres?" Richard inquires.

"I left a tray on the butler's pantry off the kitchen," Trevor moans. "Emma, would you be a dear?"

Oh, so the guest serves the servants in this household. Richard probably has to make the beds and mow the lawn while Trevor and Ping bask about. As I wander about the house like a mouse in a maze, I find a series of green glass rooms and something that resembles a toilet. It's one of those ultra-modern baths where you can't figure out how to get the water out of the faucet or how to flush the toilet. I wave my hands over the toilet thinking there's a sensor, like in airports. No luck. I know, maybe it has one of those clapper things like on TV. I try a combination of clapping my hands and jumping. Still no luck. Now I can't seem to get the door open. It's a sliding glass door that probably needs a password. I'm trapped! It will take days to find me. Then I hear a gentle knock on the door and it slides open. It's Trevor, suppressing a smirk. He makes a gentle wave of his hand over an electronic beam that I failed to notice.

Richard stands up when I return. "Did you get lost?"

Trevor fills me in. "We were discussing Irene's daughter trekking around Australia."

"I miss her so much," Irene pines.

Richard pats my knee. "Do you have children, Emma?"

I look around. "Not that I know of."

"Oh, you'd know," Richard says with a smile.

Trevor pours me more champagne and says to Irene, "This ought to be fun."

Richard winks at me. "I find Emma to be a refreshing delight."

I smile at him and say, "You make me sound like sorbet."

"Do you two want to get a room?" Irene jokes.

We bring our drinks as we continue the tour, leaving out most of Bunny's side. Richard explains that since it's identical there's no need to bother with her side, but I think it's due to fear that she would appear.

We leave the Weinstein residence in Irene's newly cleaned car. Irene looks at me. "That went well. He really seems to like you—which means he won't mind you subbing for me."

"I think he's sweet."

"Emma, even though he's married to the biggest bitch in town, he's still married."

"You're right. I can't believe I sat on his face."

Irene looks over at me and practically drives off the road. "What?!"

"Oh, it was an accident."

"Whatever you do, don't let Bunny see you flirting with him. She'll claw your eyes out and feed them to the cat."

"That's a lovely thought. Why did such a sweet man marry someone like her?"

"It was right after his first wife died. Bunny was designing his new apartment. She lured him into her web; you know how pathetic men are around stunning women."

"So that's why she gets to be a bitch. I'll bet she's a blonde."

"Yes, of course she's a blonde. There must be a law that all rich men have to marry thin blondes. But she's not stunning anymore. Well, I guess she is more like shocking, than stunning."

"What do you mean? What does she look like now?"

Irene thinks for a moment and finally says, "How can I describe her—she looks like Miss America gone bad."

"You'd think with her money, she'd get a facelift or something."

"That's just it. She did and it's awful. It's the primary reason why I will never get one."

"I thought that's what you were having done this month."

"No, honey, they found two lumps in my breast and I have to have a procedure next week."

"Oh, Irene, I'm so sorry."

"They're trying to save my breast. How come women don't get cancer in their belly fat, so they have to cut that off?"

"So are you having lumpectomies? Is that the plural?"

"Richard got me into an experimental medical study. On one lump they'll implant a tiny device that slows down the vibrations of the cancer cells—they think hyper cell vibrations cause cancer. On the other one, they're going to inject condensed stem cells from my good breast. I am the Guinea pig."

I give her a hug and wonder how she keeps her spirits up. "Irene, I had no idea."

"Well, I'll be out of commission for a while, so you'll have to take over."

"Sure. Anything you need.

"Great. I need a responsible adult to take me to the hospital for the pre-op."

I look around. "Do you know any?"

As she drops me off, Irene points out a bicycle, covered with pink triangles. She says it looks like I have a visit from the cat lady. Then I hear a loud crashing sound from upstairs and wonder if it's a cat lady burglar.

Kevin calls down from upstairs. "It's just me. Did you see my new bike? I'm going to call her Mavis."

Ursula, who has been licking the dishes in the yawning dishwasher, follows me upstairs. "Good, now we won't have to fight over my car."

Kevin doesn't look up from the TV. "Bought it for $20 from the cat lady."

"Kevin, what are you doing in my bed?"

"I'm watching General Hospital reruns. My TV is so small I can't see which side Jason dresses on."

"Maybe we should have just rented one house and shared it."

"Oh, I like my privacy," Kevin says pronouncing it using the Queen's English, "*Priv*-acy."

I notice Kevin is not looking at the TV. He and Ursula have a perfect view out the French door about four feet away—into Ernesto's window.

"Maybe Ernesto would like some *priv*-acy too."

"Puhlease. He just had some woman over. I couldn't see her, but boy, I sure could hear her."

"What do you mean?"

Kevin wrinkles his forehead in concentration. "Maybe it's been a long time since I've been with a woman. What kind of noise do you make when you're finished?"

After I process the notion that Kevin used to be straight, I consider answering his nosy query into my orgasm sounds. Using a food code, I say, "Let's see, when I'm finished eating ice cream, I make a kind of quiet 'ah.'"

"Me too. Only mine's more like an 'oh, ohh ohhh.'"

"No mine's more like an 'ahh ahh ahh.'"

"Now pay attention. Is mine sexy?" He makes his "oh, ohh ohhh" sound again.

I render my verdict: "It's gentle, but not manly."

Kevin grimaces and quickly changes the subject. "Well, this lady at Ernesto's was even worse."

"What was it like?"

"It was kind of a howl."

"Are you sure Ursula wasn't over there?"

"No. Ursula makes a low 'hooowl' sound. This lady made a high-pitched howl. Like a monkey mated with an owl."

"Kevin, I think you have a little too much time on your hands."

"What should I be doing? I can't start waiting tables until I have my pathetic waiter training on Monday."

30

"You could do a little research on your catering business," I say helpfully.

"Is that code for saying you want to go and test champagnes with me tonight?"

"Well, I've just spent the afternoon drinking Cristal champagne in a $27 million mansion with the gorgeous Richard Weinstein, but someone has to work around here."

Kevin hops from my bed. "I want to hear all about it at dinner."

"Did you know every year Dr. Weinstein flies to Costa Rica for... I think it's called the "Doctors Without Boundaries program."

"He's perfect for you! You love doctors and you don't have boundaries."

Kevin grabs a towel from my linen closet and heads for my bath. "I'm listening, I just have to take a shower after all my eavesdropping."

"Why don't you use your shower?"

"Yours is so much nicer."

I put more makeup on my old makeup and run back upstairs and throw on a little black dress.

"People in Palm Beach will think you're a funeral director," Kevin says.

I ignore him. "Let's go to the Leopard Lounge in the Chesterfield Hotel."

Kevin is giddy. "First, can we stop at a place called the Pack Rat or the Church Mouse? I heard they are having a special event that the whole town is talking about."

5

There's a mob scene at the Church Mouse. Kevin manages to score a blue Brioni blazer for $57—I sure hope it's not the one intended for Trevor. The ladies dressing room has a long line, so Kevin makes me use the men's dressing room to try on a yellow Versace dress. It's huge, but only $45, and he says I can alter it later. I am now banned from the men's dressing room after several complaints; my black dress is held hostage, forcing me to wear my new dress on our outing. We scurry out and head to the Chesterfield Hotel. On our way, we drive past a beautiful marina full of mega yachts on South Lake Drive. We park and walk along the marina, where we spot a mega-yacht at the end of the dock named *No Woman No Cry.*

"That's the perfect name for a gay person's yacht," Kevin says.

"I think it's the perfect yacht name for a man who hates his wife."

At the corner, we spot the red-striped awning of the Chesterfield Hotel. We cautiously enter the dark, cool bar called the Leopard Lounge. On stage is a sexy singer with a forlorn face. He's tuning his guitar, or perhaps contemplating suicide. He looks at his watch and begins to play, starting with "Fly Me to the Moon." He stares, and I can't help but hope he has reconsidered his demise and is planning a trip with me to another planet. I notice he has a cleft chin and wide mouth. Oh, how I love a full mouth, and I find the deep parentheses in the corners fascinating.

Kevin catches me staring at his mouth. "I know just what you're thinking."

"What? That I want to put my tongue into that sexy mouth?"

"No, he needs a little Juvéderm."

Then a woman comes over with a flute and starts turning his pages. "Here's a little something from the late Robert Palmer," he says. The woman plays a tropical sounding flute solo, then sexy mouth jumps in with, "Give me an inch. Give me an inch, girl, I'll give you a mile."

Whoa. I could sit here all day and stare at this guy's mouth. Next, he sings a David Aldo song, "Freedom." As I listen to the song, I decide that I am a girl who loves her freedom more than anyone. We sit at the bar and have glasses of Chardonnay and share a yummy crab cake appetizer with chili lime mayonnaise. This would be great, if Kevin actually knew how to share. At $18 a crab cake, it will cost a fortune to fill him up. Now, I can tell he wants to go elsewhere; he doesn't come right out and say this, of course. Instead he uses one of his clever ploys. "The singer is probably wondering why you're drinking wine in a maternity dress." Rats. As we are leaving, we hear another David Aldo song, "Someday." I hope *someday* I see the handsome singer again, and I hope I'm not wearing this dress.

We head to our car on Worth Avenue, but notice there is some sort of function at Tiffany's. As I walk farther, I notice Kevin is no longer behind me...then I see someone who looks just like Kevin inside Tiffany's waving me in. I sheepishly enter the crowded jewelry store. "Kevin, we weren't invited!"

"How do they know?" he whispers as he points with his chin to a waiter serving free crab cakes. I give him a look. He pops a caviar-topped blini in his mouth. "What? We might as well eat. It looks like none of these ladies have had an hors d'oeuvre in decades. Look at that one."

I look over and see a human Praying Mantis bent over a display case of baubles. I mistakenly nod and wave to the insect: Pudge Lichtenfelder. Rats. Now she's approaching, rapidly. From across the room, I try to guess Pudge's age. After a complicated calculation factoring in gauntness and plastic surgery, I conclude late forties.

Pudge lands near our feet. "Why, Emma, I didn't know you were on the guest list."

I'm mortified and let Kevin know it with an unmistakable look of *now look what you've done* on my face, which I then realize makes it even more obvious. I introduce him, waiting for him to laugh at the absurdity of her name.

Kevin takes Pudge's hand. "Hello, Mrs. Lichtenfelder. It's such a pleasure to see you again."

Pudge studies his face using just one of her large insect eyes. "Have we met before?"

I'm wondering the same thing but keep my mouth shut.

Kevin, sensing we are on the verge of ejection, turns on the charm. "Yes, last season. Say, is that a Harry Winston necklace you are wearing?"

"Why, yes. Are you in the jewelry business?"

"No, I'm in the catering business."

"Really? Which company?"

"All About Kevin Catering."

Pudge makes a face to the extent she can with her tightened skin. "What a stupid name."

I have to contain myself when I reveal, "This is Kevin."

"Oh. So whom have you catered for?"

I can tell by his face, Kevin's brain is in full-tilt conjure mode. Thankfully, Pudge's turbo lips are without an adequate breaking mechanism and she rolls on. "I need someone for a luncheon I'm having in two weeks."

Kevin, not knowing a soul in Palm Beach, comes out with, "Um, Bunny Weinstein?"

I give him a full raised eyebrow look that says, *Kevin!*

Pudge discharges a business card. "Call me tomorrow. Oh look, there's Cricket, the hostess."

I grab Kevin by the arm and drag him toward the exit. "What were you thinking?"

"Who would name anyone Cricket?"

"No! What if Pudge follows up with the Weinsteins?"

"I'll just say it's one of the other Bunny Weinsteins. Surely there must be warrens of Bunny Weinsteins on the island."

I sigh. "Thank goodness Bunny and Pudge rarely speak, but she is good friends with Richard."

Just when I feel we're on the precipice of a clean escape, Kevin is seduced by something turquoise and glimmering at the front door. It's a huge Tiffany gift bag. Not content with one misappropriated Tiffany gift bag, Kevin requests two, saying he needs one for his mother, leaving out the dearly departed part. That's when things start to unravel. We are asked our names, which shockingly do not dovetail with any on the actual guest list. Soon, we are loudly identified as party crashers. Kevin is without remorse, but I'm humiliated to the point I will never be able to crash another party at Tiffany's again.

6

My alarm goes off Monday at the sprightly 5:30 a.m., set for me to pick up Irene. I find her standing in front of her building with a hard green suitcase, like she is running away from 1957. She seems a little depressed, which is expected, but it makes me think it's because she is not wearing any frog accessories or duct tape.

I have trouble finding the place she refers to as "7th Heaven," and secretly wonder if it's a strip bar. Soon we are at the Saint Heaven's Hospital admissions office for her pre-surgery check up. From there she will be taken to the private clinic for her experimental procedure, then returned for post-op.

Irene tells me Richard was originally assigned to take her to the hospital, but Bunny conjured up a reason where he would have to let her down.

When I finally make it home, I get a call from an agent at Cornwall Real Estate saying he wants to show the Weinstein house tomorrow afternoon at five. Hallelujah! This is a chance to sell the house, call Richard, and sleep late. As I have trouble containing any sort of merriment, I mention the showing to Kevin. Naturally, he wants to come along after hearing all about the house and, more importantly, the house champagne.

Despite the fact Kevin has taken over most of my closet, I am able to locate my best white suit. Kevin insists on wearing the Brioni blazer, so I tell him if anyone named Trevor asks, to say he bought it somewhere besides the Church Mouse. Surely, he should be able to contain that sort of TMI.

As I drive down Ocean Blvd, it's hard to decide which to marvel at: the glistening ocean on the left, or the monumental mansions on the right. After several false entries down the wrong hedge-lined driveway, I learn to make fast getaways.

We know we have correctly identified the Weinstein estate when Ping runs out and starts washing my car. Kevin points out that Ping is wearing Prada shoes, ladies ones.

Trevor answers the door and immediately glares at Kevin's blazer. Kevin, the blazer and I are told to wait in the living room on Richard's side. The other agent is a Southern guy, his client a Middle Eastern-looking man. I'm a little nervous showing the house, but the Southern guy seems to know his way around the house from when he attended a party here. Kevin seems interested in him, and follows us on our tour.

Finally, the Southern guy tells Kevin to buzz off, and he wanders off with his tail between his legs and departs from my guided tour. With the client and agent in tow, I continue my expedition, throwing out chestnuts of agent wisdom. After a while, I notice no one is following me. The ever-efficient Trevor tells me they left a while ago; he adds that if I was wondering where my helper was, he's in the library with Dr. Weinstein.

As we approach, I hear the sound of a piano playing a Gershwin song. I peer in to see Richard gently playing "The Man I Love" to Kevin, who is swaying like he's at a piano bar.

Richard stands up when he sees me. "Oh, hello, Emma. I'm having a nice little chat with Kevin and finding out all sorts of interesting things."

"Don't worry," Kevin says, "I didn't say a word about the time you ended up in bed with the…" then he quickly covers his mouth.

Richard laughs and politely changes the subject. "How did you two meet?"

"We both applied for the same restaurant manager job in Washington. They made me the manager and Kevin the waiter."

"Then Emma fired me."

"Well, you ate all the shrimp. Plus, I hired you back."

"Yeah, when my mom was dying. She hired me back so I could get time off."

"Then he became the manager and fired me."

Trevor smirks. "I take it this was before they had employment laws."

Richard starts to play another Gershwin song, "Summertime."

"Come and sit with us. Trevor, please bring a glass."

Trevor, thinking it's for him says, "Splendid. I fancy a drink right now." He then eyes Kevin's jacket and asks if he'd like him to hang it up for him. Kevin chatters his teeth pretending to be cold and says he'll keep it on. Trevor rubs his fingers down the sleeve and asks where he purchased it. I give Kevin a gentle kick under the piano, which prompts him to come up with the ridiculous reply that I made the jacket for him.

Really, Kevin? A Brioni blazer.

Richard walks over to the sofa and pats the seat next to him. "Kevin tells me you went to Boston College. I'm from Needham, Mass you know."

"I worked at a restaurant there, Café Georges. That is, until it burned down."

Richard opens his mouth with surprise. "I believe I was there that night."

"It was Bastille Day. I think 1997."

Richard looks up, rubbing his chin. "I remember that night. The chef became ill, then some waitress ran in and poured water on his head. He nearly drowned."

I don't feel the need to confess that was me. Instead I say, "Isn't it weird? I remember that night like it was yesterday."

Richard leans back and nods his head slowly. "Now I remember you."

Really? I close my eyes trying to remember Richard as the young doctor. "I remember you! You were the doctor who helped everyone."

Richard laughs. "There you were after fire, flood and pandemonium, calmly giving people their bar tabs in the parking lot."

Kevin interrupts our trip down memory lane like a Mack truck swerving in front of us. "So where is Mrs. Weinstein?"

"I have no idea where my wife is. If you mean my mother, she's at her fencing class."

"Fencing what, jewels?"

Richard laughs. "No, swords. And don't give her any ideas."

Right then, a woman in her twenties with jet-black hair and black Goth fishnets comes in. Without a word, she plops down on the sofa, making me glad I'm not the only one with a brisk "plop."

"Hey, Dad."

"Hello, Lisa. I want you to meet Emma and Kevin. Emma is showing the house and Kevin is her friend."

Lisa waves to us. "Hi. It's nice to meet you." Then she gives me a pleading look. "Please don't sell the house."

Absentmindedly, I say, "Oh, don't worry. I usually talk people out of buying things."

Richard lets out a sigh. "Darling, we've gone over this." Richard turns to me. "My wife hates this house and wants to buy the Etherington estate, Sea Mist."

"Dad, why don't you stay here and she can go live there?"

39

Richard rubs his chin. "Actually not a bad idea. And you can go live with her."

"That's not funny, Dad. I'd end up having to kill her and then the carpeting would get all bloody."

Kevin cups his mouth and jokes to Lisa, "Always try to kill people outdoors."

"Kevin!"

Richard laughs. "Darling, why don't you go and get ready and I'll take you and Nana to dinner at Cafe L'Europe."

Lisa perks up. "Is Rabbit coming?"

"Lisa," Richard scolds, "is that the proper way to refer to your stepmother?"

Trevor contains a grin. "Yes, Lisa you should have said, 'Is *The* Rabbit coming?'"

"No," Richard says, "it will be just the three of us."

Lisa runs for the door. "Good, I can finally have lobster."

Richard feels the need for a sidebar and explains that his wife is highly allergic to shellfish.

"That would be awful," I say. "I love lobster."

"So does my mother. In fact, she was raised as Orthodox but converted to Reform Judaism because of lobster. Say, would you like to join us tonight?"

Kevin jumps in. "I'd love to."

"Sure, you can come too, Kevin," Richard politely replies.

Then I remember. "Oh, I can't. I've planned to visit Irene at the hospital...."

"There's no point," Richard interrupts me. "Trevor went today and she's not allowed any more visitors."

"You sent your butler to visit her?"

Richard gestures, patting his heart. "I think he's got a little thing for her." Trevor is hovering and promptly turns red.

Kevin gets us back on point. "What time is dinner?"

Richard looks at me. "How about if I pick you up at seven?"

"We should just meet you there. We live north of there off County on Cat's Trail."

Richard reminisces. "I just love those little Cat's Trail houses. So…quaint."

"So small. I wish I could live here." Once I realize what I have blurted out, I want to take it back.

Surprisingly, Richard winks at me and says, "Perhaps you will someday."

For once, I'm happy for my lack of a filter.

Kevin sees the affection and devilishly says, "Yes, I'm sure his wife won't mind."

After goodbyes and hugs we depart. The minute we're in the car, Kevin says, "Gosh, Emma, he is charming in that sweet, intellectual kind of way. And those ice blue eyes!"

"Too bad he's got a wife."

"It sounds like that daughter can take care of that really fast."

Kevin and I race home to get dressed. To the uninitiated, this may sound like a simple task, but with Kevin it involves a fashion show on a makeshift paper-towel catwalk—and that's just for Kevin's ensemble. Kevin whines when I don't let him wear his new blazer.

I explain that I'm worried the omnipresent Trevor will appear and demand it back, causing an English scene in a French venue.

I wear the Versace dress again, taking a moment to nip in the side seams so it's a normal size. It's now the nicest thing I own, and being yellow it can take a little butter spill. As we drive past, I look in the windows and am shocked. There is Richard—in drag! Kevin, in a high voice, concurs. We valet park and proceed anyway because we're hungry.

Upon further inspection, we deduce it's Richard's mother. She has the same face, but with a pageboy and huge black glasses. *They look so much alike one actor could play both roles.* Richard appears next to her. "Mother, this is Emma Budnjk and Kevin...I'm sorry, but it just occurred to me that I don't know your last name."

Kevin is quick to announce that it's Conway, as in Tim.

I pipe up with, "Hello, Mrs. Weinstein, it's nice to meet you."

Mrs. Weinstein looks at my dress. "Did you swipe that dress from Bunny?"

"Um. No."

Mrs. Weinstein looks at the tag. "I remember she had one custom made by Versace, but she pissed off the tailor and it came back gigantic."

Richard gets a little smirk.

I look around. "So, where is Lisa?"

"The Spanish dog walker asked her out at the last minute," Mrs. Weinstein explains.

Kevin and I look at each other, wondering if it's Ernesto.

"I thought she was dating the Holmes fellow," Richard says.

"Maybe she's sowing her oats before she gets too into the sausage man."

I give Kevin a look and whisper, "I think they are talking in code."

We are seated at a table with Richard's knee touching mine. My heart is pounding, as I find the forbidden so magical. Then he puts his hand on my leg. Whoa. I knew it. It's just a matter of time before we are in each other's arms. He'll leave that spa-going wife of his and run away with me. Then I realize it's his mother's knee and his mother's hand. She realizes her mistake and says she thought it was Kevin's leg. I guess when you're that old, your gaydar and your aim would be off.

Richard orders a bottle of Petit Syrah, and duck pate with petit cornichons. I gather petit is French for expensive. For dinner, his mother and I order the lobster and a bottle of Far Niente Chardonnay. When Richard and Kevin order Dover sole, Mrs. Weinstein tells them to get their own bottle of wine if they want any. Richard helps her crack the shells, although I think she could do it with her bare hands. She's one of those tough cookie types you don't want to mess with. Mrs. Weinstein dips a huge piece of lobster in butter and declares, "I'm so glad Bunny isn't here." Richard gives her a look, so she quickly swerves her topic. "So, what do you do Kevin?"

"I'm a caterer."

"Oh, I need one! Thanks to Bunny, all of the Weinsteins are shunned by the caterers and banned from the private clubs."

Kevin cracks a lobster claw for her. "I'd love to cook for you. Where do you live, Mrs. Weinstein?"

"I live at the Flagmore. And you can call me Esther."

"It sounds like everyone does; I mean live at the Flagmore. I'm going to cater a lunch for Pudge Lichtenfelder there."

Mrs. Weinstein's huge oval glasses, focused on Kevin throughout his babbling, now turn 180 degrees back to Richard, like an owl. That's it! She's an owl who has come back to life as an old lady.

"Is it on the 20th?" she hoots.

Kevin says that it is. Mrs. Weinstein points with her fork. "I think I'm on the guest list. She and I are friends. Well, I take that back. She and I are next-door neighbors."

Richard folds his napkin. "They have a lot in common—they both hate Bunny."

"If only I'd been faster with the arsenic," she quips.

Richard throws down his napkin. "Really, Mother!"

She lets out a full Yiddish sounding, "Whaat?"

Richard's voice drops to a serious level. "Arsenic is too obvious. You need something undetectable."

I knew he was too good to be true.

His mother bursts out laughing, complete with leg slapping. "He's kidding. It's a running joke in our family."

A wave of relief blankets me as Richard takes a cloth napkin and covers my dress. Then he offers to crack my shells for me and is soon feeding me. When our eyes meet, he accidently drops the lobster head on my lap. Feeling terrible, he tries to wipe it off.

Mrs. Weinstein quips, "Versace Schmervachey, she only paid $45 for it. Says right there on the tag. So who cares about a little lobster splatter?"

I'm officially mortified in the thrift shop dress, so Kevin attempts to save me by blurting, "Did you guys know that Emma once had a pet lobster?" As I have a big piece of lobster in my mouth, I just nod my head.

"Yes," Kevin goes on, "his name was George and she was going to get him a girlfriend and start a lobster farm in her apartment."

Richard feeds me an entire claw. "Then what happened?"

"She ate him," Kevin ends the story.

Mrs. Weinstein looks at me through her butter splattered glasses. "I can see that."

Richard laughs. "Now we'll have to have a fund raiser to save lobsters."

Mrs. Weinstein is serious now. "Did you tell Emma about the benefit, dear?" Kevin clears this throat in a shameless effort to elicit an invitation. Mrs. Weinstein is quick to respond. "You can probably help the caterers, dear."

"Our foundation is holding a black tie event," Richard says. "It's the 'Dogs are People Too!' Ball on April 19th."

As my mind is processing the premise of the party, Kevin interrupts. "Just dogs? What, are they worried that money would get into the hands of cats?"

"That's later in the season," Mrs. Weinstein says. "It's the 'Cats are Better' party."

I'm reminded of a bumper sticker and say, "Cats are dogs with bad attitudes."

Mrs. Weinstein says she has a cat. A service cat. As I ponder such a thing, Richard looks into my eyes and asks if I'd like to come. He says it in such a way that it sounds naughty, and my mind wanders from cats to his mouth on me.

Mrs. Weinstein seems to intercept my devilish thoughts. "He means to the ball."

I do a mental rummage of my closet, and guilelessly admit, "I could probably make a gown by then."

"For what you'd pay for fabric and zippers, you could get five gowns at the Church Mouse," Kevin blurts out.

Mrs. Weinstein looks appalled. "What? And have the whole town recognizing it? Emma, dear, let's hit Worth Avenue and do a little shopping."

I let out a demure, "I'd love that."

After we finish feeding and touching each other, we say our goodbyes. Richard and his mother kiss us and tell us to drive safely, like we are their little wayward stepchildren.

When we return, Kevin, Ursula and I climb up in my bed and go over the evening. We're excited about our new lives. Well, at least Kevin and I are—Ursula I'm not so sure. Kevin suggests I get Ursula a boyfriend, or maybe a cat to play with. As Kevin lectures me about falling for Dr. Weinstein, we hear the weird Howler Monkey sound from Ernesto's. He has the blinds closed, so we can't see anything. Rats. Ursula howls back intermittently, like they are having a conversation.

Then we hear Ernesto say, "I don't want to."

A woman, presumably the monkey, says, "I don't think you mean that."

"I said, I don't want to," a frustrated Ernesto grunts.

"Ha!" the monkey hisses. "I know what you are up to. "

"And what 'xactly is that?"

Kevin whispers to me. "This is better than General Hospital, and just as confusing." Waiting for the answer, Kevin and I are at the edge of our preverbal seats; in reality, we're on the floor between the bed and the edge of the French door. Right then Ursula howls to

Ernesto, so we never get to hear what *'xactly* is, but it sounds like our little dog walker has a monkey on his back.

7

This morning, I decide to visit Irene at the hospital. I feel sorry for her not having any relatives around, plus I'm curious about what sort of wild birdlike outfit she'll be wearing. When I get to her room, I see my sweet Richard has sent her flowers: white lilies. She is heavily sedated and not permitted any guests—a policy I'm sure was instituted to reduce embarrassment and blackmail. I really wanted to see Irene, but am only permitted to drop off my chocolates.

Kevin and I now have the entire day to hang at the beach, so I go back to throw on a white tee shirt, shorts and flip-flops. In an effort to socialize Ursula, I cheerfully approach other dog owners, who promptly grab their pets and flee. Could it be me? Or perhaps it's Ursula's licking compulsion.

Kevin tells me he's decided to tender his resignation at the beach club, and wants me to hand in his polyester leopard print shirt. He had wanted to just mail back the shirt with a little note saying he's moved to some place like Madagascar. I think this is too exotic sounding, especially since neither one of us knows where it is. Then I point out that with his deceitful protocol, he would not be able to ever eat there as a guest.

We take the shortcut down the beach to the restaurant, carrying the leopard shirt in a quart-sized Ziploc for easy drop off. The minute we walk in, we see Mrs. Weinstein. This is not a huge surprise, as she is a Flagmore resident and she's banned from every other club. Kevin doesn't want her to know he was going to work there, so he runs into the kitchen. I hear the manager yelling at him, saying he has no waiter for today.

"Hello, Emma!" Mrs. Weinstein says. "What is all that ruckus in the kitchen?" Kevin flies from the kitchen wearing the leopard print shirt and tries to hide behind a large patron.

"Kevin," Mrs. Weinstein says in her nasal voice, "I didn't know you're a waiter. I thought you were a caterer. Oh look, there's Pudge now."

I can tell by his pink face that Kevin is about to die, though he's soon summoned by several of the blue haired ladies who lunch.

Mrs. Weinstein invites me to have lunch with her and Pudge, to whom she introduces me as a talented painter.

Pudge lights a cigarette. "Yeah, you'll probably starve as an agent."

The manager comes over and timidly points to the no smoking sign. Pudge waves him off. "I have a doctor's note. It's a service cigarette."

Mrs. Weinstein is laughing.

Pudge exhales dragon fumes. "Say, Emma, I need my bathroom painted."

"No, I do oil paintings."

Mrs. Weinstein winks and adds, "Cakes and nudes."

"Great. She can do a portrait and donate it to the charity auction."

We order Reuben sandwiches and iced tea. Well, at least Mrs. Weinstein and I do. Pudge has a stalk of celery, and that's only because it came in her bloody Mary.

Thanks to Mrs. Weinstein, I find out a little more about Pudge, who makes frequent trips to the ladies room. Mrs. Weinstein talks fast. "Richard hired her sister to decorate his condo for him after his wife died. Then the sister, Spanky, who was quite fat, somehow died and Pudge took over as decorator and started putting the moves on him."

49

My mind wanders to the Mantis; I remember reading that Pterygota eat their siblings.

"Richard apparently was not too keen on her decorating style—frankly it's too clinical—so he hired Bunny to take over. During this process, Bunny stole Richard from Pudge. So, Pudge married a guy named Saul, who liked to say he was in ladies underpants."

I have a vision of an old man with gigantic granny pants on his head.

Mrs. Weinstein goes on. "He was actually in the garment industry. But Saul died…"

Rats. Pudge is back. Well, this gives me time to process it all.

Now, apparently, it's Pudge's turn to get the gossip on me. "Budnjk? What kind of name is that?"

"It's supposed to be Polish, but I think it was an airline reservation code."

Kevin wants to hear our gossip, so he seats himself at our table. When the manager comes by, Kevin pops up and refills Pudge's water glass. She excuses herself once more to visit the ladies room. Without missing a beat, Mrs. Weinstein continues on about Pudge. "Saul left her a zillion dollars and a lifetime supply of girdles, of all things."

The manager has taken the extra chair, so Kevin is now sitting in Pudge's seat, listening and covertly splashing hot sauce in Pudge's drink. Pudge returns and snaps her fingers at Kevin to get out of her seat, which curtails the gossip. When I subsequently relay the missing parts for Kevin, I leave out all the Spankys and the girdles and condense it to: Bunny stole Richard from Pudge.

"Emma, if you're free after lunch," Mrs. Weinstein says to me, "I'd love to take you shopping."

Kevin is now organizing our sugar bowl of Sweet'N Lows, ignoring his other tables.

"Sure," I say.

"Great. We'll just work our way down Worth Avenue until we find you a gown."

Kevin, who is now stomping his feet like a child, must be jealous he hasn't been invited along. He finally breaks his silence. "Um, I think my tuxedo may be a little too snug; I might need to go shopping with you two."

"Well, you have a few weeks to lose the fat," Pudge says.

Kevin starts to take off his apron, but the manager comes over and says he needs Kevin to stay for the night shift.

8

Mrs. Weinstein, my new best friend, and I drive off in her white Rolls Royce convertible. She's so short, passersby must think it's a driverless car coasting in neutral. She slowly drives down Worth Avenue, a tony street of small high-end shops. I think I shall need nice clothes when I start to show expensive properties, but right now who has time to bother with real estate.

Mrs. Weinstein glides past Neiman Marcus, Gucci, Tiffany, and Chanel, asking where I'd like to start. I tell her anywhere but Tiffany, remembering my last outing there.

She pulls over and makes a phone call. She flashes an elfin smile as she tells someone named Babka to meet her at Ta-Boo in a half hour. It sounds like she's talking in some sort of Eastern European secret code language. I close my eyes for a moment to focus on any remnants of an Iron Curtain accent. This is when I notice she smells like a combination of Pastrami and that 1970's perfume—Wind Song.

Mrs. Weinstein seems to know her way around at Escada, whipping through the dresses like they are book pages. While she does this, I play with the sales lady's guard Chihuahua. I'm handed a rhinestone squirrel on a chain and told this will be my evening bag. It's a Judith Leiber purse. You'd think for $1385 it would hold a wallet.

Finally, Mrs. Weinstein shouts, "Bingo!" Despite her stumpy arms, she holds a long, white-jeweled gown in the air. It's something Miss Universe would wear—Miss Universe with an extra $9500. I sure hope she doesn't think I'm buying this. I wish there was a TJ Maxx on this street. She tells the sales lady that I'd like to try it on. Before I know it, I'm holding court in the velvet-draped dressing room.

Mrs. Weinstein, the sales lady and her dog are in the audience; I am directed to take my bra off, so they can get a better look.

I step into the divine dress, but can tell it's too tight. The next thing I know, the sales lady and Mrs. Weinstein have me facedown on the carpeting, with Mrs. Weinstein telling me to suck it in while the sales lady yanks on the zipper. The dog must think this is a perfect opportunity to revive me with her tongue. The minute I turn my head, the crafty dog grabs my bra from the chair and runs off with it. I can't very well chase her, so Mrs. Weinstein says she'll get it in a minute. With everyone's help I'm soon back on my feet, where the sales lady points to the floor and says we have a puddling problem—this apparently means excess fabric at the hem. The helpful sales lady unearths a pair of 6-inch rhinestone high heels and I toddle out, transformed.

Mrs. Weinstein whips out her Visa card. "Sold!"

"No, really, it's so expensive." Frankly, I'd rather have the money, but know I must keep this to my self.

"Please, dear," she says to me. "Babka will love it."

I'm wondering who this Babka character is, and assuming he'll be at the ball, when the ladies start waving their arms at me.

Clearly not concerned with my safety, they convince me to mount the dramatic curved staircase so I can make a grand descent. I must be really out of shape, as my heart is throbbing from the one flight of stairs.

I pivot at the top of the stairs and look down to see the instigator of my heart palpitations: Richard. Grabbing the railing, I slowly descend the marble stairs, stopping on the final step.

He just watches silently while his mother and the shop lady babble in overlapping dialogue.

"It fits her like a glove."

"Didn't think we could squeeze her in."

"It helped to take her bra off."

"Oh, where is that?"

"The dog ran off with it."

Finally, Richard says softly, "Emma, you look lovely."

Mrs. Weinstein tells the lady to let it out a few inches and have it delivered. She then directs Richard to go wait for us across the street at Ta-Boo. "Wait, what time is it? Oh, order me a Manhattan before happy hour is over."

"Oh, Mother!" he laughs, as he heads out the door.

I thank Mrs. Weinstein for the generous gifts then I change back into my beach clothes. Except now I'm wearing the really high-heels, because she tossed my flip-flops in the trash. And still no brassiere. It somehow never turned up, although I don't think Mrs. Weinstein looked very hard.

After we are all settled up, we patter across the street and meet Richard at the bar. He has four manhattans all lined up. "Mother, I don't know what happened, but somehow when you order one drink they give you two." He stands up and offers his mother his seat and me the vacant one next to it.

The bar is dark, with the only light coming in from the front, reflecting in his eyes. I sit on the high barstool and he stands before me in a place called Ta-Boo.

Mrs. Weinstein beams at us and suddenly exclaims, "You two have the same color eyes. I hope you're not related."

Without needing to look, Richard replies, "No, hers are different. They are more of a pale turquoise."

He then offers me one of the glasses. "Emma, would you like one of these, or did you want something stronger?"

I give him a look. "I'll try anything."

On cue, he pours the molten amber up to my lips and we fix on each other's eyes. Finally the cherries tumble forward in a concerted effort to break our spell. The cherries cause a tidal wave of liquor to gush into my mouth and down my chin.

"Whoa doggies!" I shudder a bit. "That is strong stuff."

Richard wipes my face and laughs. "Apparently, this is what keeps Mother alive."

I toast Mrs. Weinstein. "You look great for ninety-five."

"Thanks," she quips. "I'm eighty-seven."

I'm a little embarrassed, swearing that Irene told me her age.

Then she pats me on the leg. "I just say I'm ninety-five so people will say, 'Damn, you look good Esther!' Saves a lot of bother trying to look younger."

Richard is silently watching the interaction, and I catch him taking in my ensemble of tee shirt and hooker shoes. Suddenly, Mrs. Weinstein's mouth opens wide. "Say, I've got an idea! Emma, can I commission you to do a painting of my Babka?"

At first I forget what she is talking about.

Mrs. Weinstein is now eating the cherries from her second drink. "You can do more than cakes and naked men?"

I'm half apprehensive and half confident. "Um…yes."

Richard finally speaks up. "Mother, what do you have in mind?"

Mrs. Weinstein grabs the remains of Richard's drink. "You know, a nice portrait of your head."

"I'd be happy to do it as a thank you for the dress. In fact, I'll paint the whole family. I have a whole new tube of Ferrous black I can use for Lisa."

Mrs. Weinstein hops off her barstool. "Great it's settled."

Richard appears to be processing this idea. "How long will this take?"

"I paint really fast and sloppy; I can do it in a day."

Richard must realize he is outnumbered. "How about Wednesday?"

I nod my head, welcoming that which is taboo.

9

After a dreamy drive past palm trees and gumdrop shrubs, we drop off Mrs. Weinstein. She salutes like a little sailor. "Richard, can you take Emma home and bring my car back tomorrow?"

He misses the tiny mark of the house, landing instead at the ocean. He leaves the car by the side of the road and, pointing to the moon reflecting on the water, says, "Let's sit by the sea for a moment."

I take the crazy shoes off and he rolls up his pants and takes my hand as we cross the street. Palm Beach is probably the safest place on earth, and now I feel even safer. We sit on the sand with the moon on our faces. Here I can see the sadness in his eyes. I lie on my back to gaze at the stars. "Doesn't it seem like we've met before?"

"We did—twenty years ago in Needham."

I turn my head to face him. "No, like a thousand years ago."

He gets very quiet. After a while, he kisses my forehead in an innocent way.

Then he takes my hand and pulls me to the water's edge.

"A thousand years?" he says, "You have a good memory."

"Like it was yesterday."

"Just you, me and the sea."

"I wonder if the sea remembers us."

A wave comes up and splashes us with its wet, salty reply. Now that we're sopping wet, it's time to end our day of bliss. As we head to my house, I'm secretly hoping Kevin is not holding some sort of phallic ice carving seminar in my living room. Richard kisses my cheek and says goodbye.

When I get inside, I find Kevin and Ursula waiting for me upstairs. In their own separate ways, they both seem a little mad at me. Ursula is out of dog food, and Kevin says he has to work the entire week until the other waiter comes back from his gay cruise— all because of me. I show him my new dress and he looks at the tag.

"You did *not* just spend $9500 on a dress!"

I tell him Mrs. Weinstein paid for it. Now he's really mad.

10

It's hard not to love Irene. I'm just dropping her off at the top of the Flagmore's arched upper driveway when her gigantic green suitcase gets out of control and rolls down the front entry ramp. She tries to catch it, but can't before it crashes into a parked Lamborghini. After reporting the incident to the Flagmore security staff, we are released from custody but are deemed suitcase vandals.

As we take the elevator up, I tell her the Weinsteins have invited me to the "Dogs are People Too!" charity ball, and that Mrs. Weinstein bought me a dress. Irene suddenly gets some energy.

"Oh, I just love that mother. Rumor has it she was some sort of spy for Lithuania during the war."

"She's a little sneaky. She seems to like leaving me with Richard."

"Oh no! Stay away from him."

I say I can't help it. I think I knew him in a previous life.

"Did he have a wife in this previous life?"

"I can't remember. From now on I'll look for a ring."

"Honey, I need a little nap. Will you wait for me by the pool for an hour, then come up and help me with my pills and bandages?"

"I'll have to go home and get my swim suit."

"Don't bother, I've got a whole collection of bathing suits for you."

I help Irene into her bed and she directs me to open a drawer in her dedicated bathing suit center. There, on top of all the swimsuits, is a roll of duct tape. Irene can barely lift her arm. "Honey, don't you know all the lovely uses of duct tape? I could write a book. You can use it for killing warts, and a fix a leaky radiator; and most importantly, you can use it to lift a droopy butt in a swimsuit."

Back in the drawer, I find all sorts of one-piece bathing suits; they all have little skirts and look like something Charlie Brown characters would wear. Irene can tell I'm not impressed with her selection.

"If I were you, I'd wear the one with the tags still on it."

I pull out a large skirted one with a blue butterfly print.

"Oh, maybe you'll meet someone at the pool. Blue butterflies are a sign of love!"

She sends me to the kitchen for rice pudding. When I return, she takes a huge spoonful and points to me. "You, missy, are going to make some man very happy."

"I want to make Richard happy. I think I'm in love."

"Oh, for crying out loud! You just met the man."

"Yeah, that's the trouble with love at first sight: it happens so fast."

Irene drops her spoon. "Whoa. I've created a monster. I've got to fix you up with someone fast. What is your type? What age do you like?" She pulls out a pen and starts writing it down, like it's a grocery list.

I ponder the question. "Well, my range is 22 to 72."

"That narrows it down."

"And forget tall men. Nothing lines up."

"Ok. Now, do you want a rich lawyer like Larry?"

"I hate rich men. They're all so miserable."

Irene laughs. "Ok, so you're willing to go for short, old and poor. Jeez, honey; short and old I can do, but where am I gonna find a poor guy in this town?"

"Maybe some rich person's gardener?"

Irene is petting her dog, Dr. Phil. "Emma, you were so fixated on Richard I completely forgot about Graham. He's Richard's yacht captain."

I help her put a pink dress on the dog. "Richard has a yacht?"

"Stop thinking about Richard! I'm giving Graham your number."

"Oh, I don't know about blind dates. They always result in disappointment."

"You'll love him."

"No, *the guys* are always disappointed."

11

I finally get to go swimming. When I arrive at the pool I see a sea of blue, except it's the blue hair of old ladies rubbing lotion on their blue veins. Then I see one of them waving to me with her turkey waddle arm, incognito with her huge hat and huge sunglasses. Yeah, I can see Esther Weinstein as a spy. She pats the lounge chair next to her. "Emma, come sit close to me because I don't like to have to repeat gossip."

All conversations are a bit precarious in a building that houses Irene, Pudge and an ageing Lithuanian spy.

"I just brought Irene home from the hospital. She's in good spirits now."

"Should she be drinking already? You know, sometimes I feel guilty being friends with Pudge, knowing that Irene hates her."

"Why? I don't think Pudge is so bad. Why does Irene hate Pudge so much?"

Mrs. Weinstein looks around and whispers to me. "Well, after Bunny stole Richard from Pudge, Pudge stole Mr. Reijkeboer from Irene."

I try to follow. "But I thought Pudge was married to Saul?"

The patient Mrs. Weinstein lets out a deep sigh. "This is all post-Saul. Then the very wealthy Mr. Reijkeboer left Pudge for Miss Denmark, whom he was introduced to by one clever Irene."

"Wow. I can't wait to tell all this to Kevin…if I can just keep it straight."

"Here I'll draw it on a napkin for you."

Once she finishes her chart, Mrs. Weinstein leans in and says, "What choice do I have but to be friends with Pudge? I don't want her as an enemy. She's a lot like Bunny."

"I still haven't met Bunny. I'm not sure she's really alive."

"Oh, there are a lot of people in this town who wish that."

I go for a swim in the huge, pale blue pool, blissfully floating on my back in the glimmering sun. When I finally look up, I see someone who clearly doesn't belong. She looks like a supermodel: thirty, flaxen hair, high cheekbones. When she emerges in her wet, white, mesh bikini all heads turn. All action stops as well. Everyone seems completely oblivious to their assigned task, which is to deliver heated towels to people like me when we leave the pool. As I get out of the pool, my droopy suit has expanded like baby swim diapers. I scurry over to the towel bin to find it's empty. The pool boys, now made of stone, do nothing to help me. Only their eyes move as they watch the girl with flaxen hair reapply lotion with a rhythmic motion.

Meanwhile, I'm freezing and dripping wet. I'll just have to mention this to my hostess, I think, as I run to my lounge chair. There I find Richard, sitting next to Mrs. Weinstein. He also appears transfixed by this goddess. That is, until he notices my swimming suit and bursts out laughing.

12

Wednesday afternoon arrives at my doorstep with an apprehensive knock. I look out to see Richard in the drizzling rain. Kevin answers the door. "Oh, hello, Dr. Weinstein. I'll be leaving soon, so it will just be you two…all alone."

"It's a conspiracy," Richard mutters.

I pop out of the kitchen. "Hi, Richard, I've made us some tea."

Taking off his wet raincoat, Richard says, "I wasn't sure what to wear."

Kevin shoves an entire scone in his mouth. "Wisn't wit a wude?"

After a moment of translating, Richard looks worried.

I correct him. "No, Kevin, it's not a nude. I'm doing an oil of his head."

"Sounds naughty to me," Kevin says out of the corner of his mouth.

Richard peers around the tiny living room. "Where are we going to do this?"

"My easel's upstairs in the bedroom."

Kevin raises his eyebrows and makes an exaggerated wink.

"Now, Kevin," Richard says, then cautiously follows me up the stairs, carrying my silver tea set and a jar of orange marmalade. Thinking a little music might relax him, I play a Nat King Cole album on my old phonograph.

We can hear the rain on the roof. I have Richard sit at my wooden desk, but can tell he's uncomfortable so I suggest he sit up in my bed and lean against the headboard. The mellow Nat King Cole is singing "Nature Boy." Richard swallows hard, like he's going to cry, and says it was his father's favorite song.

I ask about his father and am told he emigrated from Poznan, Poland, as a child, and was a butcher in Buffalo.

Even though it's three in the afternoon, it's dark in my room, with very little light coming in the French doors. I open them a bit and the breeze blows the sheers in a whimsical way. It's very romantic, until Kevin runs up the stairs.

"Forgot my table crumber."

He peers into Ernesto's window. "I hope Ernesto doesn't get a visit from the Howler Monkey. Well, I'm off. I'll leave you two alone."

Richard sips his tea quietly; I see his eyes reflected in the shiny silver teapot. He wipes marmalade from my lips with napkin embroidered with blue butterflies.

I tell him to relax as I mix up the paints, explaining that it takes awhile.

Ursula takes this opportunity to jump on his lap. I don't know whether it's the rain or the song, but we are both very quiet and the romantic mood has returned—until Kevin runs back in.

"Emma, can it borrow your car? It's really pouring out."

I turn the lamp on, but it's too bright. I find a pug-shaped candle and hand Richard the matches. He laughs while trying to light the wick on the curly tail. Soon the room is cast with dim shadows.

Not perfect for getting colors right, but still lovely.

Like frosting, I stir up a palette of Cerulean blue, adding Arctic white and bit of Oxide of Chromium green. Somehow I have no trouble recreating the crystal blue of his eyes. I tell him with his tanned face and his blue eyes, the painting will have Modigliani colors.

I'm finally ready, and ask him to hold still as I sketch his face.

"Which way to you want me to face?"

I take his face in my hands to try to get just the right angle. He stares into my eyes while I tilt his chin. My lips are really close to his; I want to kiss him. I want to hide right in his warm heart. I am bad. Bad, bad portrait artist.

I tell him to hold still while I slather the orange and white paint on the white canvas; I then add contrasting green to the orange to make a shadow for the frown lines around his mouth and eyes. He can't see what I am doing, as I paint. I'm completely focused, unable to juggle a conversation with my process. Whipping up a mixture of black, white and blue to make his hair, I realize I need more white and think maybe he's older than fifty-seven. Richard suddenly jerks his head to sneeze and apologizes.

Now, on to his precious eyes. I savor the painting of his eyes. I want to kiss his eyes while they are open. His eyes are so kind and watery. Like the sparkling Gulf Stream.

"Emma, when did you learn to paint?"

"I only remember it started when I baked a cake and made paint look like frosting."

"Did you study art in college?"

"Heavens no. I studied computer science. Dad thought I'd never get married and said I'd starve as a painter."

"Computer Science; really?"

"Yes, I know, people find it hard to believe. I can't even follow the instructions to change a vacuum cleaner bag."

Richard laughs. "Oh, am I allowed to laugh?"

"Yes, I love your laugh and your voice."

I tell him his voice is like Bergamot tea and mahogany wood.

He rubs his chin with his finger. "That's fascinating that you use senses other than your hearing to describe a voice. There's a medical term for that. What is it? I know, you may have synesthesia."

Now I'm sorry I said anything. Soon, he'll probably diagnose my obsessive-compulsive disorder and my assortment of phobias. I feel like a transparent bundle of neuroses on a shrink's leather sofa.

"It's a good thing, actually. Well, if you're an artist or writer. Do you find your self associating numbers with colors?"

I nod my head yes like a child. "Four has always been green to me. Five is blue. Do you do that?"

"No, they're just numbers to me. And the rest of the world."

Afraid he'll ask more probing questions, I hide behind my easel and try to capture his ears. He has nice thick ear lobes. I want to nibble on them, but keep this to myself. I try to focus on the painting again. My headboard is shiny pink; I don't know how to make shiny, plus it will clash with his skin and coral shirt, so I make it green. He's surprised at how fast I paint. He tells me not to rush, as the rain is not letting up any time soon.

Mixing up several more globs of paint, I tell him it will probably take a year to dry. I bend down to put another record on; this time a 78 rpm by Lawrence Tibbett, "Myself When Young." Richard reminisces about his father's old wooden sailboat, which had an old record player.

Wistfully, he adds that they could only play it in port as the needle skipped with the waves. He's surprised someone my age would have an old 78 record player.

Silently, he sips his tea and looks up at me. It's like a scene from a movie. When I get closer to paint his lips, I pull the candle up to see they are full, but undefined color- wise. It's then I realize I have a problem: I can't find the color to capture the sadness in his face. I guess I'll just mix in some Payne's gray. Poor, sweet man. When I get closer, my heart pounds more. I hope he can't hear my heart. If he could, he'd probably think I have some sort of arrhythmia requiring immediate medical attention.

Ursula is asleep on his lap now; hopefully her snoring covers the sound of my pounding heart. After I spend some time working on the details, I notice Richard has also fallen asleep.

When the painting is done, I carefully curl up next to him on the bed. I wonder what will happen. If anything does, I'll blame it on Esther Weinstein. It's not like I want to make love to him, I just want to love him. I know I already do. I lean over and kiss his sleeping mouth. When I open my eyes, I see Ernesto peering in from his bedroom window.

After Richard leaves, I find the little moleskin notebook by my bed and write the poem that comes flowing quickly to my head. I realize any romance with Richard will have a sad and lonely ending.

He speaks of sailboats and tea
his voice mahogany and Bergamot
The rain pelts our window
I tell him I love rainy days
He says I'm the only one
I serve him orange marmalade
from estate-sale silver
a tarnished wedding present
but not ours
I'll bring it back to life
Along with the man
Who belongs to another
When he leaves,
I reminisce about
the soul
with the rainy-day eyes
who speaks of the sea
As I sit alone with my scones and tea.

13

The angels must have read my unrequited love poem. Shortly after Richard leaves, I receive a call from the Graham fellow Irene mentioned. With a most endearing English accent, he invites me to meet him for a drink at a place called Bice, which he pronounces 'Beach-ay.' When I ask him how I'll recognize him, he says he'll be the man standing there waiting for the gorgeous woman.

"Oh, are you also meeting someone else?"

He laughs a hearty Burgundy laugh, which fades to a Riesling whimper. *Maybe I do have synesthesia.*

Channeling my inner spy, I tell him I'll wear a trench coat with a red carnation in the lapel. He replies with a sexy, "Really?" Then I realize my raincoat is back in D.C. at Larry's pool, and I don't have a red carnation, so I tell him I'll be wearing a red dress. And nothing but.

"What were you thinking?" Kevin asks after I hang up.

"I don't know. Blame it on Esther. Blame it on estrogen."

"No. You look terrible in red."

I spend the rest of the night with Kevin and Ursula, practicing our English accents as we watch *Goldfinger*. Unfortunately, the film's title has a Pavlovian effect, compelling me to run out to get a family-sized Butterfinger. *Kevin and I are like family.* Wanting to get a full night of beauty rest, we sleep until the crack of 10:00 and awake to a fierce rain. As we do not have regular jobs, Kevin and I—and Ursula for that matter—are free to take advantage of the James Bond Marathon all day today. I feel justified, as I'm on one of my five-day "Ladies' Holidays."   Not knowing what I'm talking about, Kevin says he's on a ladies' holiday too and joins me in eating and drinking.

70

The rain and the marathon linger for another day, into the day of the lucky dress. At 6:30 I pull out my one and only red dress, preparing to meet my future husband. Hey, listening to the glorious James Bond accent for thirty-six hours straight is almost enough to clean Richard's intellectual accent out of my head. With minutes to spare, Kevin assists by pulling up my zipper. As usual and without prompting, he grabs the pliers from my dresser drawer and yanks.

"I need three hands: two to pull the fabric together and one to pull the zipper up. Wait, I've got an idea."

After making odd searching noises downstairs, Kevin comes back with a huge grin and proceeds to tie a huge dog bone to my zipper and summons Ursula to assist. I lie face down over the edge of the bed and Ursula pulls the bone with all her might. No luck. In a perky tone, Kevin proposes he put the red dress on to stretch it out for me. I watch as he puts the ruffled dress over his head with glee, which swiftly fades when it gets stuck under his arms, not budging up or down.

I try to call this Graham fellow to tell him I'll be late, and not wearing red, but I think it's the yacht number on my cell and it goes to voicemail. Running short on time, I decide to give up and wear a white halter dress. My strapless bras are no doubt decorating the highway, so with Kevin's clinical assistance we tape up my breasts with duct tape. As Kevin zips me, he gets his red ruffle caught in my zipper, sticking us together!

"How could this happen?" I plead.

Kevin reminds me of the entire box of Snyder hard pretzels I consumed yesterday. I defend myself, pointing out Ursula ate the two that fell on the floor. Well, one.

Kevin can't get the dress out of the zipper without ruining both dresses. He grabs the pliers and says he will disconnect us in the car.

Getting into the car is nearly impossible with Kevin's chest hooked to my back like conjoined twins. We realize Ernesto has been witnessing the spectacle when we hear his uncontrollable hyena laugh. When he finally gets his diaphragm back under control, he helps un-tether us.

Kevin offers to drive me to my date to save time, but I have known him long enough to know he is anxious to get a look at Graham. After parking the car in a linear swerve, we race to the entrance of Bice. We look about, but see no men. In fact, the place is empty except for a two hundred pound woman wearing, of all things, a red dress.

"Oh no!" Kevin cries. "Graham probably saw her and ran."

"Now what do I do?"

"You simply tell this woman you were to have worn a red dress as a signal for your blind date and ask if any man approached her looking for an Emma."

I make my way to the bar, and notice that Kevin is still by my side. On the way, I see a dark haired man enter the doorway. Ah, I already love his jagged hairline and dramatic temples. He hovers a bit, and I'm worried he's about to escape. Perhaps he thinks Big Red is me and he's wondering what to do. I wave him over and tell Kevin that he's free to leave me on my date.

I say rapidly, "Sorry I'm late, but we had a little wardrobe malfunction." Kevin refuses to leave, so I jokingly grab the tablecloth like a cape, and drape it over Kevin's head. "Just pretend he's not here."

The man is smirking and asks if he can buy a round of drinks for the table. As Kevin and I order wine, I ponder Graham's accent. Hmm, that sounds more like a Spanish accent.

I tell him I'm sorry my red dress didn't fit, to which Kevin adds I ate an entire box of pretzels. "From now on, I'm going to think long and hard before I put anything into my mouth," I babble.

Kevin lifts his tablecloth. "That's naughty."

The man is laughing, and finally holds out his dark fingers. "Hi, my name is George."

"Emma once had a pet named George," Kevin blabs, "then she ate him."

"Oh, sorry," I say, "I thought you might be Graham." I look around and then continue. "I had a blind date, but I was supposed to wear a red dress...."

His eyes wander over to Big Red and he starts laughing. "That is why I hate blind dates."

Kevin feels the need to elaborate from under the cloth. "She's in love with her married doctor client, so they had to hurry up and fix her up with his handsome British yacht captain."

When the drinks arrive, Kevin takes the tablecloth off his head. "Look! There's that cute singer from the Leopard Lounge."

After passing our odd trio, the singer walks over to Big Red and hesitantly asks with a distinct English accent, "Are you by chance Emma? If so, my apologies for not being punctual."

I have a look of horror on my face. George gets the whole scene and bursts out laughing.

Big Red takes a very long drag on her cigarette and says in her best Mae West, "What kind of chance are you talking about?"

I call over. "Graham?"

Graham stares at Kevin wearing the bunched up red dress. Suddenly he looks at me. "Emma?"

"Hey, aren't you the singer at the Leopard Lounge?" Kevin asks.

"I sing here and there. I used to tour in a band."

Kevin asks if groupies use to throw panties at Graham. He politely says no. "Because Emma still hasn't found her underpants," Kevin continues. "She's wearing a bathing suit bottom right now."

Graham and I end up seated at the bar, sandwiched by George, Kevin and Big Red. Graham gracefully asks for a Beefeater martini straight up. I already love his accent. I just want to close my eyes and listen to him read the phone book…except I want to stare at him too.

He somehow has nice teeth for a Brit. I can only really see the lower teeth, which are short and white. His jaw is square, with a pronounced clef in his chin. At this moment, I know already that we will become lovers—I just don't know when.

Graham interrupts my daydream. "I remember you from the Leopard Lounge as well. You were wearing a rather large dress."

"Did you think she was pregnant with my baby?" Kevin inquires.

Graham, hesitant to answer, says, "Well, not your baby." He quickly changes the subject. "So, Irene tells me you're a painter. What do you paint?"

I'm so transfixed by his face I'm not even listening. What did he just say to me?

"What do you paint?" George repeats slowly.

"She specializes in naked men," Kevin answers.

I quickly give Kevin a look and say, "Don't you need to be somewhere?"

"Yes, I need to talk to my nicer friend." Kevin takes his drink and wanders down to Big Red's end of the bar, where I hear him say loudly, "You should have pretended you were Emma."

Graham folds up the cuffs on his crisp white shirt, prompting me to observe his large hands. "Did I hear that correctly, just naked men?"

"No, that's not true; I do Krimpets, too."

Graham asks how I know Irene. I give the short version and ask him the same.

"She's a friend of Trevor's. He and my father were old friends from when they were stationed at Malta in the British Navy."

"How long have you been in the States?"

He puts his lower lip over his top lip thinking and finally says, "I came to visit three years ago when the yacht was up for sale. Trevor brought Richard to meet me at a boat show. He bought the boat and asked me to stay on as captain."

"You just stayed here?"

Even though the bar is nearly empty, the George guy is inches away with his pointed temples impaling our conversation. Graham leans over and says to him, "You don't work for immigration do you?"

George shakes his head. "No. No. Where are you from, London?"

Graham takes a careful sip of his martini. "No, Batley, but I haven't been there in years." Then he gets a look like he's been in hiding, so he adds, "I've been working on a yacht in Palma."

"I've never been to Italy," I say. "I'm saving it for my honeymoon."

"Palma is in Spain," George answers, like he was on a game show.

I wonder out loud, "Did they move it?"

Graham puts an elegant, long finger on my hand. "I'll have to take you there."

I turn to George. "It's been nice meeting you," I joke, "but we've decided to have dinner in Spain."

Kevin returns and butts in, "Can the yacht go that far?"

"Yes, it's a forty meter Westport; the best there is."

"I guess I don't know my metrics—how big is that?" I say.

"It's a 130 feet," George says.

Impressed, I ask, "Did you do that in your head?"

"Do you know the Weinstein's boat?" Graham asks George.

George answers that he's seen it in the marina. I guess it's a small boating town.

Graham says, "It's a great yacht, but crossing the Atlantic is no simple undertaking. We'd have to get serious crew and refuel along the way—probably in the Azores."

Kevin bursts with glee. "The Azores! I know just what to wear."

Graham asks I'd like to get a table in the dining room. I think he wants to get away from George and Kevin. As we walk away, I look back and see Big Red has moved right next to George.

We are seated in a cozy banquette with a white tablecloth. I order the veal Masala, and Graham orders the lobster ravioli and antipasto for two.

He asks to see the wine list, puts on his glasses and spends a bit of time studying it. I'm happy because this gives me time to study his sea-green eyes. I look at the crinkles around his eyes and calculate he must be in his late forties—factoring in that Englishmen always look older than they are.

Before our wine arrives, I visit the ladies room and walk past the bar. Kevin is now talking to Big Red, and George is still sitting there.

I go back to my date with my future husband, Graham. We enjoy our wine and appetizer as I tell stories about Ursula. He tells me about his teenage children in Scotland, who have been living with his ex-wife and her new husband. I only catch some of what he is saying. It's hard to pay attention; he's so handsome, all I see are his lips moving.

He leaves the table just before our entrees arrive. Yay, I can try his ravioli. Yum! It's in a creamy wine sauce. When Graham returns he leans in and kisses me. Whoa! I make a moaning sound. He gently tries to put his tongue in my mouth. I keep my lips sealed.

"What kind of kiss is that?"

"I have two raviolis in there," I mumble.

After we finish, Graham asks if I'd like dessert. Knowing I'll need to be wearing a bathing suit at some time in the near future, I'm about to say no. Then all discipline goes out the window when he says, "I like a girl with a robust appetite like yours. It's rather sexy."

All right, one small crème brûlée won't kill me. While we wait, I turn to see the bar and notice that Kevin, Big Red and George are all watching. Graham asks if I'd like to have a drink on the boat this week. Like I'd say no. I ask if the Weinsteins will be there. He says, no; Bunny Weinstein isn't allowed on the boat anymore, and Richard will be in Ft. Lauderdale. This is useful to date a man's employee.

14

Kevin answers the door wearing a hot pink, fur-lined apron. It's his first catering gig at Pudge's. She invited me as a guest, but Kevin asked me to come over early to help. "My assistant is finally here!" he yells to Pudge.

Pudge's pad has a 1980s motif, complete with Plexiglas dining table, vinyl upholstery and mirrored walls. It's hard to believe she's a decorator. Who are her clients? Anal-retentive minimalists, who were in comas for 20 years, no doubt.

I don't see Pudge's reflection anywhere, so I ask Kevin, "So, who else is coming to this luncheon?"

"Besides you, there are only three other guests: Esther Weinstein, Lisa Weinstein and Natasha something."

"Who's Natasha?"

"She's sunning herself on the balcony. All I know is that she's about 30 and married to a hairdresser."

"Oh, good. I need some younger female friends, and I'm going to need a hairdresser soon."

"I don't think you want to hang out with her." Kevin gestures over to the bedroom terrace. It's the flaxen supermodel! Kevin waits for my shocked mouth to close before saying, "See what I mean?"

She's topless, with just a bulky towel around her waist.

Kevin points. "Look at her. I guess nipples come in three flavors," he says, "chocolate, vanilla and strawberry. Yours are strawberry."

I put my hands over my chest and start to think it's time for new door locks.

"Oh, come on. I've seen them a million times when you're sprawled out snoring. It must be an eye color thing, otherwise I'd think yours would be the brown ones and hers would be pink."

He is pointing directly at her full breasts and adds, "I think they're real. I tell you, it's enough to make me come back to the other side."

I look at her round tummy under the towel and think, yes, girl bellies and large breasts go hand in hand. I turn my head away just before she catches Kevin pointing at her.

We're saved when we hear Pudge calling in her shrill voice. Safely back in the kitchen, Kevin is in full gossip mode about Natasha. He spoons crabmeat out of Tupperware and says, "Apparently she was a mail-order bride from Russia and lives some place near the power plant with her latest husband, Pierre, who is from some awful place like Albania or Albany."

I eat crabmeat off the spoon. "She was at the Flagmore pool the other day, but her stomach was flat then."

Kevin pats my belly. "Maybe she gets into the pretzels too."

"What I'm trying to figure out is why Pudge would invite her."

Kevin looks over his shoulder. "It's called disarming the enemy."

"What does Pudge have to worry about?"

"All I know is that wives are getting traded in left and right in this town; husbands are going with the new foreign models."

"But Pudge doesn't have a husband to lose."

"Maybe she's got her eye on somebody else's," Kevin says in a conspiratorial voice.

"After what I found out yesterday, I'd say she wants to steal Richard back from Bunny and is using Mrs. Weinstein to get to him."

I peer out at the wide-eyed Praying Mantis—preying on Richard.

"We'd better talk in code," Kevin whispers. "I'm sure Esther-ay is on to Udge-pay."

Then I have my "ah ha" moment. "Maybe Mrs. Weinstein is using Pudge to get rid of Bunny."

Kevin shushes me. "Use the code."

"Kevin, what is taking so long?" Pudge calls out.

Kevin pushes a jar of mayonnaise on me. "I'm so far behind; throw this in the salad, will you?"

"So, Kevin," I joke, "how do you like working for Pudge?"

In a tone fitting Liberace, Kevin says, "Oh, I just love her." Then he winks at me. "Do you think I should give her a little salmonella?"

Pudge orders Kevin around, snapping her manicured fingers at him. Natasha finally enters in some sort of low cut Empire gown. She's chatting with Lisa and Mrs. Weinstein about homosexuality. Lisa says her brother is gay. Kevin and I come to a complete halt in our lunch preparation in the kitchen at this bit of juicy news. We have to open up the half shutters in the kitchen. We didn't know there was a brother.

Mrs. Weinstein jumps in. "But he's not over the top, like Kevin."

"I love gay men," Natasha declares cheerfully. "They don't ogle your breasts all day long, like some people."

Kevin yanks back the shutters. "I wasn't ogling, I was researching."

The crab salad course goes off without a hitch. I return to my assisting job in the kitchen, having given up posing as a proper guest. Now Kevin is spooning ice cream into little crystal bowls. "I love this catering gig. I'm learning so much about the people here in Palm Beach."

"I love it here. I can't wait to start selling some real estate."

"Emma, if I were pretty like you—well, I am pretty—but if I were a girl, I'd forget about being a real estate agent and get in on this rich husband thing before it's too late. These Palm Beach wives have it made."

"I would be happy with my singing yacht captain."

We see Natasha's eyes perk up. Besides the obvious—she's beautiful, with a palette of flaxen hair, golden skin and honey-golden eyes—there is something subtle about her look that undoubtedly makes men want to protect her. Definitely not the kind of woman you want for a best friend.

Pudge yells for Kevin to serve the cherries jubilee. I'm hiding in the kitchen watching through a crack in the louver. I wince as he pours the brandy and spills it all over Pudge. He lights the tray of cherries until a blue flame hovers about. In a second, we see that Pudge's skirt also has the blue flame hovering about. It's like it's happening in slow motion, until I wake up and fly from the kitchen with a pitcher of iced tea. I put out the fire, but Pudge is now dowsed and has a lemon slice clinging to her face. Natasha brings her a towel and helps clean up. Mrs. Weinstein promptly has a coughing fit and runs to the powder room. I follow her to see if she's ok and she bursts out laughing. "Emma, that was so funny the way you poured the tea right on Pudge's head. I laughed so hard I wet my pants."

"Oh, Mrs. Weinstein, I'm so sorry."

"It's okay, dear, I just live next door; and I've got fifty pairs of white polyester pants."

15

Graham has invited me to the Breakers Hotel for our second date. As I don't want Kevin tagging along, I tell Graham I'll meet him there. I love the Breakers and am happy I can easily walk there. A girl should always live within walking distance of a five star hotel.

It's like being in some sort of Italian Renaissance palace. The ceilings look like they're forty feet high and have ornate coral and pale blue carvings. I'm so busy looking at the ceilings I trip over the patterns on the carpeting.

I venture back to the Seafood Bar overlooking the ocean. The bar is made of an eight-inch high Plexiglas aquarium, with fish swimming under your drink. Somehow, I always seem to attract the resident eel, which sleeps under my drink, driving me to place cocktail napkins all over my section, so I don't have to see it.

As I wait for my sexy yacht captain, I wonder if the fish know they are trapped in a fancy hotel bar. I wait and I wonder, and wait some more. Now I wonder if maybe he's run off with Natasha...or Big Red. After half an hour, I get a call from him.

"Emma? Have you become trapped in a dress? Lost your knickers again?"

"Um, no. I'm here. Where are you?"

"I'm here at the bar. Oh, I should have told you the *new* HMF, on the north side."

I wander down to the main lobby, passed demure staff. I enter a two hundred-foot salon, with the same forty-foot high ceilings.

Graham is sitting at the bar. He kisses me on both cheeks and says, "I'm so sorry. We've lost our table reservation, but there is another table in an hour or two."

"I love sitting at the bar. Let's have sushi here."

They have a sake menu. He orders a trio and several complicated sushi items. I ask what he ordered, and he says sometimes it's better not to know.

"Some things you have to eat with your eyes closed," I say innocently.

His eyebrows go from southwest to northeast.

As he sips his sake, I look at his mouth and wonder where has he been all my life? It's like he reads my mind when he suddenly says he lived in Shanghai for a year, teaching English to schoolchildren. Those poor Chinese girls; they probably didn't learn a word if they stared at his lips.

After dinner he invites me for a drink on the boat. We take his car to the beautiful starlit marina on South Lake Drive that Kevin and I had visited. When he punches a code to open the gate, he half-jokingly makes me look the other way. He gently holds my hand as my heels get caught in every other plank on the dock, until we reach the huge yacht at the very end. It's the one Kevin and I saw: *No Woman, No Cry.*

He suggests I take my sandals off and gently helps me over the gangplank. He opens a heavy sliding door and we step into a beautiful stateroom. It's like a huge living room, with normal furniture, and has the same Asian feel as in Dr. Weinstein's house. It's easy to forget one is on a boat as he offers me a tour. He looks at me and says I needn't bring my purse. Adding, "there's no gift shop."

He holds my hand and points out the galley, which looks like a kitchen in a large home. Directly in front of the galley is a room that looks like the command center at Cape Canaveral. There's a ship's wheel and lots of computer screens and dials; he says this is the wheelhouse. He says Richard had the yacht customized, so it could be manned from either the top or mid level.

We go up another spiral flight of stairs to see the top open air deck; he explains the fly bridge area with another captain's wheel and dashboard of dials, along with an outdoor seating area. We go back down two more flights to a series of little cabins, each with its own bath.

"Richard hates to have a lot of staff, so Ping and Trevor help crew the boat. After Trevor left the Navy, he became the private yacht captain for Esther and her late husband."

"Is that what happens next, you become their butler?"

"God no! His sight is failing. Besides, he likes playing butler. It's not like he cleans or anything."

"Who cleans that big house then?"

"All of the maids in town refuse to clean for Bunny, so they have to hire outside teams to come in once a week."

I want to know more about this comically awful Bunny person. "How come Bunny is not allowed on the boat?"

Graham laughs. "I said I'd quit if she ever sets one foot on the boat again. I should have said I'd throw her overboard if she ever comes on, but she's probably a biohazard."

"Is she really that rotten?"

Graham sighs. "I don't know how he puts up with her. The whole town hates her."

"Really?"

"Yes. She caused a waiter strike one year, and now once a year all the restaurants close for Waiter Appreciation Day, which has been dubbed Rabbit Day."

As he talks, we tour an endless series of little cabins with built-in beds. Graham says there are five guest cabins and three crew cabins, which are in the lower aft quarters. I find a huge bedroom that, unlike the others, is as wide as the boat.

This must be Richard's master stateroom. I visit one of the bathrooms onboard and see a white bikini hanging on the back of the door. Hmm?

We go back to the main deck and Graham pours me a glass of white wine then looks in my eyes and tells me not to run off. Like there would be any chance of that. He comes back in jeans and a green polo shirt and I can see his muscular forearms.

"I should have worn something more comfortable, or at least less torturous."

He disappears down the spiral staircase again, so I begin yanking at the long piece of duct tape holding things up. He returns and catches me. "Well, I see what's holding you together." He tosses me a long *No Woman No Cry* tee shirt.

"If you look the other way I can take this off."

He pretends to cover his eyes with gapping fingers while I transform. In a posh English accent, he asks, "Is that a swimsuit bottom?"

"Yes, all my underpants are still missing, and new ones cost $135 on Worth Avenue."

Graham reaches over and picks up a golden guitar. He plays an Eddie Vedder song; "Society." It's very anti-establishment, and makes me think I could live as a poor person with him. I could cook and he could sail the boat. His voice is so smooth, like butterscotch and reedy wood. All men should go and get a guitar and sing to women. They would get way more action. I interrupt his singing and kiss him. He takes the guitar from between us and zeros in on my mouth. Then he uses the tip of his tongue to part my lips more. He laughs and says, "So much nicer without the ravioli." We kiss for the longest time. Thoughts swirl through my head, like what will our babies look like. It's a good thing men cannot read minds or, for that matter, understand a single thing we say. He pushes me back on the leather banquette and leans over me.

He starts at my forehead, kisses my eyes, skips to my neck and lifts up the shirt and fondles my breasts. "Umm. I hope I'm not being politically incorrect, but I love voluptuous women." Then he adds, "I think thin girls are overrated."

He pulls off a piece of the duct tape. I can tell I am getting very juicy and wonder if I'm ovulating.

Let's see…had cramps during eighteen hour car ride to Palm Beach and made Kevin stop ten times for Aleve and Lorna Doones—an excellent combo. While I'm doing my calculation, Graham must be still in the moment, as he appears to have gotten "enthused." He seems a little embarrassed.

"It's not what you think. It's not a flashlight."

Do men have any control over these events? I know I have to get out of here before I get carried away. "I should probably be running along."

Gesturing south, Graham says, "You aren't going to make me walk down the dock like this?"

I wonder what men must think of to make it go away.

"Esther Weinstein wants me to do a painting for the charity ball. Will you pose for me?"

Graham freezes. "Not one of you infamous nudes?"

I nod. "I'll make it tasteful."

"I don't mind if you're the one tasting." Then he puts on a faux Scottish accent and says, "But I don't want the whole town leering at me John Thomas."

I laugh. "We can leave him out. It will be just you."

He walks me to his green Jaguar in the marina lot and opens the door for me.

We arrive outside of my little house. While he is giving me a slow, deep kiss, I notice one of his eyes is open. He suddenly stops. "Do you have a husband you failed mention, or is that Kevin?" I look up, and see Kevin, peering out the kitchen window like Mrs. Kravitz on Bewitched.

"Let's save the tour for another night," Graham suggests.

"Here's your tour, just peek through the keyhole."

He kisses me. "I'd like to peek in your keyhole."

As Graham drives off into the night, I close the heavy Periwinkle wooden door behind me.

"Well? Did you have sex?" Kevin bursts out.

"Of course not!"

"Were you less than ladylike?"

I ignore him. "I'm in love!"

"Again?" Kevin says, which sounds more like "whawhen" given his mouth full of Fritos.

"This is different than with Dr. Weinstein. Graham is actually single."

"So, let's review," Kevin says, pointing with a Frito. "You've been here less than two weeks, and so far you've fallen in love with a married billionaire and now his poor, singing yacht captain."

"And he's going to pose for my charity ball painting."

"How come you have all the luck? I went over to that trendy hip gay hotel, not to be redundant, and it was swarming with lesbians."

"Well, they can be fun, and maybe they have brothers. Did you make friends with any of them?"

"There was one I thought was stalking me, until I realized it was because I was sitting next to the margarita machine. I ended up just coming home." Kevin says 'home' like it's his house. "I was watching *The Wizard of Oz*, but the flying monkeys were even scarier with Ernesto's Howler Monkey carrying on."

"He must be good." I pull the wadded up duct tape out of my purse and throw it in the trash.

"It looks like the sisters got out tonight."

"You try wearing duct tape all night."

"You took it off at the restaurant?!"

"No, on the yacht."

"You got to go for a yacht ride, while I had to sit home eating Fritos with your dog?"

"I'll be sure to ask him if I can bring an extra guest next time."

Kevin turns his back. "Don't bother. I'll ask my new best friend, Dr. Weinstein."

16

In another effort to make a friend for our only child, Ursula, we venture to the beach. There, we see our next-door neighbor, Ernesto, wearing a small white Speedo that barely covers his bronzed body. Kevin wants to get a closer look, so he picks up Ursula and decides to give her swimming lessons in the surf. Ursula quickly runs from the water, shaking it everywhere. Then she rolls in the sand and shakes all over me and my coffee.

A little peeved, I ask, "Will you take Ursula back and hose her off? And bring me a new coffee?"

Kevin takes my pug mug. "Okay, but while you're sitting here, try to get some info out of Ernesto."

Ernesto emerges from the sea in his now opaque suit. Wow! I can see the shape of things to come. Surely he's a shower, not a grower. Kevin taught me that lingo as some men are big and don't get much bigger, and some men are small and get huge. I hope there's no cartoon bubble over my head showing my thoughts. Ernesto is forced to come over because I'm sitting right near his towel.

"Hi, Ernesto. I can't believe you got in that water with the jelly fish."

"My shower isn't working, so I have to come here."

"I guess you could go to your girlfriend's and take one."

"My girlfriend?"

"What's her name?"

"Um, um…"

Ernesto escapes my subtle interrogation by saying, "I really have to be getting back."

A few minutes later I see Kevin running down the lane. "Emma! Whew, you wouldn't believe it! I was minding my own business, you know on my way to get you more coffee, when your dog decides to run through Ernesto's broken screen again."

"Oh, don't tell me you went in?"

"Well, I had to. And she was eating his cat's food, so I tried to refill it. I couldn't help but notice he had a Hermes belt sitting on the sofa, you know with the big 'H.' Well this inspired me to take a quick run up the stairs to look in his closet, and there I spotted it: a Neiman Marcus box with a pair of patent leather Ferragamo loafers. And you know what that means?"

"He paid too much?"

"No, they have sales. No, it means he's a member."

"Kevin, I can't believe you went upstairs. What if he caught you?"

"I would have made up something, like Ursula pooped up there and I was cleaning it up—that's highly plausible."

"You must have just gotten out."

"Wait, it gets better. When I looked in the drawer next to his bed, guess what?"

I'm afraid to guess.

"There was a gun!"

Now I'm worried. "You're lucky he didn't shoot you."

"I heard him coming and ran out the back door." An alarmed look overcomes him. "Oh no! I left your pug mug in his kitchen."

I look around frantically. "Where's Ursula?"

91

"Oh no. I left your pug in his kitchen too!"

My mind is racing; racing to thoughts such as, never let Kevin so much as babysit a houseplant. "Kevin!"

"Don't worry. I'll be your lookout when you go to get her back. I think that our little Ernesto has something to hide."

Kevin and I walk back and see Ernesto through the back door washing off the sandy Ursula in the garden. Ernesto hands me the pug mug saying, "This is yours, I presume."

I use Kevin's lame excuse. "I see Ursula was tempted by your little Friskies."

"I guess I'll have to fix my screen...and lock my door."

Trying to give the appearance of composure, I say, "Ernesto, thank you so much for washing Ursula."

He smiles "No extra charge."

17

Like he's my child, I send Kevin off on his bicycle with his Brady Bunch lunch pail. As a reverse commuter in life, he takes it empty and brings it home full of food from the restaurant. Just as I am peacefully enjoying my coffee with my sneaky dog, and wondering about my next date with Graham, I get a call from Irene.

"Kevin is having one of his dramas. He was run over by a car and needs you to race over here right away."

"Which hospital?"

"No, come to the lunch club and bring his new blazer."

"What?"

"He said to hurry and come the beach way."

I take the short cut down the beach and run into Kevin by the sea grape trees outside the restaurant. He grabs the jacket and exhales. "Oh, thank goodness, you are here!"

"Are you ok?"

"You'll never believe it. I was tooling along minding my own business when a huge blue Bentley suddenly ran me down. So there I am, lying on the ground with Mavis's basket crushed and Marsha Brady's face dented, when a cop comes over and asks if I'm all right. Then he starts to write me a ticket. He said he watched me ride my bike right into the man's car, and pointed to the pink scrape. Well, a crowd of elderlies soon formed and backed the policeman's version of the story. I don't know what sort of fine one gets in Palm Beach for riding a bicycle into a Bentley. Then the driver finally got out of his car. Emma, it was like a giant golden god appeared. It was lust at first sight. His name is Hudson DuPont, III. He was on his way to the Flagmore Club and invited me to lunch. He's waiting for me on the outside terrace."

I peer around the sea grape and see a chunky forty-something wearing a navy blue blazer to hide his unfortunate hippopotamus hips. Kevin rips off his animal print shirt, revealing his tee shirt. I'm thinking Kevin should keep his leopard on for Hudson's hippo, but am focused on more important matters than Safari animals. I ask, "Don't you have to wait tables?"

He taps my shoulder. "That's where you come in."

"What?"

"I can't let my soul mate find out who I really am."

I say, "I wouldn't be caught dead waiting tables at my age."

"Where did I hear that excuse before?"

He had me there. "But I don't remember how to wait tables."

"It's very simple. You take the order, then bring the food."

Kevin puts on his lucky blazer and sunglasses and sneaks around the back.

I reluctantly put on the shirt, and am instantly summoned by a customer—Irene. She's in my section and wants an iced coffee. I start to explain the Kevin update and how I got stuck in this horrible shirt.

"Yeah, saw that coming," she mutters.

I spy an incognito Kevin laughing on the terrace and think this is okay. He was just in a car accident. He would do the same for me. Well–maybe not. As I'm figuring out the iced coffee, the manager comes up behind me and bellows, "What do you think you are doing?" I'm petrified and want to run. "That's decaf!" he exclaims.

On my way back to my section, I notice Mrs. Weinstein exiting the ladies room. She has toilet paper trailing from the back of her pants as she traipses through the dining room to Irene's table. I catch the tail and break it off.

"Thanks, Emma. I thought someone was following me." She takes a seat with Irene. "I just had a thought. Richard is taking the boat out on Sunday, and I'm sure he'd love it if you two could come along."

Irene looks sad. "I'm starting chemo, and chemo and sea sickness don't mix, but Emma you go."

My mind ponders this fresh fantasy: Richard, Graham and me together on a yacht sailing the high seas. I wonder if they will fight over me; possibly a duel with swords along the gangplank.

Mrs. Weinstein waves her hand over my face. "So is that a yes?"

"Oh, I think I can squeeze that into my schedule."

"Good. Meet me in my lobby around noon."

The minute the manager heads to the kitchen, I see Kevin frantically waving to me from the terrace. He gushes as he introduces me to Hudson DuPont, III.

"Did you hear the tale of how we met?" Hudson asks in an overplayed, lockjaw accent.

I manage to keep my mouth shut, as I don't want to say anything incriminating against Kevin, or Mavis the bike. Then, I can't contain my latest news. I tell them all the wait staff in my section, meaning me, have been invited on the Weinstein's yacht on Sunday. If only Kevin worked here, he'd be invited too.

Kevin is having a fit. "May terrace guests come?"

I say I don't think so.

Hudson gets up and says he has to get going, which is a good thing, as the manager spots Kevin on the terrace. The minute Hudson leaves, I hand Kevin his shirt and he is back in his section, hoping for a yacht invite from Mrs. Weinstein—but it's too late, as she has just left.

Irene tells me she ordered me lunch and to have a seat. While we wait, I get more gossip from her. Apparently, Mrs. Weinstein's husband died and left a lot of money to Richard, but it all went into Bunny's name because of his belly button lawsuit. Kevin is listening in, ignoring all his other customers, who are yelling at him. When he leaves, I tell Irene benign details of my date with Graham.

"I was hesitant to introduce you because he works for Richard, but I knew I had to get your mind off Richard."

"You know I would never do anything with Richard."

"Good, because he's probably going to stay married, and you don't want to be on Bunny's bad side."

"That's too bad. He doesn't seem very happy."

"He makes do. It will be fascinating to hear how you handle it with both Richard and Graham on the boat on Sunday."

"I had drinks on the boat with Graham."

"Don't let Richard know Graham has been entertaining you there. If he ever lost that job he'd have to leave the country."

"Really?"

"Sure. Most captains are foreign citizens who can stay on the boat, but not on land."

"Maybe he should marry a nice US citizen so he can stay on land."

18

After a little pug nap, I peek out the window and see a blue Bentley with a pink triangle-insignia bike protruding from the trunk. Kevin, dressed in his new used blazer, returns with Hudson in tow. Kevin offers Hudson a Corona from my kitchen and they join me in the garden.

"So, any lawsuits filed against Mavis the bike?" I gently inquire.

Hudson waves his hand. "I prefer to not have the authorities involved for such a small matter."

Feeling like a third wheel, or training wheels on their date, I decide to go upstairs to paint. Like most tortured artists, I find myself in a compositional debate. Sometimes it's whether to paint a man sitting, standing or leaping in the air. Often, practicality is the determining factor, as a leap is hard to maintain. Today's debate is between a mango and an avocado. With still lifes of food, the determining factor is always what I can resist eating until it's finished. I decide to paint the mango, so I can make guacamole. I'm in the little study area off my bedroom and I can see out the open screened window. I have a perfect aerial view of the garden and can see that Hudson needs to get his roots re-touched. At first I thought they were gray, but as I study his clock-wise swirl, I see blond roots, not gray. Who dyes their hair darker? As I set up my easel and mix my paints, I can't help but listen to their loudly whispered conversation.

Kevin talks into his Corona like it's the cone of silence, pointing to Ernesto's window. "Somehow he supports himself as a dog walker and a massage therapist."

Hudson plays the game too, talking into his beer bottle, which makes the conversation echo. "I've seen him around."

"He's from Brazil or Peru. Which one has the nude beaches?"

Hudson dismisses him. "I've no idea. I've never been to either place."

Now I can tell why Kevin has a hard time having a relationship with anyone. Here he is with a prospect, and he's staring into another man's window. *What a busybody.* I mix my oil paints and continue to listen in.

"Maybe I'll just have to make an appointment," Kevin says in a snappy tone.

Hudson sounds surprised. "What, for a dog walk?"

Ursula, who is sleeping on my bed, knows the word "walk" and looks up at me.

"No, a massage. I'll be right back."

As I cut up the mango and arrange it on the blue plate, I see Kevin cut through the garden and knock on Ernesto's back door. Then he disappears inside.

A moment later I see Kevin emerge, looking a little grumpy. "I find that a bit curious. He says he's not taking any new clients; then after he thought I'd left, I heard him booking a one way ticket to Brazil." Kevin takes the last sip of his Corona and, like some Phillip Marlowe character, says, "That's where troublemakers go."

I've just made the first few brush strokes of orange on the canvas when I realize I'd better run downstairs to get a Corona before they are all gone.

"Hudson, would you like some guacamole?" I call out through the screen door.

"Why, yes, Emma. I haven't had good guacamole since I was in Belize." As I'm trying to picture just where Belize is, Kevin quickly joins me in the tiny kitchen and we have to practically dance backwards each time I open the fridge.

Grabbing the last beer, Kevin says, "Isn't he just fab? He's an international businessman, and he has homes all over the world."

I try to catch a lime that is now rolling quickly into the living room, thanks to the tropism of the house.

"Kevin, do you think you should be looking at Ernesto so much when you're here with Hudson?"

Kevin stands by drinking his beer. "That's not an accident. It's part of my plan to make him just a wee bit jealous which is phase one of my patented luring system."

I mush the avocado and squeeze the lime on it. "I don't know. It could backfire on you."

Kevin squeezes the used lime into his beer. "You just wait and see who gets invited to the Colony for dinner tonight."

I chop red onion and cilantro and add it to the guacamole. Kevin grabs the Tabasco, but the inner sprinkle lid is missing and half the bottle goes in. Kevin shrugs his shoulders. "That's okay, we'll have Hudson try it first."

I grab the huge bag of Tostitos Hint of Lime Chips, thinking they are the best invention of the twentieth century. Thinking this is phase two of Kevin's patented luring system, I watch as Hudson takes a chip full of guacamole and starts coughing. Believing Kevin is going to save him with a frosty Corona, I stay on the sidelines so Kevin can be a hero. With a graceful solution not in the offing, Hudson grabs Ursula's outdoor water dish and pours it on his face. In a hoarse voice he says, "Very good guacamole, Emma." Kevin smiles adoringly at him.

"Where is Ursula?" Kevin asks.

I yell for Ursula, then look next door. "I hope she's not over at Ernesto's eating his cat food again."

"Emma, have you ever seen Ernesto's cat?"

"No, now that you mention it."

Kevin presses his lips together and nods his head. "Cat food, but no cat. Very suspicious."

Hudson is rinsing his tongue off with the hose over by the tree when I see Ursula inside our screen door. I let her out and Hudson looks down and points to the terrace—there are blue and orange paw prints all over. I go inside and find multi-colored paw prints all over the floor, and the sofa. It's like the Family Circus kids with their zigzag dotted lines.

Ursula jumps up on Hudson, getting paint prints all over his pants. "Stupid damned mutt!" he yells. It's not his usual lockjaw, more like a Michigan accent. Ursula runs back into the house and finds a safe place to hide behind the claw foot tub. She surely is offended at being called a mutt. I see Kevin try to kiss Hudson, who resists his affections.

Kevin runs in. "I must have guacamole breath. Hurry, hand me those Asteroids!" He grabs the tin of white mints and gobbles 10 in front of Hudson, who's followed him into the house. Hudson recoils from Kevin's kiss again and says he has to leave; he has to meet up with some friends who just flew in on their Learjet.

Later, Kevin and I eat the remaining guacamole, which we determine must not be fattening because eating it is so painful. After a fruitless Google and ZabaSearch for one Hudson DuPont III, I conclude he is a dubious poser. Kevin, naturally, concludes he is a fascinating social recluse.

19

I wake up next to Kevin, who has taken over as the requisite snorer. Apparently, Ursula has decided to live out the rest of her days in seclusion behind the tub, which is fine with me. I'm certain she is bemoaning the fact she's an only dog, with no one else to blame for her misdeeds. Surely, she is lamenting the lack of thumbs to write to Dear Heloise to inquire as to how best to remove oil paint from fabric.

Today is my first day at sea and I have no idea what to expect—or wear. I am to call Mrs. Weinstein to check the weather.

In her Boston voice she says, "It's going to be windy and gusty."

"So you're cancelling?"

"Hell no! It's so boring when it's calm. I want some adventure."

Settling on a big terrycloth cover-up and a one-piece suit, I walk over to the swanky Flagmore. The whole elevator ride I'm secretly hoping I don't run into her next-door neighbor, Pudge.

The double door opens and I'm greeted by a man who looks just like Ping. On further inspection, I realize it's Ping on reassignment. He welcomes me into what could be Zsa Zsa Gabor's pad, with Louis XIV gold furniture. I hear Mrs. Weinstein calling in another room for Ping to come and pet her Pyewacket. Ewe! Mrs. Weinstein and the Chinese cook? Didn't see that coming, although they are the same height. A minute later Mrs. Weinstein appears in the doorway petting a Siamese cat. She's wearing a little sailor suit prompting Ping to ask, "You boat captain now?"

She has white Capri pants and a blue and white-stripped shirt and a little captain's hat. If there is a designated place to attach jewelry, she has it covered. If she falls overboard, it will be Tiffany's fault she sinks.

She salutes me, then all of her vivacity comes to a screeching halt when she focuses on me. "Oh, Emma, is that what you're wearing?"

"Um. I thought so."

She peers behind me. "Did you bring a valise? We're going to have dinner in Lucaya, so you'll need something to wear for cocktails and then something for dinner. And for heaven's sake, bring underpants!"

I ponder all of the things I have learned to do without in my life.

"Don't worry, dear, we'll stop at your place and I'll help you find something." She has Ping pack up three drum-shaped Louis Vuitton suitcases for the trip.

Mrs. Weinstein drives me to my humble little house. She follows me up the stairs and casts a wary glance at Irene's gigantic runaway suitcase which has been on the lam in my closet. Ursula follows us up the stairs and jumps on my bed. We suddenly hear the bed yelp a high-pitched and distinct, "Ouch." Our heads swivel to catch two pairs of men's hands pulling up the covers over their heads.

Esther Weinstein seems unfazed. "Good morning, Hudson and Kevin."

Hudson calls out a polite, "Hello, Mrs. Weinstein," as he escapes from under the covers fully dressed.

I'm embarrassed and start wadding dresses into the suitcase. Kevin fires random clothes from under the fortress toward the clam shelled suitcase. I'm relieved I don't have to venture towards the occupied bed. Then, an announcement is broadcast. It seems someone occupying the bed is unable to take on the responsibilities that encompass Ursula, and shall be unavailable for the remainder of the day.

Rats! I won't be back until late, and it's too hot to leave her outside tied to a tree. I hate the thought of asking Ernesto, the gun-owning Brazil-goer, which could lead to trouble.

Mrs. Weinstein pets Ursula. "Just bring her along. She's so cute."

Kevin, in some sort of fit, wrestles with the sheets and emerges yelling. "What? I don't get invited but that bad dog does?"

"Just so you know, we're not talking perfection in the house training department," I say to Mrs. Weinstein.

Mrs. Weinstein winks. "Kevin's not house trained?"

"She meant Ursula," Kevin snips.

"She'll be fine, besides the upper deck is waterproof."

She pulls the suitcase by a leash, like she's walking a pet through my narrow living room. Mrs. Weinstein touches the sofa. "I just love this fabric! I've never seen this with the little dog prints all over." I laugh and think I'd better not tell her of Ursula's latest disaster.

Mrs. Weinstein compliments me by saying, "Emma, that's smart thinking bringing a gigantic suitcase. You know how these three-hour tours can turn out."

"Well, I really couldn't focus on what to pack."

"Who could with two men in your bed."

When we get to the marina, the hyper Ping stops within inches of the water, hitting the brakes like it's some sort of Michelin Tire commercial. He startles Graham who is on the dock, loading supplies for the boat. I thought he'd be wearing a captain's outfit, but he's wearing a white Polo shirt that says *No Woman No Cry* on it.

My mind replays the tape of him lifting up my shirt and kissing me. I wonder if he is playing the same tape in his head.

"Emma, what are you doing here?"

Guess not.

Mrs. Weinstein looks at him through her huge glasses. "Oh, you've met Emma?"

Graham takes her bag. "Yes, Irene made the acquaintance for us."

Mrs. Weinstein looks around. "Oye. Where's Richard?"

I'm holding Ursula's leash and trying to lead her over the plank, but she's not budging. Graham gets a concerned look. "He's in the wheelhouse. Did he say it was all right to bring your dog?"

"Don't worry," Mrs. Weinstein says. "We'll get Trevor to take care of Ursula."

"So Trevor works in the house, on the boat and he takes care of dogs too?" I ask.

"Lucky me," says Trevor, who has appeared on the gangplank.

"Graham, why don't you put Emma's valise in my cabin, that way she can take a bath."

Does she think I'm her child? I guess motherliness is far-reaching.

Graham takes the huge green suitcase and carefully angles it to squeeze down the limited staircase. "Heavens, Emma, it's only a day trip." Graham is all business as he says, "We'll see you in the main salon after we embark. Meanwhile, I'll be on the flybridge."

"Okay," I say, not knowing exactly what he means. I guess when I feel the boat moving, it will be time to go upstairs. I'm in the queen's suite, with white carpeting and a real bathtub. I put a patchwork of towels down on the carpeting for Ursula, just in case. I think I'll just stay down here to keep myself from committing any sort of faux pas. Too bad I couldn't get Kevin invited on this trip, he would have loved this. All the same, this will be wonderful: a day at sea with my new boyfriend, Graham, and my fantasy husband, Richard. Perfect. Then I look out the porthole and see a pair of long tanned legs. Who could that be? I head up the stairs to see her face. It's the flaxen-haired Natasha.

20

She's wearing a very tight, white tank top and little white shorts and has a tiny white suitcase. As I walk to the back deck, I see Richard is there, but he doesn't seem to see me; he appears to be held captive in some sort of tush trance. Finally, and only after Ursula knocks a silver wine bucket off its stand, does he see me. "Oh, hello, Emma. I see you brought the famous Ursula." She gives him a long lick.

He gives me a little hug. "Have you met Natasha? She's helping out as our stewardess today."

Rats! "Yes, we've met. That's great she's helping."

I retreat to my cabin to apply more makeup and whatnot. I'm in mid–wee when I hear an alarming, high beep. Then I make out Graham's voice directing us over some sort of Big Brother speaker system. It seems we are to report to the mid-deck immediately for safety instructions. I race up the stairs, still zipping my dress. In no hurry, the other guests meander in calmly so as not to spill their drinks. Natasha, looking impeccable, saunters in last. *Must work on my saunter.*

After we are all seated off the main deck, Graham comes out with a huge orange bag and solicits audience participation. With no takers, he grabs my hand and pulls me to his side, which would be romantic if he didn't place a huge, orange life vest over my head. Then he proceeds to zip up the front and directs me to start blowing in the little tube. I must look like an orange cow. Natasha is preoccupied with pointing and laughing.

Right then, my cell phone rings a ridiculous "She's a Brick House" ringtone that Kevin programmed in my phone. It's an agent who wants to show the Weinstein house. Mrs. Weinstein says to have Kevin do it, adding, "How hard can it be?" Richard gives the okay, so I call and direct Kevin through the logistics.

After I hang up, Graham resumes the exercise with Mrs. Weinstein by his side. We learn nautical things such as where lifevests and fire extinguishers are stowed thanks to Mrs. Weinstein, who is motioning like a flight attendant. Somehow, the life preserver zipper goes off course, and I'm stuck wearing the thing passed the allotted safety announcement period. Then, without words, Mrs. Weinstein grabs my phone, shoves me next to Richard, and snaps our picture. Our first picture together and I'm wearing the hideous orange contraption.

I order a chardonnay from Natasha and she laughs at me, actually using the word, "Ha!" She says to get it myself...and to get her one while I'm at it. I glare at her as she takes a little red mesh bag of tiny cheeses and exits the side door to walk around deck to the bow.

As I open the wine fridge for a bottle, I say to Mrs. Weinstein, "Well, she's a big help."

Mrs. Weinstein pulls me aside. "I just figured it out. Richard is just saying she's part of the crew in case his wife finds out he invited her."

Graham calls out to Richard. "We've got a swan on the bow." Richard has a little smile on his face as he mumbles that he's needed up front. I'm really curious how this whole boat thing works, so I wander past the galley to the main deck wheelhouse and sit next to Graham as he mans the controls. He's got his hand on the throttle and is looking very serious. He's gorgeous when he wears his little wire glasses.

I look out front, and there is Natasha, sunning herself. Now she's down to wearing a tiny aqua bikini and looks like she's been on a diet— maybe that's why she's kind of bitchy today. The bikini is mesh with oversized holes, allowing for lots of peeping, which Graham and Richard are now doing. Mesh bikini? I wonder if that was hers in the bathroom. She has her tiny yoga butt parked against the glass. Then she takes her top off, right in front of Richard and Graham! That's not a good idea. Graham could crash the boat. I'll have to tell her to move or put some clothes on.

Now I'm glad I brought my dog on this little outing, so I can let her out to pester Natasha. I push Ursula out the side door onto the walk; she seems enthusiastic about this latest mission involving the possible snatch of a wedge of cheese. Graham has stopped his seriousness and the engine has been cut as we all watch through the green-tinted windshield. We watch Ursula stop to sniff the wrapped triangle of cheese, then suddenly she takes a quick lick with her long tongue sideways across Natasha's pointy nipple. Richard and Graham burst out laughing.

Natasha jumps up and makes muted screaming sounds, through the thick windshield. Now she's turning toward us, giving a full frontal view. Well, this wasn't such a good idea. Now she's shoving my baby away—Ursula could fall overboard and be eaten by a shark or something. I signal for Ursula to abort mission and knock on the windshield and gesture for Natasha to cover up. The guys half jokingly yell at me for spoiling their view and I'm ejected from the wheelhouse. Graham starts up the engine and we head up the Intracoastal at full speed.

I was just concerned about safety, I mutter to myself as I return to the main salon with Mrs. Weinstein. There is a soothing voice singing "Get It Through Your Heart" through the sound system. Richard comes back in the salon with pliers and dislodges me.

"I miss R.P." he says, woefully.

I must have a question mark on my face.

"Robert Palmer." Trevor fills my glass while filling me in.

"Bunny killed him," Mrs. Weinstein whispers.

"Mother, it was an accident."

Mrs. Weinstein turns to me. "My poor Babka is in denial."

Richard slips back to the wheelhouse, presumably preferring to ogle Natasha rather than being psychoanalyzed by his mother.

I stop the conversation for a moment with raised hands. "Wait. Bunny killed the singer that Graham loves? No wonder he hates her."

They look at me like I'm clueless. Finally, Mrs. Weinstein says, "No, silly, Richard liked him too. He named his dog after him."

Trevor quickly fills me in. "It was a scorching day and Bunny was to pick the dog up from the veterinarian's office."

I know where this story is going and let out a loud, "Oh no!"

"It seems it was Last Call at Neiman Marcus. Although she says she cracked the windows and only ran in for a minute, she came home with numerous dresses, indicating she must have been shopping for some time. She didn't even notice the dog was dead in the car. Richard and I were in the study when she came bounding in and started pulling dresses out of a shopping bag. When she was nearly through, Richard asked how RP's heartworm test went. Bunny got this horrible look on her face, worse than normal, and said she'd be right back."

Poor Richard.

Mrs. Weinstein and Trevor take turns catching me up on Weinstein folklore. I find out that Richard went to Harvard Medical School and that his first wife, the mother of his children, died of cancer ten years ago. He married Bunny a year later. His thirty-two-year-old son lives in Paris. This is useful gossip that I can't wait to tell Kevin.

21

We pass beautiful homes on the Intracoastal on our way to the ocean. We will maneuver through the inlet between Singer Island and Palm Beach to head south in the ocean to Lyford Cay in the Bahamas. Once we get out far enough and away from boat traffic, we'll have a light lunch of lobster salad and pomegranate ambrosia, accompanied by a light little Pouilly-Fuissé. I could get used to this.

When I ask if we should wait for Graham, Mrs. Weinstein says, "No, dear — he's staff."

Natasha, thankfully, has put her mesh top back on and has covered it with a sheer white blouse. A lot of good that does.

Richard sits next to Natasha and pats her leg, saying she's getting too much sun. I look to see if she has any inferior features. Rats! None. Wait! She has huge, long feet. I take another look and decide the culprits are her toes. Why, they look like fingers. How could anyone possibly ever love her? I solemnly rejoice in my discovery. Then she bends over with the pretext of lacing up her Grecian sandals, and suddenly her curved little fanny is right in Richard's face. The poor hopeless man was just about to make a toast, when the train goes off the tracks.

Finally Trevor saves the day. "Sir, try, 'Bottoms Up?'"

Richard turns a lovely shade of magenta. I'm wondering exactly when Natasha is leaving the country, so I ask her, "How long have you been in the States?"

Judging by the little smirk on his face, Richard seems amused that I'm jealous of Natasha.

"I moved here in September. Why?" Natasha says guardedly.

Mrs. Weinstein helps me with, "So do you get to stay because you're married?"

"No, my husband is from Algeria. We both have tourist visas."

Graham seems to have left Ping at the wheel to listen in. He smiles at Natasha and says, "You could always stay on the boat and work."

Trevor, who is running around frantically, mutters, "Is that what you call it?"

Mrs. Weinstein suggests we take naps in our cabins so the crew can have their lunch. She then directs Trevor to draw a bath for me. He mutters that he's busy, and my cabin doesn't have a tub. I guess no one is aware of the cabin switch.

That's ok; I know how to work a faucet.

I bring Ursula down to the cabin so I can keep an eye on her and fill the tub with a hot bubble bath. Mrs. Weinstein walks into the hallway and yells, "Richard, will you bring me some champagne? Trevor is busy and Natasha is useless."

In a minute, Richard walks in the door of my new cabin with a half bottle of pink champagne. He sees me in the tub, and thankfully I'm covered with bubbles.

He looks away. "Oh, I'm so sorry; this is usually Mother's cabin."

"She wanted to switch so the dog would have more room."

Richard has a nice smile on his face. "You look lovely all soapy."

"I guess doctors like clean women."

"All men do."

He tries to look the other way as the bubbles start bursting. He pours me a glass of champagne and asks if I mind if he joins me. I wonder if he means in the tub.

He pours himself some champagne in a water glass. "That mother of mine is up to some of her old tricks."

He looks at me with his crystal blue eyes and they linger on mine for a moment. Rats! I finally meet someone who makes my heart beat like a hummingbird and he's married. Plus, he's my client. What's the worse that could happen? We have a torrid affair, his wife kills us, I lose the listing.

Richard nervously gulps his bubbly. "I'd better be going before the bubbles burst." I guess he's thinking he'd better get out of danger. I'd better stay away from him too; focus on the very single Graham, I think.

Ursula is getting antsy, so I decide to stroll around with her to see what everyone is up to. I love this—I can see into all the rooms if I walk around the outer deck. When I walk past Mrs. Weinstein's room, she waves to me and closes her blinds. I walk down the starboard outer deck and can see into Natasha's cabin. I see her legs, and can see the arms of a man in her bathroom. I'd know those muscular forearms anywhere—it's Graham!

I go back down to my cabin to sulk a bit. Before long I hear the sound of a bell, indicating the 5 o'clock signal to start drinking again. I wish I was sharing a cabin with Kevin so he could consult on what to wear. I think I'll wear my pale green silk dress, despite the fact it's all wrinkled; it's a perfect match for my flat rubber-soled sandals. Then I realize it: I've leapfrogged straight over my mom and have become my grandmother.

"Honey, did you sleep in that dress?" Mrs. Weinstein says. "Go back to your cabin and I'll send in something nice."

I wait in my cabin, missing all the fun. Then I peek out see Natasha slinking by in a beautiful, wrinkle-free dress and high spiked heels.

Bitch trying to steal my man in a wrinkle-free dress and heels.

Finally, Ping knocks on my door and says, "New dress for you. So don't look so bad." He hands me a nice navy and white St. John knit dress that must belong to Mrs. Weinstein. Nice to know I'm the same size as an eighy-seven year old.

When I climb the front stairs by the wheelhouse, I see Graham standing at the top.

He turns slightly. "Oh, there's sleeping beauty."

I don't have the nerve to call him on being in Natasha's cabin, so I murmur a meek little, "Are you going to join us?"

Graham sighs. "Unfortunately, the crew has to work."

"Someday, you'll have your own yacht like this."

"Not on a captain's salary. I'll never be a rich man like Richard."

As we have more drinks, Trevor and Ping prepare more food in the galley. Mrs. Weinstein tells us Ping grew up very poor outside Hangzhou, China. He apparently won a contest singing "What's New Pussy Cat" by just saying the words phonetically; he then took the prize money and moved to Canada. There, he met the Chinese architect who had designed Richard's house for the prior owners. Ping became the houseman and stayed on after the sale. Actually, he hid in the house for a week before anyone noticed; for days they wondered who made breakfast every morning.

We hear a faint cry coming from the galley, then see Trevor, who is wearing rubber gloves, carry a guilty looking Ursula out of the galley. She still has a lamb chop in her mouth. "Sir, we shall be serving rack of lamb for four."

I'm mortified. "Ursula! Bad dog!"

"Why did you bring your stupid dog?" Natasha asks. "And why did you get such an ugly dog? She looks like someone from Siberia."

I pet my baby dog's hurt feelings.

22

With gray skies and strong gusts threatening our expedition, Ping is dispatched to the aft deck to "batten the hatches." Soon, we feel the boat slow down and dip with every wave.

"Richard!" Graham yells out.

Richard drops his fork and runs to the wheelhouse.

Mrs. Weinstein pulls her lamb chop out of her mouth. "It's always something."

Richard emerges from the wheelhouse with a serious look. "We've lost our satellite—it blew right off the top."

Graham comes down and chats with Trevor. "We have a storm brewing in the north and can't cross the Gulf Stream to head back. We need to get to a safe anchorage."

"We should continue east to Lyford Cay," Trevor offers.

My head swivels from Trevor back to my sexy Graham.

"Without a Navi system, I'll have to go by chart," Graham says as he disappears to the wheelhouse.

I want to follow him, just to watch him with his glasses and his big tanned arm unfurling a chart. Oh, how I adore smart men with big tanned arms and little glasses.

"Thank goodness we brought a case of champagne," Trevor says.

"Yes, that's fine for me," Mrs. Weinstein says, "but what are the rest of you going to drink?"

While they're blabbing away, I'm pondering the Natasha/Graham scenario. He didn't really invite me, Mrs. Weinstein did. Hmm.

Ursula takes the distraction as an opportunity to grab Natasha's lamb chop and runs around the salon. I'm trying to catch her and she brakes abruptly, causing me to trip over her and hit my lip on the edge of a marble buffet.

I feel hot, rusty blood in my mouth.

Richard pats me, "Look, Mother, our first injury."

Mrs. Weinstein barely blinks. "We usually have three or four."

I see drops of blood on the white carpeting.

Richard sees the look of concern on my face and says, "Here, come over to the sofa."

"Sir, why don't you take her into the galley so she doesn't hemorrhage all over the carpeting," Trevor says.

We head for the galley, but Ping kicks us out. "Eww. No blood in kitchen."

Richard puts a napkin on my lip and guides me downstairs with a gentle hand on my back. Maybe no one will notice we're missing. Maybe we'll disappear into a cabin and he'll kiss me all over. Even the places that bleed. Say, that's naughty. Doctors are somehow never grossed out and never have a naughty, leering nature. That must be two classes they have to take.

I tell him we'd better put Ursula to bed so she doesn't trip anyone else. On the way to my cabin, Ursula pushes her nose into Natasha's cabin.

"Doesn't your dog know how to knock?" She yells out.

"No, she missed charm school."

"And obedience school."

Little does she know that Ursula was kicked out of Pup Academy on day one, and had to be sent home on the Wag Mobile.

Richard tells me to wait in my cabin and goes to get his medical kit. When he returns, he starts gently washing my lip...and staring into my eyes. I want to kiss him right there. He says he's just going to bandage it up for now, because it would be too hard to stitch it up and that lips hemorrhage easily as they have a confluence of nerve tissue. He puts a beige bandage on my upper lip and smiles at me. I must look ridiculous.

"You're not going to be able to eat now."

I'm in love. I wonder if he feels the same.

He kisses my forehead and says, "You'll be fine. I'd better get back upstairs before my mother starts rumors. "

I'm sitting below deck and the boat is making me a little nauseous. I wonder how long it will take us to get back. A minute later the door bursts open and there is Natasha holding Ursula by her harness.

"Your stupid dog got into my suitcase and started eating my new Belgian dark chocolates."

"Ursula! Give me that."

"She got her slobber all over the box, so I let her have the rest."

"How many chocolates did she eat? Oh no, dark chocolate like that can kill a small dog."

"Really? How unfortunate." Natasha says flatly.

I grab Ursula and run up the stairs, calling for Richard.

Trevor winces at my bandage. "He's in the wheelhouse."

I run there, and find my two favorite men studying the dials.

I glare at Graham. "Your girlfriend gave Ursula chocolate."

Graham avoids eye contact, focusing not on my lips, but my bandage. "My girlfriend?"

"Yes, I saw you in her cabin."

"Oh, a wee bit jealous, are we? There was an air gap leak in her head."

Actually, I believe that. Then I realize he's talking about her bathroom.

"All right, you two." Richard calmly says. "We don't have much time. Emma, go to my medicine cabinet and grab the hydrogen peroxide."

"Hydrogen peroxide? Should we go to the top deck so we don't bleach the carpet?"

"I don't think that's a good idea," Graham says. "You and the dog could end up overboard in this weather. Well, maybe that's not a bad thing…the dog, I mean."

I start to think this could have been Natasha's plan all along to get rid of both of us.

Richard fumes. "I can't believe anyone would give a dog chocolate. Grab the dog and let's go to my cabin." I love it when he goes from soothing to angry. He does it with such restraint.

I watch as he tries in vain to get a spoonful of peroxide down the dog's mouth. Richard looks at the dog's eyes. "Go ask Ping for some bread."

Bread?

I run up the stairs to find Ping, who is butchering a duck. I guess that's what Chinese cooks like to do in their free time.

Without wasting any parts of duck or parts of speech, Ping says, "I busy. You look bad."

"I need it now." He looks at me like I'm a bossy guest and hands me one slice of bread. When I return to Richard in the bathroom, I see he is rubbing Ursula's belly and she is licking him.

"Here little girl, you'll be fine."

He looks up at me as he pours the liquid in a bowl and soaks the bread. Ursula is not too keen on this recipe, but Richard shoves the wet bread down her mouth. We put Ursula in the empty tub and wait as we bump along at sea. I look at Richard and hope we get stranded on a tropical island together.

After a few minutes of silently waiting, orange vomit and diarrhea spew out of my baby. I can't help but say, "Eww."

Richard leans back. "That didn't take long."

"That's good. Richard, you don't have to stay with her. You go and finish your dinner."

"After all this, I'm not very hungry anymore."

"Boy, if I were a doctor I'd be so skinny. I don't know how surgeons can operate and then eat a sandwich."

"I'm used to seeing blood."

"Do you miss operating?"

"I don't practice in the States anymore, but once a year I help out surgical teams in war zones."

"That's really sweet of you. And brave."

"Frankly, it's more fulfilling than sitting on a yacht."

We sit in the bathroom staring into each other's eyes. As I am fantasizing about having a honeymoon with him, he finally says, "We can expect a night of vomit."

119

Well there goes that fantasy.

"Emma, why don't you go back upstairs and ask Trevor to move your things into my cabin."

I wonder if we are going to sleep together. Richard must read the look on my face, and he says, "And I'll move into yours—actually mothers—so we can keep Ursula held in a shower stall."

I guess everyone knows she's an escape artist. When I return to the dining room, Mrs. Weinstein and Trevor are looking a little soused. Graham comes out to report that we are going to try to dock in Lyford Cay."

"I guess we're all sleeping on the boat," Mrs. Weinstein says.

"This should be amusing," Trevor says.

Mrs. Weinstein has a big smile on her face. "Well, Emma, we couldn't help but notice that both you and Richard have been spending some time downstairs."

"Richard wants me to move my stuff into his cabin; you can have your cabin back, although I wouldn't plan on taking a bath any time soon."

Trevor and Mrs. Weinstein look at each other. Mrs. Weinstein's eyebrows somehow reach above her owl glasses.

Richard returns. "Emma, she should be fine, so you go ahead and get some sleep. If there's anything abnormal, be sure to wake me up."

"What do you mean by abnormal?"

"You know, excessive panting. Or if she stops breathing, come and pound on my door."

"Oh my god! How can I sleep?"

"I'll have Graham run down and check on her in a few hours. There's no reason for everyone to stay up all night."

We head back down and peek over the shower door to check on Ursula.

"I'm so sorry. I never should have brought her."

It's nearly 11:00 now, and I'm really tired. The rocking of the boat actually makes me sleep. Some how, I didn't pack any sort of nightgown in all that commotion, so I'll have to sleep in the altogether. Richard's soft sheets smell so good, just like him. I wish he would climb in bed with me.

23

As the wind hits the windows, I awaken in the middle of the night to check on my poor Ursula. She's now sleeping on a patchwork of icky towels on the bathroom floor with a big bowl of water. Someone must have paid her a visit awhile earlier. As I sit on the floor to pet her, Richard opens the door and sticks his head in and gets an eyeful.

"Emma, I'm sorry. I would have knocked but I didn't want to wake you."

He grabs a white dress shirt from his closet and tosses it to me.

He joins me on the bathroom floor with his medical bag and pulls out a stethoscope.

"I want to check her heart rate. That's the real danger you know. Heart attack."

"How does it sound?"

"I don't know yet." He puts his finger on my bandaged lip to shut me up.

I stare into his kind eyes, just inches away. He has a little gray stubble on his chin, which is kind of sexy. My heart is pounding.

"Your dog will be fine," he says as he pulls the stethoscope away from Ursula's chest. Then he puts it on mine.

Ahh! He can hear my hammering heart. He'll know I love him.

His forehead contracts into a worried look. "Young lady, have you had a lot of chocolate or excess caffeine this evening?"

I bob my head several times. "Yes, that's it." Lying, I add, "I think I had five Red Bulls."

"Don't do that again." He fishes through his bag and hands me a pill. He kisses me on the forehead and shuts the light off.

The next morning, I take a bleary-eyed look at the nautical clock on the wall and it looks like it's five of six. I must be the first one up. At the end of my bed is a white peignoir and sheer white robe. Must be from Mrs. Weinstein, or maybe that Natasha because she felt guilty about being a pug killer. It goes well with my hideous bandage. I peel it off, revealing a bruised, swollen lip.

I wander up the stairs with Ursula; it's very bright up here. Ping is serving everyone coffee. He looks at his watch. "11:30, lazy bone."

Trevor fails to contain himself. "Well, if it isn't Rip Van Wrinkle."

Mrs. Weinstein hits him. "It's before noon. You owe me five bucks."

"Good morning, Emma," says a cheery Richard. "I see both my patients are looking well."

"That looks nice on you," Mrs. Weinstein says. "I brought it just in case I got lucky."

Richard looks at the white opaque gown. "Now you've ruined the fantasy, Mother."

"Oh, that was you?" I say. "Thank you."

"Who's looking out for you, kiddo?"

Now that the wind storm has passed, we are safely on our way home. Apparently Graham was able to reattach the satellite, which had fallen into the inflatable tender.

We dock back in Palm Beach, a complicated maneuver involving Richard, Ping, Trevor and Graham. It's not exactly a regimented chain of command. Each time it starts with Graham calling out an order to Trevor, who outranked him in the British

Royal Navy and therefore tasks Ping with the command, who then ignores it, whereupon Richard sheepishly follows the command. Ping, Graham and Trevor begin unloading the contents of the boat onto a cart as Natasha emerges from the boat with her suitcase. With the musical cabins, I wonder who slept where and with whom.

We pile into Richard's tank-like Maybach. I like the way he drives in a steady manner, without all the spastic braking and accelerating like most men. After dropping his mother off, he parks and steps cautiously into my little house. Kevin is comatose on the sofa in his Hugh Hefner robe, which has become askew revealing his designer skivvies. Ursula commences her lifelong mission of reviving all things horizontal with her tongue.

Richard does a quick check of Kevin's vitals. "Just making sure he's not dead. He appears to be suffering from overindulgence."

We head to the back patio, where Richard holds my dog and rubs her belly; he's so kind. I wish he would rub my belly. Richard looks up at Ernesto's window and starts laughing. "I like your little setup here. We don't have any interesting neighbors like that."

I can hear Ernesto singing "Lady Marmalade" in the shower.

"Did you know your street was a popular venue for artists in the 1930s?"

"No, I thought it was just dog walkers and masseurs."

Richard pats me gently. "I'm so glad you came on the boat."

"Oh, I loved it. I'm just sorry I brought Ursula." Ursula looks up at me, insulted.

Richard pats her belly. "It wasn't her fault."

"I forgot to feed her. See, this is why it's good I never had kids; I'd forget to feed them."

Richard laughs. "No, they'd remind you."

I see Kevin in the kitchen, so I go to ask about the house showing. "Did they seem interested?"

Kevin sees Richard out back and makes some sort of gesture toward Ernesto's house and makes an "ahh ahh" sound.

Richard passes through and says he has to be leaving. He tells me to call if Ursula starts acting strange. I ask how that will be any different.

After he's gone, I fade down the wall. "Did you think Richard likes me by the way he petted my dog?"

"I have no idea. And stop thinking of him! Do you want Bunny to kill you?"

"You're right. I should focus on Graham. Although I think he's got a thing for that Natasha."

"Can you blame him? Anyway, I have so much to tell you."

A minute later, Graham is silently standing at the door looking irritated with my baggage, and my suitcase too. Kevin, annoyed by the distraction, practically jumps up and down.

The ever-polite Graham peers through the screen. "Hello, Emma, I've got your things. Hi, Kevin. Did Emma tell you about all the trouble we had?"

"No, we keep having interruptions."

Graham backs out saying, "Well, I won't keep you. Emma, I wanted to see if you had time for dinner this weekend."

Wasn't expecting to hear that. Must feel guilty about something.

I've got to get my mind off Richard, so I say, "I'd love to."

Graham stands at the front gate. "I'll ring you first thing tomorrow to compare our schedules."

Kevin breathes a sigh. "Emma, I can't wait to tell you what happened at the Weinsteins' house, but let's get out of here first."

24

We get a nice little table outside at a cafe called Cucina's where we can gossip with abandon. Kevin is dying of a hangover and persuades the waitress to get him a cheeseburger even though it's not on the menu.

"Did you remember to ask about Richard's son?" he asks.

"Yes. Mrs. Weinstein says he graduated from Cornell, and now he's a product designer in Paris. Apparently, he invented some ingenious iPad part that's a high powered mini microscope, but Bunny went and blabbed and someone stole the idea before he could even get a provisional patent."

Kevin ignores my comprehensive research. "But did you ask what arrondissement in Paris? I'd need to know that up front."

Falling into the shelter of the menu, I veer off. "So, how did it go at the Weinsteins?"

Kevin's eyes dart about as he conjures a reply. "Well, remember a while ago when I was trying to reset the stove clock for Daylight Saving time?"

I think I know where this story will end. Kevin was probably an hour late, but will argue it's not his fault and will proceed in piling the blame where it belongs, that being on the rotation of the Earth or little schoolchildren.

"I really would like to complain about this setting of the clocks forward, but I don't know who to call. Anyways, I was running a little late and somehow forgot to bring the keys. So I'm ringing the doorbell, hoping that the Weinsteins had some secret servant who was also not invited for the boat ride who could answer the door."

I can just picture Kevin poking the doorbell like an ADD sufferer with too much caffeine.

"But no one answered the door. So I thought I'd just use a credit card on the lock like they do in the movies, and then I heard the strangest sound: kind of like a monkey swallowed an owl. And I thought, could there really be two people who make that noise? It must be Ernesto's girlfriend. What is she doing here? So, I walked around to the back and looked; no, it was more like a peer. I peered through the hedge to the inner courtyard and saw this tall, naked blonde woman and deduced it must be Bunny Weinstein."

"Really? What did she look like?"

Kevin purses his lips. "Hmm. Well, to be polite, I'd say she was beautiful once, but is quickly sliding down the hill. And she's got huge boobs. They're fake I think, along with her lips."

"How can you tell?"

"Because when she and I were fighting in the kitchen they didn't move."

Now, I wonder which part he's talking about.

"So, it's pretty obvious she's paying Ernesto for the deluxe massage."

"While her sweet husband was on his boat."

"So all that time it was Bunny Weinstein over at Ernesto's. Two people couldn't possibly make that same sound."

The news is slow to sink in. "Was anyone else there?"

"No, she was alone. And right then I heard the doorbell ring up front. I knew it must be the other agent, so I ran around to the front and met the other agent and an elderly pair of twin sisters."

"Elderly twins? Perfect! They could each have their own half."

"So I told them the lock was broken and raced to the back patio calling, 'Yoo-hoo, realtor!' so as to alert the naked Bunny woman."

Kevin's Coke arrives. He begins sucking it down and I can feel the life come back to him. He goes on rapidly. "So, this bare-naked Bunny had scampered into the house somewhere—and I mean scampered. I think she was looking for her cell phone. So I started doing that complicated thing you agents do, like wave your hands and say, 'This is the living room, this is the kitchen.' I did it loudly and clearly so the Bunny would have a heads up."

I can barely stifle a laugh at Kevin as a real estate agent, thinking the video would serve as a valuable training film by our Errors and Omissions insurance providers. He is oblivious to all the contract negotiations, inspections, and legal issues that realtors have to deal with to get to settlement.

"And right then the homelier twin, although it was debatable, asked, 'Who owns this house?' and I was of course pleased to be among the useful, so I said it was a doctor and his second wife, who needed separate wings to stay married. They seemed to like that, so I thought I'd add a little household lore."

"I'm afraid to ask. What did you say?"

"Well, missy, I simply said I was an agent helper because the actual agent is on a yacht with the owner. Then the other agent said he could tell I wasn't an agent."

Trying to follow his rapid pace. "So where was Bunny all this time?"

"That's anyone's guess. So I had to rely on my superb detective skills—mainly, I avoided all places that smelled like Creed Fleurissimo perfume. She must bathe in it."

"So you managed to show the place *and* avoid her?"

"Well, somehow it came up that I was really a caterer to the glitteratti, and so I offered the trio some refreshments. That's when I found Bunny, in the kitchen.

So I quickly pushed the galley door shut, and thankfully only caught one of the homely twins' hand in the door.

I'm now bewailing the clearly lost deal; the vision of a homely twin caught in a door, will forever replay in my head.

"Heaven forbid they should see the unrobed lady of the house. So I offered them refreshments on the terrace, and then one of the elderly twins says, 'We love champagne. We haven't had any since—brunch!' They had matching mannerisms, including bending over when they laugh, like your mother. So I left them on the terrace, and while I was musing about in the wine cooler, I found a lovely 1959 Cristal champagne. Right when I was selecting the appropriate glasses, that bare-assed Bunny comes up from behind me and grabs the bottle!"

"Oh no!"

"Well, I was trying to be quiet, and so was she, so we had a silent little tussle in the kitchen. Those things are slippery."

I dare not ask what things.

"Then she bartered by offering two bottles of Dom Pérignon, and so I finally let go."

"Did anyone see her?"

"Well, while I'm slowly sipping my champagne, the pushy other agent says impatiently, 'This isn't the only house on our tour, so we really should finish up.' I said, 'Grab your glasses ladies,' even to the man, and I took then up to Bunny's wing, knowing she was still in the kitchen. We were making our way to Bunny's bedroom when we heard someone—a burglar! Well, if ever there was an occasion that called for a piercing scream, that was it. First I screamed, then the other agent screamed—like a girl I might add—

then the twins screamed. Even their screams are synchronized. Well, who do we find?"

"Dare I ask?"

"Ernesto! To think all this time he was in the closet."

"So you right about the Hermes belt indicator."

"No, he was literally in the closet."

"What did you do?"

"Well, Ernesto said he thought he heard a burglar, so he hid. I quickly explained to the homely twins that the household came with Ernesto the dog walking massage boy."

"I guess they didn't want to buy the house."

"Well, no, but they wanted to buy Ernesto."

"So you left then?"

"Well, I simply couldn't leave your client alone with Ernesto, so I thought I'd stick around and guard the premises."

"Oh, you had to finish off the champagne by the pool?"

"Well, yes. And right then Pudge Lichtenfelder called and said she needed me to prepare a little lunch for six on Wednesday."

"Really? She's giving you another try?"

"Her regular caterer quit on her. Plus, she found out I "held" that case of Veuve Clicquot as payment. Of course she didn't see it that way, and says I have to work off $480 or she's calling the police. I'm meeting her at her pool on Monday. She said not to wear a banana hammock—like I'd do that in front of all those horny blue hairs. Although there is that hot pool guy. Hmm."

"Kevin, today is Monday."

He looks around frantically. "Oh. I completely forgot." He rings up Pudge in a panic. "I'm so sorry, but I've been detained at Cucina's. No, it's not my fault; Emma is having some sort of nervous breakdown. Yes, come by, she's just wrapping it up now."

Oh brother!

I put up with this because I can't wait to finish my story. "Guess who was on the boat as our stewardess?"

"I don't know. Ping?"

"Natasha. And I saw Graham in her bathroom. That is before she tried to kill my dog."

Kevin is all girl-friendy and says, "I wonder why Pudge is friends with her. Oh, Pudge is on her way. You'll have to tell her all about the boat ride, she'll be green."

I show Kevin the photo of Richard and me. He grabs my phone and texts himself the photo then pokes away at his phone. In a minute, he proudly says, "Here, this is what your baby will look like!"

"Kevin!"

"Hopefully, Richard has not been fixed."

"I have another date with Graham, but I can't get Richard out of my head. He wasn't even mad when Ursula threw up on his yacht."

A few minutes later, Pudge shows up looking all Palm Beachy in an Emilio Pucci shift and a Dolce & Gabbana bag.

Kevin can't help but blurt out, "Emma just got off an *overnight* yacht ride with Richard!" He holds up his iPhone. "Yes, this is what their baby is going to look like."

I grab the phone. "He's just kidding."

Pudge takes a drag from her cigarette. "Really? Just the two of you?"

"No, the captain was there too."

Smoke spouts from her nostrils this time, conjuring up the Praying Mantis again, this time with antlers. Finally the insect says, "Come on, I'm sure his mother was there."

"Well, yes. And that Natasha friend of yours was there. She's awfully flirty for a married woman; practically sat on Graham's lap the whole time."

Pudge crosses her long legs. "She's after Richard. There's no point in her divorcing for Graham—a man with no money and no green card."

Kevin and I look at each other, not even bothering to be subtle.

Right then his cheeseburger and fries show up. Soon he is happily inserting a haystack of French fries in his mouth and having them protrude, while shaking the ketchup bottle fiercely at the plate.

The Mantis, for surely she doesn't pray, says to order her a Caesar with no cheese, croutons or dressing; we wonder why she doesn't just say a bowl of lettuce. I decide right then and there I'd rather be curvy than have to forgo the joy of food. If the waitress ever comes back, I'll get a cheeseburger too.

Pudge can't seem to sit still and leaps up to say hello to Cricket Farling. Pudge says to cancel her salad, as she doesn't want to be seen eating. Kevin protects his remaining fries by pulling them back out of arms reach and then takes another mouthful of his burger. Before Kevin gets to tell me any more, Pudge returns.

"Are you two talking about me?" she says suspiciously.

"No. We were talking about, um…insects."

Pudge lights up another cigarette. "Kevin, what are you going to serve at my party? And please tell me it's not anything flaming."

Kevin looks a little green around the gills; I can tell he's nauseous from the smoke. He coughs and says, "I was thinking of watermelon martinis. They're probably not flammable."

Pudge leans in with her slim thorax. "If you're going to set anyone on fire, I want it to be Bunny."

"Why are you having Bunny Weinstein to your party if you don't like her?" I can't help but ask.

Pudge leans back in her chair. "I have to. It's my turn to host the Committee Luncheon for the 'Dogs are People Too' ball."

"Who else is on the committee?"

Pudge crosses her wings and says, "Esther, Bunny, Richard and Hudson DuPont. I'd invite you, Emma, but, you know, you're not on the committee."

Kevin claps his hands. "You can come and be my assistant."

I can see the wheels in Pudge's head turning, trying to come up with a reason not to have me. Finally she says, "I'm sure Emma will be too busy on Wednesday."

"I'm free, and I can't wait to meet Bunny Weinstein."

Pudge thinks for a minute. "No. I don't want any amateur caterer at my party. I've got enough liability just having Kevin."

Looking slightly appalled at Kevin's table manners, she says, "So, Kevin, tell me what you're going to serve for food?"

I can tell Kevin has spent no time thinking of a menu; he seems stumped, or else he's just starving. He stalls for time by attacking an oversized chunk of his cheeseburger, getting ketchup all over his face.

I start to describe the fine cuisine I was served on the yacht. "Kevin, didn't you say you were serving baby lamb chops with pear and Calvados compote, with a salad of Boston lettuce and candied walnuts and aged gorgonzola cheese?"

Kevin nods his head, taking another bite and pointing to his good burger.

"Marvelous!" Pudge says. "Say, girls, this has been fun, but I've got to get a facial. Bye."

The minute Pudge is two feet away Kevin gulps his coke and says, "Poodle." She hears him and he tries to cover by saying, "Poodle cakes; that's my pet name for you!"

25

There is a dulcet message on my phone. It's Richard, inquiring about Ursula and my lip, in that order. I love his voice! Men think women like flat abs or a fancy car, when in fact we care more about a deep voice, kind eyes and manly hands. Richard is perfect for me. Why doesn't he see this and leave his wife?

As I was not invited to Kevin's luncheon, even as helper, I am curious about what sort of calamities ensued. I return from a real estate class to find Kevin sleeping in my bed with Ursula. She wakes and makes a loud *cluck cluck* when she drinks from the water glass by the bed.

"It was fabulous." Kevin mumbles. "Did you know Bunny and your Graham are singing a duet at the ball?"

"Bunny can sing?"

"No, but that doesn't stop her. Richard and Graham are writing a new song that lowlights her voice. Do you want me to imitate them imitating her? They sang it as a duet in A minor."

"No, I just want to know who you set on fire."

Kevin sits up. "No one, this time. But, naturally Pudge arranged the seating so that she could sit next to Richard, and Bunny was next to my Hudson DuPont III. Did you know my Hudson is going to hire Pudge to decorate his London flat? I hope she has another style besides Lenny the XIV. So anyway, Pudge is talking and putting her hand on Richard's lap every few seconds. I had to come up with a diversion. So at the last minute, I spilled Perrier-Jouët Rosé all over Pudge and Richard."

"Oh no."

"I'm always thinking of you, Emma."

My mouth drops open in shock. "Did Pudge get mad at you? I hope you realize she's your only client."

"No. I made it look like Richard's fault. And he never gets mad."

"Yes, that's partially true. But it's more like he gets mad, then silently swallows the anger."

"Those are the types who end up going postal. Watch out."

My mind wanders at the thought of him gunning down his wife at the post office.

Kevin sighs. "Frankly, I don't know why Bunny hasn't killed Pudge yet, what with her blatant flirting with her husband."

Despite feeling a little guilty about flirting with Richard, I nod my head. "Yes, it's despicable."

"You should talk. Besides, I kind of like Bunny Weinstein."

I can't resist saying, "That's great; when you have the fan club meetings, you can book a table for one."

"I feel sorry for her, especially when Pudge insinuated Bunny was some sort of gold digger."

"What exactly did she say?"

"'You are a gold digger.' Right in front of everyone."

Kevin takes a gulp from the water glass by the bed and continues. "Well, there was a tussle. Not a major one; who would want to undo all that work? So, then Esther Weinstein tried to change the subject; she told my Hudson she used to date his great uncle, Walter. Then Hudson says he went to Austria or Australia, with him in the summer of 1980. Then Esther Weinstein says that's impossible because the Walter fellow died in the 1950s. So I think that ol' Esther has a little memory problem."

"You don't think Hudson could have the wrong year?"

Kevin scowls at me. "No. Then, and I knew this was coming, they start going over final plans for the Dog Ball, when Pudge announces Bunny will be in charge of dog patrol."

"They let you bring your dog inside the Breakers?"

"Well, probably not your dog. But anyway, you should have seen the look on Bunny's face! Her mouth gaped open and eyebrows practically went over her head."

Kevin continues like he's telling a ghost story. "All of a sudden Bunny becomes violently ill, all over her new Gianfranco Ferrier white pants. She just bought them and they had to special order them, you know, because they don't carry daddy long-legs pants at Neimans."

"Did you serve spoiled food again?"

Kevin shakes his head. "It wasn't me this time. Pudge pulled out a caviar jar that must have been left over from when she had a party for Mamie Eisenhower."

"So did Bunny just run out?"

"Well do you think Bunny was just going to leave in shame?" he asks Ursula. He uses his hands to shake Ursula's head no. "Of course not! So as Bunny was leaving, she went into the powder room and must have flushed a Chanel purse down, because a few minutes later water was spewing all over Pudge's new faux zebra rug; I thought, good for Bunny!"

I look at Kevin with pity. "Do you ever wonder why you are the only person on the planet who likes her?"

"What's not to like? She's my favorite new client; and she asked me to cater her pre-ball party."

"That's wonderful." I'm starting to think it's weird she would choose Kevin to cater her party, then I remember all of the caterers in town refuse to work for her. I'm glad for Kevin, and he can gather useful info.

It's like Kevin reads my mind. "I think it's also because I didn't blab about her being home alone with Ernesto; so don't you tell a soul about that."

"Um. Okay," I say, as I mentally tally up the people I've already told. "So did the apartment flood?"

"Pudge snapped her fingers at me to mop it up, but I told her it wasn't in the scope of my employment. Hudson DuPont III of course wouldn't even know the purpose of a mop; so Richard called the front desk people, but they were having a staff meeting, so he had to stay behind to mop it up."

"Ah ha. I'll bet Pudge was anxious to get rid of his mother so she could be alone with Richard."

"Esther Weinstein was having too much fun to leave, although I think she wet her pants laughing. Pudge said she was worried that she might slip on the marble floor, so she asked Richard to carry her into the bedroom. Esther followed them, saying she wanted to watch a William Holden movie, *The World of Suzie Wong*. So the four of us sat on the bed and watched the movie."

"How did that go?"

"Well, William Holden is a painter in Hong Kong and is supposed to marry this banker's daughter, but he falls for the poor Chinese prostitute."

"No, how was it between Pudge and Richard on the bed with you and Esther Weinstein there?"

"Esther and I sat between them. Then she wanted Mai Tais with maraschino cherries to get with the theme, and she sent me over to get some frozen egg rolls from her freezer…and some fresh pants, including underpants. I'm trying to stay in her good graces in case she needs me for a job someday."

Yes, you have to start somewhere. You can put "Underpants Valet" on your resume.

26

Graham has the day off and has taken me to the Four Seasons Hotel. I love having an English boyfriend who likes posh places. I'm starting to even *fantasize* with a British accent. I could get used to this, as we are waited on hand and foot while we read the London Financial Times Weekender and order crab cake sandwiches. It's the perfect way to while away a Sunday afternoon by the pool.

I give him the wistful glance I practiced on Kevin earlier. The key is to make eye contact, but not to linger so long they think you are having some sort of catatonic stroke. I wonder if he's feeling the same way, or is he just better at the wistful glance. Then he tells me he has to leave the country. *Rats!* It seems Bunny Weinstein called the INS on him in retaliation for a comment he made about her fine character. I'm really starting to hate this Bunny person. He says Richard is trying to sponsor him for citizenship, but that could take a few years. The fact that Graham was employed illegally, with no green card, and an expired passport has messed things up a bit. He's in the lounge chair next to me and he looks so sad. Those are his looks: subdued wistfulness and sad. As he talks, he looks up at me with his sea-green eyes. I have to alternate between staring at his eyes, his mouth or his cleft chin; it's just too much to take in. Graham says the only way he could stay around would be if Richard flagged his boat in a foreign country.

That is not the only way—he could marry me.

After lunch, I lure Graham back to my place. I find he's easily lured, despite me saying it's to start his oil painting. He brings in his guitar from the back seat, so he can practice his song for the ball. When we walk in, Kevin and Ursula are downstairs watching the movie *Avanti!*. Without us asking, Kevin gives us the synopsis of how Jack Lemmon has to share a hotel room with a beautiful stranger because it's the last room in all of Italy. Kevin says he has to wait and see how it ends, like there's a big mystery. This means

Graham and I can't get into too much hanky-panky during our painting session.

Grabbing a Stella Artois for Graham, I lead him upstairs to my room. Oddly, Ursula stays downstairs, but I think it's because Kevin is making popcorn. Food can easily sway a dog's loyalty.

When Graham gets to the top of the stairs, he sees Richard's painting. "Oh, I see you've still got him in your bedroom." *Bedroom. Headroom.* I am reminded of the rainy day when I painted Richard's portrait. This will be different being a nude and all.

Touching the wet paint, I say, "He's not ready yet."

Like I'm making frosting, I whip up batches of flesh tones and beiges.

Graham looks up from tuning his guitar. "Are you having trouble making navy blue?"

"What? I'm not going to paint your shirt."

He gets his signature panicked look. "I said I wouldn't take my clothes off."

"When?"

He stops tuning and enunciates. "I distinctly recall saying, 'I'll let you paint me, but I'm not letting the whole town leer at my John Thomas.'"

"I know, it's just a painting of you, naked. There's no other guy in it. It's not a Kevin painting."

"John Thomas from *Lady Chatterley's Lover*."

Shaking my head. "I've got no time to paint Lady Chatterley, or her lover, just you."

"My todger, my tackle, my penis. I don't want it in the painting."

After my brain returns from a long wander, I say, "Why didn't you say so?"

Graham comes up behind me, laughing; he kisses the back of my neck and holds my breasts. "We'll do that kind of painting another day. If you need one for the charity ball, I'm happy to sit for a proper portrait."

I pout. "But Esther says it won't bring in the big bucks unless you're nude. How about if I paint you from the backside? I'll make it impressionistic."

He says all right, but to look the other way so I don't go getting any images in my head to add later.

I put a playlist on my iPad, starting with Mumford and Sons, "White Blank Page."

He nervously takes a gulp from his beer and faces the wall, then lifts his polo shirt over his head and tosses it on the chair. Somehow—probably due to other distractions—I'd failed to notice a faded tattoo of a rose on his upper left bicep; I decide to leave it out of the painting as it could bring the value down with society ladies. I put my painting pallet down to take in the scene of his broad shoulders and chiseled lats. He turns his head to catch me looking and gets a little smirk. To get back on track, I look down at my palette and mix vigorously.

Then I hear the distinct sound of his fly being unzipped, and the rustle of his trousers falling to the floor. Nice bum. So athletic, with such narrow hips. Ahh! He turns slightly in the process. I can see a bulge as he begins to remove his short boxer briefs.

He catches me again. "I told you not to peek."

Squeezing burnt umber from a tube onto the palette, I try to make the two varied tones of his tanned legs and his white bottom. He's facing the wall, completely naked now; he looks so divine from the back.

143

"How should I stand?"

I come behind him and arrange his limbs. At first I compose a regal pirouette, to which he says, "I'm not a freaken ballerina."

Taking his limbs to try other poses, I run my lips along his sun-speckled shoulders. He whimpers and says he's ticklish.

We settle on a masculine pose where his legs are spread and his arms are crossed in front of him. I tell him that's better, as I won't have to paint his full hands. Hands are always tricky.

While I'm folding his arms, I steal a peek at his full package. He says he feels odd being naked while I'm fully clothed. Wordlessly, I take off my dress leaving only a pale pink slip.

He turns fully to me. "Now that's more like it."

It's difficult not to take in the scenery. The natural light is fading, so I turn the gooseneck desk light on to create interesting shadows on his backside. I decide to make a simple blue background, with steely blue for shadows. Since I'm not painting his face or hands, this shouldn't take long.

"Awfully quiet up there," Kevin calls from downstairs. "Must be up to something."

Graham exhales. "I hope he doesn't come up."

I run downstairs and direct Kevin in no uncertain terms to go to his own house and take my dog with him. He unplugs my small TV and noisily takes it back to his hovel, with Ursula and the TV cord in tow. While I'm down here, I pour myself a big glass of Malbec; it is well known that master painters need wine to loosen their stroke.

When I reach the top of the stairs, I see Graham has lost the pose and is sitting on my bed, lightly covered by the white sheet. I get a good imprint of "him." It's resting on his thigh and running halfway down his leg. Whoa! I get another view when he gets up and squats over my iPad to find a new playlist.

144

He resumes his formal pose, except now he's standing at a bit of a side angle. Grabbing a charcoal pencil, I do a quick loose pencil sketch and then begin slathering paint on the canvas. Okay, I'm having one of my bliss moments. I love being a painter.

Whipping up a batch of Zinc white, I try to match the untanned parts of Graham's narrow butt. When I slather it on the canvas, his butt looks like it glows in the dark, so I tone the brightness down and wonder if a little burnt sienna is in order. When I bring my paintbrush over to compare Graham's skin with the paint tone, I get some on his butt. He looks behind himself. "What are you doing?"

Quickly, I try to wipe it off with the nearest thing I can find on the floor—yesterday's panties. Now he has paint all over his backside. I take some linseed oil and rub his left cheek. During this, I accidentally brush my hand on the back of his truffles. They are like lambs' ears, so soft I can't stop my self from doing it again. "Whoops, just trying to get the paint off your little behind."

He pretends to be indignant. "Oh, I get it—this is just a ploy to see me naked and touch my parts."

"No, hold still, I'm going to be very serious now."

I go back to my easel. When I look up, I see a long "puppet shadow" of an erection on the wall. He gets very quiet. If I were painting his face, I'd use Alizarin crimson.

I don't want to say anything, but I decide to include the shadow. These things can fade quickly, and it's always a shame to waste a good erection. I'm glad I stirred up the steely blue in advance. It really does resolve the flatness of the painting.

Just as I thought, the shadow disappears. Graham says he's getting a little tired holding the pose and asks if he can take a break. He sits back on my bed and wraps the sheet over himself. He watches me as I try to fill in the background. Then he comes behind me still wrapped up like Julius Caesar, and points to the "enhanced shadow."

"What the hell is that!" he says in an agitated tone.

"Well, I don't know if you don't."

"You don't think I'm going to have the whole bloody town see me having a freaking stiffy!"

"I think it gives the painting dimensionality and character."

"Character all right."

I grab him. "Wait, I only have a little left to do. No one will know it's you."

"The first thing out of Esther's mouth will be, 'We have a painting of our excited singer.'"

"Don't worry, I can paint over it. I'll turn it into wainscoting or something."

He sits back on the bed with the sheet over him, arms crossed. Aptly, the Glen Hansard song "All the Way Down" is playing.

"I wish I had another canvas. I'd love to paint the look on your face."

His pout goes away and he pulls me onto the bed. He traces his fingers around my lips. "I'd like to paint you in this little see through thing." He then traces my nipples through the shear slip.

When I look down, I see the shadow is back. This time it's straight up, prompting me to wonder how I'd ever paint something from aerial perspective. He has his tanned fingers on my white thigh. I suppose I should have tested my paint tone on my own thigh, then I wouldn't be in this predicament. The pale pink slip has a ruffle-trimmed slit up the center. He reaches his fingers into my matching pink ruffled panties, then rolls them down and tosses them across the room. He gets up, and I see the long shadow move across the room. He shuts the lamp off and we are lit by the streetlight out front. I watch his tanned middle finger disappear into my white tenderness.

27

I awaken to hear someone coming in the back door. Presumably, it's Kevin and Ursula returning.

"Emma, are you asleep?"

"Yes."

Kevin yells from the bottom of the staircase. "I saw your lights were off. Ursula chewed the end of your phone charger and swallowed it. I suppose it can wait. You have a few bars left on the charge."

Now at the top of the stairs, he sees me in bed with Graham and the half-finished naked painting. "Oh. I thought he was gone."

This doesn't stop him from sitting on the end of the bed and saying, "You'll never believe how it ended."

"Let me guess, Jack Lemmon ends up with Juliet Mills."

Graham is clearly embarrassed and tries to hide.

Ursula spits out the chewed up phone part and jumps on the bed. She trots up to lick Graham's ear. "Err...I've got to get up early. I think I must be going." Not wanting Kevin to see him, he carefully wraps up in the sheet, grabs his clothes and hops down the stairs.

I glare at the clueless Kevin, who picks up Graham's boxers. "He forgot these."

Once again, I remind Kevin of his actual address, and he goes and pretends to live there as a reclusive movie star.

***

After a few quiet days of painting, I'm distracted by the sound of Kevin giving loud directions, presumably to Hudson DuPont III. I look out the window and spy the well-dressed hippo.

He is standing in front of his blue Bentley, rubbing his fingers on the bicycle dent. Of course Kevin is not ready, so I have to run down the stairs to let Hudson in.

Without unclenching his teeth, Hudson manages to say, "Emma, we're off to The Breakers; why don't you come along?"

I try to come up with a reason not to go, and pull out my little calendar book hoping I have a conflict. Then I see it; it's Graham's birthday! I had asked him that first night and had forgotten I'd written it down. I send him a text on Kevin's phone.

Hudson and I sit for what seems like hours, as Kevin performs his one-man fashion show down the stairs. I look up and see Graham standing in the doorway wearing a jacket and white shirt.

"So, you've come back to finish the pose?" I call out.

"Not bloody likely. I'm afraid you'll have to find another model."

As I ponder finding a matching torso to model, he enters and says, "I've come back to take you out; your mobile must be dead."

Hudson extends the Breakers invitation to Graham, who says he was planning on going there with Richard tonight, but Bunny derailed his plans.

Kevin enthusiastically waves us on, so we pile in back of the Bentley.

I can see Hudson in the rear view mirror and wonder if his jaw had been wired shut after some horrible auto accident.

Hudson's buttonhole of a mouth barely moves. "Graham, I've been thinking of getting a yacht and would need a foreign captain like you."

"I'm perfectly content working for Richard."

"But don't you have immigration issues?"

Graham looks a little peeved. "Is that any of your business?"

"My yacht will be in the Mediterranean in the summer and the Bahamas in the winter."

Kevin smiles like a child. "Wow."

"You're going to reposition it twice a year? Not very likely."

We pull up to The Breakers and Hudson tosses the valet the key in an overt attempt to look cool—were it not for the underthrow.

Hudson directs us to the back bar, where his phone rings and he has a brief conversation in Spanish.

"Isn't he so continental?" Kevin gushes.

Hudson leaves, saying he has to visit his "executive suite" for a moment. Kevin and I gawk at the majestic lobby with Michalangeloesque paintings on the forty-foot ceilings. I look around the lobby, realizing this is the same hotel where we will be having the ball next week, and maybe where I will someday have my wedding.

Kevin, Graham and I claim the three remaining seats at the seafood bar, hoping another will free up before Hudson returns. Graham asks what we'd like, but Kevin and I are in a debate over the Jalapeno Margarita or the Basil Martini, deciding on nothing. Realizing this could take awhile, Graham goes ahead and orders his James Bond martini.

Hudson reappears in the doorway, adorned in a blue ascot. After a brief pause to make sure everyone notices him, he sashays over to the bar, and appears miffed that we didn't save him a seat. With the actual snapping of fingers, Hudson signals the bartender and indicates the presence of a vacant seat at the far end of the bar, thus forcing the bartender to gently ask each patron to kindly shift one seat to the right. Graham and I bond our relationship a little further with a knowing eye roll. After this little mambo, Hudson barks out an order for a bottle of #5175.

Without delay, a bottle of champagne wrapped in a cloth is poured for us and we toast to Graham's birthday. Kevin asks how old he is; Graham answers 43. I'm glad I didn't guess 47. Soon a huge display of crab claws on ice arrives, also at the request of Hudson. Kevin is soundlessly basking in Hudson's extravagance, while Graham is reeling off the names of possible ships for Hudson.

Hudson explains that as a child he spent his time on his father's two hundred-foot yacht in Monaco.

Graham asks who built the boat.

Hudson thinks a while and finally says, "I know everything about yachts; it was a Burger."

"Impossible. Burger never made a boat much larger than forty-seven meters."

"I love it when you talk in metrics," I say to Graham. "How long is that in feet?"

"One hundred fifty-four feet."

"Oh. Perhaps it was a Palmer Johnson," Hudson, says.

Graham sips his martini and furrows his brow. Kevin lets the bubbles of his champagne go to his head, oblivious to all the boat chatter.

"Did I mention I'll be attending the Monaco boat show?" Hudson says. "Once there, I'll get a better idea of what I want to purchase."

Kevin's ears perk up. "Can I go? I've never been to Monaco."

"If you'll put up with me until May."

Graham's face becomes a sudden scowl of doubt. "The Monaco Yacht Show is always at the end of September."

Hudson appears to be conjuring up a cover for his error, but is saved by the arrival of the hotel manager. After a brief discussion, where Hudson looks like he's sweating bullets, he tells us he has to take an international conference call upstairs. He gives everyone but Graham double air kiss and leaves.

"Isn't he dreamy?" Kevin gushes. "And now I get to go to Monaco and look for yachts!"

Graham tips back his martini. "I wouldn't count on it. I think he's a bloody phony."

Kevin is shocked. "But he's a DuPont."

The bill arrives, and I whip out my Visa card and hand it to the bartender before Graham can do anything. I hear a beep from the credit card machine and the bartender says my card has been declined. Although this has happened once or twice before—ok, actually dozens of times—I'm mortified.

Graham pats me on the head. "Looks like someone has been shopping."

Kevin picks up the bill and makes a grand charade of clutching his chest.

I grab the bill. "$1,927! There must be some mistake. Wait, I see why. We had nine colossal crab claws at $32 a piece—but worth it."

Graham looks over my shoulder, enumerating the bill: "#5175 Perrier-Jouët, Fleur de Champagne; Epérnay 1990, sixteen hundred dollars. No wonder." He shakes his head. "I'll get it. Bloody DuPont should be paying with that champagne he ordered."

Kevin hides behind a large patron, presumably to avoid getting involved in the bill.

Boy, I feel guilty with it being Graham's birthday and all. "Want us to chip in? I have some twenties, and Kevin's card might work."

"That won't be necessary."

Now that the bill has been paid, Kevin reappears. "We should have ordered a bottle of Chardonnay; it's only $36." He disappears, saying he wants to check on Hudson.

Optimistically, I offer, "I'll be rich when I sell the Weinstein house."

Graham tucks his card away. "Emma, you can't count on that for income. You do realize the house was on the market prior to this for three years with the darling Ms. Lichtenfelder. The only people who would ever buy it would be a couple who hate each other."

"Well, that shouldn't be too hard to find."

Graham looks at me like I'm dense. "People who hate each other don't buy houses. They get divorced or murder each other." He puts his wallet away. "But, I wish you luck selling the house."

We finish the rest of the champagne, and I sip it slowly for once, knowing how expensive it was.

After a while, Kevin returns. "Oh good, you saved me some." He pours himself more and relaxes in his seat. "I'm sure that as Hudson invited us, he would have wanted to pick up the tab."

"Is he coming back down?"

Kevin regales us with his escapade. "I wanted to find Hudson's room, but they are pretty tight-lipped at the front desk. So, I remembered he said he was in the HMF suite, which must stand for, pardon my language, Huge Mother F— Suite, so I followed his scent. At first I thought I was outside the wrong door, because I could hear his voice, but he was speaking in Spanish again. Then I heard him repeat a credit card number. I wrote it on my arm in case we need it for the next bottle."

"Kevin," Graham says, "you don't think it could possibly stand for Henry M. Flagler? Furthermore, does it occur to you that eavesdropping and credit card fraud are against the law?"

"How can it be a crime? He's my boyfriend."

Graham laughs and shakes his head.

"You didn't go inside?" I ask.

"No, what if he saw the numbers on my arm?"

"I'm starting to wonder about your Hudson DuPont III," I say. "I think we should do a little more investigating."

"Oh, here we go," Graham says. "I'd better have some bail money ready."

28

Having lost our Bentley ride, the three of us amble home on foot. Kevin halts at the entrance to a little gourmet market, *Amici*, and says he'll catch up with us in a minute. When Graham and I reach the house, Ursula follows us as we venture out back on the balmy last day of March. I light some candles to get in the spirit.

If there was ever an occasion, I guess this qualifies, so I dig out the special bottle of wine Larry and I were to drink on our first anniversary. I can only connect the dots in retrospect, and know that I was meant to be here at this moment, sitting outside a cottage named Larry. Not with Larry. The wine made the road trip down to Florida wrapped in a dress and yoga mat; as did I.

Graham holds the bottle gingerly, reading aloud through his little glasses. "Chateau Margaux 1983. Grand Vin. Now that was a very good year." I wonder if he means for wine or his life. He does the honors by decanting into two large glasses, and says we need to let it breathe awhile. Maybe everything needs to breathe for a while.

He remembers he left his guitar here and goes up to my room to retrieve it. When he returns, he begins singing an old Frank Sinatra song, "It Was a Very Good Year." I find more candles in the kitchen and smile at Graham as I light them one by one. He looks contented. I'm not. I just realized I could have gotten him a gift at one of the Breaker's shops.

Soon we hear Kevin entering the house breathlessly and holding up a paper grocery bag. "I got four filet mignons! That nice Al guy threw in one for Ursula. I'll just put these under the broiler and serve you two a nice dinner."

I am sent to borrow butter from Ernesto for our asparagus. I find him eating alone from a can of black beans, so I invite him and his butter over to join us. This also rounds out the party, though I think Ursula is not too happy about sacrificing her steak. We have a beautiful dinner and find out some more about Ernesto, as Kevin and I pepper him with questions. Graham politely stays out of it, enjoying the wine.

We learn Ernesto was never married, but was engaged to a woman who was a swimsuit model until she got fat. It wasn't clear whether the fat ended the engagement or the modeling, and I didn't dare to ask. He says he's here temporarily from Rio, where his mother had a beautiful home by the sea.

Graham finally asks what neighborhood, having visited there a few times. When Ernesto tells him, Graham is surprised, saying it's a very upmarket neighborhood.

"It sounds nice," I say.

"Yes, she won the lottery a few years ago and bought a big house."

"How lucky is she?"

"But then she died."

We all look down, and I can tell Graham is glad he stayed out of the questioning for the most part.

Ernesto bites off the top of his asparagus. "She was poisoned."

I say, "I'm so sorry," while my brain wonders how to politely inquire further.

Kevin quickly changes the subject by inquiring about Graham's adventures as a teenage singer in London in a cover band. Yes, women did throw panties at him. Never swimsuit bottoms. He says it's a young man's game and he always preferred to be on the sea instead of in a smoky bar.

After dinner, Kevin pulls out pink cupcakes and lights little candles. He really is adorable, and I'm sure he feels guilty for the Hudson episode. Graham looks grateful for the effort. Ernesto

156

disappears to his house and returns with a fancy box of individually wrapped cookies from Brazil. Then he says, "Yes, fish cookies," and we take a pass.

Not to be outdone by fish cookies, I run upstairs and rummage through my dresser thinking of what I can give Graham for a present. My eyes land on the unfinished painting. It's not going to the auction, so I carefully bring it down. Ernesto takes one look at the shadow and asks, "What's that on the wall?"

I say it's not quite finished, and hand it to Graham. He jokes, "Thank you. I'll pick it up when it's dry next year," and then takes an incoming call. "It's the harbormaster; the boat alarm is ringing. Probably the water maker." He kisses me goodbye, saying it's nearly midnight. We make plans to meet tomorrow night.

After everyone leaves, Kevin appears with a wet paintbrush and not only enhances the shadow, but creates a large "shadow maker." He stands back. "Ta da."

Definitely not going in the silent auction, as it will generate loud gasps.

29

Graham meets me for dinner the following night at the romantic Italian restaurant, Renato's, not far from the marina. The A/C has been over cranked inside, to the point where the windows have dew, so I suggest we have dinner outside in a leafy courtyard by the fountain. Graham silently complies even though I can tell he's hot. It's so hot, I don't feel like eating and only order a Caesar salad; he has stone crab claws, and feeds me. I have concluded that men like putting things in women's mouths. Well, I don't know about other mouths, but *I've* noticed a trend. The patient waiter must be dying in the heat in his white tuxedo, and he tries to get rid of us by refilling our Sancerre after each sip.

After dinner, Graham walks me the two blocks to the yacht, inviting me aboard for drinks and a song. He leaves me in the salon while he goes below deck to change. When he returns, he pulls me into the dark galley, where he opens the fridge and pulls out a pitcher of pre-made margaritas; a pitcher of premeditated passion if you ask me.

I say I want to watch the moon; it's a fat mandarin orange. He leads me to the upper deck, which is clean and white, like a rooftop beach. It's so sticky and hot I want him to pour a drink over my head. I'm only wearing a long turquoise sundress and panties. I'd lose at strip poker in two draws.

He's wearing shorts and a white linen shirt. He'd lose in two as well.

When I sip my drink and report that the rim has sugar not salt, he says they look alike in the dark. He takes a gulp of his drink and kisses me full, squirting some in my mouth. When I do the same it runs down his face. He laughs, then disappears down the spiral staircase.

He comes back up with a guitar, a grin and a roll of paper towels.

While he sits on the captain's bench playing a haunting Nick Drake song, "Joey," I lean my hips against the dials. When he finishes singing he tells me not to sit on the instruments, then he puts his glasses on and talks like a teacher, explaining what the various dials are for: depth finder, oil pressure, water temperature, etc. As he says this, I only hear: pressure, oil, deeper, faster.

He puts on a playlist of Bob Marley songs then stands behind me. I press my hips into his loins with the rhythm of the music, "Jamming." As I face the bow of the yacht, he reaches into the sides of my loose dress. Ahh! He even sighs with an English accent. He kisses the back of my neck.

Hopefully no one can see, as we are up high in the marina with just the soft, red glow of the fly bridge lights.

My hands are leaning on the dashboard. *Really not sure what I'm ready for.* Now, he has his hands tightly on my hips. I can see his reflection in the glass; his eyes look half closed, like he's in another world. I want to say, "Penny for your thoughts," but know not to.

He takes my hand and says, "Naughty girl. Now look what you've done to the teacher."

He unties the drawstring of his pants and lets them drop to his ankles, his long, gauzy shirt hiding his assets. He looks around and says, "Don't worry, no one can see us."

He laughs a little and pulls me to the white, padded lounge seat just behind the captain's bench and gently lowers me onto my back. He pulls my dress over his head like a tent. He puts his tongue on me, and then stops to open my legs more with his tanned hands. My mind drifts to the first time I saw his face; well the first time ever I saw his mouth. I wanted it on me. That would be a good song; maybe Roberta Flack will sing it.

159

Graham takes a break and looks up at my face. His full lips always look like they are waiting—waiting to say something profound.

His tongue is forceful and exuberant, and before long I'm traveling to a place called ecstasy. When I reach my stop, I can hear myself echo on the water. *Ahhhhh.*

He gets up to stand over me; the front of his shirttail is lifted by his thoughts. I run my tongue around the rim of my sugared glass, then run it along the rim of his sugar cane. Before long, I've returned the favor, as he lets out his own respiring cry.

Dripping with salty sweat, he collapses on me and we lie there panting with the now, "watery moon."

***

I wake up in a tiny cabin below deck all alone. When I resurface, I find Graham on the back deck, engrossed in his favorite English newspaper, the Guardian. He says Richard is coming on board soon, and I'd better get off the boat. He's all business, making me wonder if this will ever work. Is he scared? He helps me over the gangplank and says he'll pick me up for the party on Saturday. I have a nice walk of shame down the dock, carrying my shoes.

When I get home, I find Kevin and Ursula waiting for me. Kevin puts a sign above Ursula's head saying, "Lost Mom. Not wearing collar, but answers to Delilah."

Despite his attempts at humor, I am grateful to have him tend to my dog during such outings. When I remind him of the ball, he becomes a frantic mess—well even more so. Although he has a couple of days, he has yet to prepare for the cocktail party before the big ball.

We head to Costco, where I push the cart chocked with family-sized packages of caviar, cheese and jumbo shrimp, to name a few.

I'm sure people think Kevin and I have a pack of fat fancy kids at home. As we stand in the endless line, I replay the Graham night in my head. I tell Kevin little parts of it, mostly because he needles it out of me by dangling various tantalizing foods in my face. The other people in line also seem curious about my escapade with Graham, judging by their hand-cupped ears. I am grateful that Kevin and I have our code words "eggplant" and "parfait" for his and her *fun*.

30

It's the day of the big "Dogs are People Too Ball," and Kevin is engaged with his human resources recruiting task—at the beach. Someday, he may come to regret not casting his net wider than the hot surfer dudes at the end of our street.

As much as I'd love to witness the spectacle, I bow out of playing his fake assistant to take a bath; it's the first time I've had uninterrupted time in my own bathtub. Despite a natural aversion to water, my little peeping pug watches me bathe by inching her paws along the side of the iron claw foot tub like a can opener.

I want to be clean for my date with Graham. Guess we'll have to wait until after the ball to have any sort of resumption of activities, although he's picking me up, so we could do a little something before. Hmm.

Just as I'm zipping up my gown without any 'helpful' assistance from Kevin, Graham calls to say Bunny has held him up and he can't get away. I'm really starting to hate this Bunny woman, and am thinking of joining the committee to kick the rabbit off the island.

Ernesto has agreed to watch Ursula while I'm at the ball. It seems the repute of my pug has resulted in banishment by the local kennels. I peek over at his place to make sure I'm not interrupting anything; I can see he has helium balloons hovering by the ceiling, and wonder if Bunny is making a visit. Kevin thinks it's one of his sex tricks. I hope he doesn't give my dog helium to make her bark funny. Actually, that would be funny, but probably dangerous. Dogs are invited to the ball, but Ursula is staying home, as I want to be able to return to The Breakers sometime in the future.

At 5:00 I toddle over. Ernesto opens the door in a tuxedo, which seems a little overdressed for pet sitting, even for my princess.

He says he got a last minute invitation to the ball and to the Weinstein's party and he planned to just bring Ursula with him. *What?* For a moment I consider just tying her up in the backyard. Then I have a vision of her strangling herself, running in front of a Dodge Dart, and then being eaten by raccoons. (Pet owners live in constant fear.)

Well, the good news is now Ernesto can give me a lift to the party. He says sure, putting Ursula in the back of his convertible. It's so hot out I have put Kleenex under my arms until we get to the party. Rats! I forgot my Judith Leiber squirrel purse. Now, I have to penguin walk in the tight dress back to the house, and figure out how to squeeze my cell phone in the purse.

As I reemerge from the screen door, I feel like Cinderella. I wonder how this evening will turn out. Graham and I will dance the night away under the stars, then he will take me back to my place and we will be alone: no pug, no Ping, no Kevin. We'll finally do "it" the first time and he'll glide right in, and tell me I'm his true love.

Better get some Astroglide if I want true love.

Instead of staying in the back of the car, Ursula is compelled by some Darwinian force to bond with a maternal lap. Oh well, fawn dog hair doesn't show up much on a white dress. As we drive down Ocean Boulevard, past the endless hedgerows, I note that Ernesto finds the Weinstein driveway on the first attempt and wonder if he routinely sneaks over for a little cottontail. I see Graham in the motor court parking cars, and he doesn't look too happy about it. His British sneer is drawing his face tightly. I guess it's more Bunny's fault than England's.

Trevor answers the door in his royal manner, and the first thing out of his mouth is, "Not this creature again?" He takes Ursula by the leash and says he's going to tie her up on the side of the house. He points to the Kleenex still under my arms and says, "Might I suggest a visit to the powder room? I'll come and save you if you lock yourself in again."

After a quick visit to the powder room, Ernesto and I walk together to the back terrace. I wonder if people think I'm with Ernesto—although, he does look like a bronze god tonight. Oh, do I just fall in love every damn minute?

As if he can tell what's going through my head, Ernesto makes a hightailed departure to the bar.

I look out back to the Intracoastal and take in the lovely scene. There is Irene, playing "Afternoon of a Faun" on her ancient harp in the far garden. It looks like she has a dead parrot on her lap, but then I see that it's Dr. Phil dressed in a matching green feather outfit. One of these days Dr. Phil is going to get a complex.

Graham resigns his post and comes out. After taking a moment, he compliments Irene's dress, and she replies, "Where else can I wear this ? Although I suppose it would be good to dust the house in."

There is a huge ice sculpture in the center of the hors d'oeuvres table. I know it well, as Kevin carved it next to my head one morning last week; it has been in the Weinsteins' deep freezer since then. Kevin is really good with a chain saw, which I think is how he survives as a caterer. Most of his sculptures are literal and 'enhanced' sculptures of David. This one appears to be a woman with her mouth open, and it looks like she's drinking from a fish fountain. It must be symbolic of something.

It's hot out here. I'm shvitzing on my new $9500 dress, which means even though I kept the tags on and well hidden, it's becoming less likely that I'll be able to return it to get the money to buy food. I hate that.

Speaking of chainsaws, I peer into the kitchen and it looks like Kevin is running around with his head cut off. Better not go there.

I see Lisa Weinstein with her huge, black Bouvier dog. Wow. People do look like their dogs—I wonder if I look like a pug. She's wearing Goth gloves and a short dress with torn, black fishnets.

"Hi, Emma. Love the Cinderella look."

"Hi, Lisa." Somehow I say, "Love the stepsister look."

Lisa makes another hole in her fishnets. "I hate this. I just do it to piss off Bunny. Do you like my fake tattoo?"

She lifts her arm to show a huge spider under it.

"I hope your dad knows it's fake. You don't want to shock him."

"He knows. Even my grandmother knows. She's always helping me figure out ways to annoy the rabid hare."

"Where is your grandmother? She picked out this dress."

Lisa puffs on a cigarette and juts out her chin. "She's over there smoking with Trevor. I think they did it this afternoon on his trawler."

At first I'm wondering what they just did, then confusion turns to full-scale shock. "Lisa, do you really think so?"

"I came over early and heard all sorts of noises."

Now I wonder if she's talking about Bunny Monkey.

I change the subject by offering her champagne, but gather she's the kind of person who would probably drink absinthe.

"No, thanks. Hey, did you come with Ernesto?"

"No. He just gave me a ride. He's my next door neighbor."

Lisa throws her cigarette on the ground and pulverizes it with her foot. "Cool." She looks up toward the house, and I turn and see Richard escorting his mother down the terrace steps. His tan stands out against his white jacket and tie.

He looks gorgeous.

When he reaches me, Richard kisses me and says, "Emma, you look lovely."

"Thanks to your mother. This is the dress she bought me."

"Don't spill all over it now," Mrs. Weinstein blurts out. "You still have to wear it to the ball."

Richard looks around then whispers, "Emma, did you come with Ernesto the dog walker?"

"No. Just caught a ride. Graham was supposed to bring me, but your wife has him parking cars."

Richard looks up at a back window. "I don't know what's taking her so long to get ready. She's still in the tub."

"I'm sure it takes awhile to soak out the malice and venom," Mrs. Weinstein mutters.

"Mother!" Richard remands her. Then adds with a smirk, "You know it won't come out."

Mrs. Weinstein tries to be helpful. "Lisa, will you go up and see what's taking your evil stepmother so long?"

In a minute, I see Lisa tip-toeing up the back stairs with an extension cord and a hair dryer. She has a devilish smile on her face.

Richard turns to the side yard. "Isn't Irene's harp playing exquisite? It's too bad the neighbors have their horrible dog howling."

Poor sweet thing has no idea it's Ursula.

On my way to check on her, I stop in the kitchen to see Kevin. He hides behind me. "Oh, Emma. These people are driving me crazy. Every time I turn around that little Ping is right behind me. I think he's trying to hump me like a dog."

I survey the messy kitchen and notice Kevin is working alone.

166

"Where are your new recruits?"

"Surfs up; plus, they didn't think I'd pay them."

I don't want to get stuck cooking in my new dress, so I look around and ask, "Have you seen Graham?"

Kevin's preoccupied as he fills twenty-four champagne glasses in one pass; as they overflow, he takes a slurp from each one. Without looking up from his siphoning, he says, "He's out by the pool."

When he's gotten the glasses to toasting level, he adds, " Oh, everyone wants to know what that horrible howling is. They probably think it's Bunny having an orgasm."

I wander out back and see Trevor serving canapés and cursing. "So delighted to have selected Kevin's vast catering enterprise."

Graham comes up from behind and kisses me on my slick neck. "I'm so sorry I couldn't pick you up. You're not dating the dog walker now?"

"No. Kevin would be jealous. So, you're the captain and valet car parker?"

I can tell he's getting a little steamed, which I find adorable. "I had to help Kevin lift the sculpture and whatnot. I don't take orders from the lady of the house."

I start to wonder if there really is a lady of the house, or if they all killed her off years ago. Perhaps they're in on a household conspiracy to feign her existence. Maybe they sit around all day and make up horrible Bunny misdeeds to keep the spirit alive. Must run this theory past Kevin, but on another day.

Irene takes a break from her harping and finds me in the house with Graham and Ursula. She whips out a doll-sized pink wig with an attached rhinestone tiara. "It's for your dog. She can wear it to the ball," she says as she tucks it on Ursula's head and adjusts the chinstrap. Now, my dog looks like Tina Turner.

Graham is laughing, and says, "I'm sorry to break the news to you, ladies, but your dog is not allowed. It's in the contract with The Breakers. Esther told me."

Suddenly, we hear a loud crash and a scream from the nearby kitchen.

31

Graham looks at me and we bolt through the door, where we find Lisa Weinstein bent over and making a strange sound, like a dull saw going back and forth on wet wood. Oh, she's laughing, which I determine when she makes an inadvertent snort. She's bent over Ernesto, who is on his knees; apparently she was horsing around and hit him with a huge lamb leg right on the nose. I race over and he turns his head toward me quickly, which sends a trajectory of blood flying out of his nose…straight on my new dress! Naturally it gets on the lap area, not that there is any good place for a bloodstain. Dammit! $9500 of Mrs. Weinstein's millions down the drain.

Richard runs in, completely disinterested in the state of my gown, and gives Ernesto the medical once over. Graham is directed to get ice, and Kevin to get towels. Instead, Kevin just stands there screaming.

Hudson appears out of nowhere and volunteers to go upstairs to fetch towels.

Trevor takes a sponge and tries to clean my dress, but soon realizes he is wiping my 'lady parts' and turns red. Graham gets a cute smile, but now I have a larger red spot and it looks worse. Mrs. Weinstein appears with a white scarf and ties it around my waist to hide the stain. She hands Trevor a twenty dollar bill. "I thought she's at least make it to the ball without wrecking the dress."

I notice Lisa and Ernesto holding hands. Kevin and I look at each other, remembering that Ernesto is doing Lisa's evil stepmother.

Now that my gown looks like something out of a Stephen King novel, I decide I might as well spoil the look further with girl belly. I say I want to get something to eat, so Graham guides me to the buffet and hands me a little, blue Tiffany plate, which prompts me to try to read the bottom of the plate without spilling the food. "Looking for your wedding china?" he says with a little grin.

He's a mind reader. "Oh, no, I just didn't know Tiffany made plates. I nervously add that I knew about the diamond rings, but not about the plates. Kevin proudly marches out with a tray of the largest prawns I've ever seen, so large they look mutant. There's also raw tuna wasabi sauce, which reminds me of the time I ate a mouthful thinking it was guacamole. One never makes that mistake twice. There are even little tiny lamb chops with a raspberry glaze. This is going to be tricky to eat in my white dress. But if I don't eat, the champagne will start to get to me. I should have pre-eaten. The party looks to be a success, with no fires, floods or locusts, and I hope Kevin gets more business from it. Graham and I are quietly eating at an old French wrought iron table, listening to Irene play "Claire de Lune." As she plays, her bat wings waddle in rhythm with the song.

When she's done, the homely twins take over the harp. Trevor offers her a grasshopper, but she says she doesn't feel like drinking, so we know she must be sick. She tells us that while she awaits her experimental treatment results, the doctors are giving her chemo. Her face looks the color of her dress, and Trevor says he's sorry he brought up the grasshopper.

Concerned, Graham calls Richard over and they conclude Irene should lie down. She plops down on an inflatable raft by the pool house and says, "This is fine. I can watch the goings on from a distance."

Graham is the master of grace, and of course says nothing about the fact she looks like a dead peacock. As we walk away, Ursula gets loose, runs over and starts barking at the peacock. Irene gets up to push her away and the raft makes a series of farting sounds. Ursula smartly runs from the scene. "It's not me this time," Irene yells. "It's the raft."

Graham and I head to the buffet, where there is a cluster of ladies pointing at Kevin's ice sculpture and saying, "Oh my." Hmm.

Ice sculptures in Florida are never a good idea. It's melting all over the tablecloth and soaking the little canapés. Now I hear ladies gasping.

Graham points to the sculpture and starts laughing that full laugh of his, which fades to an adorable whimper. I look at the sculpture, which has melted considerably: the woman is still recognizable, though a bit more impressionistic, but the fish has melted to look like a something obscene, and water is still flowing from the fountain!

Irene bursts out laughing. "It looks like the woman is giving "eggplant!"

Feeling the need to alert Kevin to this state of affairs, I look in the kitchen but can't find him. Ping runs to the terrace door and yells something in Mandarin. Without saying a word, Trevor approaches the work of art and flings a white tablecloth on the phallic figurine.

Where is Kevin? When I finally find him, I think it best not to mention the ice sculpture at this point, as it's probably just a puddling problem now. He and Hudson are in the pool house drinking with my dog. She has a sign around her neck saying, "I just pooped in a $27 million house."

I tell them not to give Ursula any more champagne, and ask them to keep an eye on her while I'm at the ball.

"Oh that's all right missy," Kevin says, "you just go to the ball and leave your ugly stepsister here to clean up."

"Kevin, didn't you know? You're my guest," Hudson says.

"Oh, I was hoping so, but no one said anything. I brought a tuxedo just in case. Emma, will you keep an eye on things in the kitchen?"

Feeling like the stepsister now in my ruined dress, I help Ping prepare hors d'oeuvres and drinks. Suddenly the lights go off and the air conditioner hum makes a screeching halt.

32

Frankly, the party now has a calmer tone with just the sound of the harp strings. I go back out to the terrace and see there are battery-powered security lights around the perimeter.

Richard comes over to Graham. "Shouldn't the generator come on?"

"I was just thinking the same."

Irene emerges from avian death and jokes, "What's the matter, Richard? Forget to pay the bill?"

Graham walks over to the pool house and suddenly all the lights and electronic noise come blasting back on. "That's peculiar. The main breaker must have been thrown."

Ping finds Kevin drinking in the pool house and chases him out with salad tongs.

Trevor comes out and rings a bell, announcing there is a shuttle bus and everyone might as well head to The Breakers for the ball.

I ask where Bunny is and Richard throws his hands up. "She's not ready and wants someone to bring her iced tea. Kevin, can you arrange that?" While Kevin's brain is clearly trying to come up with a reason to get out of it, Hudson, oddly, volunteers.

Irene decides to stay behind as well, and Trevor helps her up the stairs to rest. Ursula follows Dr. Phil up the stairs, barking all the way. Pudge is left without a ride and resorts to purring into my Graham's ear; next thing I know, she and Natasha are riding with us.

The well-trained Graham complies with all disparate female requests on the two-mile trip to the hotel, including simultaneously running the heat for nearly-naked Natasha and the air conditioning for the hot-flashing Pudge. I am glad of this, as it diffuses the reek of smoke and perfume.

As we glide down the tree-lined entrance of the majestic Breakers Hotel, I'm thinking my life is picking up. Here I am in a ball gown, with my handsome knight in shining armor. I'm so glad I moved to Palm Beach.

Because Pudge is wearing six-inch Jimmy Choos, Graham is directed to forgo the valet parking and illegally park at the fire door by the ballroom. As we enter the ocean-front ballroom, we see Lisa and Ernesto nearby with Lisa's huge Bouvier dog.

Richard and his mother come by. "I hope that doesn't turn into anything serious," Richard says into my ear. I think it has to be terrible to be a father, send your daughter to the best schools in the world, and she ends up with a questionable dog walker. Hmm. Would now be a good time to tell him we found Ernesto in his wife's closet?

There's an eight-piece orchestra playing "Some Enchanted Evening." Despite the fact Graham is holding my arm and it's an official date, Natasha grabs him for a dance. Before he can conjure up a tactful line to cut her loose, he is holding her close. As I stand alone, a swollen toad of a man asks me to dance. What do I say to not hurt his feelings? Finally, I conjure up, "I am terribly sorry, but I have a partially broken leg." The Toad stands nearby looking sad.

When Graham returns with Natasha, I suggest Toad ask her to dance and point to her perfectly good legs. Without apology, she answers Toad with an abrupt, "You must be joking," before glaring at me and stomping off.

Hallelujah! Graham finally takes my hand for a dance. Toad is still standing there, so I must feign a slow moving limp. By the time we get to the distant dance floor, the orchestra has stopped playing and put on a tape. "Brick House" is now immortalized as our first song, and therefore the song we must dance to at our eventual wedding. As we're dancing, I look over and see the diminutive Mrs.

Weinstein boogying up a storm with Trevor's waist. She Watusis over to us, grabs Graham and pushes him over to Natasha. Then she yanks Natasha away from Richard and has him dance with me. I'm glad my first public dance with Richard is not "The Hokey Pokey." It's "When I Fall in Love." As we dance, Richard's lips are on my ear asking, "What has happened to your leg?"

"Oh, I broke it five minutes ago." Richard doesn't seem to hear me and I don't feel like explaining. I have my body pressed to his, and hope he can't feel my heart pounding.

Pudge is reeking of Joy— the perfume, not the emotion— as she hovers about. She is trying to cut in to dance with Richard, who avoids her by holding me. I am worried that Graham is feeling a little annoyed, but every time I try to cross the room to dance with him, Mrs. Weinstein grabs my arm or has some sort of ersatz seizure.

Graham seems to be getting a little quiet, but it's hard to tell because he's quiet anyway. He finally gets away by going up to the stage and making an announcement. "I'm here to sing a duet, but fortunately my singing partner is missing—sorry, unfortunately—so, I'll sing a solo." Graham launches into an old, poignant song, "Portrait of Jennie."

"Oh, my gosh, I almost forgot," Pudge says and runs off. We see her order a pack of minions to drag the painting of Graham up to the stage for the now not so silent auction.

During his song, Graham catches a look at his enhanced portrait. When the song is over he stomps over to me, looking furious. He points to the now elongated puppet and shadow. "What is that doing here? I believe we talked about this."

"Don't look at me, it was drying in Kevin's house."

"And that was safekeeping?" he huffs.

Mrs. Weinstein pats his shoulders. "It should go fast. I've already bid a grand."

Graham covers his face.

Richard's phone makes a horrible car honking sound. "It's a text from Bunny," he explains. "She wants me to go back and get her."

"No taxi driver will have anything to do with her," Mrs. Weinstein says. "Graham, why don't you go, your car is on the service road."

Graham is all too willing to get out of here. Natasha says she's tired and asks for a lift home. Hmm. I think that no good will come of that lift.

33

Richard, sneezing from Pudge's scent, takes my arm and guides me through a subtle room divider into a vacant ballroom. Suddenly, a dog barks; it's a seeing eye dog with his master, a teenage girl. She's seated at a grand piano. Her head swivels to catch the sounds. The girl tells us her dog was disturbed by the other dogs and she had to leave the ball. I can see why all the social climbing dogs at the party would annoy her service dog.

The girl politely asks if we mind if she plays the piano. She begins a very complicated piece by Vivaldi. When she finishes, Richard gently asks her if she can play Satie's, "Gymnopedie." Without a word, she begins. When she gets to the part where the volume and tempo become engorged I have tears in my eyes. Richard takes my hand to dance. We are invisible to the world. Only the seeing eye dog can see us, and I'm sure he's seen it all. The girl plays on, this time Vivaldi's Four Seasons suite. Richard and I take a seat on a little pea green velvet lounge against the wall. I have never felt so at peace. When she plays the Autumn sequence, Richard falls asleep against the wall.

As I rest with Richard, replaying the evening thus far, there is a sudden ruckus. Kevin, whom everyone knows wasn't officially invited, has knocked over a cart of crème brûlées. No, wait—it's Dr. Phil. He's on a leash…that Kevin is holding. They flee and run straight to the bar. Richard and I return to see everyone from the party is at the ball, including Big Red and the homely twins. I would love to chat with them about the house, but they are always out of limping range. I look around and see dowagers dancing with hired men; I see Dobermans dancing with dachshunds.

Mrs. Weinstein gets up to announce the winners of the cutest dog contest and there is a collective booing amongst the losing dog masters. Big Red has a fat Irish setter who wins best behavior. The Toad's bulldog wins as the ugliest dog. He doesn't seem too happy, but it's hard to tell with that face. I think of matching the two up, but worry that it would be unfair to their future children.

Mrs. Weinstein goes back to the microphone to co-host the silent auction. Just as Graham expected, she takes away all doubt. "I can't find our singer, but we've got this spiffy painting of him."

"I pray that she doesn't know the term 'stiffy,'" Trevor mutters.

Everyone turns to look at the painting. Graham would be mortified.

"I've already bid a grand, who dares to beat it?" Mrs. Weinstein says.

"We do!" the homely twins call out. "We'll bid two thousand."

Mrs. Weinstein glares at them; the bidding goes on, finally ending at $14,000 to the twins. Graham should be proud.

I find Kevin across the room and demand to know how the painting ended up here. He gets nervous. "Pudge sent someone over to pick it up this morning. It's for charity you know."

I frown at him. "Graham is furious with me."

"She coerced me. Said she'd report me to the police for taking the case of champagne."

Mrs. Weinstein announces, "Our singers Bunny and Graham are mysteriously absent, but Emma and Richard have agreed to sing the duet." Richard and I look at each other in disbelief as the spotlight turns on us. We are dragged up to the piano on the stage. I sort of know the song from Graham playing it, plus Richard has the sheet music in front of him at the piano. It's alternating *his* and *her* verses, with some overlapping. Richard begins the melody and nods for me to sing:

Donna Drejza

"I walked into the room
You were dancing, you were singing
Fly me to the moon.
I'll take you there soon.

She walked into the bar
I was minding my own business
playing Venus and Mars
Her eyes looked like stars.

Will you sing me a song?
Your mouth is so inviting
your voice is so strong.

When she looked in my eyes
I knew I was in trouble
I knew I was in deep.
my heart made a leap.

Will you sing it to me?
You don't need to hit the high notes
You can play midde c.

She sat next to me
she said she'd turn my pages
my legs became weak
I hadn't felt this for ages.

Will you write me a song?
doesn't need to be a good one
doesn't need to be long.

My heart was beating faster
I kept losing my place
when I looked at her face.

Somehow, we dovetail the verses nicely, but I think it was due to Richard's strategic winking. That is until he loses his place and knocks the sheet music on the floor. We are met with a round of applause, initiated by Mrs. Weinstein, who comments that we make beautiful music together.

Thankfully, Trevor saves us as he hesitantly approaches the microphone on the stage. He proceeds to sing a very poignant rendition of "Try to Remember." Who knew he could sing? His voice falters with emotion as he hits the last haunting refrain. I have tears in my eyes, so Richard helps with a handkerchief and puts his arm around me. This just might be too much affection for a married man to show in Lilliputian-sized Palm Beach.

Right then there's a blinding flash. It's the society photographer for the Palm Beach Post snapping our photo. "I hope that doesn't end up in the Shiny sheet tomorrow," I say.

Kevin tries to capture the attention of the photographer, but Hudson puts his hand over the lens and runs off. I pull Kevin aside. "Did you notice how Hudson doesn't want his photo taken?"

"Surely you know that fabulously rich people do not like press."

"Tonight, you should try to poke around his room."

Right then Hudson reappears, and I wonder if he heard me. He tells Kevin his suite is being re-papered and is a complete mess. Trevor steps over and reminds Kevin he has to clean up at the house tonight. This prompts him to depart with Hudson in a taxi.

We stay a bit longer and all walk out to sit by the ocean. The ball is ending, and still no Bunny; Graham seems to have gotten waylaid by Natasha. I wonder what happened to them.

After an endless wait for the valet, Trevor, Mrs. Weinstein, Richard and I leave the ball. Mrs. Weinstein says to stop off at

Richard's house so she can have a nightcap and so I can retrieve my howling dog.

When we get there, Richard fumbles for his keys before he realizes someone left the front door open. Trevor and Mrs. Weinstein venture in and disburse to various rooms. The main power is off, prompting Mrs. Weinstein to return and announce, "We're outta here, Trevvy."

Without waiting for me, they are off. Another one of Mrs. Weinstein's not so sinister plots to strand me with her son. Richard guides me past the motionless fountain, through the dark foyer, with the red emergency lights creating long shadows on the walls. We hear raucous laughter, which tempts us to follow the audible lead to Richard's study. There we find Kevin, Hudson and Irene's dog, Dr. Phil.

With cigar-lit faces and drunken mirth, Kevin announces Dr. Phil's green feather gown has won him an award for best dressed. The prize is a free dog therapy session. They toast the dog's style, causing Richard to notice their choice of drink. He points to the half-full crystal bottle of Courvoisier L'Esprit. I recall Kevin previously enlightening me as to the suggested retail value: $9500 a bottle. Egad! One could buy a dress for that, he teased.

"Saved you some," Kevin says.

Richard walks away, laughing. "It was my wife's cognac, not mine."

Kevin's face instantly contorts into terror. Hudson, looking stressed, takes the opportunity to pour himself more—well past the understated mark on his grand snifter. I take a moment to notice how perfect they look together: Kevin, Hudson and Dr. Phil; like they are in a European ad for wristwatches or cognac—but not $9500 cognac.

I ask if anyone knows where Graham is.

"Well, not that it's my job to track the staff," Kevin says, "but someone who looked just like him," he breaks into laughter, "only without the 'shadow' stopped by." He notices my tense eyebrows and sobers up. "He and Ping went to the boat for the night."

"Have you seen Irene, Lisa or my wife?" Richard inquires.

"Haven't seen Irene, but she could be sleeping in the garage for all I know. Lisa and Ernesto were just leaving when we got here. They must have awakened your wife, because I heard her playing the piano on her side. Well, I'm not sure if 'playing' is the right word."

Richard smiles. "She needs a little practice."

"Your wife's gone to bed and said not to bother her," Hudson adds.

He speaks with a bit of a tense tone, but not in his usual lockjaw. I guess it's hard to keep that up.

Kevin, stepping back into caterer mode, offers us the last drop of the cognac. Kevin must feel a tad guilty. "Don't worry, I think you can get another bottle online from the Liquor Snob."

I ask where Ursula is.

Kevin starts laughing. "I think you'll find her wearing a sign around her neck saying, 'I ate an $845 pair of Christian Louboutin shoes.'"

"Oh no! Who let her back in the house?"

"I couldn't take the howling, so I let her in."

"I hope, for the dog's sake Bunny doesn't find out. We'd better hide them." Richard quips.

Kevin takes a deep, warm gulp. "Already tossed them. I've seen her shoe collection—she'll never miss them."

Richard and I walk into the kitchen for champagne and it looks like a flour bomb went off. There's broken glass on the counter and sauce all over. Like a little rumba robot, we find Ursula systematically licking the floor. We find the chewed up sign too.

Richard picks up a Styrofoam container. "It looks like your dog got into Lisa's leftovers."

Kevin has followed us as far as the doorway. "Who knew that a dog could open up a refrigerator? Did you know she can get into messy corners with that tongue?" Kevin makes an attempt to put stuff in the fridge, but a huge frozen lamb leg keeps getting stuck. Richard takes a bottle of champagne from the fridge and carefully steps over Ursula, who is focused on her assigned task. Kevin informs us that he and Hudson are leaving with Dr. Phil. Richard and I look at each other without saying anything, sensing a collusion to keep us together this evening.

Alone with Richard—except for his sleeping wife, we sit under the stars by the pool and laugh about the evening.

"Did you see when the most congenial dog jumped onstage and started humping Pudge's leg under her gown?" Richard asks.

"At first, I thought it was Ping."

Richard tells me that they have a boat ride planned for tomorrow. "I'm sure my mother has already invited you."

"Yes, but I have an appointment tomorrow to show the house, remember?" Rats. If Bunny had let me the other day, I'd be free as a bird.

Richard looks at his watch and notes it's midnight already. He points out that I'm effectively stranded here, and suggests I stay over in one of the guest rooms. Well, I suppose just this one time. We walk up the curved staircase, like we are going to bed together. Ursula follows us up, doing her bunny hop on each step. I wonder where he'll put me. He pauses at the top of the stairs and doesn't seem to know what to do. I see his gentle hand on the railing. The moon is shining through the front window; it looks to be a badly hung quarter moon.

Ursula has no patience and pushes her nose through the double door on his side. I snap my fingers to call her back, but she ignores me as usual. Richard winks and dances his index finger, indicating for me to follow him. When we pass through the double doors, he whispers, "We don't want to wake her, so I'll take you on my side."

I follow him down the wide hall, where he opens a door to a huge room decorated in leaf green—my favorite color. He says he'll be right back and silently steps away on the thick carpeting. I climb out of the sequined torture chamber and my body gives off a silent sigh. Thankfully, I find a wrapped toothbrush and soap, as my purse does not make an adequate overnight bag. When I come out of the bathroom naked, I find sweet Richard sitting on the bed.

He covers his eyes a little. "Here, I brought you something to sleep in. It's Lisa's, but I'm sure it will fit." It's a Snoopy tee shirt, probably from when she was twelve. I turn away from him to put it over my head. He brings me a glass of water from the bathroom and tucks me in. "Emma, I had a wonderful time tonight."

"I did too. Thank you."

Richard looks at me and suppresses a yawn. "I can't believe I have to be at the boat by eight. The boys want to do a little fishing. You sleep as late as you want."

I turn off the light, knowing that I probably look hideous. "Don't worry, I'll get up early and be out of here. I don't want to run into Bunny."

"Oh, you won't run into her. She sleeps until noon and then has breakfast in her suite."

He pulls the covers up to my chin. Then he kisses me on the lips. "Emma, I think I'm falling for you."

Whoa! Before I can think of a reply, he's gone and I hear him closing doors to his room next door. This is weird; sleeping in his house with his wife in the other wing. Before long, I hear Richard snoring on the other side of the wall as the beds are butterflied against the wall. His heart is beating just a few feet away. I'd love to sneak over and climb in bed next to him, just to feel him breathe. I guess this is the next best thing. Ursula is also snoring up a storm; when Richard exhales, Ursula inhales. I'll never get any sleep.

34

The next morning, I wake up wondering where I am. The room is so huge it's probably twice the size of my little pillbox cottage. Ursula wakes up and we wander around a little; it feels like no one is home. It's a safe bet Bunny is still sleeping, so I try to be really quiet. As I descend the stairs, I can tell the main power is back on, as the fountain has resumed its rain dance. Ursula and I wander down the hall to the kitchen, which is still a huge mess. I'll have to do a little cleanup before the clients come. It's just like Annette Benning had to do before her open house in that movie, *American Beauty*. First I'll need a cup of coffee, but find myself in a vicious cycle, as I need coffee before I can decipher the fancy Italian espresso maker. After loud groans, presumably in Italian, black mud dribbles from the system and spews all over the counter. Oh well, can't get any messier.

I sit at the kitchen desk dipping Stella D'oros in my sludge as I replay the evening in my head.

Did Richard really tell me he was falling for me, or did I dream that part? If only he didn't have that bothersome wife—lazy bitch, upstairs sleeping all day. I could be living here and sleeping next to his little beating heart. This is bad karma to think about a married man. Nothing good will come of this. If Richard and I had an affair, his jealous wife would surely find out, and she's probably not the type who would divorce him and move on; she would be vindictive and kill me or make me a social outcast in Palm Beach—and then kill him. I wonder what she's like; I could find out any minute.

I've got to clean this place up before the clients come over. Ursula's ears flap as she follows me around, knowing we are on some sort of emergency mission. I start picking up the dirty glasses from Richard's library; that is, until I'm distracted by old photos. Oh, there's Richard on his wedding day, arm in arm with a blonde. Hmm. Based on Kevin's detailed description, I would have thought

Bunny was taller; maybe it's the first wife, but would think she'd have dark hair like Lisa. Maybe there was a secret middle wife.

As I start down Bunny's side hallway, I find two more dirty brandy glasses. Maybe she had a gentleman caller over last night and was serenading him on the piano. There is her cell phone on a side table in the hallway. I'm tempted to take a peek at who she had over, but with my luck she'd sneak up behind me and I'd juggle it in the air like a nervous clown.

Boy, the things a realtor has to do; I grab the dirty glasses and go to the kitchen to run the dishwasher. The only thing that's remotely clean is the travertine floor, which, thanks to Ursula, looks spic and span—except for the bloodstain on the wall.

Every time I open the freezer side to hide things, that stupid lamb leg falls out. There's dried crab dip all over the cabinets and huge fingerprints all over the stainless subzero. As I am cleaning, I realize I have no car to drive home. I'll have to call a taxi and have them pick me up at a neighboring address. Guess I'll have to put the dress back on. It's still hanging on the shower, and now the dried blood looks rusty brown. I'll have to explain this to the drycleaner, leaving out the details: girl hits the dogwalker on nose with a leg of lamb, which had nothing to do with the dogwalker shtupping the stepmother. I think that would be a good movie title: *The Dog Walker and The Stepmother*.

Maybe I should look around Lisa's room for a comb in case the mystery snoozer emerges as one of the living. I make my way upstairs, with Ursula following. It's funny that they keep her bedroom intact like a Lisa shrine, even though she has her own apartment in Delray Beach. I hope she doesn't mind. Her room is an odd combination of pink and Goth: like a little girl suddenly turned rotten.

Ursula is rooting under Lisa's bed. "Ursula, stop." Ignoring me, she pulls out a glow in the dark rubber stick and starts chewing on it, causing it to make moaning sounds.

Then I realize it's a vibrator and think this Lisa is one weird chick. I think Lisa would be mortified if her dad ever found it, so I throw it down the laundry shoot. She must not have lived here since she was twelve. A child with a vibrator. Maybe I shouldn't have any children with Richard, imaginary or real.

Now time for just a little peek into Richard's room. How cute; he made his bed. This is a good sign: he's a neat person, and neat people always marry slobs. I'm a match made in heaven. I'll bet Bunny is irritatingly neat, and that's why they're a mismatch. I pull back the covers a little and see Richard's pillow, and bury my face in it. I can't help it. It smells just like him, kind of like honey and butter.

Boy, I wish I could have gone on the boat trip. All thanks to Bunny Weinstein. I should have had her show the place today. Yes, that's probably the secret to being a stress-free agent. I should have the client do my work while I'm on a yacht with her husband. Now that all this party business is over, I'd better get cracking on the real estate, starting with this sale.

I lose my train of thought as I wander into Richard's bathroom. This is a fabulous place for a curious girl. Not to be nosy, I just want to see what kind of aftershave he wears. We'll, it's nice to see he's not a complete neat freak. There's trash on the floor—a prescription bag from Fedco pharmacy. Knowing the clients are coming, I'd better do a little cleaning before I leave. When I put the paper in the trash I feel a slight stab, so I rummage through the paper and find a syringe. As I wash off my hand, I wonder if Richard is a diabetic. Carefully, I pull it back out of the trash to examine the syringe, but it's just got little lines and numbers on it, but no writing. Maybe he does his own Botox. How wonderful would that be to have free Botox. Another reason to marry a doctor. I'll have to watch to see if my hand becomes paralyzed in a few days.

Maybe I'd just better check out his medicine cabinet to see what it could be, so I know what I'm going to die from.

I open it up and there's a whole pharmacy of prescription bottles. Lipitor: that's for cholesterol. I know this because my mom takes those.

As I'm cleaning, I spot Richard's black leather Patek Philippe watch on his tall dresser. That should be put away in case clients have sticky fingers.

Boy, you pay all that money and it doesn't even have the correct time; it says 10:40, but it must be only around 9:00.

Plenty of time for more coffee, I think as I head back downstairs to the kitchen where I find dirty fingerprints all over the stainless SubZero. Oh, the things a real estate agent has to do. I pull out some Fantastic spray and put on some rubber gloves to finish cleaning. Everyone on the Eastern seaboard knows I don't clean my own house, yet here I am spraying my listing with Fantastic, hoping the stuff will live up to its name. Given all the glass, maybe I should use Windex.

I stop in Graham's little office near the side of the house, just to make sure I have not overlooked anything. Hmm. Another neat freak, as I suspected. Here, I notice a file folder labeled "crew updates." I see one for Natasha. Hmm? I peek inside wondering what exactly her job title is.

My phone alarm goes off. Oh no! It's 10:54. I guess when the power went off all of the clocks were off. There's no way for me to go home and change. I guess I'm wearing this to show the house.
Right then the doorbell rings, which starts Ursula barking. When I walk out to the entry, I see five heads peering in.

With Ursula by my side, I open the front door. There, an entire limb of the Aggarwal family tree greets me. Unfortunately, they have caught me in the unintentional pairing of a white Escada evening gown with yellow rubber gloves. While they are no doubt wondering how I ever get dressed in the morning, I am secretly praying to St. Joseph that they buy the house.

Most people don't know that when they were coming up with various saints, they came up with one, St. Joseph, and dedicated him exclusively for real estate agents.

They come in the house in a neat clump. The family consists of a sixty-something mother, her husband, an ancient grandmother, the grown daughter and her seven-year-old son.

Feeling the need to explain the mess, I go on about a huge party here last night and about how the caterer didn't have time to clean. The mother complements my gown; she probably thinks that agents wear evening gowns to show houses in Palm Beach. I say I wore it last night and didn't get home. Then she looks down at the blood spot and doesn't say anything.

While we are viewing Richard's study, I wonder what order to show the house in. We proceed down the wide glass hallway that runs the length of Richard's side of the house. I suppose I'd better show them the kitchen to give Bunny a little more time. The elderly grandmother touches things, but never says a word.

The little boy, Monty, runs over to Ursula, who has relocated the vibrator and is making it moan. Other than the telltale sound, and the fact that it vibrates, it looks like a harmless green stick. The grandmother says, "What's that Monty?"

I'm humiliated. "It's a dog toy," I say, grabbing it from Monty. He instantly starts to squawk, so I have to give it back.

After showing them the pool and the view, we go back inside and I think of riding them up the elevator, but it's been left upstairs. Also, I'm not sure if the capacity is five adults plus one boy. I decide to lead them back to the front and up the curved stairs.

With Monty as the new leader, we reach the top. I begin with Richard's side, praying that Ursula doesn't pull out any more 'dog toys.' While they are marveling at Richard's burled wood dressing closet, I discreetly pull Richard's pillow out again and do a quick sniff. Of course Mrs. Aggarwal catches me doing this.

When we're done with Richard's side of the house, I ask them to wait a moment; I peer into the inner sanctum, and I'm relieved to see no signs of Bunny. Hmm. Her bed is made; I guess she remembered I was to show the place today. I look and see the Aggarwals turn in unison, like meerkats, admiring the suite.

Then we enter Bunny's gigantic bathroom, which has a hairdryer on an extension cord. Very unsafe. I'll have to mention this to her when I finally meet her. She has dozens upon dozens of jars of lotions and creams that cover her marble counter top. Now I see reason number 1,357 why Richard dislikes her: she's a slob. Her melted ice tea from last night is still on the counter as well. I quickly pour it down the drain, thinking they really should get better staff around here.

When we finally emerge from Bunny's suite, my assistant Ursula gets impatient and starts to get a little too sniffy by the grandmother's sari, so Ursula is demoted to her previous position as just my dog. I put her in an enclosed bathtub on Richard's side for the remainder of the tour.

The rest of the family is waiting in a pack on the stair landing, where old Grandmother gives me a thumbs up. Yay!

Then the middle matriarch, Mrs. Aggarwal says, "We would like to put in an offer."

I like the way the women decide everything and Mr. Aggarwal is just the car driver. The grandmother is clearly going to block the family with a slow descent on the steep staircase in her swishy sari, and I don't have time for that.

"Let's take the elevator down."

189

The little grandson and the grandmother fight over who gets to press the button; clearly button pressing is a family compulsion. With a ping the doors open. Suddenly there's a chorus of screams, like they rehearsed in their car on the way over. I look inside the elevator and think this can't be good. There's a dead body.

35

The Aggarwals re-scream in horror, and the grandmother, who can barely move, runs down the front stairs at a surprising clip. Holding my breath, I take a closer look at the purplish woman lying on the floor. The woman is long—tall lying down and has blonde hair. This must be Bunny Weinstein. Just to be sure, I look again and notice the large breasts, which are upright like Kevin described.

"Mother, put Monty in the car," the doctor/daughter commands in a stern voice. Then she takes a closer look at the body and announces, "She's dead."

The rest of the Aggarwals flee the scene while the unruffled daughter orders me to call 911. "Tell them you have a deceased woman and to send the police."

Not having had that same medical composure class, I cry out, "The police?"

"This was no heart attack. Look at her mouth."

There's a piece of duct tape flapping over her mouth, and dried blood crusted on her head. The bottom few inches of her body are purple, like she was floating in an inch of ecru paint.

"Looks to me like suffocation. I see petechial hemorrhage."

Eww. I have to step into the elevator to use the phone. The curly cord dangles over the body. A red-soled shoe has fallen off her not so lucky rabbit's foot. Lucky for me, that wasn't her last pair of Christian Louboutin's.

"Hello? Hello?" I cry like I'm some deranged telephone operator from a 1940s movie. I can't remember what she just told me to say.

It's all starting to hit me as I struggle to get out, "I'm a real estate agent and I was showing a house to my client, when the little boy had to go to the bathroom and we decided to take the elevator. Then we found a dead lady with duct tape on her mouth. What? Oh, the address?"

I give her the address on South Ocean, and answer more of the dispatcher's queries. "She looks completely dead. No, I am not going to touch her."

The doctor/daughter appears from behind me, which makes me jump out of my skin, and grabs the phone from me. "Hello, this is doctor Aggarwal-Patel. I've just arrived on the scene of what appears to be a homicide. The deceased is a woman, about fifty. No. No gunshot wounds, just edema, bloating, lividity. Looks like suffocation."

I pull the loose duct tape off. "I'm sure that's not helping."

Aggarwal-Patel hands the phone back to me and stares as I give my name and the address, again, to the dispatcher.

Peeved, Aggarwal-Patel says, "I hope I don't have to fly back from Delhi to testify. I'm just visiting my parents you know." She gets up and marches down the stairs.

Soon I hear sirens getting louder, then come to a winding halt in the motor court. My, they have good service here in Palm Beach. I run down the stairs and open the front door and see a police car. The Aggarwal family, minus the daughter, is already packed into their car. I'm guessing that now they don't want to buy the house. The father is prompted by one of the officers to roll the window down; I'm sure he regrets the action, as the family is directed to get out of the car and line up by the garage. I hear them chatter amongst themselves in Hindi—or whatever they speak.

The gist of which is probably, "Damn it, Dad! You should have floored it."

The police enter with guns ready.

"No need for guns," I say. "She's already dead, and there are no bad guys here."

They come to a halt. "We got a call for a signal 7," says the skinny one with red hair.

The other officer introduces himself. "I'm Officer King and this is Officer Cain."

The red head says, "You can call me Rusty and him Luther."

"And I told you, Rusty," he corrects his colleague, "we're not supposed to use the codes anymore."

"But that's my favorite one: dead body."

Hearing the words makes it even freakier. I lead them to the downstairs elevator door and press the button.

"The door must be stuck. Wait here, I'll get her."

They look at each other in apparent disbelief as I dash up the stairs. The elevator door seems to be ajar due to the shoe, and I see no reason to have them drag the body down the stairs and get blood all over the place. Throwing the stiletto inside the elevator with the stiff body, I send it down to the awaiting officers on a solo journey. From the top of the stairs, I hear another emergency vehicle in the driveway.

I peek down to see a van marked Crime Scene Unit. Luther has taken the initiative to lead the orderly Aggarwals into the living room, presumably for questioning and not for tea. The CSI team, an Asian guy and a tough looking woman, unload equipment from the van.

We meet at the back elevator, and when I press the elevator button they yell at me, saying I'm contaminating the scene.

We all wait quietly. "Isn't it always hurry up and wait?" I offer. Finally the door opens.

The CSI pair and Rusty take one look and must be repulsed, because they are oddly silent. I guess they're not allowed to scream. I'd be terrible at their job; it's probably a good thing I'm a real estate agent. I hear another siren, and soon a man who appears to be some sort of police captain, ambles in. He must have seniority, judging by his bald head and stakeout belly. He looks to be in his mid-sixties and has a "seen it all" manner about him, steadily asking where the victim is.

He directs the CSI woman to start "a crime scene log," then points and orders Rusty to seal off the perimeter and cordon off this area. Rusty is having trouble starting the roll of yellow police tape. He eventually gets it, and begins marking off the doorways. It's hard not to laugh as he gets the tape all twisted and tapes the captain into a corner. The captain swats at Rusty, and I am reminded of Skipper and Gilligan.

The CSI guy, who looks like he'd be a neat and tidy person from the way he carefully touches things, says things to the girl to write down. "Positive for edema, but free of stab wounds or bullet holes."

Luther peers over their heads. "I see a little bruising around the eyes."

"She looks puffy to me," Rusty says.

"She's showing signs of bloating."

I say maybe that's why she didn't make the party.

"Party?"

"Yes, Bunny had a party for fifty people here last night and didn't bother to make an appearance."

194

The CSI woman takes an obsessive number of pictures of the exact same shot, turning the head slightly to reveal a small amount of blood on the elevator floor. You couldn't call it a pool of blood, more like a slurp.

The captain gets on his police radio and asks, in what sounds like an upstate New York accent, how long until the detective arrives.

I see Luther go up the stairs and immediately think I should have made the bed this morning. The boss introduces himself as Captain Lacey and asks my name.

"Emma Budnjk, agent," I say in an official sounding voice.

He directs Rusty to get the spelling of my name, so I go on. "B as in boy, U as in Ursula, D as in dog, N as in Natasha, J as in Jacuzzi and K as in kitten."

He shakes his head. "Could you start over again? I'm caught up in a weird image now."

"What exactly happened here?" Captain Lacey asks me.

"I have no idea. I was just about to sell the house, and found a lady lying in a slurp of blood."

Without looking up from his clipboard, he barks, "Name of the victim?"

"I'm not positive, but I'd say it's Bunny Weinstein. I could be wrong. I wouldn't want you to call her parents and get them all upset—I'm just guessing she has parents; she could have been raised by wolves for all I know."

"What makes you think it's Bunny Weinstein?"

"Well, I've never met her, but Kevin said she had" —I use air quotes—"'huge fake melons,' but he's a caterer, so he always talks in foods."

We all look down at her upright breasts in her orange evening gown. Mr. Aggarwal, who has deviated from his assigned waiting spot, ogles her.

"And my friend Irene said she had the worst facelift in all of Palm Beach."

We all look at her face, which has been pulled into a permanent smile even though she's got nothing to smile about.

"Yeah, everybody was talking about it last season," Rusty says.

Captain Lacey gives him a look. "Rusty, just try to get the facts."

I kneel down for a closer look and can't help but say, "Whoa, that *is* a bad facelift. I didn't notice when I was taking the duct tape off her mouth."

"What?" Lacey bellows. "She had duct tape on her mouth, and you took it off?"

"If someone had just taken it off sooner, she might not be in this predicament." I pick up the piece of spent tape. "See, there was a little slit in it. I don't know if that matters."

"Yes, it does. Thank you for pointing that out."

He shakes his head and looks at his clipboard. "This is the Weinstein residence isn't it?"

"Yes, it's my listing. Well, it's really Irene's. I'm her helper."

I notice the captain has sparkly Irish eyes, as he looks at me quizzically. "You've got her place listed and you've never met her?"

"She's always getting massages, so I interact with the husband."

He exchanges glances with Rusty, who can't seem to keep his eyebrow from arching up.

Captain Lacey gestures to me with his outstretched chin. "Rusty, be sure to get *her* address and phone number." He looks to the CSI team. "What's it look like?"

The guy answers mechanically. "It looks like a blow to the head and petechial hemorrhage indicating possible suffocation."

"That's just what my daughter said," Mr. Aggarwal says. "She's a nephrologist."

Captain Lacey yells for someone to send the doctor/daughter over. Soon, the entire Aggarwal family comes over in a traveling clump. Mr. Aggarwal, who clearly wants to get out of here, exclaims in a singsong Hindi accent, "We just came here to see the house. We didn't do it."

"We think she did it," his wife chimes in, indicating me.

Suddenly the mute Grandmother adds her two heavily-accented cents. "She was wearing rubber gloves and cleaning up blood when we arrived." She doesn't miss a second in pointing to the bloodstain on my dress and says something in her native language.

I'm starting to think this looks bad, and wonder what Marlene Dietrich would do in this situation.

36

Captain Lacey confirms that Luther has the Aggarwals' contact information and says, "You can leave now."

I breathe a sigh of relief. "Oh good, I really can't wait to get out of this dress and take a shower." I start to grab my purse and Captain Lacey, who doesn't look up from his clipboard, says, "Not you."

Moi? Now I'm ruing my keen curiosity and the resulting blood residue. The Captain points to a chair and tells me to sit tight until the detective arrives. The elevator door keeps closing on Bunny's long foot, but the Captain directs the CSI people to leave the body in the elevator. Apparently the body stays put until the medical examiner arrives.

"Based on preliminary visuals of rigor, liver and algor mortis," the CSI woman tells the captain, "we estimate the victim died 14 - 18 hours ago. It's difficult to determine, as we believe the temperature in the elevator may have fluctuated, and we do not believe the body was moved."

"That's weird," I say. "Kevin said he heard her playing the piano last night when he returned from the ball."

"Did he say if he actually saw her play the piano?" Captain Lacey asks.

"Well, no. He assumed it was her, because no one else was home."

"14-18 hours? Can't you narrow it down?" Captain Lacey asks the CSI couple.

"The Medical Examiner may be able to provide a more accurate range, but you may have to rely on indicative acts."

"What's that?" I ask.

"Let's say she had come down to the party, or ordered a pizza at 9:00, we'd know she died after that." the Captain explains.

Luther comes in. "Captain, the dog is licking up the blood on the wall."

We all go into the kitchen, and see dirty dishes and spoiling food all over. The captain falls back. "Oh my god! Luther, cordon off this area and don't let anyone in. And get that dog out of here!" the Captain says, shaking his head.

Luther gets really wide eyed. "I'm not going near that dog. I think she's some kinda rabid pig."

"Is that your dog?" the captain asks.

I say, "Yes, but I got her used from the dog pound, so she was already bad when I got her."

"Do you always bring your dog when you show a house?"

In a tone that suggests it's obvious, I explain, "I was going to take her home this morning but had no ride, and they don't usually let dogs in taxis; not that a taxi would pick up from this address."

Captain Lacey is scratching his head. "You lost me. You started to say you were going to take her home this morning and — Rusty, are you listening?"

Rusty looks up from playing fetch with Ursula and the vibrator. "What?"

"Rusty, you take over," Captain Lacey says.

"You got her at the dog pound? My aunt Ruby had a pug and the dog only had one eye. She used to always say, 'Nothing sadder than a one-eyed pug.'"

Captain Lacey stomps his foot. "Pay attention, Rusty! She said she was going to take the dog home this morning."

Rusty doesn't follow where the Captain is leading, so the Lacey takes back over. "Miss...Buttinski, is it?"

Used to the mistake, I simply say, "We pronounce it, Budnjk."

"So, Miss Budnjk, where were you this morning?"

I look around. "I was here," I say in a naïve voice.

"Rusty, start writing this down." Captain Lacey looks at my dress. "Did you sleep here?"

Right then the door opens, and in comes a familiar face. It's George, the Latin looking guy from on my blind date with Graham.

"Hey, George! How have you been?" Captain Lacey says. "This is Detective Perez," he introduces George to the team.

"Were you with Ft. Lauderdale Vice?" Luther asks.

"Yes, he was a star," Captain Lacey says, "then he went with the Coast Guard."

"Thanks," George says. "They just called in from West Palm. I guess you guys don't have too many homicides on the island."

"Last one was 1995."

George turns and recognizes me, judging by his, "Hello, Emma."

Captain Lacey looks very surprised. "You two have met before?"

George Perez winks. "Yes, it was a blind date."

Captain Lacey gets a look, like he thinks the detective and I have had sex. Now I can see that George is playing with me.

"It was my blind date with someone else," I feel the need to add.

"As I recall," Perez says, "it was with a British yacht captain, so you would get over his boss, Dr. Weinstein."

Whoa. Mustn't blab so much to complete strangers in bars.

"Wait," Captain Lacey interrupts. "This Dr. Weinstein?"

Detective Perez winks at me, again, which I feel is inappropriate for official police business. "Bingo."

I can tell Captain Lacey doesn't know what to make of all this. Finally, he clears his throat and gets down to business. "The victim is believed to be Bunny Weinstein; CSI is estimating time of death as 14-18 hours ago. They are recommending a serum tryptase blood test by the Medical Examiner."

"Well, it couldn't have been too late last night, because I was here the whole time, except for when I was at the dog ball."

Whoa. I am a blabber-er. Must find some police tape for my mouth.

Detective Perez steps away. "I'll come back for the abridged version. I want to look at the victim."

He walks back to the elevator. He has such a strong presence we all feel the need to follow him. The CSI pair have put a sheet over Bunny and all you can see are her twin peaks. When the detective pulls back the sheet, he recoils. "Ay yai yai! That should be a crime."

We all look at him. Finally, Rusty says, "In the state of Florida, murder is a crime. Maybe not in Cuba."

"No, I'm talking about the facelift. Look at her earlobes— they're sewed into the seam."

I wonder who did the facelift, just so I'll know not to go.

Detective Perez, who is wearing a sexy Euro-looking suit with an open shirt collar, opens the port-holed kitchen door. "Ay yai yai!"

I follow him in, nervously spraying Fantastic on the fridge. "I tried to clean up a little."

Detective Perez takes both my hands in his big dark hands, which is sexy until he yells at me. "Don't touch anything!"

"I don't know what came over me. I usually never clean."

"When did you clean up? Hopefully not after you found her."

I feel this is a good time to stop talking.

"Please tell me the CSI guys already handled the kitchen."

"Yes," Captain Lacey says, "I had them do it before she and Rusty could contaminate it anymore."

"I've got an idea," Perez says, and proceeds to stretch surgical rubber gloves on my hands and secure them with police tape.

As Rusty tries to hold off the determined Ursula, who found more blood spewed on the wine cooler, Lacey calls the CSI people back in to take a sample.

"Don't worry, it's Ernesto's blood," I say.

Detective Perez looks down at my dirty white evening gown. "Did you sleep in that dress?"

These men are so nosy. "Are you kidding? Have you ever slept in a strapless dress?"

The guys all start laughing, and Detective Perez smiles and says, "No, I can't say I have."

"She slept here last night with Dr. Weinstein," Rusty says in a gossipy tone.

Detective Perez's mouth opens wide. "Hey, didn't I see you in the paper with him this morning?"

Yay, I finally made the shiny sheet!

Then I remember to be indignant. "I slept in the green room and he slept in his room next door. Nothing happened."

"You slept with Dr. Weinstein, while the wife was home, and somehow woke up with a bloody dress?" Detective Perez theorizes.

Rusty, not realizing this is Perez's way of charming interrogation, points out, "No, remember she took the dress off?" Trying to imitate me, in a high voice he adds, "Have you ever slept in a strapless dress?"

"Rusty," Captain Lacey says, "let her answer the questions."

I point to my dress. "I know, isn't it terrible? I tried to get the stain out with Spray 'n Wash, but I'll have to take it to the cleaners tomorrow."

"Would it be too forward to ask how the blood got on your dress?" Detective Perez asks.

"Oh, I'll bet you're thinking this looks bad. No, this isn't Bunny's blood; I never even met her until this morning—if you can call that meeting. This is Ernesto, the dog walker's, blood."

I can tell the ageing Captain Lacey is trying to compete with the sexy young Detective, when he exclaims, "Are you saying you killed Ernesto the dog walker too?"

I laugh. "No. No. Lisa Weinstein hit him on the nose with gigantic leg of lamb."

Detective Perez takes the power back as he runs his fingers on the bloodstain, which, due to its location on my lap, is a bit flirty. "How did it get here?"

"You shoulda been here—the blood was flying."

Detective Perez swaggers out of the kitchen and asks the crew, "And just where is the husband?"

Captain Lacey cringes a bit. "We haven't seen him. But we haven't had time to properly search the premises."

"He, Trevor and Ping went out on the boat early this morning," I say, trying to be helpful.

"What time was that?" asks Detective Perez.

"I have no idea; I'm not a morning person. I got up around 9:00, but actually it was more like 10:30 because the power went off last night."

Detective Perez's eyes open wide. "Really? What time did the power go off?"

"I don't know. All I know is it went off during the party, and it was off when Richard and I came back to the house."

"What time was that?" Captain Lacey inquires.

"Around midnight."

"Who was here when you two came to the house?" Detective Perez probes.

"Kevin was here drinking Bunny's cognac with Hudson."

"The same Kevin who wears ladies dresses and tablecloths?" Detective Perez asks patiently.

"Yes, the very one. Kevin was the caterer last night. They had fifty people."

Captain Lacey whistles. "Woo hoo, fifty people. Oh boy. Do you have the names?"

"Let's see: our gang, plus Cricket, Pudge, the homely twins, Big Red..."

Detective Perez starts laughing. "Are you kidding me? Someone names a baby Cricket?"

"You don't happen to know their legal names do you?" Lacey asks.

"No, and I'm sure Kevin doesn't, but Bunny does." Then, remembering she's dead, add, "Well, she did."

"Does anyone actually know Bunny Weinstein's legal first name?" Detective Perez asks.

Full of info, I say, "Yes. It was in the listing agreement. It's Felicia and her maiden name is Lake."

I reel off more names. "Don't forget Hudson, Pudge and Natasha."

"I'm writing this down," Rusty says, "but who is Hudson?"

"That's Kevin's new trust-funder boyfriend."

"Wait a minute." Captain Lacey says. "Does that guy drive a blue Bentley? I remember he was cagy in a bike versus car incident."

"Yes, he stays at The Breakers in the HMF suite."

"Yeah, well I've seen him around and I think he's full of shit."

I nod my head. "That's what Graham says, although he didn't use that word. He's English you know."

"So, Kevin was here throughout the party until midnight, when you saw him leave with the Dupont guy?" Perez asks.

"No, they both went to the ball for a while, then they came back to clean."

Rusty shakes his head. "He didn't do a very good job."

I try to defend Kevin. "Well he didn't have any staff."

Detective Perez exhales. "They had a big party with fifty people and then everyone left and went to the ball, and some of you came back. Is that correct?"

"Well, everyone except Bunny Weinstein."

"She stayed here at the house?"

"Graham went to get her for their duet, but she never made it. Hudson said she'd gone to bed early."

"Who's Graham?" Captain Lacey interrupts. "I'm getting very confused."

"He's the British Yacht Captain," Perez says.

Remembering the text, I run over to Bunny's hall table and grab the cell phone. "I don't have my glasses. Look on this phone to see if it's Bunny's."

Rusty grabs it from me.

"Rusty, did you just get your fingerprints on that?" Captain Lacey yells.

"I hate to eat cookies with rubber gloves on. She has Stella D'oro biscuits."

Captain Lacey is so mad he grabs the phone, before realizing he's now contaminated it too. "Now see what you made me do."

Detective Perez throws his hands up. "Go ahead and look for a text."

"Here it is. 10:14. *Come back and get me.*"

"So that is her phone," I confirm.

"She must have died after 10:14," Captain Lacey says.

Detective Perez leans over the body. "She looks deader than that. Maybe the killer just wanted us to think she was still alive at 10:14."

"Wow! You're good," I say.

Captain Lacey tries to recover. "Why was her phone in the hallway? Not in her pocket or purse?"

"Ladies do not have pockets," I say. "Besides, she could have been having drinks over there. There were two dirty glasses on the side table. I could barely get—"

"Hey, we need some help over here!" Detective Perez yells to the CSI people.

I must get a funny look on my face.

"Don't tell me," Captain Lacey says, "you put them in the dishwasher."

I think the detective is going to have me ejected out to the car park; instead he appears to be controlling a dimple-inducing smirk.

Regaining his composure, Perez looks around and points to me. "Is she the only one here who ID'd the victim?"

"Yes," Captain Lacey says.

Perez shakes his head. "But she's never seen her before."

"I just assumed it was her because of the, you know, enhanced breasts and facelift—and by the fact she was in the house."

Perez gets excited, like Ricky Ricardo. "Facelift and fake tits! That's half the town."

Lacey shakes his head. "We've got to get someone to ID her; and let's get the husband and the captain and the damn cook in for questioning."

Rusty looks over at the body and winces. "Are we done now? The Elite Removal van is here."

"Oh, good. Do you think they can get this blood stain out of my dress?" I ask.

The detective and the captain start laughing. "No, Emma. They only remove bodies."

"Where is the damned medical examiner?" Detective Perez demands.

"He's on his way," Rusty says. "He said he's always curious about new ways to kill people."

"Thank you, Rusty, for the update," Perez says.

"Do you have a way to reach the husband on the boat?" Captain Lacey says to me.

"I have his number in my phone."

Detective Perez looks at Captain Lacey.

I exhale. "Do I have to be the one to tell Richard? Shouldn't that be someone else's job?"

"Where are they going on the boat?" Detective Perez asks.

"I think they are going to the Bahamas for the day. The mother likes to bring back rum."

Detective Perez looks at Captain Lacey. "Let's alert the Coast Guard."

"Anyone know the name of the boat?" Captain Lacey asks.

Detective Perez stifles a smile. *"No Woman No Cry."*

37

I'm sure they're thinking they are damned lucky I was here to give out all this useful info. When they grill me, I tell them that Lisa, Ernesto, Trevor, Mrs. Weinstein, and Hudson were in the house after the ball. They remind me that I've left out Richard and Kevin.

"Don't leave," Detective Perez says to me. "I want to look upstairs."

Feeling like the little hostess, I ask Rusty and Captain Lacey if they'd like coffee. They say they'd love some. Detective Perez hears them and yells down the stairs. "No. Don't let her make coffee. She'll contaminate the scene."

"But we really want some," Rusty whines.

Detective Perez comes back down the stairs. "Then you make it, Rusty, and put the gloves back on in case CSI missed anything." Detective Perez looks me up and down and finally says in a non-official, sexy sounding voice, "You know we're going to need that dress."

"But if it doesn't get to the cleaners right away the blood stain will be permanent. Can you have someone drop it off when they're done? I like the Tropical cleaner on County Road because they put things in nice little boxes."

Detective Perez laughs out loud. "You're joking, aren't you?"

I look at him in shock. "No, it's a $9500 dress."

Luther whistles. "Holy mackerel! You coulda bought a car for that."

Trying to trip me up, Detective Perez asks, "Dr. Weinstein bought you that dress, right?"

I correct him. "No, Mrs. Weinstein did."

"You're doing her husband and she buys you a dress? You got balls, girl."

"I'm *not* doing the husband, and it was his mother who bought the dress."

"I hope someone is keeping all this straight."

"Do you think someone broke in and killed her?" Rusty says to Detective Perez.

"Did you see any signs of forced entry?" Detective Perez asks Captain Lacey.

"No. Who would need to? All the terrace doors were wide open."

"And the front door might have been left unlocked. I'll bet Kevin left them open; he does that at my place all the time," I say.

"We still don't have positive ID." Detective Perez says. "She could be someone else for all we know."

"I think I recognize her from the paper," Captain Lacey says, "but then I think all those ladies with blonde hair and huge lips look exactly alike."

"Me too!" all the men chime in.

"Emma, who else could positively ID her?" Perez asks. "Hopefully someone who's not on his way to the Bahamas."

I scan the party list in my head. "Let's see, Kevin has met her."

Perez asks for the number, so I press Kevin's number and hand him my cell phone. He stares at me as the phone keeps ringing and I get nervous. "I'll bet he's still sleeping."

Then I hear Kevin pick up. He sounds out a groggy, "Hello."

"Hi, this is Detective Perez," he says in a deep, official voice. "I'm here with Emma Buddinski."

We all listen in as Detective Perez presses speaker. Kevin says, "Emma, are you getting a DUI?"

"No," I sheepishly say.

Detective Perez continues. "Kevin, we've found who we think is Bunny Weinstein dead this morning."

Kevin lets out a loud, high-pitched girl gasp, which prompts Detective Perez and Captain Lacey to give each other communicative looks. I'll bet there's a police training class called, 'Are you thinking what I'm thinking?'

"Kevin, we are going to need you to identify the body."

"Why do I have to do it?" Kevin whines. "Can't Ping or someone else do it?"

"Kevin," Detective Perez says, "can we send a squad car to pick you up?"

"Um...I'm in Ft Lauderdale. Isn't this something that can wait a few days? I mean she's not going to run off."

"Kevin, we'll need to talk to you when you get back to town."

"Emma," Captain Lacey says, "we can't wait that long. Who else knows her? A friend?"

"Friends? She wasn't exactly friendly."

"Do you know anyone who'd want her dead?" Captain Lacey asks.

"Um—let's see—how about the entire town."

"I've heard she wasn't very well liked," Rusty says in a mock society voice.

"This will be fun," Detective Perez says. "Fifty sets of fingerprints, all with motives."

"Well let's get her ID'd first," Captain Lacey says. "Who else should we call? "

"My friend, Irene, knows her."

"Is that the lady who makes dog outfits?" Rusty says.

I'm glad Irene is becoming well-known on the island. "Used to, but now she just makes dog hats and wigs. She's coming out with a line of pug wigs. Want to see Ursula's?"

"Enough you two." Detective Perez is getting antsy. "Was she at the party?"

"Yes, she was here, but didn't go to the ball."

"Irene—what's her last name?

"Ahr."

He has his pen ready, waiting for the next letters. "R…what's the rest?"

"A-H-R."

"What kind of name is that?"

"Do you want her to come or not?"

He nods his head, so I press Irene's contact number and she answers right away. He introduces himself and delivers the news on the speaker phone to get her reaction.

Instead of gasping at the news, Irene says, "Huh? I guess it's not a huge surprise."

"Why do you say that?" Detective Perez asks.

"All that silicone probably got to her."

"If it's alright, we'll send officer Cain to come and get you."

"Okie Dokie, but I'm in my housecoat and a little nauseous already; I can't imagine what will happen if I look at a dead lady."

38

Detective Perez and Captain Lacey walk the entire house, with Ursula following as deputy dog. As they descend the dramatic staircase, they repeatedly concur that something happened in the kitchen; it has crime scene written all over it.

By now, I'm officially dying in this dress. Detective Perez sees me squirming. "Why don't you change and bring the dress down?"

Wanting to be compliant, I run up the stairs, but then realize I have the same problem I had this morning—and all my life—of nothing to wear. Releasing myself from the torturous confinement of the zipper, I slither into a large, forgiving towel. I wonder if I might borrow something from Bunny. Knowing she's not in her room now, but not fully processing that she's never coming back, I wander over to Bunny's side and look in her closet. Creepy would be the word to describe the atmosphere in her closet. Maybe I should just wear the towel.

Boy she has a lot of clothes. I pull out a light blue Chanel dress that would look lovely for day. Right then a man's voice sounds behind me, and I'm so shocked I nearly drop the towel. "Did you get that from Bunny Weinstein's closet?" Detective Perez is standing behind me.

I grab the towel up around myself. "I'm sorry, but I don't have any other clothes. Lisa's are too small, but I suppose I could wear something of Ping's."

"Who's Lisa? Her daughter?"

"No, she's Richard's daughter from his first marriage."

"So she was here at the house before the ball?"

"Yes, she was here before and after the ball. Then she left with Ernesto the dog walker. Hey, that's who you should talk to. Kevin thinks Ernesto and Bunny were having an affair."

The detective's cool façade is finally broken. "Bunny Weinstein was having an affair with a dog walker?"

"Well, I've never seen them together, but I did hear this woman who makes kind of a—we call it a Howler Monkey sound. We heard that at Ernesto's—he lives next to me, in Moe."

"What kind of sound are you talking about?"

I look at my feet and modestly say, "You know."

Detective Perez looks at me seriously. "No, I don't know."

Red-faced, I try to demonstrate. "Aahhh. Oww."

Now Detective Perez gets what I'm talking about and is embarrassed. He grabs my gown, which is wadded up on the floor, and says, "Do you really think you're ever gonna wear this dress again?"

"You're right. I'll probably never even fit in it again."

Not wanting to wear anything of Bunny's, I'm forced to put on the Snoopy tee shirt; I've never been so grateful for underpants in my life.

Detective Perez proudly carries the gown down the stairs and Ursula and I follow.

I see Irene standing over the body. She's wearing her Sunday housecoat and carrying an empty milk carton. Without looking up, she says, "Like I wasn't vomity enough."

She and Rusty are trying to keep Bunny's low-cut gown from revealing her severe cleavage in an unladylike manner. Handing Rusty a donut-shaped piece of duct tape, Irene says, "Stick this under the décolletage."

"Gee. Thanks Mrs. Ahr."

"No prob. Keep the roll. You can use it to pick up evidence."

"I just heard back from the Coast Guard," Captain Lacey says. "They've located the yacht and are headed back."

I ask how Richard took the news.

"He broke down and sobbed."

My poor baby.

We hear a scream and look up to see Luther running up the stairs, with Ursula chasing him. "Luther get down here; she won't bite you." Captain Lacey says.

"She keeps licking my ankles."

"Let's get her and that dog out of here, so we can focus on the murderer."

Detective Perez offers to give me and Irene a ride home. I guess it's all right to leave the CSI people there. I ask them to be sure to lock up. Rusty follows me out to the car and discretely asks how to flush the toilet.

With Irene getting ill in the back seat, I elect to sit in the front with the handsome detective and my pug. Irene thought it necessary to tape the wig back on, as Ursula always sits on the driver's lap, sticking her head out the window. Everyone votes to drop Irene off first, then the detective drives right to the Three Stooges, without asking for directions or landing in the ocean. He sees Kevin's mangled bike. "If you ever want to cover up your affair with Weinstein, I'd go with the lesbian angle."

"I'm not a lesbian, why would you think that?"

He points. "Your bike has hot pink triangles all over it. That's code for lesbian."

My mind retraces all of the places I've taken the bike. "That's Kevin's. It's all mangled because it was hit by a car. Well, more like, a car got hit by it."

"The Bentley? Oh, that's the Kevin we're talking about? Can you imagine getting a RWI citation for riding a bike hungover?"

Boy, there are no secrets in this town. Changing the subject, I point to Moe. "That's where Ernesto, the dog walker, lives."

"He's on my list, but I'll get to him later."

When I finally walk into my door, I realize what a long night it's been. It seems like a month ago that I walked out the door feeling like Cinderella.

It was yesterday.

Overnight, I have fallen from my perch as glamorous Cinderella— to lover in a triangle with a wealthy doctor and his young laborer. I have somehow fallen from potential thriving real estate agent to penniless murder suspect.

39

I'm so tired I can barely make it upstairs to my bed. Ursula keeps growling at my Snoopy tee shirt, so I change into a ribbed tank top and hope she doesn't have a problem with the ribs. I collapse on the bed to contemplate the last twenty-four hours. Ursula joins me, no doubt thinking she has a fascinating life compared to most pets. I wonder if she suffers from nagging self-doubt like the rest of us: why hadn't she been the one to discover the dead body? Why hadn't she been able to close the Aggarwals on the house? My dog must be skilled at compartmentalizing, for she is now soundly asleep. Probably concluded that compared to a cat, she did her best.

After several hours, Ursula decides it's high time for me to get out of bed. I hear her drinking out of the toilet with a loud slurping sound; this is her way of letting me know her water bowl is empty and I'm a negligent mother. I stumble around bleary eyed, thinking she has a lot of attitude ever since she got the Tina Turner wig.

It's only 9:00 p.m. Like a mother hen, I wonder where Kevin is, and look back to Curly, but don't see any lights on. Surely, if he were around he'd be over here pestering me. Did Bunny Weinstein really die? Or was it just a bad dream? Or maybe good dream. It's bizarre that I never met her all this time. Maybe that's why I'm not too sad. I do feel sorry for Richard. What if he loved her?

What if he killed her?

Despite the new circumstances of having my previously married soul mate suddenly freed up, I waver for a moment on the ramifications of loving a murderer.

I am abruptly jarred from my deliberation by a forceful knock on the door. Ursula lets out an absurdly fierce bark, no doubt praying the intruder will never see her actual size.

When I look down through the windows behind my headboard to the front door, I can see the top of a man's head. It's hard to tell who it is because he's pacing. Then he stops: it's Graham.

Every girl's dilemma is what to prioritize in the fleeting seconds before opening a door. I run down the stairs and opt to brush my teeth in lieu of putting on pants.

"Emma, I tried to call, but your mobile went straight to voice mail."

Standing in the doorway still half asleep, I say, "Somebody changed my ringtone to 'Get Down on It,' so I shut it off."

Graham looks serious as he passes through my tiny door and sits at my scaled-down rattan table. As a habit from my waitress days I inquire, "How about a drink?" Graham looks very tired and has more creases around his eyes than normal. When I open the fridge I notice all of the wine is gone, leaving one lonely Corona. Ursula, the usual suspect, is off the list, so that leaves Kevin. The only other libation left is my emergency bottle of Veuve Clicquot. No woman's fridge should ever be without a bottle, for when handsome British men drop by—in sexy khaki pants. Having been lax in the housekeeping, I manage to find only a clean red wine goblet and my pug mug and carry out the champagne. Handing him the icy bottle, I say, "Let's have this. Will you open it?" When he looks at me with that "what a princess" look, I tell him champagne corks are a known safety hazard. To appear busy, I press my iPod of random, haunting songs. I turn the dial to Lisa Hannigan singing "Needles." Graham pops the cork and pours. He bites his lip and says, "I hope the neighbors don't think we're celebrating anything."

I love the way he pronounces it: en-a-thing. I love English accents. Maybe I should have moved to London. It's not too late. I could take a boat tonight, like they do in the movies. Now I wish I had a fur cape—it's what one wears when running off in the night with a handsome British yacht captain.

Graham waves his hand across my distracted face. We look at each other; neither one of us dares make a toast. This is the first time

I've had champagne and not toasted, but then again, this is the first time I've had champagne after finding a dead body. Graham takes a swig.

"I heard the waiters in town are celebrating the demise of Bunny by giving complementary champagne."

Hoping Richard doesn't hear this news, I ask how he is.

Graham exhales. "I think he's in shock."

My mind veers from sexy Brit to poor, shocked Richard. He's probably in some sort of languid stupor, with Trevor having to spoon cognac into his mouth, just to keep his color.

After another swig, Graham says, "Life is strange. One minute Esther was doing a charade for some movie with Audrey Hepburn and Albert Finney—"

"I know that one! *Two for the Road.*"

"Very good. Trevor was getting close; you know he can practically read Esther's mind?"

"I think they secretly do it."

Graham gets an impish look. "Trevor and Esther Weinstein?"

"Well, can't you just see her with her big glasses getting all foggy, and he would have a feather duster and tickle her."

Graham pauses. "Is that your fantasy? A feather duster?"

I blush as I sit on the sofa, and fold my knees. "Where was Richard?"

"He was at the helm. I let him take the helm sometimes. He's especially keen on manning the wheelhouse when Natash...."

"What?" I blurt out. "Natasha was on the boat?"

Judging by his face, he must be sorry he opened his mouth. "Well, er—yes. She was there by the dock in the morning. We didn't really need her."

"Did she go with you to the house to get Bunny?"

"No, I dropped her off at her car by Cucina."

Graham tries to change the subject. "Where was I? Oh, I turned and noticed the Coast Guard was trailing us." He pours more champagne—perhaps to get me off his trail—and goes on. "My first thought was that the registration on the tender boat had expired. Then I remembered a few of us are a little behind on our INS forms and I've got that vexing passport problem."

"Yes, let's see: Ping, Trevor, Natasha and you."

"It would have been the climax of an INS officer's career."

I love it when British men say climax. Makes the mind wander.

Graham is oddly chatty tonight and continues. "So, I thought I'd better take over. When I went to the wheelhouse, I noticed Richard looking so happy and content."

"Did Natasha have her top off?"

"Well—maybe just for a wee bit, but she put it back on when the Coast Guard pulled us over. They asked for Richard Weinstein. For a moment, I thought he was about to be arrested, although I can't imagine him committing anything more serious than smoking in an elevator."

"Speaking of crimes in elevators, you don't think he killed her?"

Graham takes a huge inhale, a huge exhale and a lengthy pause before responding. *If only I used that breathing technique prior to babbling.* Finally, he says, "I don't think he's capable, although I'm sure the thought crossed his mind."

"I hope you didn't tell the police that."

"Of course not," Graham quickly says. "I'm indebted to Richard."

"What did the Coast Guard say?"

"They called Richard to the back deck and said his wife had been found dead in their home."

I'm so curious. "Did he scream?"

"No, he didn't scream. We're not talking about Kevin or Ping; but his whole face dropped and suddenly he looked about eighty."

"I'm sure the police noticed that he was shocked. Was his mother right there?"

"Yes, Esther was standing next to him and didn't muster a flinch."

"I imagine when you're that old, a flinch is hard to muster."

Graham has a lose tassel from a pillow in his fingers. "What does it take for you to muster a flinch?" He runs the tassel over my bare shoulder.

Ursula, who seems to be listening with rapt attention and now wearing her wig again thanks to Graham, turns her head to me when I say, "Then what happened?"

"The Coast Guard relayed that the Palm Beach Police requested the presence of our company and gave us an escort up the Intracoastal, with bridges raised."

Ursula seems to nod her head, as if to say, "That was nice of them."

"They probably did it so we wouldn't flee to the Bahamas. Even Ping came out from the galley when he heard the news."

"Was he crying?"

"No, he didn't look particularly distraught. Ever since the Robert Palmer dog incident, he was no fan of Bunny."

He takes the tassel and runs it over my bare thighs. "Sorry, I don't have a feather duster."

I have a feeling that things could get a little friendly, so I run up to put on better panties. As I'm routing through my dresser, I hear Graham coming up the stairs. In the nick of time, I change from the white cottons to the purple lacey ones. He sits on my bed and sets our drinks on the dresser. Then he sees the picture of Richard. "Why wasn't that painting auctioned at the charity ball?" he asks in an irritated tone.

They'd have to pry the painting from my hands, is what's running through my head. I try to come up with something fast. "I told you, Esther said only the nudes brought in any money. Did you know your little fanny brought in $14,000?"

He laughs. "My fanny? Do you know what that term means for Brits?"

"I am afraid to ask. Anyway, between the two of us, we could make a fortune."

He shakes his head. "Now what were we talking about?

"The police station."

"Right. When we reached the boat slip, the Coast Guard waited for us to dock, then the police met us in the marina parking lot."

"Really?"

"Yes. Then a chap named Lacey suggested we follow them back to the house for questioning. There was an odd web of police tape about the place."

I laugh at the thought of Rusty taping the police chief into a corner.

Graham throws down a pillow. "Bloody Hell! I can't believe she's dead."

He leans against the headboard, and I prop myself up on pillows facing him at the foot of the bed. I think of the time he was here with his shadow. Studying his full lips, I ask if he has any Italian in him. He says a little and asks if I have any Italian in me.

"No, but I'd like to." I realize too late it sounds naughty, especially when he gets a sudden smirk on his face.

Graham takes another long, slow taste of his drink, which means he's thinking. Then he gives me a little kiss. I give him a look like I want another kiss. So he does, and this time it's very slow and gentle.

After the kiss, my curiosity prevails. "Why didn't you bring Bunny back to the ball?"

There's another, longer pause. So long, I try to seductively sip champagne like in the movies, but instead spill it down half my shirt.

Graham laughs. "Did you do that on purpose, so this would get cold?" He runs his fingers over my now chilled, wet nipple.

"No, but I'll remember that."

He winks at me. "Yes, excellent technique."

"No, I'll remember not to drink champagne lying down."

Without a word, he takes his glass and artfully drips champagne on my other nipple.

"Whoa, that's tingly."

He laughs that deep laugh of his, and this time there's no trailing whimper.

I want his baby. Are we going to finally do it? Am I ovulating? Am I out of dog food?

Wait a minute; he never answered my question. Can't carry child of murderer.

Pretending I'm a police interrogator, I ask, "So, Mr. Peel, why didn't you bring Bunny Weinstein back to the Breakers?"

Graham smiles. "Yes, Detective Budnjk. After I'd driven back to the house, I'd noticed a text from Bunny saying she'd gone to bed. Ping was there, so we loaded up the car and I went to the boat."

Good alibi, I think. "Do you think she could have had a guest in her library?"

"I have no idea. Why?"

"There were dirty cognac glasses in her library. Kevin and I think she's having a fling with Ernesto," I blurt out.

Graham practically chokes on his champagne. "The dog walker?"

"Yes, he lives right there," I say, pointing to Moe. "We've been hearing this high pitched Howler monkey sound."

Graham's eyebrows form a question mark. "What do you mean?"

"You know—when she's finished."

"Are you referring to after she's finished having a sexual orgasm?"

I hide my head under my pillow. "Yes. That's what I mean."

Graham reaches his fingers into my panties, whispering, "I've forgotten what sound you make."

I return him to the conversation at hand. "Ahem. When Kevin was over at the Weinsteins to show the property, he says he heard the same sound. Then he found Ernesto in Bunny's closet."

He waves a dismissive hand. "He was the dog walker, then became part-time security."

Graham takes my face with both hands and goes right for my mouth with his. There is ardor in this kiss, like I'm a fountain and he's been in the desert his whole life. I hear the haunting Neil Hannon song, "If..." playing downstairs. The melody makes me want to roll around on the sheets with a handsome man.

The mind reader takes my wet tank top and pulls it up, revealing my chilled breasts.

Then his tongue is on my nipple, tickling it. He kisses the other one, saying we don't want to leave her out. God, he's sexy! He pulls my top off.

Then I spot the 'shadow maker' in his pants. Whoa! It practically reaches diagonally to his left hip. Ursula is probably going to start barking at it.

He takes his shirt off and throws it on the desk; there's that smooth chest and great abs. Then he's back to kissing me passionately again. I'm so glad I brushed my teeth instead of putting clothes on. He's making little circles with his finger, then rolls my panties off and kneels over me. It's amazing that all guys know exactly what to do—and a few can actually do it well. He tosses them on the floor and Ursula runs over and starts sniffing and snorting. We laugh.

He parts my legs and rubs his face on my tummy. I can tell he's about to go in for the feast because he's really quiet. I reach down and find I'm already a little slippery from spilling the champagne on the pink party hats. He parts me with his tongue.   I feel a ticklish jolt. Boy, am I glad I took a shower when I got home and shaved my legs again. These are the thoughts that go through a girl's head during foreplay. It's very quiet. He reaches up to hold my strawberry nipples between his fingers; he's coordinated. I guess you'd have to be to sail a $16 million yacht with all those dials. I look down at the top of his head and it looks so different from the one that was pacing out front.

Reaching down, I undo his belt, thinking he must be really uncomfortable with all the crowding in his pants. He stops, kneels up and takes his pants off. He's wearing short white boxer briefs. He pulls them down and his middle extremity springs back up like a diving board. He tosses his briefs on the chair, safely away from Ursula.

Should we do everything but "it?" Where is this turgid thing going to fit? People should be careful what they wish for; there is such a thing as too big. I'm so into this; I think I must be ovulating. I think men can tell—it's like I'm giving off a "hey sailor" scent. Boy, does he have good timing; the next time I may have my period or something—or he could be deported.

Hmm. He's back at it, and patient. I'm trying to get there, but I can't relax. The normally mellow Nina Simone is singing that fast song from the *Thomas Crown Affair*, "Cinna Man."

The hyper song increases in tempo for over ten minutes and I can't very well stop in mid-lick to go turn down the volume. Graham's working away; you'd think guys would get bored doing this and wish there was a football game—or a cricket match—projected on my stomach. Hey, that's a great invention!

I wonder what he's thinking. I'll bet he's thinking I'd better hurry up or he'll lose altitude. Ok, focus. He reaches up and feels both breasts. They are full and fluffy now. The song finally ends—and I jolt up in release. He wipes his slippery face on my inner thighs. "Did you enjoy that?"

Um. Yes. Are we ready for "it?" I wonder what he calls it? Kevin once called it crepe Suzette. As in, "Well, it's not like I had crepe Suzette and then had to call her the next day."

While I'm pondering away, Graham asks in a reticent voice, "Have you by chance got any protection?"

At first I'm wondering if he means a gun, then I realize he's politely asking if I have any condoms. I start a mental inventory of my medicine cabinet and my secret box. Yes, I do have some left over from before the Larry days, but wonder about the expiration date. Graham must sense my hesitancy, as evidenced by my non-response. Before he derails the train, I quickly say I have some, leaving out the expired part. I stand up fast, but fall to the carpeting.

"Are you all right?"

"My knees are weak."

"Tell me where they are and I'll go."

With careful instruction, I direct him downstairs to the bathroom, to a pink box under the sink. He gets up and runs down the stairs. Ursula must think he's going to the fridge, so she follows him. Ah, a moment to think. Am I really ready for this?

I hear footsteps out front; suddenly the front door opens and slams shut. I look down from my window and see a receding red hairline. What unfortunate timing. Why doesn't Kevin go to his house?

I hear the refrigerator open and a noisy shuffle of pans and bottles. In a moment, I note the unmistakable cracking open of the lone Corona. Then I hear an "Ah" with a distinct English accent. This is followed by a high-pitched "Ahh!" There are quick footsteps and lots of door slamming.

Figuring out what just happened, I wonder if blind people go their whole days connecting the sound dots. I'm just glad Kevin didn't think this was a good time to regale me with the ingredients of his latest meal. Graham slinks up the stairs and fills me in.

"It seems I have just run into Kevin. I'm sure he did not appreciate me running about completely starkers."

I laugh. "I wouldn't be so sure of that." I'm sure Kevin has a permanent image of Graham's gifts etched in his mind. I know I do.

Graham takes a huge sip of his champagne and sets three condoms on the nightstand. Three? He's optimistic. He looks down at himself. "You'll have to get me going again." I reach down and

228

he's soft now. I guess running into a gay guy will do that. I lean over him, and put my tongue in his mouth. I can feel his blood flowing south again.

"Are we ready for that?"

"You tell me," he whispers in my ear.

I don't answer; I have to think, but it's really hard to concentrate now. Should I or shouldn't I?

The light beaming through the blinds reveals his tender eyes. "If you don't care to, I can just lie here in agony." He says in that elegant English accent.

How can I say no to anyone with that accent? I make a mental note not to move to England, unless I want to have sex with every odd chap in the local pub. I can almost taste the pint of ale and smell the wool. Back to the matter at hand. I don't answer, and he takes full advantage of the lull by sliding about my opening. Finally he says, "I wasn't planning on doing ena-thing like this today."

Whoa. We're really going to do it. I had all that extra time to consider the ramifications of this act and squandered it. I can't very well say 'never mind' now.

After a little help from me, he looks down and says, "Back in business."

He doesn't waste a second tearing the condom wrapper open. I love that sound. Uh oh, he chose the green ones. I hope he checked the expiration date. He hands me the condom.

Naturally, I put in on the wrong way. Then I get it right, and roll it halfway with my one hand. Suddenly his uncut skin rides back up and the condom goes flying off; like a helium balloon losing air, it's aloft and then finally lands on the floor. Judging by Ursula's vehement barking, she must suspect a new form of flying invader. After a mutual gale of nervous giggles, Graham releases another flying green condom. I guess being uncircumcised he's used to this happening, so his bringing up three could mean he's more practical than optimistic.

This time he takes over the precautionary measures, then safely pokes about my fountain.

I think this warm-up act is, in fact, underrated. He gently gives a push and I let out a sharp "Oooh," like I've been goosed. He laughs and starts working his way into me. When I look down, I see he's only inserted half of himself, yet I'm all filled up. Once he's in me, he stops for a second, and it's quiet. Then he pushes again and lets out a deep moan. I love to make him happy. He kisses me on the lips again, but his mouth is hard this time. My face is parallel with his neck, where I can smell his sandalwood and musk aftershave; his neck is slick and tastes a bit salty. As he pushes into me, I note his faultless rhythm. I love a rhythmic thruster. Some men do an abrupt "surprise" thrust. It's been my observation men gleefully overvalue the element of surprise, never realizing that women hate all surprises. I wonder who trained him. I'll bet he's just naturally tender.

With each thrust, I let out a gentle, "Oooh." I'm so wet it's a slippery procedure. "That feels so good," I say. He's panting and getting faster and manic, and forgets to kiss me.

"I'm going to come," he announces abruptly.

I like a man who gives notice. Well-trained all around. Then he lets out the biggest breath and a loud, deep "O." Yes, I detect the English accent. My dog makes a yodeling sound to match.

Graham collapses next to me. Then he looks down and says, "Uh oh."

This is not what one expects to hear at a time like this. Does he already regret this? Did he just remember something, like he's married?

"We have a little problem."

"What?" I dare ask.

"Don't move."

"Well, I wasn't planning on going anywhere."

"It seems I'm out, but the condom is still inside you."

His forehead looks even more worried than usual. Gently and carefully he puts his pincher fingers up me; slowly tugging the condom out, he lets out an authentic sigh of relief and flops back down next to me. I look over at his eyes and he smiles at me, but doesn't say anything. When I kiss his ear, he sighs again. We lie side-by-side, reminding me of the time I was lying here next to Richard when I painted his portrait. Why would I think of Richard at a time like this—when I have just been loved by a handsome young Brit.

I pull the sheet up over us to block out the streetlight. From an aerial view we probably look like a dead married couple. We just lie there and watch the ceiling fan circle our heads. Well, now we've done "it." Now, I'll probably fall in love and act all funny around him. It's too bad making love only works on women. My experience is that it just makes men afraid. Women in love, and men afraid—that's what makes the world go round.

What have I done now? Something that can never be undone.

40

My bliss is interrupted by the roar of a deep snore, making me worry this could be a deal killer of any forthcoming marriage. It would be like being married to some fat old man like Ernest Borgnine after a night of heavy drinking—especially if he drank a lot too. Then I look down and identify the ubiquitous Ursula sawing wood at the foot of the bed. Was she there the whole time watching us? I'm glad dogs are known to exercise discretion regarding the bedroom activities of their masters. While they are appalling voyeurs, they are at least discreet. Not that my dog would have that virtue.

Then I detect an alternative snore; it's mercifully softer and emanating from Graham. I wonder how guys manage to fall asleep so fast. My theory is that God makes them fall asleep so they'll stick around for at least fifteen more minutes before they disappear forever. He's so cute when he sleeps. His eyebrows really do turn down like a sad child who dropped his ice cream. And that dimple in his chin! I feel strangely compelled to stick something in there.

He lies on his side to take the role of outer spoon. Implanting myself as inner spoon, I think that I would like to have his baby. Perhaps this thought leaks out of my head, for he suddenly he mumbles, "What? I already have two kids. Don't need anymore."

I don't say a thing, but must give a look of displeasure.

He softens his tone. "Do you want children?"

I think for a while. "I did—until I had Ursula."

He laughs. "Oh, worried you'd be a bad mother again?"

I give him a look that says, *Not having your child.*

At around four in the morning, I hear Ursula miserably trying to jump up on the bed. For some reason, she keeps missing and falling backward.

When she sees I'm awake, she looks up at me from the floor pleadingly with her sad cow eyes. Why can't she make it? She alternates between a pitiful hopping and an even more pathetic full leg collapse.

Graham wakes up with a stir. "What was that?"

I say something's wrong with Ursula.

Graham looks at her. "She looks hammered."

"Ahh." I look down at my now empty champagne mug.

I look under the bed and there's my blotto dog. When I walk down the stairs Ursula tries to follow, but she slips on the wood. It's probably best that she get some fresh air, so I deposit her in the front yard with a huge bowl of water and little regard for what passersby might think. Tomorrow, there will probably be a sign around her neck saying, "# of Days Sober = 0"

41

When I awaken, I find no snoring man or dog—just a cold indentation in the bed. So this is how it goes—from warm intentions to cold indentations. Grabbing a top, I clomp down the stairs following the trail of the man who got away. Hmm. I distinctly smell that glorious of all morning smells: coffee and toast. Wondering if Ursula, after years of careful observation, has mastered the art of making breakfast. Oh, wouldn't that be great? No, it's more likely Kevin has performed the good deed; he's no doubt sprawled out on my sofa pretending to read the Palm Beach Post, while desperately pinning away for the uncut version of Graham. As I peer out back, I spot my baby Ursula sitting upright on a garden chair reading the paper. Wow, she is well trained. Upon closer look, I notice my beloved Graham, who has in fact not fled the country after making love to me, but appears to have brewed coffee, made toast and tended to my pet.

He looks up. "Good morning."

Now there's the kind of intimacy I'm afraid of. He's here at my place in the morning. I hate company in the morning, especially perky English company.

"I can guess what you're like without your coffee, so come out, I've made you some." His hair is messy and his clothes are rumpled. "I think your dog is a bit whacked today."

I look at Ursula; the fur is all messed up on her head, just like a hungover person.

"You left her out front, but somehow she ended up here," Graham says matter-of-factly.

"Must have been Kevin."

Graham takes a sip of his tea and looks up from the paper. "I found her tied to a tree with this note stuck to her head."

I look at the lime green sticky note, which has odd, illiterate handwriting. Graham reads it out loud, exaggerating the bad grammar. "Your dog ate cat food. She look bad. Ernesto."

"I hope she's going to be okay."

Graham pets Ursula's head. "I'd worry more about the champagne than the cat food."

When I laugh, Graham grabs me from behind, putting his arms around me. "I had a nice time."

"What," I joke, "when I was interrogating you?"

He kisses my ear. "No, just after that."

Recapping the evening, I get that lusty pang in my stomach, as I sit on his lap with a thud, making him spill his tea.

He kisses the back of my hair. "My legs are falling asleep."

When I get up, I notice the headline of the paper. In huge print, it says: 'DEAD SOCIALITE — No one liked her anyway.' I gasp and point.

Graham catches my eyes. "I've already read it. You'll be glad they misspelled your name."

I hold the paper out far with my arm, not feeling like running all the way upstairs to get my glasses, which look nerdy.

Graham catches my far-sightedness. "Here, I'll read it to you."

I sit and pet Ursula's sticky head as he reads:

Palm Beach socialite Felicia "Bunny" Weinstein, second wife of renowned cardiologist Richard Weinstein, was found dead in her home yesterday morning by realtor Emma Budinski.

The socialite was last seen in her bedroom, during a party held in her home catered by "All about Kevin" catering. Naturally, the police thought it was another case of food poisoning. Foul play is suspected and an autopsy is underway.

I close my eyes, so I can focus on his elegant voice as he continues.

She was a fierce charity-goer, but was a less than a popular figure in town, with some old-time residents taking to the streets and breaking out in dance upon hearing the news.

Several upscale local restaurants served complimentary champagne to patrons and relieved staffers. Bunny Weinstein was to have attended the "Dogs are People Too!" event.

When Weinstein failed to arrive for the charity auction, the Weinsteins' marine captain, Graham Peel, was dispatched to the residence; it's presumed that he was the last to see her alive."

I look at Graham and realize I may have just made love to a murderer. My face must convey this suspicion, for he lifts his glasses and turns to face me. "What are you looking at? Would I be sitting here reading the Sunday paper to your dog if I killed her? Hell, I'd be drinking a Dark and Stormy in Barbados by now."

Abandoning any doubts, I murmur, "Sorry, go on."

He winks at me. "Now, where was I?"

"It's presumed that he was the last to see her alive."

With a little smirk, Graham continues.

According to the realtor, who gave the lead detectives volumes of information, the home was revisited by several of the partygoers on the evening in question: the elder Mrs. Weinstein; Trevor Heath; Ernesto, the dog walker; Kevin, of All About Kevin Catering; Hudson DuPont III; and Ping Wu, the cook and reluctant first mate. Dr. Weinstein and the realtor were the last to return to the residence, and both stayed the night. The next morning, the realtor

236

discovered the younger Mrs. Weinstein dead in the elevator, dashing all hopes of a romantic breakfast in bed with Dr. Weinstein.

I grab the paper. "It doesn't say that."

"No, but the police might think it."

I cover my mouth. "How could they think that? Okay, go on."

Captain Lacey, of the Palm Beach police, states this is the first murder they have had in Palm Beach since 1995. He says there was no sign of forced entry as the caterer apparently left all of the doors completely open. Detective Perez is questioning several suspects, many with motives, but no alibis.

"I was probably taking my life in my hands sleeping next to you last night," Graham says with a serious tone. I realize he's joking when he kisses me. "I know you didn't do it."

I kiss him back, wondering what to name our future baby.

"The police seem a bit suspicious. You might want to watch what you say to them in the future. Or get a lawyer."

"A lawyer? I don't have any money."

"If the police start to read you your Miranda rights, then you'd better shut your yapper."

I put my hand over my mouth. "I'll try."

Graham pats his chest. "They told me not to leave the island."

"I can't believe they are worried about you when there are some many others."

"Let's see, Richard, Pudge, Esther, Lisa, Trevor, Ping—yes, there's quite a list."

"I don't think Richard would do it. I'm not so sure about Esther."

"She hated her, but not enough to do this. Now Lisa...that girl is a little crazy."

I have a realization. "Maybe Lisa and Ernesto conspired to kill her. They left the ball before we did and stopped at the house."

Graham pats my lap. "Emma, the police are quite capable. Once they do the autopsy and investigate, they will find the culprit."

"Maybe it's that suspicious Hudson DuPont."

Graham nods his head.

I leap up. "Oh no! He could be in Kevin's bed this very minute."

42

The screen door opens on the little yellow hideaway, aka Curly. A man stumbles out in my favorite marabou pink peignoir. It's Kevin, looking like he might need the hair of the dog to save him. In a strange twist of events, I'm the only one in the world without a hangover. Graham purposely avoids eye contact with Kevin, and says he has to get back to the boat. He disappears out the side yard.

I follow Kevin as he sleepwalks into my kitchen and pours a cup of coffee. After a few sips, he seems to awaken. "So, how was it?"

"Glorious. Sublime—oh wait, I'll put it in your terms. It was Cherries Jubilee!"

"I can imagine. Actually, I don't have to imagine. I drank the leftover Grand Marnier in my place and heard every word."

My mouth gapes at the thought. "What? Did you think it would go bad?"

"Well, when the condom got stuck…then..."

"Thank you for the recap. I meant the Grand Marnier."

I pcek out the kitchen window when we hear voices out front; it's Captain Lacey and his new sidekick, Rusty. Kevin evaporates out the back door just before I open the front door. They say they have more questions for me and that they are also looking for 131 Cat Trail, the house where Kevin is supposed to live.

We hear yelling and growling, as Ursula apparently feels this is a good time to initiate a round of tug-a-war with the pink peignoir. I'm sure Kevin's sorry he's borrowed it, and now it's too late to

239

break away. The police walk to the back and see Kevin cowering in his chiffon.

"Kevin," Captain Lacey says, "why don't you sit a moment and talk to us, or are you late for an Auntie Mame revival?"

Kevin plunks down in his hammock and hides in his pink cocoon.

"Tell us about the food you served the other night."

I listen in as Kevin goes on about the lamb chops and the duck.

"Do you have any of it left?"

"Sure. I put it in the back of Emma's fridge."

Trying to be a cooperative witness, I go to the fridge and pull out the Saran-wrapped food samples, which were hidden in the drawer.

Rusty grabs a duck leg and starts gnawing on it.

"Rusty, it's not for us!" Captain Lacey says. "We need to send it to the lab."

"Oh, why didn't you say so."

"Emma, what did you do when you went back to the Weinstein residence that night?"

I experiment with various responses, but all are fraught with perilous conclusions. "We assumed Bunny Weinstein was upstairs sleeping, so Richard and I sat out by the pool discussing business and whatnot." I leave out the part about him saying he was falling for me.

Kevin interrupts to ask if he can swap houses when I'm in jail.

Captain Lacey, emphasizing the seriousness of the matter, asks Kevin, "What did you and this Hudson DuPont III do when you returned to the Weinstein residence?"

Kevin turns from pink to red, so we know some kind of tryst happened. Finally he says, "We went back to clean the kitchen." Then he must realize this is not a good alibi, so he says, "I was so tired from all the catering, I thought I'd take a little break in the library."

"Did you see any signs of Mrs. Weinstein?"

"No, I assumed she was at the ball. I wouldn't have been drinking the Courvoisier if I thought she might be home."

"Is that stuff any good?" Rusty interjects.

Captain Lacey rolls his eyes. "Did you hear any signs of people in the house besides you and this Hudson fellow?"

"It was dark and shadowy; all I could hear was the wind howling and the tree scraping the windows like the fingernails of a dead man trying to scratch his way in to kill me."

"It sounds scary," Rusty says.

"It wasn't windy that night," Captain Lacey points out.

"Well, who could hear anything with that dog of hers making that incessant licking sound." We all look over at Ursula, who's sitting on a chair demonstrating her incessant licking sound. She has a "what, me?" look on her face.

Then Kevin says, "Oh, I forgot. I thought I heard someone playing the piano, but I realize it could have been Ping, attempting to play 'Chopsticks.'"

"What time was this?"

"Frankly, it's all a blur now."

I think this is the perfect time to change the subject, and ask the police if they ever made it over to Natasha's house.

"Yeah, Captain," Rusty says. "When can we go see the hot Russian Chick?"

Captain Lacey ruins my theory. "Detective Perez says he has proof Natasha never went back to the Weinstein house after the ball."

Captain Lacey's police radio goes off with a call that requires him to leave.

Kevin does a little dance in the pink peignoir when they leave, except they have merely paused and turn back and witness the spectacle that is Kevin.

"Don't leave the island," Captain Lacey warns.

Kevin makes sure they're gone and drags me into his little house and up the stairs. "Emma, this is bad. They're accusing me too." His voice gets even higher. "I can't take this kind of pressure! What if I have to go on the lam? What would I wear?"

"I can tell you what not to wear."

43

Even though I'm exhausted, I simply can't sleep until I share my love- is- a- many- splendored -thing adventure with someone. Kevin apparently only likes fresh gossip, so the only one to call is Irene, who has been known to sit patiently through less than riveting tales of tax deductions. Plus, I feel the need for a little of Irene's five-cent therapy. She's at the pool and says to hurry over before she forgets. Now that I'm a murder suspect, I find it best to skulk under the entry ramp in lieu of the lobby. When I get to the pool, Irene yanks me over to the private Jacuzzi, where we can "natter" about sex and murder. She's wearing a neon orange bathing suit with matching beaded turban, defeating all efforts to look inconspicuous. Over the bubbling waters, I launch my theory that it might be Lisa or Ernesto who killed Bunny.

Irene shakes her head in dissent. "Lisa is too smart to hit someone over the head. Now, I could imagine her tossing a radio in the tub." I'm sure it's hard for Irene to follow with the beads rustling every time she moves her head, so I ask, "But what about Ernesto?"

Irene shakes her head so much I'm losing my train of thought; she finally says, "But you say he has a gun? Then he's out because he would have shot her. All murderers have their own little patented system. They really get themselves into a rut."

I wonder how Irene knows this. "What about Hudson?"

"I don't know this Hudson DuPont fellow. Pudge is the one who knows him. He wants her to redecorate all of his homes. I think she's just doing it so she can say she's an international decorator."

I ponder Irene's theory-of-the-minute. "I wonder how she met him."

Irene slathers suntan lotion on her wrinkled face. "They met at The Breakers bar. Oh, I almost forgot! How was it with Graham?"

The Jacuzzi shuts off as I gaze up at the sky and gush. "He made my insides quake."

Irene slaps her hands together, which splatters the lotion. "Ah, I miss that. My uterus doesn't quack like it used to. Well, not since I lost it in my hysterectomy. Well, it's not lost, they've got it in a jar of formaldehyde."

"You'll be happy to know Graham is making me forget all about Richard," I say, trying to change the subject a little.

"Well, guess what, honey? Richard is no longer a married man."

I get up to turn the Jacuzzi back on. "It hasn't registered in my brain yet."

"Isn't it interesting—you liked Richard more when he was unavailable."

"That's my type! Unrequited and unavailable."

She looks over at the back of the Flagmore. "Now everything has changed."

Raining on my reverie, Irene says, "Emma, you do realize that now no one is going the buy the house. What are you going to do for money?"

Somehow, I've been in denial about this. "I suppose I could paint. Maybe Richard can have me paint his whole family."

"You need to stay away from him until the dust settles. The police think you were having breakfast in bed with him."

My mouth falls open in shock. "Have you been talking to Graham?"

Irene waves her wrinkled hand. "Bunny had it coming. The amazing thing is that it didn't happen sooner."

"Irene, why didn't you tell me I was getting into such a messy situation?"

"Hey, you needed the commission, and I needed a helper.

"I do think it's bizarre that I never laid eyes on her when she was alive."

Irene slaps her leg again. "See, the cops are never going to suspect someone who's never met her. To know her is to hate her."

"I wonder who did it."

Right then the timed Jacuzzi jets shut off again, just in time for the whole world to hear Irene announce, "I'll bet Pudge killed her."

Everyone at the pool area looks over to our location.

"But she was in the ballroom the whole time," I whisper with my hand over my mouth, "except for when she was in the ladies room."

"Do you really think Pudge would get her hands dirty on this? She'd hire a hit man. And what a perfect night to do it when the whole town was watching her."

44

As I lie in bed, a gentle rain is pelting the roof. A Jeff Buckley song, "We all Fall in Love Sometime," plays while Graham licks whipped cream off my lips. I silently direct him to go lower. Then I hear Kevin's jarring voice, saying I have no filter. I realize I've been dreaming, and it's Ursula licking my face. Kevin pokes my shoulder to awaken me, and to alert me to the appalling lack of service in my fine establishment. It seems we have no handsome Englishman to make us coffee, no coffee filters and no dog food. Once again, Ursula will dine on duck pate. Judging by the look on Kevin's face, I think he misses Graham too. It's been five days, and I haven't seen or heard from him since our glorious "it" night. I wonder what's happened? Maybe he's deep into planning our wedding.

Kevin says I probably scared him away. Scared him away? Why don't men call after sex? So rude! Probably ran off with someone. Or the rascal probably did kill Bunny and has fled to Barbados. Either way it's not good. Kevin and I can't find an umbrella, so we drive the few blocks to Publix to get dog food and filters. At the front of the store, we see the Palm Beach Post—with a front photo of Bunny and Richard! I'd been trying to stay away to keep him out of my mind. *My poor Richard.* Kevin can't understand how my mind just toggles from Graham to Richard. That's just it; they're never in my head at the exact same time—it's like there's a love lever in my brain.

Kevin thinks it would be appropriate to send Richard some flowers. As I am low on dough, Kevin suggests buying flowers at Publix and delivering them myself. I like everything about this plan. Richard will take me in his arms and say he's finally free. Then that rascal Graham will be there at the house and get jealous. He'll kiss me and say I'm his, that he missed me this week and was pining away with love, but didn't want to rush things.

Kevin snaps his fingers in my face to awaken me from my tryst trance. After a spirited debate between the roses or the tulips, which look too romantic, we compromise on a little jade bonsai plant with a blue butterfly stuck in it. Kevin doesn't want to go to Richard's, as he's afraid the police might be staking the place out. He says he'll just walk back to his hovel to watch his favorite Richard Burton movie, *The Sandpiper*.

Winding my way down the misty Ocean Drive, I find the windshield wipers are lulling me into a stupor. I reminisce about the first time I came to this house with Irene. It was way back when I was young and innocent—two months ago. Before I have a chance to knock on the door, Trevor opens it in his best imitation of Lurch. Without waiting for me to speak, he says, "If you are looking for Graham, he's not here."

"No. Why, where is he?"

"It's a secret."

"I promise not to tell."

An unrestrained gale of laughter flows from Trevor. When he finishes, he jokes, "I can keep a secret, it's the people I tell secrets to who cannot. He's gone to the Bahamas to work out his immigration issue. So it's on the QT."

"He went on a cruise all by himself?"

"No, he took my boat and needed crew; he went with Ping and...."

"Natasha?" I guess.

Flustered, Trevor says, "Strictly business. He'll be back in a day. Meanwhile, if you are looking to bring some cheer to Dr. Weinstein, he's in his library."

Trevor guides me down the glass hallway, where I find Richard lying on the leather sofa like that first day. I think it might cheer him up if I sat on his face again, but Trevor might think otherwise. Upon hearing my voice, Richard pops up, revealing eyes that are red and puffy.

He looks so sad and vulnerable that I just want to hold him. He's wearing his bathrobe and gets up to greet me with a kiss. "Emma."

I return the kiss, but it somehow lands on his nose. "Richard, I'm so sorry."

Trevor hovers about. "Emma, would you like anything? Coffee? Tea? Scotch?"

I look at my non-existent watch. "It's a little early for drinking."

"Oh, now you tell him," Richard jokes.

"I'll have coffee if it's not too much trouble."

"Oh, I was betting you would choose the Scotch. The police have the kitchen sealed off, so coffee preparation will be cumbersome. " He exits in that subtle way of his.

I hand Richard the little bonsai.

Feigning cheerfulness, Richard says, "Thank you, Emma. Maybe they'll let me keep this in my prison cell. Did you know I'm the prime suspect?"

"Well, I might have read that somewhere."

"But I don't feel so badly because Trevor is the number two suspect, then Graham and Ping respectively."

"Me too," I say helpfully. "I think because I was the one to find her. Well, it was really the Aggarwals; they screamed first."

"Watch what you say to the police, Emma. Perhaps you should retain an attorney."

"I don't even have money to buy dog food, and I think lawyers cost more."

Trevor reappears in the doorway. "The good ones do."

He's returned with a little tray of tea biscuits, milk and marmalade, apologizing for the absent coffee.

Richard pats my hand. "You must need a little something to tide you over." He walks over to his desk and pulls out his checkbook.

He scrunches his brow and then surrenders. "How the hell do you spell Budnjk?"

Trevor clears his throat. "Sir, do you really think it's a good idea to write a check to a beautiful suspect that can be easily traced by the police, days after your wife has been murdered?"

Richard sighs. "Oh, you're right, old man. Have we got any cash in the house?"

Trevor hands me the milk and says to Richard, "I'll go to SunTrust first thing."

Still playing the "beautiful suspect" part over again in my head, I say, "Oh, that's ok. I don't even have a lawyer—except my old boyfriend."

"Would he be the one who cheated on you with the leggy blonde who was not his sister?" Richard says, with a little glee.

Surprised by his attention to my details, I say, "Yes. I guess I should find someone else; probably someone local."

"Better hurry," Trevor quips. "Defense attorneys are in high demand this week."

"They can't suspect everyone in town. Who else has a motive?"

"The whole town," Richard and Trevor blurt out in unison.

Richard begins a loud, deep, extended laugh as Trevor enumerates: "Waiters, hairdressers, and we mustn't forget the Girl Scouts."

I choke on my milk. "The Girl Scouts?"

"Yes, Bunny terrorized a flock of them in front of the market one day. A little freckled one cried so hard she ruined her merit sash."

Richard smiles again. "I suppose they won't be attending the service."

"When's the funeral?"

"Attendance would be dismal," Trevor says, "so this might as well be it."

"Boy, that would have been one tricky eulogy."

"I would have said something like, 'She was unfailing in her...'" Richard muses.

"Heartlessness," Trevor finishes the line.

Richard gets up and shuffles in his slippers to his piano. He begins to play a DeBussy song, "Reverie." The rain is really pouring down now and the palm trees appear to be waving goodbye. I sit and watch Richard's graceful hands on the keys as he glances at the sheet music.

He turns, kisses me on the cheek, and says that will be his signal for me to turn the page. I hope it's a long song.

The doorbell suddenly disturbs the reverie. It continues to ring, making me think it's Kevin or the Aggarwals.

Richard leaves the piano and hunkers down on the sofa. "Don't answer it, Trevor."

Trevor carefully peeks out the edge of the huge window. "It is Ms. Lichtenfelder."

"What is she doing here?"

I look out and see Pudge dressed in black with a mesh veil over her face, like Elizabeth Taylor in *Ash Wednesday*. I guess Pudge got the memo. She's holding an umbrella, balancing a huge floral arrangement on her bony hip, and pressing the doorbell with her pointy elbow.

"There's no use ducking down," I say. "She can see us."

Trevor sips his scotch. "He who lives in a glass house should have blinds."

Richard hides his face under a pillow. "She is the last person I want to see."

"I thought you were friends?" I ask, dipping my cookie into the milk.

"No, we all hate her. Trevor invites her to everything just to irritate Bunny."

Trevor's smirk flashes back. "Then let's invite her to Bunny's unarranged arrangements."

Richard contemplates that for a moment, then directs me to let her in. I guess it's Trevor's day off.

I guide Pudge down the glass hall; she is wearing a black, mermaid-cut dress and toddles to keep up. She waits until she has an audience to yell at me. "What took you so long the answer the damned door? My dress was getting wet!"

She takes this opportunity to give Richard a big hug. He largely ignores her, then returns to the piano to resume his rendition of "Reverie."

Pudge has only been here for a minute before she starts giving orders. "Trevor, be a dear and get me some champagne."

Trevor gives her a judgmental, sideways glance. "Oh, someone feels like celebrating?"

Pudge lights up a long, thin cigarette and exhales. "Why, of course not."

Trevor pours himself more scotch from a crystal decanter. "I'm off duty."

Pudge appears to assess the hierarchy and barks, "Emma, dear, go get me a bottle of champagne. The good stuff."

I'm thinking I might as well join in at this point.

"Please do not enter the kitchen," Trevor says, "try the wet bar by the dining room."

Returning successfully with a bottle of Louis Roederer Cristal, I stall as I slowly peel the heavy foil off the neck of the bottle, hoping I don't actually have to open it.

"Oh, I suppose you're used to the twist off kind," Pudge says.

I hand the unopened bottle to her, hoping she loses an eye.

Pudge is fidgety as she takes a long drag on her thin cigarette. "What are you looking at?" She waves the smoke away in a futile effort to protect our lungs.

"Nothing, you just look so happy."

"What? Do you expect me to cry over Bunny and get all puffy? Sure, I'm upset. I just lost my best enemy."

"That's a novel alibi."

"We loved hating each other. That's what keeps women on their toes—otherwise you get fat."

Ignoring Pudge, I bask in the calm soulfulness of Richard's playing as he concentrates on the sheet music for DcBussy's "Afternoon of a Faun." Instead of kissing my cheek, he gives me a wink when it's time to turn the page. Still good, as a wink is a secret kiss.

Feeling like I'm in a subtitled black and white French film, I watch as his gentle fingers move; they make an effort to reach over the ordinary ivory keys, to get to the eccentric black keys.

When he finishes, Trevor commences a subtle interrogation—as a good butler should. "So, Ms. Lichtenfelder, did you remain for long at the ball?"

Pudge lets out a blast of smoke. "Come on! The whole town knows I got a lift from the damned dog walker. I'll never live that one down."

Ernesto is probably thinking the same thing about her. I keep quiet, focusing instead on my burgeoning detective skills. Is Pudge lying? I close my eyes to hear any quiver in her voice. Nothing. I guess nicotine takes care of quiver. Then I notice it: the one thing that makes me conclude Pudge could never sneak in and kill someone. At least, not without leaving her calling card—the smell of smoke and Joy perfume.

Richard furrows his brow. "Pudge, did you leave before we did?"

Pudge nervously pours herself more champagne, causing it to foam over the edge. "I don't know; I left after the drawing for the most congenial Rottweiler."

Abandoning silence, I say, "You weren't there for that one."

"Well, then I left after fattest pug. Didn't your dog win?"

I'm about to protest again, but Richard cutely puts his finger to his mouth indicating for me not to talk. I love him. His bathrobe is light blue, which makes his eyes even bluer; I want to hold him.

253

"Who was it who won the drawing for the USAir lifetime pet travel pass?" Trevor asks casually.

Pudge waivers. "Um. Let's see—I can't remember his name."

Trevor shakes his head. "You didn't pull his name out, Esther did."

I can't help myself. "I remember they pulled out that famous guy's name, but he was the one who donated the prize, so there was a debate as to whether he was eligible. Then everyone started chanting, 'Get Judge Pudge! Get Judge Pudge.'"

Richard is facing the piano, but I can tell by his shoulders he is secretly chuckling.

Pudge tries to defend herself. "I was in the ladies room for god's sake.

Then someone came in and shut the lights off, so I had to feel around like Helen fricken Keller to find the light switch before I could apply my lipstick."

Trevor shakes his head. "Esther said you had your lipstick tattooed on in 2003."

Richard starts laughing. "Trevor, behave."

"Well, I was the chairperson; I couldn't possibly go up to the podium all disheveled."

I'm curious. "How did you get disheveled?"

Pudge looks at me. "Please, Emma. There were a lot of handsome men there, and I was very popular on the dance floor. "

We all look skeptical.

"I was there the whole time and I have a perfect alibi." She looks at me and adds, "I'm not so sure about some people."

Trevor is now sitting on the piano bench with Richard, ready to turn a page. He and Richard remind me of Richard Harrison and his sidekick in *My Fair Lady*.

Richard plays "I've Got a Crush on You."

I'm sure Pudge thinks he's playing it for her, judging by the gush she lets out.

Then Richard jokingly sings in Trevor's ear, "I've got a crush on you, sweetie pie."

Pudge blows out dragon-like smoke. "Oh, come on it's so obvious—it's Graham."

I jump up and say, "How do you know he wasn't with me?"

Pudge looks at me like I'm a pathetic child. "Hello? He went back to the house alone during the estimated time of the murder. And now he's suddenly hiding out in freaking Freeport with Boris and Natasha."

Was I the last to know?

Trevor stands up and announces, "I've known Graham since he was a lad in Batley. He would not hurt a soul."

Pudge jumps in like she's Angela Lansbury. "And who now has immigration issues thanks to Bunny."

Richard comes back to the sofa. "I can't believe Bunny called the INS."

Pudge slides over next to Richard. "Darling, whom do you suspect?"

Trevor lets out an, "Ahem, Sir."

"I know I shouldn't talk, but Natasha seems to have some interest in my becoming single. I suppose I shouldn't have invited her on the boat."

"Perhaps you should not have played "The Girl with the Flaxen Hair." Trevor quips.

Pudge stomps her foot indignantly. "You invited that little married skank on a cruise and not me?"

Trevor can't help but add, "And she stayed all night."

Pudge sulks. "How come I never get invited on the boat?"

"Well," I say, "maybe it's because you just accused the captain of murder."

"Now that Graham is a suspect in a crime, he'll surely be denied a new visa."

Trevor and Richard glare at her.

"Poor Emma," she says snidely. "There goes your boyfriend."

Richard looks up. "He's your boyfriend, is he?"

My face must say, 'Oh no, how did Pudge find out?'

"Oh, come on. We all heard about your quaking lady parts."

I can feel my face becoming warmed by the embarrassment.

"Actually, once he returns, Graham is required remain in Palm Beach until the police are finished with their investigation," Trevor points out.

Richard shakes his head and falls back on the sofa. "I can't believe she's gone. I wasn't very nice to her at the end."

Trevor pulls on his foot. "Sir, watch what you say."

Richard takes my hand. "Oh, I trust Emma."

I love his hand on mine. So warm, so firm. The switch has tripped back to Richard now—and he's single. Number one murder suspect, but who can be picky?

Right then, a truck engine revs up and pulls away. Pudge jumps up. "Oh no, there goes my ride. Richard, will you give me a ride back to the Flagmore?"

Richard looks irritated. "How did you get here?"

"I'm having my car detailed; I made the florist drive me here."

I volunteer to drive her home, only to rue the offer instantly.

After saying our goodbyes, Pudge climbs in my back seat, like I'm her chauffer. She lands on a squeaking toy encrusted with dog hair. "Tell me you don't drive real estate clients in this car."

"Until Ursula gets her learner's permit, I have to drive her to the vet every month. She's a cancer survivor you know."

Pudge brushes off the hair. "Why don't you just get rid of that ugly dog?"

"Because I love her."

"Let me tell you something: Love ruins everything."

"Remind me to needlepoint that on a pillow."

45

When I get home, I find my curly-tailed pet is missing. As all pet owners can attest, my first thought is she's been kidnapped; my second thought is she's out breaking and entering. I am relieved to see Kevin scurrying into his Curly cottage—with my dog.

"Don't worry. It's just me."

"Oh, I thought it was the authorities. I'm a prime suspect, you know; my fingerprints are all over the place."

"Kevin, I think you are the only non-suspect. The cops are under the impression you were the only one who actually liked Bunny." I look around. "Where's Hudson? Did you find out anything more about him?"

Kevin adjusts his bathrobe and says in a sultry voice, "Like what?"

"Like why does he have blonde roots? Like is he a murderer?"

"You're the one in love with two murderers. How dare you accuse my Hudson."

"He was there at the approximate time of the murder. What was he up to?"

Kevin opens a chilled Starbucks espresso. "When the power went off for the fifth time, I heard a noise. But it was dark, and you remember how Richard said no candles? Well, I couldn't see a thing and I thought it was an intruder so I grabbed that golf club that Trevor was swinging, but you know I don't know how to swing a club. I couldn't possibly take golf lessons after I found my mother with that Danish half-finished transsexual golf pro. So, I was in the kitchen sipping the rest of the Veuve Clicquot, when Hudson said he thought he heard a burglar in Bunny's butler's pantry; not to be confused with the upstairs east or west wing butlers' pantries. Frankly, they should color code them, because east and west are confusing when you're lying down. Anyway, I ran to the pool house, but I was scared to death, which is *not* the way to go with my pale coloring.

I dashed back for a moment to get the champagne; it was just going to go flat, and if this was the end—I wanted a stylish exit."

"A burglar? How come the police don't know about this?"

"Well, my thoughtful Hudson was concerned that such an incident might impact your impending showing. Then he concluded it was probably just Dr. Phil giving Ursula a little romp on the sofa."

My mind wanders to the concept of this, and the thought of Irene as a pet in-law.

"Hudson was anxious to go to Ft. Lauderdale, but I wanted to stay. Then that little Ping came back to get his Tom Jones music and said I had to stay and clean up. Did you know he does a perfect, "What's New Pussy Cat?"'"

"Yes, I did, though it's more like "What's New Puddy Cat." Wait, you went to Ft. Lauderdale after that?"

"No, neither one of us could see straight, so we came here and drove down the next morning.

Newly irritated, I say, "Why didn't you wait for me and Ursula? Then I wouldn't be a suspect."

"Well, I thought you wanted to stay with Richard—and who knew?"

"Yes, who knew a woman would be murdered."

"Well, I didn't," Kevin belts out.

"Who else was at the Weinstein's house when you were there?"

"Ping came in and out. He was yelling at me in that horrible high voice of his. Your dog somehow opened the fridge and got into Lisa Weinstein's leftover lobster dinner. I think that stupid lamb leg kept the door from closing. Ursula left such a mess that I had a stern talk with her and off she went."

"What time did Ping drop by?"

Kevin looks exasperated. "Emma, let's review: I'm drinking cognac with a hot trust funder at a mansion. Do you think I'm keeping track of the Chinese cook?"

I open my mouth in shock. "So maybe Ping killed Bunny Weinstein!"

Kevin sips the last of his coffee. "I wouldn't put it past him. Anyone who likes Tom Jones can't be normal."

"My mother likes Tom Jones."

"Then you get my point."

He opens the fridge and sees we have no food; not even dog food.

"I'm overdrawn at the bank," I say, "and barely have space on my last Visa card. What are we going to do?"

"I know, why don't you ask Esther Weinstein for a job?"

46

Upon Ursula's insistence, I go back to get the elusive Iams MiniChunks dog food. It's that, or stock up on lipstick and caviar—no doubt, her favorite forms of sustenance.

This time I write it down and march to Aisle 7, not stopping at the free samples, lest I get distracted. When I'm in the checkout line, whom do I see? Lisa Weinstein.

She's wearing white pants and has blond hair! I wouldn't have recognized her if she wasn't right in front of me, and if the cashier didn't say, "Here's your I.D., Lisa."

"Hi, Emma!" She seems abnormally happy, like she wasn't just accused of murdering her stepmother kind of happy.

Wondering how to property deliver condolences in the express checkout line, I touch her arm and finally come up with, "I'm so sorry about Bunny."

Lisa utters a curt, "No worries."

Then the cashier lets out a pert, "We have cake left. The union workers had a party in the break room when we read about her in the paper."

Looking at Lisa's perfect hair, I can't help but comment, "I didn't know you were a blonde."

"Yeah, I'm over my Goth phase."

"I'll bet your grandmother likes it better."

"No, she liked the darkness. Say, she's having lunch all alone at the club; you should stop by."

Thinking this is perfect, I calmly say, "I suppose I could."

"I just came back from a weekend in Connecticut." She flashes a huge ring. "I just got engaged."

"Really! Who is the lucky guy?"

"My old boyfriend, Johnny."

"I'll bet your dad is excited."

"He doesn't know yet. I want to tell him in person, but he's playing tennis with Graham and Natasha."

The cashier's head is alternating between Lisa's face and mine, like she's watching a tennis match.

I'm shocked, for many reasons. "What?"

"She used to like Graham, but she's after my dad now that he's a free man."

A stabbing pain punctures my chest. I do love Richard, and don't want him to get away. Still stunned, I manage to recall and say, "But *she's* married."

"Not for long."

47

Ursula is just going to have to wait a little longer for her Iams MiniChunks. She'll probably just put her nose up anyway, after living off lobster and duck pate for the past week. The universe and Lisa are telling me I need to see Mrs. Weinstein. In fact, Lisa drops me— and the dog food off at the club. When I walk in, I notice the service is better, and can't help but think it has to do with Kevin's departure. When I reach Mrs. Weinstein's table, she silently pats the chair next to her for me to put down the huge bag of dog food, like it's a third guest. She asks me what I want for lunch; I look at her as she is slathering mayonnaise on a BLT, and stirring an iced tea. When I order a matching BLT, she tells the waiter I'll have a salad. She pats my belly and says this is a crucial time for me, that I can eat BLTs when I'm eighty-seven.

"I'll bet you're excited about Lisa's engagement."

"Oy! That was hard to arrange."

"How did you do that?"

She smiles. "You don't think I've lived this long without learning a few tricks."

When I tell her she looks great, she pauses. "I've never been happier. But I can't go around saying that with the rabbit dead and all, so I try to rein it in."

Yeah, I can see that.

"Emma, it's important to act normal in times of supposed tragedy. You don't have to be normal, just act it."

I pat her liver spotted hand, which makes me think everything in this town has spots. "Your poor son. He seems in shock."

"The shock is that my Babka kind of loved her. You know, in that awful bickering kind of way."

An iced tea arrives for me, and I hesitate to put sugar in. "Who do you think killed her?"

Mrs. Weinstein takes a bite of her crunchy-looking BLT. "It could have been just about anyone, but I can't believe they suspect my sweet Trevor."

Judging by the look on her face, I say, "You love him, don't you?"

Mrs. Weinstein puts down her sandwich, which now has a big lipstick- rimmed bite mark. "He used to take me for a ride on his big trawler every Sunday morning."

My mind drifts at this image; I hope she's talking about a boat.

"I've been in love with him since 1967."

"Really?"

"I remember it like it was yesterday. The radio was playing that trendy Donovan song "Wear Your Love Like Heaven." It was Trevor's first day as the captain of my husband's yacht; Trevor must have been nervous for he pulled away from the dock and still had a rope tied, so part of the dock followed us to Boca. I loved my husband, but when I was *with* him, I'd close my eyes and pretend I was with Trevor."

Whoa! So she's got the love toggle too. She looks sad, and I wonder whether this tender moment is the right time to tell her she has mayonnaise all over her face.

Instead I come up with, "Why didn't you two ever get married?"

"Very simple; he doesn't love me."

What can I say after that? Definitely not mayo on your face time. "Oh, I don't believe that. Look at the way he sneaks vodka into your morning orange juice; or that time he fished your glasses from the toilet. Now that's love."

"It's hard to love someone when you're in love with someone else."

Not for me.

My plain salad arrives with little fanfare and I get back to the matter at hand. "So, who does Trevor love?"

"Why, he loves your friend Irene. If only I could be sixty-nine again. If only I could *do* sixty-nine again." She bites the lipstick parts off her sandwich and gets a far away look. "Frankly, I always thought it was too much going on at the same time."

Is she still talking about the sixty-nine position, I wonder.

I shake my head. "This is really sad—all this unrequited love."

"Most love is unrequited," Mrs. Weinstein says wisely. "It's hard enough to find someone to love, let alone have the exact same person love you back."

There is no hope for me.

I spill out, "I'll probably end up all alone like you."

Ignoring the slight, she says, "You won't end up alone; the question is whether you end up with Richard or Graham."

"I'm worried they'll both fall in love with Natasha. Well, I'm not sure love is the right word."

"The word you are looking for is lust."

"I can never tell the difference between them."

"It's easy: lust is short. It wouldn't be lust if it lasted."

265

Sounds like a perfume ad, or maybe a condom ad.

Newly optimistic, I conclude, "So, I don't have to worry about Natasha because everyone lusts after her?"

"Actually, I've seen her naked; that's the kind of lust that could linger."

I realize I've got big problems now. Natasha could get them both and I'll end up all alone with Kevin and my dog—and Mrs. Weinstein.

She must notice my sorrowful look. "But even love doesn't last forever."

Now I must look like I'm going to jump out a window, for she yanks a piece of bacon from her sandwich and puts in on my salad. "The only love that lasts forever is unrequited love."

I nod in agreement. "Yeah, you can't make that go away."

Mrs. Weinstein waves her bejeweled hand in her signature "Oy" like gesture. "So one of them chooses her, and you get the other one. I just hope my son picks you."

Little does she know that I've gone to the dark side with Graham.

"Too bad you shtupped Graham."

48

After lunch, Mrs. Weinstein drives me and the dog food home. Riding with her is like sitting in a living room with a slow change of scenery. How does she ever get anywhere? Then it hits me: Maybe I should be her driver.

"Do you need help with anything? You know, maybe driving or running errands?"

She looks at me like I'm pitiful. Probably thinks I have to live on dog food. "What? Out of money again?"

I nod my head.

She pats my shoulder. "Then go for Richard."

As she stops in front of my little house, she looks up. "How's that painting coming along?"

"It's done, it just takes awhile to dry." I feel guilty offering to paint her whole family, and she still hasn't seen one painting.

"Say, I've got an idea! You can help me with Lisa's wedding. Are you a good planner?"

Despite the fact I can't plan a bologna sandwich, I say, "Yes! I was made for planning."

"Good. They're getting married in Nantucket in June."

"That's great. I'm glad she's not with Ernesto."

"Ernesto? That was just to annoy Bunny. It's amazing how much easier things are without her."

She's right.

She turns to me. "I can't wait to tell Richard about this. I think you and he just might have to take a little trip up there to look for reception sites."

"Yes, that would be fun—if only we could leave town."

Pushing the periwinkle door open, I am sucked into a dark, empty shell. I miss the olden days when Kevin and my dog were waiting for me in my bed. That's what it takes to make a house a home. Kevin's lights are on, so I wander out back.

Because it involves me and love, I can't wait to tell him the new gossip. He's in his little bed upstairs with Ursula on his lap. "Kevin, that was a great idea! Mrs. Weinstein says I can help her plan Lisa's wedding."

"Lisa is getting married?"

"Yes, to some guy named Johnnie from the Holmes Sausage Company."

"Sounds like a porno film."

"No, it's a wedding and it's going to be in Nantucket, sometime in June."

"Did you ask if I could cater?"

Changing the subject, I say, "Oh, and Mrs. Weinstein thinks that between Richard and Graham, whoever doesn't marry Natasha will marry me."

"Isn't she already married?"

"Yes, but now Natasha wants out so she can marry Richard. She was playing tennis with Graham and Richard earlier today. That is one girl we need to keep married."

Without looking up from his miniature black and white TV, Kevin says, "You need to reverse your usual home-wrecking tactics."

"Yes, and it's probably much more difficult."

"What do we know about this husband of Natasha's? Maybe we need to do a little investigating."

"All I know is his name is Pierre and he works as a hair dresser on the island. But I don't know which salon."

Kevin quickly determines that Pudge will know the whereabouts of Natasha's husband. "But," he expounds, "I'll need a pretext to call, otherwise Pudge will get suspicious and blow the whole thing and Natasha will end up divorced and then be free to lure Graham or Richard and you'll end up an old maid."

Kevin has such a way to inspire accessories to crime and mischief. I've got it: after Pudge gets nosey, Kevin will slip that he's "heard" Natasha is trying to frame her husband for Bunny's murder and we need to alert him to this. Pudge will blab away because she'll want Natasha to be blamed for the murder instead so Natasha won't be able to steal Richard.

Blab she does: Pierre Abdoula, 5'9', medium build, black hair, dark eyes, forty-three years old, from Casablanca, Florida license plate H456GH, works until 5:00 p.m. at the salon on Worth Avenue.

"Perhaps I should get my hair cut," Kevin offers. "You know, for research purposes."

"I'll bet he charges a fortune. If we're going to be good spies, we'll have to stay within our budget."

Leaving our spy dog at home, we race down to Worth Avenue. Hovering out front in the car, we duck down and watch discreetly through the shop's plate glass window.

While I stay in the getaway car, Kevin enters the facility and asks for Pierre. I can see his lips move in an exaggerated manner to shape the word "Pierre." The receptionist points to a handsome Middle Eastern looking man with dark hair and large eyes—the man who is massaging the shoulders of an attractive woman. Kevin and I look at each other with "this can't be good" looks. Waving my hands, I indicate for Kevin to get the home-wrecking woman out of the way. As directed, Kevin shoos the woman away and points to his own hair. He must have asked how much a haircut costs, because the Pierre guy points to the price list on the wall. Then I see Kevin indicate with a shocked look that the price is too high. It's like watching a pantomime on steroids. Pierre throws his hands up and goes back to fondling the woman's shoulders.

Kevin opts for a manicure from the receptionist, oblivious to his assigned task. Pierre walks out the front door with the woman.

After a torturous half hour of Kevin nodding his head and the manicurist apparently divulging secret data, Kevin emerges from the salon in a giddy manner. In what is probably an attempt to look inconspicuous, he slips into the back seat, but immediately starts flailing his hands in an indication for me to hit the gas petal.

Then I realize he is flailing his hands to dry his nail polish.

Kevin catches me looking. "It's just a clear gloss."

"It's pink!"

Kevin shakes his head with impatience. "Well, I couldn't very well get a hair cut—it was $140! Although with a haircut you get free champagne."

"What did you find out?" I ask as we drive up County Road.

"If you want a spy to leak, you have to buy him a drink. Let's go to Buccan."

After we park, and find seats at the bar, Kevin and I order a bottle of Rue de 33 Rose.

"That's strange," Kevin says. "My manicure was $33, Natasha is also thirty-three." Then, like he's on a game show, he shouts, "Name three things with the number 33 that are pink and divine!"

"Boy, how can I compete with a thirty-three year old?"

"We could send her a case of chocolates to make her fat."

I love gay men. Who else would go to such lengths to help you fight the competition?

Kevin takes a gulp of his wine. "She is a Russian mail-order bride, and Pierre might have already been married to another postal client, that he returned, so they can have the marriage annulled."

Nodding my head in satisfaction, I say, "That manicurist was good. We need to keep Pierre married."

The bartender looks up, like he knows Pierre. It's quite possible because they work in the same area.

Kevin says in my ear, "We need to talk in 'vegetarian.'" Meaning, we need to talk in code where we substitute a same letter vegetable for a person's name. "Pea knows that...what's a vegetable that begins with N?"

"I can't think of one. How about Noodle?"

"Pea knows that Noodle sometimes spends the night on the boat with Green Bean and Rhubarb—I knew I'd get to use Rhubarb someday," Kevin thunders.

Focusing on the night in question, I say, "But I was there and Mrs..."

I can't think of a W vegetable at first, then joyfully I say, "Mrs. *Watercress* was there too. Did you tell her that nothing happened?"

Kevin answers with an exasperated sigh, "The goal was to get information. I couldn't very well be going on about that. And did you know that Pea was the hair dresser of Broccoli Watercress," he winks at me, "and that he hated her."

"Well, who didn't hate Broccoli Watercress?" I say, knowing its Bunny Weinstein.

271

"I liked Broccoli Watercress."

"How can you stand that?" the bartender says.

We look at him, irritated, and wonder if he's talking about vegetables or Bunny Weinstein.

"But here's the really good gossip," Kevin says. "Pea was at the house before the party getting Broccoli Watercress ready for the ball—hey, that even made sense."

"Maybe he did it. Nobody ever really saw her again."

Kevin leans in conspiratorially. "The manicurist says Pea seemed shocked and wondered who killed Broccoli Watercress."

"Maybe he's just a good actor."

The bartender is hovering nearby, pretending to wipe off glasses.

"The manicurist said Pea said that Noodle didn't come home that night."

"Wow, you found all this out?"

Kevin leans back confidently, until he almost falls off the bar stool. "I should be a detective."

Nodding in agreement, I say, "Yes, and catering can be your cover."

"Actually, I'd want to be a private eye. I wouldn't want all those police rules."

"So where did Noodle stay that night ? And why didn't Pea go to the ball?"

Lowering his standing slightly, Kevin acknowledges, "I didn't think to ask."

So much for his detective skills.

Wracking my brain for H and D vegetables to represent Hudson DuPont, I give up and ask, "What about Ham Dumpling?"

Kevin looks at me. "You want to order an appetizer?"

I do a large wink. "No, ham with an H and D as in dumpling?"

Kevin finally gets it. "Oh, you mean Ham Dumpling III? He's going to Nantucket this week."

"That's were...Lima Bean Watercress is getting married. I hope you get invited to the wedding."

"Yes, I'd love to go to Nantucket."

I pay the bill, praying my last card goes through. "I can't believe we just spent our last dime on French wine and a manicure."

Kevin waves his hand. "We are so *Breakfast at Tiffany's*."

As we leave, the bartender says, "Bye now. I sure hope the police let you guys leave town for Lisa Weinstein's wedding.

49

Kevin and I make our way back to the house and assess our sorry state of affairs. Other than sofa cushion coins—we have no money. Bunny Weinstein never wrote Kevin a check considering she was busy being dead. He says I'll have to ask Richard for the money. I haven't made a single dime since I landed in Florida, plus I've spent a fortune on recent vet bills and my festering Visa bill. The thought crosses my mind to take out a loan from the friendly Bank-of-Mom, but then realize at thirty-nine I'm officially too old and it would be pathetic. When I sadly ask Kevin what we're going to do for money, he cheers me up in his best Scarlett O'Hara voice, saying we should think about it tomorrow.

He opens my fridge and gasps; this makes me worry there might be dead body parts, or worse, moldy cheese. Squeezing into the kitchen and peering into the open fridge, I see it: except for the requisite ketchup, our larder is empty. This is pathetic; we have no money and no food. Here we are in the land of the uber-wealthy, quietly starving.

Right then, like she's got some sort of mother's intuition, my mother calls. She says she has expiring USAir miles and is coming down next week.

Kevin and I are excited about Mom's visit, though our excitement soon dwindles back to hunger. Kevin says he just spent half his net worth on Wonder bread and olive loaf, but it's missing from the fridge. He looks about the kitchen. "We have a cold cut kleptomaniac in our midst." We naturally look at the prime household suspect: Ursula. Perhaps I've been a bit negligent in the pet care area, what with being a realtor/painter/murder suspect. My poor baby. Her tail is between her legs and she keeps looking towards the sofa. Upon further inspection, we find the loaf of bread, which has bite marks through the plastic wrapper. Then we find the empty cold cut package.

Ursula, long the master of Houdiniesque tricks, has apparently learned to open the fridge and make her own sandwiches. Now what are we going to do? Kevin says not to fret and whisks out the back door.

He returns with a frosty bottle of Veuve Clicquot from his purloined case. It's a good thing dogs don't have thumbs and therefore can't pop a champagne cork. I ask Kevin if he has any actual food at his place and he skips out the back door again. This time he returns with water crackers and a tiny jar of Beluga caviar he says was "left over" from the party at the Weinsteins'.

How ironic that, because we're so broke, Kevin and I have had to live on champagne and caviar these past few days. Ursula joins us, and we are happy for her company until she sticks her long tongue into our caviar. My darling aardvark is quickly relocated to the front yard; Kevin then constructs a sign for her neck which says, "Will bark for Beluga."

Upon his return, Kevin laments, "We are poor as church mice, but we are happy."

"Yeah, we don't need money; we can do all sorts of things for free. We can ride the escalator up through the butterfly mobile at Neiman's."

"We can eat crab cakes at Tiffany's."

"We can ride yachts for free."

"Ahem," Kevin says. "I wonder what that's like."

Then I come back down to reality. "Too bad our double seasonal rents are due."

Kevin plops down on the sofa. "You'd better start praying to the seasonal rent angel."

"I've got the experts on it. Irene asked her friend Billy Benson to put us in the prayers at St. Edwards. She said he works miracles."

I notice Kevin doesn't seem too worried, and I wonder if he has secret money stashed.

He reads my mind. "What? I was only making $6 an hour and I never seemed to get any tips."

There is nothing to do but pray this passes. Being patient souls, we turn on the TV, where there's a brief bio of Jack Lemon before the feature film—*How to Murder Your Wife*. Kevin and I look at each other. We need to watch this! Apparently, Jack Lemon has a party and, well, one thing leads to another.

Jack has too much to drink, and an Italian stripper jumps out of a cake at a party for judges, and, naturally, Jack wakes up married. Hence the title. Kevin and I decide they should make divorce easier, so you don't have things like this happen.

A gentle knock on the screen door disrupts our musings. Thank goodness it's during a commercial. It's Trevor; he is wearing a raincoat even though it's a hot and sunny day. He asks to come in, but we're hesitant because it's so messy—that, and we're eating his Beluga caviar. He sees the painting of Richard, now displayed in the living room, and touches it gently. "Oh, still not dry."

He hands me two envelopes, one labeled *Kevin* and the other *Ms. Budnjk*. Kevin grabs his envelope and holds it up to the sun, then does a little thank you dance. It's money, and Trevor says not to breath a word of it. After we thank him and his sponsor, he makes a quick exit into the Maybach, where an incognito Ping is waiting as the wheelman.

No sooner than Trevor has gone, Ernesto appears at the screen door. "Your dog ate my butter." He opens the door and pushes Ursula in. I'm concerned that my dog has the ability to break loose, sneak into houses and open refrigerators. If only she were trained to bring the food home, I'd let it go. I wonder if Ernesto saw the money transfer. I'm starting to think I should close our front door, but who wants to suffer the consequences of darkness and claustrophobia?

After we ignore Ernesto to the point where he leaves, we open up our envelopes. $4000 for me and $3000 for Kevin. Yeah! We can pay the rent on our two houses and buy food. We dance up and down until Kevin realizes I got more than he did. He asks what mine is for. Frankly, I really can't say. I guess as a consolation prize for losing the Weinstein listing. The commercial is over and we're back to our movie, so Kevin turns up the volume. Right when they announce *How to Murder Your Wife*, I look up and see Detective Perez standing at the door.

50

The detective is not wearing a jacket, and we can see his gun in his shoulder holster. Hmm. He's kind of hot. Maybe I'm suddenly attracted to him now that he's completely off the table. You can't date the man investigating you, but no harm in studying his face and fascinating hairline. I find men with slightly receding hairlines and jagged temples to be so attractive. However, I must emphasize the "slightly" part.

While I'm staring at his hair, Kevin's eyes are directed lower; he is no-doubt busy trying to determine if Perez is a "shower"or a "grower." The poor, hot detective has to try to do his job while being assessed by ogling suspects. He looks around and exclaims with a slap of his thighs, "So, Palm Beach people really do sit around all day and drink champagne."

Kevin offers him some and looks surprised when he accepts— and irritated that he has to go and get another bottle.

Detective Perez stares at the painting of Richard.

When Kevin returns, Detective Perez says to him, "You're just the man I want to talk to."

"Then you have the wrong lady," Kevin jokes in a high voice.

Detective Perez laughs. "I need to know everyone who was in the house that night, including the names of the catering staff."

Kevin, leaving out the part about the hot surfer dudes, explains, "My staff was detained elsewhere. The guests were the usual people. You know, that little man who is always at the bar at the Leopard Lounge with the white shoes; that lady who lost 200 pounds and now has surgical arm seams. And that guy who is about eighty with a wife who is about twenty-five."

Detective Perez stops him. "That could be half the town. You don't know any of their names? "

Kevin pauses. "No. I think only Bunny knew, and maybe Richard."

"Dr. Weinstein said he never paid any attention to his wife's friends, or her for that matter."

"What about that Natasha?" I say helpfully.

Perez gets a smile on his face, indicating that he might like her. Oh brother. He'll probably let her off the hook and have to frame someone as cover.

"What about Natasha's husband?" Kevin interjects. "He did Bunny's hair that afternoon." After the words slip out of his mouth he realizes it's too late; then he makes it even more obvious when he gasps and covers his mouth.

I can see the vignette playing out in Kevin's sorry little head now. If Pierre goes to jail, Natasha will have to get rid of him to find a husband to support her and pay for her highlights, forcing her to steal Richard or Graham, and I'll end up single because Kevin is a blabbermouth.

But it's too late.

Trying to create a distraction, I blurt, "Hudson went up to Bunny's side two times during the party; once to get towels and then to take her iced tea."

I sense that Kevin is annoyed with my disclosure, mostly judging by the abrupt swivel of his head in my direction.

Detective Perez has a smile on his face as he pours me more truth serum and encourages me to go on. Kevin goes for a quick save of Hudson by saying he remembers that he saw Ernesto on an earlier occasion, in Bunny's closet. He swore he'd never tell because Bunny said he'd never cater in this town again if he did. "But now she's dead, so I guess it's okay to blab."

Kevin makes an exaggerated gesture next door to Ernesto's and drags Detective Perez over to Moe.

The minute the coast is clear and the detective is gone, Kevin locks the wooden door and we tiptoe upstairs where the acoustics are better. We sit on the floor by the French door with the lights off. Unfortunately, Ursula is taking noisy delight in a rawhide chew, so we can only make out every other word. Ernesto says he left the blah blah with Lisa Weinstein.

He says they had a dinner at wha wha, and then came back to the house but the party was over, so they went to blah blah's apartment. Detective Perez asks Ernesto if he ever had sexual relations with Bunny.

Boy, he doesn't waste any time.

Ernesto says she liked tantric massages. Detective Perez asks if Ernesto gave Bunny one that night.

Ernesto evokes Ricky Ricardo again. "We didn't see her. And there was no way, man, that I'm gonna knock on her door when I'm with the hot daughter."

"Makes sense," Detective Perez says.

Kevin and I nod our heads.

"What about that DuPont guy?" Ernesto says. "Have you talked to him?"

Kevin realizes that I ratted on Hudson and hits me while he has the chance.

Detective Perez thanks Ernesto, then yells, "Ok, Kevin and Emma, you can get off the floor now."

51

Graham—probably thinking I could use a free meal—calls and asks me out to dinner. Yay, he's back! I suppose I'd better focus on him in case Richard decides to opt for the Russian mail-order bride. Kevin and I spend a large portion of the day rummaging through my closet in search of the perfect dress—then we lower our expectations to a dress that's free of rips and stains. As I'm lacquering my face, Kevin proposes all sorts of lofty goals for my evening so as to ensure a future date. Most fall into the category of moderation in all things, including talking, drinking, and eating. Although I think that last one is just so he can eat my leftovers.

There is a gentle knock on the door. I peek out the kitchen window to see the gorgeous Graham wearing a navy jacket and tie. Kevin wastes no time in asking Graham about our dining destiny. Worried that Kevin will devise a ploy to tag along, Graham and I make a speedy exit.

As Graham drives down the lane, I tell him the police were over grilling us; I say we ratted on Ernesto, who fingered Hudson. With this new murder in my life, I'm starting to talk like a gangster. Graham says to be very careful about talking to the police. He's lovable when he's protective. I can't wait to be with him again tonight.

We pull up to the elegant and understated Colony Hotel. As we enter the lobby, we hear a golden voice flowing from the Royal Room. It is the charming Steve Tyrell singing, "I Can't Give You Anything but Love." Maybe it's a sign about a future with Graham.

After we are seated in the dining room and have our drinks, I get down to business. I tell Graham that Bunny had an in-home appointment to have her hair done that afternoon by Pierre. Expounding on my theory, I point out that he could have been the murderer because he once caused Bunny's hair to turn circus clown orange and she threatened to ruin him by telling everyone at the Everglades Club.

Graham wonders aloud if Bunny had the INS and hit men on speed dial.

I tell him Pierre is the very same Pierre who's married to Natasha.

Graham looks a little peeved. "How do you know all this?"

"Kevin is a new client of his salon."

"And did that just happen by accident?"

"We were curious as to whether he would be getting divorced from Natasha."

"Why would you think that?"

"Lisa told me Natasha is after Richard now that he's back on the market."

Graham looks crestfallen. "Has she been with him, too?"

"Too? Oh my gosh! Were you ever with Natasha?"

Graham sees the upset look on my face. "It was a long time ago."

"She's been married for a while, so that means you had sex with a married woman."

"I had no idea she was married," Graham says sincerely. "She didn't wear a ring, or complain all the time."

After dinner, we cut down Worth Avenue to the yacht. We decide to go there instead of my place because Kevin has a date with Hudson, and I have a feeling they will end up in my bed. When we land on the yacht, we hear Ping crying.

Graham looks concerned. "Ping, what are you doing here?"

Ping replies in mixed Mandarin. "Tai Boo. Trevor fire me. Wha bu yao fandian."

I really can't understand what he's saying. "Ping, where have you been living?"

"I live pool house. So have go lao mom's."

Graham translates. "Lao means old; must be Esther's place."

"I try hide. But lao mom find me under bed with Spanky girdles."

Graham pats his shoulder. "Calm down. I know you didn't do it. Ping, why don't you sleep here in one of the cabins?"

The sweet Graham puts Ping to bed in a tiny crew cabin on the yacht. Graham's never looked more adorable.

We relax on the back deck on the mid level, alone. Graham pulls out his guitar and plays me a David Gray song, 'This Year's Love." There's a breeze blowing and I am in heaven.

Ping calls out from his porthole. "You play "It Usual" for me?"

Graham laughs and tries to play the old Tom Jones song "It's Not Unusual." Ping comes out in his pajamas and rocks to the song. When the song's over, he puts his hand over his mouth in realization and says in his broken English, "Ah, you want alone, so have sex. I not listen."

He runs away with his hands over his ears.

Graham leads me inside to the galley. He opens the fridge and asks if I'd care for dessert.

"Sure, what do you have?" I peek in and see one piece of key lime pie wrapped in Saran wrap with a scrawled note: *No eat.*

Graham pulls out a can of Reddi-Wip. "Just this."

He takes my hand and leads me down the steps to "Lao Mom's" suite. The lights are dim as he pulls me onto the high, burl wood bed. His eyes stay on mine as he unbuttons his shirt and tosses it on a chair. He lifts my dress over my head, but it gets stuck. Now I can't see. He unhooks my black, lacey bra. "Do you like to be blindfolded?"

I say no, I want to see what's going on. His pants, heavy with cell phone, keys and wallet fall to the ground; I see that he is commando, and ready. He has a sexy tan line right below his flat abs, bisected by diagonal flexor muscles. Must have gotten a tan in the Bahamas. Who wants to be blindfolded and miss all the sexy man lines?

This feels different than the other times. He pulls down my lacey thong, and throws it across the room too. What's gotten into him? There's a narrow band of mirror along the side of the bed. I can see my whole horizontal naked body, and his naked torso as he kneels over me. He sprays whipped cream into my mouth and pushes his tongue into me. Got to get some of this stuff! He takes the whipped cream and writes something on my breasts and stomach.

I look down. "What does it say, 'I jov?'"

He laughs.

I say I can't read without my glasses. He laughs again. "Don't be running upstairs now. I'll read it to you."

He takes his finger and underlines the letters as he reads them. "I-L-O-V-E-Y-O-U."

"You do?" I'm shocked and flattered.

He slowly and lovingly licks the words from my breasts and belly and looks up at my face. Somehow, I think of Richard doing this.

"I don't want you doing this with Richard now."

He can read my mind.

284

Ahh! He's nibbling my ear, then kissing my neck, then my breasts. Ahh...he's licking me everywhere. No loud music this time and, yay, no dog watching. He's good. The second I "arrive" he pulls on my legs and hoists them over his shoulders. There's barely any clearance between the high bed and the low ceiling, which is thankfully padded. He wastes no time in entering the dollhouse. No questions, no asking, just in.

Wait, that sounds like an ad for Jiffy Lube.

He's not as tender as the last two times. I hope he doesn't become rough. That really scares me.

"Oh, I have forgotten condoms. I hope that's not going to be a problem."

We really should have a little chat about things like this.

I turn sideways to see his chiseled face in the mirror. "We're probably okay this week."

"Good," he pants.

I look around and remember the time I switched with Mrs. Weinstein and had this room. I hope Mrs. Weinstein doesn't mind we're doing this on her bed. Then I remember switching to Richard's cabin. That was when Richard saw me half-naked; seems like ten years ago.

Ahh. Graham is breathing hard and comes quickly. "Sorry, it was so sudden."

"Can we do that again?"

He shakes his head. "No, not just yet. Besides, we're out of whipped cream."

Right then Ping pounds on the door. "You eat whipped cream! Now have no for pie."

I wake up in an empty bed and venture to the back deck in a *No Woman No Cry* tee shirt. Graham is reading the paper and reaches up to kiss me on the lips. "How did you sleep?"

"Fine." I lift my shirt and put my sweet nipple in his mouth. "You forgot to lick the 'U' off."

Graham turns and says, "Ahem."

There is Ping, sulking in his pajamas.

52

Kevin greets me at the door as I stand there in my tee shirt, holding my dress. He shakes his head. "Look who the cat dragged in."

I pirouette in. "It was lovely. Well, I take that back—it was sensual and sexy."

"Do tell. But first I have to notify you we are completely out of food." He opens the cupboard and the fridge. "Look!"

Yes, the fridge is empty. In fact, the entire galaxy of our kitchen is vacant except for a can of peas and the bag of dog food. Now that we are newly flush, we wonder if we should dine at the Four Seasons or be semi-practical and go to Publix. We have lobster on our minds. Falling clearly into the semi-practical category, we opt for store-bought lobster; plus, it's a snap to make if you have them steam it for you.

When we get to the Publix, who do we see practically skipping up and down the cereal aisle? Trevor, with a huge smile on his face—a face previously reserved for scowls and sneers. Kevin and I wonder if Trevor, as well as the majority of Palm Beach, can trace their high spirits to the absence of Bunny Weinstein. I wager he's also happy Ping is out of the house. We bypass dawdling elders in the produce section to investigate further. Trevor says hello and cheerfully asks where the biscuits are. I ask if he means dog biscuits and he gives me a very British look, enunciating in an American accent, "Cookies." With some experience on the matter, I answer aisle six.

He explains that Ping always did the shopping.

Kevin butts in. "Do you think Ping killed Bunny Weinstein?"

The activity of the store comes to a screeching halt. It's so quiet you could hear the clams opening. Trevor pauses. "No, I believe the dog walker did it."

There's a collective gasp in the grocery store. A nearby sushi buyer blurts out, "But she didn't have a dog!"

Trevor responds to the woman. "That is correct, madam."

"Do you mean Ernesto, who spent the night with Lisa Weinstein, even though she is newly engaged to the heir to the Johnny Holmes Sausage fortune?" I say to Trevor.

"Precisely," Trevor says as he puts leeks in his basket. "It's all on the security tape."

Kevin gets really fidgety. "Umm. Was I on there?"

"Would you be referring to the moment where you dropped the entire duck on the floor and then wiped in on your apron before serving it to the guests?" Trevor says with a straight face. "Or are you referring to your escapade in the master's library where you were trying to woo Mr. DuPont?"

Kevin gets more nervous. Finally, Trevor relieves him by adding, "Unfortunately, the power outages compromised many sequences of the security tapes, so many of your antics have not been preserved."

Kevin lets out a sigh. "There is a God."

A nosy cantaloupe buyer interrupts. "So, what's on the tape? Does it show Ernesto killing her?"

"I'm afraid not," Trevor says. He walks away from her and says to us, "Then we'd all be off the suspect list."

"Well, what's on it?" Kevin blurts.

"Let's just say the tape captures Ernesto hiding in her wardrobe with helium balloons."

I'm concerned. "Did Richard see the tape?"

"Part of being a good butler is to protect the feelings of the master; only the police have seen it."

"I saw a gun at Ernesto's house," Kevin tattles.

"But Madam Weinstein was not shot," Trevor whispers.

The other shoppers repeat him, like in an opera: "She was not shot."

Trevor smiles and asks how Irene is, then offers, "Why don't you two ladies stop by on Thursday?"

"Okay, what time?" Kevin replies.

"I was referring to Miss Budnjk and Ms. Ahr."

"Oh."

"I suppose it would be all right; we could use your culinary services."

"Even better! That way I can drink and get paid."

While we are checking out of the grocery line, we spot the ubiquitous Natasha in another checkout. I wave to her, and she smiles and gives a hearty wave back. She must have new happy meds, I suspect. She's wearing a trench coat again, making me think she gets cold wearing all that see-through clothing.

I prompt Kevin to see what she's buying, thinking it could reveal plans to ditch her husband and steal my future one. Like a good deputy, he does and reports back with amazing detail: snack size Butterfingers, Snyder's of Hanover jalapeno pretzel pieces, Stouffer's family size lasagna, and Claussen bread 'n butter pickles. No wonder she gets an occasional belly, with all that sodium.

53

Thursday rolls around quickly, the way Mondays tend to, but with much more whimsy. Irene, wearing an iridescent green caftan, is my wingman—or better, flylady—as we make our way to Richard's house. Kevin answers the door wearing a professional chef's outfit, except for his hat, which is more like a fez with a pom-pom on top.

"Welcome to Maison Weinstein."

Irene toddles past him like she owns the place. "How's it going?"

Kevin, talking to the back of her head, says, "The police were here again. Figures I'd be here when they show up."

I follow Kevin's pom-pom and Irene's flying caftan into the kitchen. "What do they want now?"

"They wanted to look in the refrigerator again, but I think that Rusty was just hungry. And they wanted to look at old security tapes. God, I hope they don't find the one from homely twin day."

Kevin is clearly not ready for guests, as evidenced by the state of the kitchen, which could only be described as immaculate. Irene, who long ago forwent decorum, rummages through the cupboards, unearthing a jar of olives and a box of Triscuits.

Enjoying the comfort of the Weinstein kitchen, I say, "I sure hope Richard wasn't around today in case they found tapes of Ernesto and Bunny."

"No, Richard went to pick up his mother. He worries that when she drives she will slowly kill people; I guess he thinks sudden death is better."

Irene pops a cracker in her mouth. "Emma told me that you are suspects."

Kevin is trying to open the jar of queen-sized olives, struggling like an old lady. "Hello? You are too, Irene."

Irene nearly falls off her bar stool. "I am?"

"Oh, I think you just got thrown in the group because you were here after the party," I say. "Didn't they tell you?"

"No. Captain Lacey said to stick around, but I thought it was because he likes me."

Changing the subject, I ask Kevin if Graham is here.

"Well, besides trying to prepare for a soirée, and assisting in a police investigation, it's not part of my job to keep track of the marine staff."

When I head out of the kitchen to look for Graham, Kevin finally offers, "I think he's on the yacht."

"Where's Trevor?" Irene inquires, fluffing her caftan wings.

"He went to the yacht to try to persuade Ping to come back. He was supposed to help me."

Irene spots two egrets mating by the Intracoastal, and gestures for us to relocate the party outside. Despite the serene setting, Kevin's *Night of the Iguana* festival is not going as planned. It seems someone (Kevin) drank all the Weinsteins' Grand Marnier last week; the avocados are not ripe, and the salsa fell off the roof of the car. So far, it's just Irene and me, making do with a bottle of tequila and a bag of chips.

Richard saunters out to the terrace. "Hello Irene. You are looking well."

Mrs. Weinstein joins us. "What kind of party is this? Are you drinking from a bottle of tequila?"

291

"It's Patrón, and we're pouring it into glasses first," Irene explains.

"It's your fault for yelling at Ping," Mrs. Weinstein says to Richard. "Trevor had to use Kevin to cook."

Defending Kevin, I say, "It's supposed to be a Richard Burton, *Night of the Iguana* theme."

"Okay, I can put up with that, as long as there are schoolmarms and nymphets," Richard says.

Right then, we look up and see Ping stomping into the house in his ladies shoes, trailed by a grinning Trevor.

"He's back," Richard says with a huge smile.

Mrs. Weinstein licks the salt from her hand and downs a shot of tequila. "Did you know I found him hiding under my bed? The good news is I found this girdle I'd lost in 1993."

Not wanting to hear any more girdle tales, I ask Trevor, "Did you see Graham on the boat?"

"I believe I might have," Trevor says awkwardly.

"Is he coming back for the party?" Richard asks.

Trevor replies that Graham has been detained with boating matters. "He's required to take the yacht to Nassau sometime this week; it seems there's an issue with the paperwork in the Bahamian flagging."

Sometimes it's handy to love two men in the same household. You can find out a lot.

Mrs. Weinstein takes a sip and announces, "Lisa has planned her wedding on the weekend of the 26th of June in Nantucket. Her brother, Mark, is flying in this weekend to help with the details."

Kevin returns with a small cracked plate of saltines and butter. "I'd love to go."

"We'll have to have the wedding here if the police don't wrap this up by then," Richard says ruefully.

Mrs. Weinstein pours herself more salt and tequila. "I don't mind, but none of my friends would be caught dead in Palm Beach off season."

"If you end up having it here, I could probably arrange my catering schedule," Kevin says.

"It had better not come to that," Richard says.

Trevor unexpectedly appears with a silver tray of champagne, caviar, and a smirk.

Feeling the need to veer off Kevin's failed catering skills, I blurt out, "I have an idea." Then I realize I'd better test it out on someone first. "No, I'll tell you later."

"People my age don't have later," Mrs. Weinstein retorts. "Tell us now."

"I was thinking, if we need to help expedite this investigation, we could invite all the suspects out on the boat. We'll ask prying questions, put together the clues, and in no time find our culprit."

"Better bring an extra case of truth serum," Mrs. Weinstein says.

"That would be a lot of people, if we count everyone with a motive," Richard says.

"We will just invite the official suspects," Trevor says. "I'll do a guest count. Let's see, Richard, Esther, Graham, Ping, Lisa, Ernesto, Emma, Mr. DuPont, Irene, Pudge and myself."

Irene, pouring tequila into her champagne, says, "It sounded like fun, until you invited Pudge."

"And don't forget the suspicious Natasha," I add. Right after I say it, I regret it.

"What day is this?" Kevin asks excitedly. "My new Ralph Lauren white linen suit will be ready soon, and I was looking for the right occasion to wear it."

"But you aren't one of the named suspects," Mrs. Weinstein points out.

Kevin looks forlorn. "But I could help with the questioning and establishing of motives. My pants will be ready by the weekend."

Richard, after a long consideration, finally says, "All right let's do it. We have to take the boat to the Bahamas anyway."

Like he had a choice.

"Emma, what a brilliant idea," he adds. "No one gets off the boat until we figure out who did this."

Mrs. Weinstein, now a little sauced, asks, "When is this?"

Everyone responds in unison. "This weekend, after Kevin's pants are ready."

Now that everyone is on board with the plan, the guest list and the date, Kevin suggests we devise a theme. He says we will need it to disguise the true intent of the party. Without much debate, and inspired by Kevin's pants, it's decided that it will be a Great Gatsby theme. As everyone prattles away with glamorous ideas, I realize all this diversion is unnecessary, as most of us know of the mission.

Plus, Kevin has a genetic inability to contain any secret. We all decide not to tell Graham of our true intent for the cruise. He'll think it's a crazy idea.

54

After much planning (chatter) on Kevin's part, the day of the Great Gatsby party has arrived. Kevin left early to drop my baby off at an out-of-town kennel—or so I thought. As we board the yacht, the first thing I notice is that Ursula is here. And someone, possibly with the help of the haberdashing Irene, has taped a chef's hat to my dog's head. As much as I enjoy having my precious dog around, I worry she'll do damage. I spy the culprit, Kevin, wearing a matching chef's hat.

Ping enters the salon and announces, "I now guest. Kevin cook for everybody." Ping orders a Mai Tai from Trevor, who ignores him. Wanting to keep in good stead with the staff, and feeling a little guilty about the whipped cream incident, I make Ping his drink. At least, I think that's what he wanted—all Chinese words sound like someone demanding a cocktail. "Ni Yao Mai Mai."

Natasha apparently missed the Gatsby memo and is wearing a trench coat. She's probably stark naked underneath, and will surely find just the right moment to feign discomfort and shed the Burberry. She looks a little bloated, so maybe that's why she's wearing it; I'd be suspicious if this sort of thing didn't happen to me all the time. Mrs. Weinstein toddles over the gangplank wearing gigantic pearls and a flapper dress, which does not cover her flapper arms. She doesn't seem to care as she tirelessly shoos Natasha away from Richard.

Pudge, looking like morning was invented in spite of her, plops down next to Richard in the salon wearing a nice beaded number. Mrs. Weinstein, never resting from her quest to safeguard her son, directs Pudge to her cabin by saying, "Hurry, it's first come first serve; or you have to share a crew cabin with Ping." Pudge flies down the stairs with such vitality we all speculate she must have actually eaten something today.

Next, I see a guest in a blonde wig and sunglasses, shuffling over the bridge. A mystery suspect? Didn't see this coming. Finally, the new suspect says in a raspy voice, "What? Blondes have more fun." It's Irene.

I'm seated on the white sofa between Richard and Irene. Trevor serves scones with orange marmalade and clotted cream. All is calm until Graham begins a serious conversation with Richard involving the timing of the tide. Evidently we need to leave, but Lisa and Ernesto are noticeably absent. Hmm. In my little mental calculation, this gives them extra check marks in the "murderer" column.

We wait over an hour, at which point Trevor is ordered by the temperamental crowd to pop the bubbly. This is what can be expected of a group who is easily bored without our spirits. I'm perfectly content sitting here in the main salon with an open view of the golden aft deck overlooking turquoise waters. Ah. It was an auspicious move to come to Palm Beach—that is, except for my continuous poverty and the pesky little murder situation. I wonder how this cruise will turn out. Maybe there will be a fistfight over my heart, hopefully between Richard and Graham. Richard will say he loves me more, but I'll have wild sex with Graham. Hudson will propose to Kevin, and maybe offer to buy the Weinstein residence. And someone will figure out who murdered Bunny and we'll all be free. Yes, that is what I predict.

Now that no one cares anymore, Lisa and Ernesto appear. They galumph down the dock to the side of the yacht, looking noticeably disheveled—so much so, everyone points and says so. This is what happens when angry mobs are kept waiting and given champagne. Ursula takes this moment to bark vehemently at them, presumably for holding up the show. Lisa tells us she's not coming, her dog is ill, and heads back down the dock. Richard says he's relieved, as there's no need to get her too involved. Mrs. Weinstein whispers to me that she arranged for the dog to appear to be sick. I wonder how one does such a thing.

After dramatic nautical exercises involving engine noises, yelling and dock lines—we depart.

Forgetting that we may have a murderer on board, I'm worried about going out to sea with this inebriated group.

Graham disappears to the wheelhouse; Kevin, Trevor and Ping squabble in the galley, and Natasha goes straight to her cabin, with a wedge of chocolate cake. I make a mental note to switch to her diet of salt, cheese and cake. Irene borrows Ursula and goes down to her cabin for a late morning pug nap.

Mrs. Weinstein, wasting no time, draws names from a silver bowl on the dining room table. With no luck fishing for Ernesto's card—probably because he doesn't have a 'dog-sitter, masseuse, security guard' card, she simply calls him in to the main salon. Richard calls out from the galley, "No waterboarding now, Mother."

Mrs. Weinstein has somehow elected herself as chief interrogator. Through her thick, round glasses, she zeros in on her first subject's darks eyes. "So, Ernesto, where does your family come from?"

"Peru."

I can't help but butt in. "I thought you said you were from Brazil."

"We're from Brazil and Peru," Ernesto coolly explains.

Mrs. Weinstein strikes, like she's Barbara Walters. "When did you start the affair with Bunny Weinstein?"

Ernesto nearly spits out his morning beer and looks around to see where Richard is. "I didn't start it. She started it when she said she'd pay extra for the deluxe massage."

Whoa. I'm a little worried Mrs. Weinstein will ask what that entails, then the next thing we know she'll be in a cabin with Ernesto.

Mrs. Weinstein leans in. "Tell me about the night she died."

Ernesto leans back. "I was at the backyard party, then I was called upstairs, but I didn't want to do anything. I like Lisa now. That was the last time I saw her."

"I'm curious, where was Pudge?" Mrs. Weinstein says out of the blue.

"As I was getting ready to leave, I saw her run back into the house. Maybe she did it."

Volunteering as co-interrogator, I ask, "We gave her a ride, so this must have been just before."

"She and one of the twins went upstairs to fix their lipstick and stuff."

I instantly think of the old homely twins, secretly hoping they will buy the house despite the recent stigma.

Mrs. Weinstein looks sideways. "What twins?"

"Didn't you know?" Ernesto says. "Natasha has an identical twin."

Mrs. Weinstein chokes on her drink. "Oh, thank god. I thought I was getting early Alzheimer's."

Twins?

Richard is standing in the doorway. "This explains the personality variances."

The light bulb goes off in my head. "And why Natasha turns up everywhere."

"They share a green card; that's why they both call themselves Natasha," Ernesto continues, "and both pretend to be married to Pierre..."

I interrupt him. "Oh my god. Did you tell the police this?"

298

Mrs. Weinstein has processed this already. "That's the perfect alibi. One Natasha at the ball; one Natasha killing Bunny."

Bursting with this fascinating bit of news, I run into the galley to tell Kevin. The engine noise has tapered, and all on board can hear his high-pitched squeal. "So I'm not crazy! I wonder if Graham knows this."

Right then we hear the yacht throttle down to neutral. Then we see Graham standing in the galley with his arms crossed.

"I wonder if Graham knows what?" says Graham, waiting for Kevin to respond.

We follow Kevin to the salon as he rubs his hands on his apron, brimming with excitement as he relays the juicy gossip. "Natasha has an identical twin also named Natasha!"

Graham's forehead lifts an entire inch at the shock of it all. Then he tips his head and appears to be replaying the Graham and Natasha tape. "You've got to be kidding."

Kevin is practically jumping up and down. "Did you have a ménage à trois?"

Graham gets that adorable sad look where his eyebrows turn down as he pauses. "I think if I was having my way with two at the same time, I would have bloody known they were twins."

"It's easy to tell them apart," Ernesto explains calmly. "One is pregnant and one isn't."

Graham is clearly shocked and confused.

"Yeah," I say, "well the pregnant one must be the one married to Pierre."

Right then Natasha appears, sans jacket, looking very pregnant.

Now petrified, Graham exclaims, "There really are two of you!"

"So what if I have a twin?" Natasha says defensively. "I came to visit my sister and decided to stay."

Richard, attempting to get things straight, says, "But you can't both be Natasha. Are you the one married to Pierre?"

Natasha points to Graham. "No, I'm single. And I think this is his baby."

Graham doubles over. "Dear god."

"It's most likely yours, but it could be Pierre's."

"You shtupped your sister's husband?" Mrs. Weinstein quips.

"He was my boyfriend first. My sister stole him from me."

"Nice girls," Graham says.

"You should know— you were with both of us."

Trevor enters carrying a tray of tea sandwiches. "This is better than *Downton Abbey.*

"Bloody fucking unbelievable," Graham mutters.

Kevin feels the need to conjecture out loud. "Can you imagine if Graham got both of them pregnant? And imagine if he got both of them pregnant with twins?"

"Shut up, Kevin," Graham and Richard say in unison.

Mrs. Weinstein takes this moment to leave the room. I'm not sure if this is part of her interrogation tactic, or if she just has to whiz.

"And no, neither my sister or I killed Bunny. We think Esther did it."

The gang reels back at the thought.

"It's wrong to accuse an elder lady," Trevor says.

"What makes you say that?" Kevin asks.

"Hello? Look at her," Ernesto adds his two cents.

"Now, Natasha," Richard asks, "why would you suspect my dear old mother?"

Kevin, nibbling on one of Trevor's expertly trimmed tea sandwiches, interrupts. "Well, she has the least to lose by getting caught—at her age a life sentence would be, what, six months to a year?"

"Kevin, don't you have some catering to do?" Richard huffs.

Natasha backs herself onto the sofa. "When Pudge and my sister left to go to the ball, she said Esther came back to the house because she left her Hermes scarf; I saw her up in the window and it looked like she was trying to strangle Bunny with it."

"You've got it all wrong, Natasha," Mrs. Weinstein says from the doorway. "It was a Chanel scarf." Then she turns and walks away.

We all look at each other.

Graham asks for a word with Natasha, meaning he wants us all to leave; we understand this, but we want to hear the gossip, so we linger.

"Never mind, I've got to tend to the boat," he says, as he pulls Natasha to the wheelhouse.

Kevin grabs my hand. "That's okay, I need some help in the galley with the baklava."

I follow him. "You're making baklava?"

301

"No, I just like to say the word. If we open the spice cabinet door, we can hear up into the command center room."

Kevin opens the cupboard door and we each quietly pretend we're looking for something. He's right; we can hear into the wheelhouse even though Graham has shut the door.

"Let me see if I have this straight," Graham says firmly to Natasha. "You're saying I made love to you nine months ago?"

"Yes; don't you remember?"

"So that wasn't you these past few months."

"That was my sister. I can't believe you could do that!"

Kevin and I gape to each other in quiet shock.

I feel breath on my neck and turn to see Trevor hovering right behind us.

Graham lets out and audible sigh. "But you also had relations with Pierre nine months ago?"

"Yes, it's either you or Pierre who is the baby's father. Well, most likely."

"Most likely? There were others?"

It seems our little Natasha is pretty, but not too smart—getting pregnant *and* not knowing who the father is. Or maybe she's really smart and will end up married with a cute baby.

"I think it happened when we were in Harbour Island."

"So the two of you each did the two of us. Well that's lovely. Just lovely."

Kevin, Trevor and I all muffle our shock. Then we see the pregnant Natasha waddle by the galley.

"You can all come out of the pantry now," Graham calls out.

Kevin, Ping and Trevor make themselves busy. Graham calls out to me, so I enter the not so private wheelhouse.

He looks at me with his sad eyes. "Emma, I'm really sorry about all this. It's a bit of a mess."

Not knowing quite what I say, I muster a jolly, "Happens all the time."

Graham sighs. "Really? Impregnating an illegal Russian twin who's having an affair with her sister's husband, happens all the time?"

Graham gets serious. "Once the baby is born, they'll do a paternity test; hopefully it's not my baby."

I ponder what to say. As much as I think I want a baby, do I want one with someone so cavalier about accepting one?

Kevin appears in the doorway, pretending to need something. "But what if it *is* your baby?" he asks Graham.

"I suppose the worst case scenario would be that it's my baby—or worse my twins, and that she's the murderer and the twins will grow up to be little murderers." Graham lets out a hearty laugh, then reins it in when he starts to think about it.

Trevor saves us. "Kevin, I believe you are needed in the galley."

After Kevin shuffles off, Graham puts his hands on my hips. "I wish you were the one who was pregnant."

Kevin shrieks an uncontrollable happy shriek in the kitchen.

When I return to the salon, I find Ursula sitting upright at the dining room table. Mrs. Weinstein, the local pug whisperer, declares, "Ursula thinks she's a person. I'll bet she thinks she's the reincarnation of Winston Churchill."

I notice that Mrs. Weinstein is re-tying her scarf in a crafty knot. What if *she* murdered Bunny? She certainly hated her. Kevin is right; she's got nothing to lose, as she'd probably die before she finished her court appeals.

55

Trevor has set the table for lunch for six, plus Winston, and is pouring a lovely Chateau d'Esclans rosé in tall crystal glasses. Kevin and Ping are serving Dover sole and risotto in a wrangling sort of manner. Through the tinted sliding door, I see another table set out back, where Ernesto and Hudson are seated at the children's table; they are given plastic forks and cups.

Natasha, having let the cat out of the bag, must not feel the need to hide in her cabin, and has now beached herself on a wide lounge chair on the aft deck.

Back inside the main salon, Richard pats the seat next to him. "Here, Emma, sit next to me."

I look at him and wonder if he's ever had sex with any of the Natashas. I'll be sure to notice if he pays attention to her and her belly. Suddenly, Marilyn Monroe emerges from the lower staircase—then we recognize the saggy face of Irene under the full platinum head of hair. Irene plops down. "This is fun! Compared to cancer, that is. I haven't been out of the house in weeks."

Pudge injects herself on the other side of Richard; without missing a beat, she says to Irene, "That's not true. You were at the cocktail party."

Irene, waving her hands to disburse the scent, says, "Yes, but I never made it to the ball."

Pudge apparently decides to take over as *The Closer*. "How long did you stay at Richard's house?"

"Trevor made me some green Jell-O just before he went to the ball. I had to wait for it to set."

Trevor is hovering nearby. "That's correct."

"I've lost track. So you and Natasha left before Irene?" Richard asks Pudge.

I'm nervously wondering where Richard is going with this.

"Yes, which means Irene was the last to see Bunny," Pudge declares.

Although Irene looks furious, I'm glad to see color in her face that isn't drawn on with a brush.

Fuming, Irene says, "Well, even though I'm not Bunny's greatest fan, I couldn't let her to go to the ball with that big black hair sprouting from her upper lip."

"I noticed that too," Kevin says.

Mrs. Weinstein laughs. "How could you miss it?"

"It was growing straight out, like a wire. She probably couldn't see it looking straight on—like that time you had one, Emma, and you only saw it from the passenger side mirror and it looked like a car antenna."

I shoot an outraged glance at Kevin.

Irene, trying to recover, says, "Now I remember! I hadn't realized that Kevin had taken Dr. Phil to the ball, so I was searching the house and ended up in Bunny's bedroom. There she was, trying to catch the whisker."

Pudge, looking smug until she drops a mound of risotto on her lap, says to Irene, "So, you admit you were the last to see her alive."

"Yes, Pudge, but I certainly didn't kill her. I tried to help her pull out the whisker, but I didn't have my glasses; I'd left them by the harp. So I peeled off some tape from my bracelet and put it on her lip."

"Everyone knows duct tape is your calling card," Kevin says.

"Well, I planned to rip it right off, but she wouldn't let me."

Mrs. Weinstein lets out a big, opened-mouth laugh. "She just had Gore-Tex put in her lip. No secrets in this town."

"She said she was going to use olive oil to get it off, so I left. I didn't feel like going to the ball, so I just went home."

Curious, I ask, "Was anyone left at the house besides Bunny?"

"I believe that left Ping," says Trevor.

Ping runs out of the galley with a cleaver in his hand yelling, "I not kill her. Her bell ring. I run up. I see tape mouth but no sound come out. She look like she want drink tea. I go get knife."

I say, "That's why you were running up the stairs with a knife on the security tape."

"She not let me cut tape off face. She make me poke hole and get straw; but she see sugar on bottom and no want drink tea."

Pudge says, "Likely story. We've got the cook who hated her, on tape with a knife. Can we go home now?"

Ping takes off his apron. "I re-quit."

We see Trevor standing in the doorway with a lobster pot. He does not look amused. In a moment, we see my dog's head pop out the top like a jack-in-the-box.

"Miss Budnjk, it seems your delightful little pet has fallen into my sticky pudding. I had it cooling on the side deck as a surprise for Irene, and now it's ruined!"

"Oh. No! I'm so sorry."

After I finish helping Trevor wipe pudding off my dog's hind legs, I return to the salon.

"I've got it," Richard says, after thoughtful reflection. "That explains the petechial hemorrhage caused by temporary suffocation."

"What sticky pudding?"

"No, the duct tape."

"But what about the electrical burns on her arm?" Irene asks.

"Did the police tell you that?"

"No, I saw them on her arm when I had to identify her."

"Isn't Lisa an electrical engineer?" Kevin asks. "What does she think happened?"

Richard gives Kevin a look. "Let's leave Lisa out of this."

Unwisely, Pudge reveals, "I saw Lisa go up to her wing with an extension cord during the party."

Richard huffs. "Bunny asked her for it. She needed sixteen outlets for all of her devices." He glares at Pudge and leaves.

Irene pours some of the fine rosé in her large, now empty water glass. "I'm surprised the house hasn't caught on fire yet."

"I am surprised she hasn't electrocuted herself," Kevin quips as he heads out to the back deck.

"Perhaps," Trevor says helpfully, "she's the one who blew the circuit breakers."

Pudge looks around to ensure Richard is out of ear shot. "Okay, if it's not Ping, then I think the spooky daughter did it."

Like she's in Vegas, Irene throws wadded up cash on the table and says, "Why don't we have a bet? I bet a hundred that DuPont guy did it."

Pudge, sounding a little tipsy, points to Irene. "I changed my mind. I'll bet $500 that you did it."

Irene defiantly stands up in her royal caftan. "I know I didn't do it. So, you're on."

Trevor, balancing a tray of petit fours, says without missing a beat, "I'm in. I'll bet Kevin did it."

The entire room chants, "No! Kevin liked Bunny!"

Trevor sighs patiently. "But he's so inept he may have done it by accident."

"I hate to say it," Mrs. Weinstein whispers in her deep smoker's voice, "but as much as I adore Graham, he looks very suspicious. He stopped by the house during the ball, and she did try to get him deported. And she got him fired from his singing gig."

I've never been mad at Mrs. Weinstein, until now. "I'm sure Graham wouldn't kill anyone."

"Well, in that case, we'd better come up with an alibi for him. Emma, why don't you say you were doing the hokey pokey with Graham that night too?"

"As much as I'd like that in the newspapers," I say sarcastically, "he says he was on the boat."

"Besides, Emma spent the night with Richard," Pudge says.

Mrs. Weinstein pulls down her glass and smiles. "Was that in the papers?"

"I didn't sleep with Richard," I quickly say to the mixed company.

The calculating Pudge swirls her champagne. "How very convenient for you that Bunny's out of the way. I'm changing my bet to Emma."

I look at Pudge and see the evil that she is. She's the Bunny runner up.

"Well, I'm taking my hundred off DuPont and putting it on you, Pudge," Irene says.

309

Kevin walks in and asks what Irene is talking about.

Irene throws a pile of crumpled twenty-dollar bills into the pile. "I used to think DuPont was the murderer, but now I'm changing my bet to Pudge."

Pudge stomps her long foot. "I'd never try to kill Bunny."

"Yes, you did," Kevin says. "Remember you were trying to give her salmonella?"

Mrs. Weinstein waves her blue veined hand. "Oh, great idea; I never thought of that. That way everyone would think it was Kevin's salmonella salmon. Say, this sounds like a conspiracy between Kevin and Pudge."

"What?!" Kevin shrieks. "I have never knowingly poisoned anyone with salmonella. Botulism, yes, but never salmonella."

Everyone nods their heads, and Kevin feels the need to divert attention to another culprit. "I think Ernesto did it."

Hudson walks in looking pompous and sweaty. "I think the piano player did it."

There is sudden chorus of, "What piano player?"

"Yes, we heard a piano player in the house that night. But I think it could have just been Bunny on her last recital." Kevin says.

Irene shuffles across the room with her huge pocketbook and pulls out a wallet with a frog clasp and starts peeling off new crisp tens. "Need change for a hundred?" she asks Kevin?

Richard returns from the upper deck. "What are you wagering, Irene?"

Irene, looking mortified, rolls up the crisp tens and deposits them in her brassiere.

"It must be something, with all that money on the table," Richard says softly.

For once, all tongues come to a halt.

Finally Hudson explains. "They're placing wagers on who killed your wife."

Richard mutters, "That's very thoughtful of you." He goes out the side door without looking at us.

I feel awful, and I'm glad I didn't have any cash in my brassiere. Thinking he needs a friend right now, I follow him out to the deck.

He looks out at the sea. "I can't remember whose idea this was, but it was foolish to come out here."

"I think it was Kevin's; remember he had those pants he wanted to wear?"

"Who knows who killed her. Maybe I don't want to know."

All of a sudden, I have a dark jagged feeling that Richard might have killed is wife. He had the most motive. What if he killed her while I was sleeping in the green room? That would be awful if he had to go to jail—after the prison term of having to live with her all these years.

The ocean is spraying a salty mist on our faces; Richard gently wipes my face with his sleeve. I look into his light blue eyes and see the pain. What was dark and jagged has turned smooth and light.

Richard pulls me in and kisses me on the lips. It is so gentle, I can feel the softness of his lips—and the softness of his soul. I quickly look back to see if anyone saw. Sure enough, there's ol' Mrs. Weinstein with her nose up to the glass giving a thumbs up.

Then I look and see Graham at the wheel. He must have just witnessed the kiss too. I wonder if I should I give up on Graham?

"Better head back inside," he says, "it might be a bit rough for you two."

As we enter the wheelhouse, we hear a high-pitched scream. I assume it's Kevin, but Richard says it's Ping. Then we hear an excited, "Piaoliang nushi LEAK wha da hongsa xie!"

Graham interprets. "Pretty lady leaking something red."

Pretty lady must be Natasha. "He must mean blood," Richards deduces.

56

Richard races up the stairs. When I follow him, I see Natasha sprawled out on the white padded lounge. We are greeted by a hopping Ping— who is pointing to his red suede shoes.

Ping calms down enough for broken English. "She wet best shoes." I see Esther blocking the bottom of the stairs, forcing Graham to climb up over the rail from the lower deck. I guess Ping was manning the wheel. Natasha is breathing hard and moaning in agony. There is no blood; the red must mean his Prada lady shoes.

"I think she's in labor," Richard says.

Judging from the look on Graham's face, I'd say he's in shock.

"Graham, how long before we can get to shore?" Richard asks.

He doesn't answer. Perhaps he is calculating nautical speeds—or processing that he is about to be a father.

"Kevin," Richard calls down in an urgent tone, "get my medical bag from my cabin."

Richard looks at Graham and asks, "How long to the nearest medical facility?"

Finally Graham says, "About two hours to Nassau, four if we head back to Florida."

"Throttle up to Nassau; I don't want her to deliver on the boat."

"How long until she delivers?"

"I can't tell without doing a pelvic exam."

"Why the hell did you get on this boat?" Graham yells at Natasha.

"I was afraid to have the baby at home in case it looked like Pierre," Natasha yells back.

"They have these places in America," I say, "they are called hospitals."

"I don't have insurance. And I don't want to be deported."

"Kevin, how's that bag coming?" Richard yells. "And bring up clean sheets. Nothing the dog slept on."

We can hear Kevin telling everyone, "Natasha's having her baby."

Soon Irene and Mrs. Weinstein join us on the upper deck with their drinks, like they're at a Red Hats party.

"Everyone, back downstairs," Richard commands.

I try to hightail it, but Mrs. Weinstein is blocking the stairs. Richard grabs the corner of my skirt. "You stay, Emma."

"But shouldn't Graham help you? He's the one who started this mess."

"Graham, as much as I'd like you here, we need you to man the boat."

Graham heads down the stairs. "I can steer from the fly bridge once I sync the system up here."

"Emma," Richard says, "you're going help me; fathers-to-be make terrible assistants."

Mrs. Weinstein flops her wrist in an indifferent wave. "I've seen my share of births. It's an awful mess. Come on, girls."

I'm left alone with Richard and the moaning Natasha.

"Natasha, do you want to be moved downstairs?" Richard asks. "We can get you to a cabin."

Natasha starts to get up and falls.

"Let's just have you stay here."

Kevin finally emerges with Richard's medical bag and a pile of sheets. "I brought two sets. I don't think you want that baby goo all over your 900 thread count Pratesi sheets, so I took these from Ping's bed." They are Spider-Man sheets.

"Fine. Thank you." Richard pulls out his stethoscope and puts it to Natasha's belly. He gets an adorable little smile. "The baby has a good heart rate." He then calmly takes Natasha's blood pressure.

Kevin takes the opportunity to inquire, "So, Natasha, whose baby do you think it is? You know, if you had to narrow it down."

Natasha glares at him.

"That will be all Kevin," Richard pronounces.

We hear Kevin go downstairs and ask, "Hey, Irene, do you want to start another bet?"

"Natasha, it's just us now," Richard says. "I'm going to drape this sheet over you and take a look."

She smiles up at Richard and pulls a seductive move with her hips as she tries to pull down her panties. She can't quite reach, so Richard has to give them a yank. Without batting an eye, he puts his fingers and thumb under the sheet.

He pats her knee. "Natasha, I'd say you are dilated over nine centimeters, but not yet crowning."

"Is that good or bad?" I ask.

"It means she could deliver soon."

We look out at the waves and hear the engines roar.

"Natasha," Richard says urgently, "we really need to get to a hospital. I don't know any of your medical background and there could be complications. You really shouldn't have come on the boat."

"Are we in the United States?"

"I believe we're in Bahamian waters."

Natasha folds the sheet around herself. "I want my baby to be an American."

"Well, perhaps you should have thought of that sooner," I can't help but say.

Richard taps my hand. "Now, now, Emma." He then takes the sheets and starts making a little hammock under Natasha's legs, all the while asking her nosy questions like, *Is this your first full term pregnancy? Do you have any medical issues?*

He's so sexy.

Kevin pokes his head out the spiral staircase and asks if we need anything.

"No thank you; we'll call you in case we do," Richard says in a distracted tone.

"I can stay up there," Kevin says helpfully. "What if the baby pops out looking just like Graham?" Kevin wonders aloud to no one in particular.

Richard, now irritated, tells him to go back downstairs. Then Richard softens his tone and suggests Kevin find some soothing music for us.

Kevin seems to take on the role with serious contemplation. In no time, he announces he has compiled a soundtrack for our trip. He blasts the lively Phil Collins song, "We Wait and We Wonder."

The sun is setting on Natasha, and I have to admit she looks lovely with the glistening patina. She says she is sorry. I wonder for what: having sex with Graham? Having his baby? It's like she's a different person; oh wait, she is. This must be the nice Natasha.

Graham comes up and starts pressing buttons and levers on the helm station on the top deck.

He keeps looking back at Natasha, then makes a little sheepish smile at me. He looks back to Richard. "I've checked our location; unfortunately, we have an easterly wind and the Gulf Stream is pulling us north at four knots per hour, so it will be longer than I thought to take her to Nassau, even if we maintain eighteen knots."

"She's pretty far along, so it will be close."

Richard asks Natasha some more questions that sound very personal to me, so I cover my ears.

While Richard is busy holding her hand and she's busy sweating bullets, I wonder what everyone is doing downstairs. The mid-deck guests are so gossipy, that I imagine that those of us on the top deck have gone up in status to prime murder suspects.

Natasha has another contraction—this one very loud. Even Graham can hear it over the engine noise. He looks back with that sad look, which is combined with his new panicked look. Richard lifts the sheet over Natasha again and takes a peek.

I must say it's rather sexy the way he has his hands on her knees and pops his head under the sheet for a peek. When all this is over, I will remember to add sheet peeping to my repertoire. Oh, how my mind wanders. I'm glad Richard can't read minds.

Right then Richard gives me a little wink.

Graham catches this, and Richard suddenly asks him about the yacht's emergency kit. Richard writes down a list of items for me to gather. Zipping past the main salon, I observe the usual suspects lounging around with apparently nothing more important to do than drink and point fingers. There's a pile of money on the dining room table, causing me to suspect they've resumed their nasty gambling habits. Ernesto and Hudson are not in the salon; I imagine they have gone up higher on the suspect list.

I am to summon Kevin to take over as nurse. In his best *Gone with the Wind* imitation of Prissy, he mimics, "Miss Scarlett, I don't know nothing 'bout birthing no babies."

"Well then help me find the items on my list." I read off: "plastic zip ties, latex gloves, warm towels, fishing line."

"So, having a baby is like going fishing?" He pokes me, "What if it's his baby?"

"How can I get mad at him? He knew her before he knew me."

"Would you say, exactly nine months before he knew you?"

"I would have never guessed she's that far along. My stomach's bigger the morning."

"She looks like a thin woman who ate a watermelon," Kevin opines.

"Well, let's just hope the watermelon doesn't look like Graham."

"I think if it's his baby, you should go for Richard. I mean, now that he's single and all that."

"Kevin! Help me find the stuff." We continue to poke around and I ask how things are going with Hudson.

"He heard that four people had bets on him as the murderer, so he's below deck in exile with his beloved Lagavulin."

"Please tell me that's scotch."

"Emma, look!"

When I do, Kevin is holding a pistol. Thankfully, holding it at a distance, like it's a mildewed sock.

"Maybe Graham is planning to shoot her!"

"Kevin, wipe your fingerprints off that!"

"What if it's Graham's baby and he killed Bunny and now he's planning to kill us all!" Kevin says in a high, panicked tone. "What if Natasha is just the cover? What if she's not really pregnant and she's just fat and moany?"

"Kevin!"

"The captain always keeps a gun to fight off pirates." We turn to see Mrs. Weinstein standing in the doorway.

"Pirates!" Kevin yelps. "Oh my gosh. I'm a pirate magnet in this outfit."

Mrs. Weinstein turns to leave. "Richard says to hurry up."

Kevin helps me find the scavenger hunt list of items, then says he has to attend to an important matter—meaning he's afraid to help out as nurse. Just as I'm about to carry my loot upstairs, I overhear Graham delicately asking Richard on what exact date he thinks Natasha became pregnant. Richard answers that he can't tell just by looking at her, but he can calculate by adding 280 days to the date of her last menses. Richard wastes no time in asking Natasha when she had her last period, which sounds rather personal to me.

We hear her answer. "I have no idea."

"Okay, what's 280 + I have no idea?" Kevin whispers to me at the bottom of the stairs.

"It was before we all went on the trip to Harbour Island," Natasha says.

"That was the middle of August," Richard says. "Let's see…just as I thought, she's at about eight months, not nine.

"That was me back then—then my sister took over these past few months."

"Oh god!" Graham cries.

Pretending to not have heard a word, I leave Kevin at the bottom of the stairs and climb up.

"What took you so long?" Richard says.

Richard shakes his head. "I hope we get back in time. I can't very well do a C-section on a boat.

"Why not? "

In a solemn voice he answers. "She would die."

57

Now, I feel awful about all of my evil thoughts; well, most of them.

"Kevin, please ask Ping to come up," Richard calls down the stairs. I guess he realizes that I'm just as slow as Kevin.

A second later Ping's head pops up the spiral staircase. "Ni Yang?"

Without looking up, Richard commands, "Bring me your good knives."

Ping nods his head. "Ah, you just kill her now?"

"No, of course not," Richard says. "I want to select one just in case."

"Ni bu my good Henckels knife on girl."

"I'll get you a new set," Richard reassures Ping.

After a few minutes, Ping hesitantly pops up with his boxed set of fancy knives.

Richard pulls out two and tells Ping to sterilize them and bring them back, along with the rubbing alcohol.

Ping nods. "Miss Emma, you hear new knifes for me?"

"Yes, Ping, I'll make sure he gets you a new set."

Natasha moans again and Graham pushes the throttles for more speed.

Richard silently stares at his watch, then announces that the contractions are one to two minutes apart. He has a very serious look on his face.

Ping emerges up the stairs holding the two knives on foil. "All clean." He runs away before anything can start oozing or screaming out of Natasha. The engines are so loud we can barely hear anything, except for Natasha's agonizing moans. Graham looks back at her with a mixed look of adoration and fear.

It will all work out: We will make it back in time; Natasha will deliver her baby and it will look just like Pierre; then Graham and Richard will both ask me to marry them; we'll start our own island country where I can say yes to both. Richard waves his fingers in front of my far away face.

Graham returns to the top deck and parks himself on the captain's seat and takes back over the helm. He plays a haunting Gemma Hayes song on the sound system, "November." Probably means something to him.

It's peaceful and the sun has just about set. Richard has a glow on his face, the setting sun reflected in the sparkle of his eyes. He's never looked so handsome in his life. He looks as me, so I make an effort to turn my face in just the right direction; maybe I'll get that sun-sparkled look too. Then, maybe he will love me.

Richard yells for Kevin to bring us some water and Natasha has another one of her annoying contractions. Richard checks her blood pressure and the baby's heartbeat, then puts his hands under the sheet again. I kind of want to look—the way people like to look at car wrecks—but I know not to ask.

Right then, my darling Ursula runs up the stairs; she has somehow has been cajoled into wearing a little cap made of a Styrofoam cup and a rubber band. I suspect that this bit of pet millinery is the work of Kevin, not Irene. Even Natasha laughs, which inspires Ursula to run over and begin an enthusiastic cleaning of Natasha's sweaty face. This initiates a cycle where Ursula takes a long swipe and then Natasha giggles. I can't get over the difference between this Natasha and the one from the other day.

Finally Graham puts an end to the lick-fest by picking up Ursula and depositing her next to him on the captain's bench. "Why are her feet red? Did she step in paint again?"

I am reminded of the time she stepped in blue paint—that seems like five years ago—and also of the time Ursula ate the chocolate. Wait, the time Natasha tried to kill her. That must have been the evil Natasha, the thin one. I'll have to update my latest plan in my head, factoring in the new, nice Natasha.

"You're past nine centimeters," Richard says to Natasha. "At ten, you'll be at your second stage of labor—delivery." Apparently they didn't teach the metric system in Russia, because Natasha doesn't seem to realize that this is vital info.

I start to wonder if I'm the best person for this task. It's clear that Ping, even though I've seen him butcher a duck, is too high strung for this. Kevin is too silly. Mrs. Weinstein is too old and unsteady for any sort of cutting. Pudge is just too mean; but that may be a good thing. Trevor is much too reserved to have anything to do with lady parts. Hudson would not want to mess up his hair; plus he's up to something, I can feel it. What about Ernesto? He's a massage therapist and could surely massage the baby out like a turkey giblet. What about Irene? She's had a kid before and she's pretty much shockproof. An abrupt grinding and scraping sound interrupts my thoughts.

"Fuck!" Graham yells.

"What was that?" Richard asks.

Graham shakes his head. "Could have been anything; could be a coral reef." He says the bad news is that with a composite boat we might have sustained some damage. I'm sent down to summon Trevor. It takes a bit to persuade Trevor up the stairs, knowing what is unfolding in Natasha's world. He appears, shielding his face from her plum position. He takes over the helm as Graham goes to investigate.

Graham runs back up. "The fuel tanks have been perforated, and now they're taking in water. We're fucked."

Trevor volunteers to man the engine room; I think to avoid any chance of being conscripted into midwifery. Suddenly the engine sputters, so Graham lets up on the throttle. This makes the engine sputter more; that is, until it comes to a grinding stop. Graham and Richard look at each other.

"Thank god!" Natasha says. "I couldn't stand that racket."

Graham lets out a loud and pithy, "Bloody fuck!"

I guess "bloody fuck" means things are worse.

"Both engines stalled. Emma, watch the helm and listen if I call with instructions; and don't sit on anything." He quickly heads down the stairs.

I have to deliver babies and captain a boat? Do they want me to cure cancer too? I sit at the wheel with my first mate, Ursula, awaiting instruction. I remember that hot night when Graham taught me all about the various dials. I guess I should have paid attention. But who would have predicted this?

It's getting dark out and the boat is rocking sideways in the massive waves. I take this tranquil moment to pretend I'm Elizabeth Taylor and I'm stranded at sea with Richard Burton; I've nothing to wear except a tattered, lacey slip and we have to share a cabin for undisclosed logistical reasons, and he's hot so he has to sleep naked next to me. There's no younger, prettier Natasha around in my fantasy. That would have made a sexy movie. With a little grin, I say to Richard, "What if we get stranded here?"

"We'll be all right," Richard says in a serious tone, suggesting he is not having the same fantasy. "It's Natasha I'm worried about."

Kevin pops his head up the staircase. "Why did we stop? Are you ready to cut her open?"

Richard is unfazed by Kevin's irreverent comment. "No, we've got engine trouble."

"Maybe you shouldn't have let Emma drive," Kevin mocks.

I take Ursula's paws and place them on the steering wheel so it looks like she's sailing the boat. "No, Ursula is the new captain. I'm busy delivering the baby."

"Emma, are you going to practice doing a C-Section on her?" Kevin jokes.

Natasha screams, indicating she fails to see the humor in things.

"Oh, this will be fun," Kevin says. "We're stuck at sea with a murderer, a pregnant woman and, pretty soon, a noisy baby."

"I'll be happy when she delivers a healthy baby," Richard says.

"What are you going to name it?" Kevin asks Natasha in a girl-friendly way.

"Graham, if it's a boy, and Natasha if it's a girl."

Kevin slaps his head. "What? Like your family needs another Natasha!"

"By the way, what is your legal name?" Richard asks Natasha. "We'll need it for the birth certificate."

"Why don't you just put down Anastasha Porochovsky," Natasha answers in a roundabout manner.

Oh, I get it; she's the anti-Natasha.

"And whom shall I say the father is?" Richard asks in a diplomatic voice.

Natasha exhales. "Let's just wait and see who it looks like."

Kevin, obliterating any diplomacy, blurts out, "Well, that's nice. You can't even narrow it down a little bit?"

"Kevin, try not to upset her," Richard says. "Kevin why don't you watch the helm until Graham returns. Emma, you run down and get Ping."

Natasha looks worried. "Oh great. Might as well kill me now."

58

Descending the staircase, I notice the main salon has a new festive décor. Frantic, Irene asks, "Where's Kevin? It's already started."

I see Pudge holding hands with Ping. Wait a minute—they're marching down an aisle made of paper and Mrs. Weinstein and Irene are throwing flowers. Pudge is wearing a white nightgown and looks completely looped. I ask Irene what's going on.

"Well, considering that Ping is illegal and all that, and Pudge needs a cook, Esther and I decided they should get married."

Tiny Ping is looking up at the towering Pudge. Graham is passing by, and Irene holds him back until he curtly says, "I now pronounce you man and wife. Now can I leave?" Judging by the brevity, he must think they're playing a game of charades. I see Irene with her notary public seal pressing away. Boy, she sure is making this authentic. I guess she brought it in case we had a confession.

Graham escapes the party and quickly climbs to the top deck, so I follow him for the yacht update.

"At first I thought we had just had fuel contamination, but someone has mysteriously opened the cover of the electrical panel and poured in a liquid—something that smells a lot like champagne; now we have water damage on the electronics."

"Thank goodness we still have electrical power," Richard says.

Graham says, "That's surprising, because the black box regulates the electrical as well."

Right then, the lights flicker and go out. All electrical humming stops.

Graham, evoking his sailor vocabulary, cries, "Bloody hell!"

I look at Richard and say this can't be good.

"No," Graham says, "it's bloody fucking bad."

"Did my wedding disco lights cause a short circuit?" Kevin says.

"We're fucked," Graham says. "We have no engines, and now no power."

"Can't you switch us to some sort of emergency generator?" Richard asks.

"Unfortunately, there's only a battery bank, which won't last long. Besides, this boat is too sophisticated. Everything runs off the computer. Once that's damaged, the systems fail."

"What can we do?" I ask.

"We'll have to call BASRA—Bahamas Rescue," Richard says.

"I hope our friends at the Palm Beach Police aren't listening in," Graham says in hesitant tones. "We weren't supposed to leave the US, so I didn't file a Notice of Arrival, or float plan."

Richard shakes his head. "I see your point. But we can't stay here, especially if we have medical complications."

"Let me try to get ahold of my mates at the salvage tow. I doubt they can get us up and running, but they can tow us back."

"Natasha," Richard says softly while patting her hand, "it looks like you'll be delivering at sea."

I wonder how all this will play out, and when we'll ever get off this boat.

It's quiet, and getting very dark. Richard thinks of moving Natasha down to a cabin, but Graham points out the cabins will be pitch dark. At least up here we have some moonlight.

Natasha is sweating and panting, a lot—not a pretty process by any means. Right then, Natasha has another one of her deafening contractions, which causes Ursula to run away. Richard glances at his watch. "Did you call for help yet?" he asks Graham.

Graham looks exasperated. "I've sent an EPIRB distress signal to the Bahamas rescue, and I also signaled Larman. His tug can rescue us, but he's a ways away."

"You might as well help Natasha. You won't want to miss this."

Even I can tell that Natasha is ready to pop. I pray it's a natural birth, but probably not as much as Natasha does. I can tell Graham is stressed out, and he avoids looking at me.

Richard peeks under the sheet and says she's fully dilated. Natasha grips Richard's hand and says she needs drugs, fast.

"The only thing you could have is an epidural, but it's too late now; plus, I haven't got one."

Boy, this is going to be painful. Richard rummages around his medical bag for a while. Natasha screams again and the sound carries on the water. Good thing no one is around or they'd probably think we were killing people at sea.

"Do you want me to ask downstairs if anyone brought any good drugs?" I say helpfully.

Richard calls for Kevin, who pops up like a weasel.

"Kevin, send up a shot of bourbon."

"If you're having one, I'll have one too," I say to Richard.

Richard laughs. "No, it's not for me. It's for Natasha."

Natasha perks up. "Is there any Cristal left? I don't like bourbon."

Graham sighs. "I think I need a shot too."

Kevin, like he's a waiter, points to us individually. "Ok, so one shot of bourbon, one glass of Cristal and, Emma, did you want a glass of Cristal since I have to open a bottle?"

I look at Richard and he nods his head. "Just a little; I can't have you and Graham smashed."

Graham is holding Natasha's hand. I guess it's the gentlemanly thing to do.

Kevin climbs the stairs holding a bottle of Maker's Mark and a bottle of Cristal wrapped in a towel. He pulls a stack of plastic cups out from the pocket of his apron and pours drinks for everyone but Richard. "Trevor wouldn't let me bring real glasses up here. Personally, I think it's a shame to drink Cristal out of plastic."

Natasha takes a chug, then has another contraction. Kevin disappears down the stairs saying he's got things to do.

Richard looks under the sheet. "I see the crown."

Natasha lets out an ugly howl. Our waiter took off with the bottle, so I give her my champagne. The remaining lights flicker.

Richard calls to me, "Emma, will you get the commercial flashlight from under the dashboard downstairs. I can't wait for Kevin. And please hurry."

I run to the wheelhouse as fast as I can and grab a huge and heavy flashlight; my heart is pounding as I run back up the stairs.

"Put it here by her thighs," Richard says urgently.

Graham kisses her forehead tenderly. I wonder if he attended the births of his other children, or did he stay in the waiting room smoking cigars—leaving it all a smoky mystery.

The boat is dark—except for the flashlight that's shining up Natasha's legs. Her belly shows up as a big shadow under the sheets. I look at Graham—Mr. Shadow Maker.

Natasha lets out a torrent of Russian words at Graham. I suspect these words are not in any schoolbook. Soon our DJ Kevin is on it—blasting Glen Hansard's, "Drown Out," to drown out her Russian screams.

Richard looks under the tent and says she's crowning. The tent collapses on the flashlight and Richard quickly pulls the tent away. I guess modesty goes out the window at a time like this. Oh, nice bikini wax—I'll have to get one of those. Suddenly there's a baby's head coming out of Natasha. It's surreal looking under the partial moon. Richard yells at Natasha to push really hard. She decides this is a good time to bite my hand. I cry in agony, but let her do it again, wondering why she doesn't bite Graham—he did this to her.

Kevin decides this is a good time to ask if we need more champagne— and if we have any musical requests.

Richard responds with a curt no.

Natasha pushes and bites again. All of a sudden, a gooey, slippery baby comes out. Richard's whole face changes; a huge smile replaces the focused concentration. He holds up the slippery baby and Natasha and Graham sob with joy.

"What a beautiful boy," Richard says, looking relieved. I guess delivering a baby at sea is stressful.

Richard tells me to shine the flashlight on his watch and pronounces the time as 8:21. He takes a good look at the baby, who makes a loud cry. Graham silently covers the baby's eyes in a tender way. Natasha is a weeping, bloody mess on the sofa. I'll bet even Fantastic won't get that blood out.

"Is he all right?" Graham asks in the softest voice.

Richard wipes off the baby, who still has a scary looking umbilical cord hooked to him. Richard smiles. "He's small, but perfect." Richard takes two of the zip ties and tightens them around the umbilical cord. "Graham, would you like to do the honors?"

I'm so glad he didn't ask me. Richard hands Graham one of Ping's Henckel knives and directs him to make the cut. Graham pauses for a moment, probably still wondering if this is his baby. Right as he makes the cut, Kevin pops his head up the stairs, looks at the umbilical cord and promptly faints, falling down the stairs.

Mrs. Weinstein yells up the staircase like a fight referee. "And he's down!"

Richard ties off the cord and hands the baby boy to Natasha, who looks up at Graham. This would be a lovely bonding scene—if he wasn't my boyfriend. Richard leaps down the stairs to take a look at Kevin.

Thinking no one is looking, my dog takes this opportunity to sneak off with the bloody umbilical cord. For a moment I ponder casting myself in that lovely chase scene, but decide to continue playing my current awkward role. Plus, it's worth the price of admission to see the look on Graham's face when Natasha tells him she wants to name the baby after him. He holds the baby up under the moonlight to study his face. The baby has huge eyes like Natasha, and I don't see any resemblance to Graham; but it's just a baby, so it's hard to tell. I guess they'll need the test.

Richard comes back up and says that Kevin hit his head, but that he'll be all right. Richard pulls out his stethoscope and examines the baby, then checks Natasha out. There's so much blood it looks like a crime scene. Richard asks me to hold the flashlight while he carries the baby to the bathroom sink to wash him off. When we're in the bathroom alone, I ask, "Do you think it's Graham's?"

Richard pauses, lets out a deep breath and looks closely at the baby. "Frankly, it's hard to tell. They tend to resemble the father at birth, but I have to say, this baby looks just like Natasha."

332

We both look at the baby again. Richard shakes his head. "I can't tell."

"Too bad the baby can't talk yet; we'd know it was Graham's if he had an English accent."

Richard laughs, but it levels off as he probably wonders if I'm being serious. I stare at his face as he attempts to fashion a makeshift diaper out of paper towels and duct tape.

The Jeff Buckley song, "We all fall in Love Sometimes," plays in the background.

We emerge from the bathroom and hand the duct-taped baby to Natasha. For a moment, we all seem to be in exhausted sigh mode. The moon casts a beautiful light on the glimmering Natasha.

It's oddly quiet downstairs, and Richard says, "They must be up to something."

The baby is sleeping, and it looks like Natasha is about to fall asleep too. Feeling like I'm chaperoning a honeymoon, I ask if I may be dismissed to go and check on Kevin. Richard says not to leave yet, then hands me a roll of paper towels and points to the blood and goo. Despite all the advance warnings, it didn't occur to anyone to put paper towels down first. Yuck. I could never work at a hospital.

Right then we hear a loud bang, then another.

"What the hell was that?" Richard says.

"Sounded like a car backfiring," I say.

A sleepy Natasha says, "Good. I'll take a ride home."

"It's a gun!" Graham yells. "Emma, hold the baby!"

Richard and Graham dive down the stairs.

I hear screaming and shrieking, so I know Kevin and Ping have been spared. Richard pops up and gestures for me to hand him the flashlight.

Kevin scurries up the stairs and hides under a clean sheet.

I poke the sheet. "What happened?"

"I don't know. We were just about to serve the wedding Jell-O—that's all we had—then boom! Someone was shot.

"Oh my god! Who?"

"I couldn't tell. They made me leave."

I hand Kevin the duct-taped baby. "I'll go and see."

Kevin holds the squirming package at arms length, like it's an alien. Natasha quickly grabs her baby back.

Before I can head down, Irene comes up the stairs munching on a box of Triscuits. "Didn't see *that* coming."

Just as she's about to fill us in, we hear Graham calling for help on the radio. He says he can't give the exact location, because we've drifted.

We look at each other in shock.

Richard comes up the stairs and, not seeing Kevin under the sheet, announces, "Hudson is dead."

59

Kevin lets out a high-pitched gasp, then a wail. I find his shoulders and rub them under the sheet. Poor thing.

"Was it suicide?" Irene asks with a full cracker in her mouth.

"He was shot in the back," Richard answers gently.

"Can't do that with short arms," Irene quips.

"So it was murder." I conclude.

"We don't know that yet," Richard says. "It could have been an accident. Graham's gun is missing from the wheelhouse."

Kevin sobs. "I loved him. Even his cankles."

Mrs. Weinstein's head appears up the stairs. "What a cute baby. Think it's Graham's?"

"Mother, I told you to stay in your cabin," Richard scolds her.

I was getting hot flashes in there, like the old days. Plus, I want to know how Hudson is doing."

"Whed," Irene mumbles, another full cracker in her mouth.

Mrs. Weinstein opens her mouth wide, suggesting major shock. "What?"

Natasha translates without emotion. "Dead."

Richard feels the need to reassure the group. "Yes, it's true. Don't worry, Graham has locked Ernesto down in his cabin."

"You think he shot Hudson?"

"He's the most suspicious one. I'm sure Trevor didn't do it, or Ping. And everyone else was up here."

Graham comes up the stairs and takes possession of the gurgling baby. He says Ping is hiding in his cabin with Ursula in case anyone is wondering.

Graham plops down on the white leather seat. "Well, whose great idea was this?"

I try to hide. Finally, Richard takes the focus off me, "Graham, is there any chance we might have drifted back to US waters?"

Graham looks up distractedly. "I haven't a clue. Of course I'm curious about whether this is my baby, and who shot Hudson, but what I'm most curious about right now is who whacked our computer system."

I notice Mrs. Weinstein's eyes darting like fish in her thick glasses.

"Will you just look at this floor?" she says. "Can't anyone give birth without making a mess?"

Irene tries to relate to her. "You should see the aft quarters. Blood splatters all over the walls and on the deck."

I watch Graham quietly adoring the baby. He's never looked more handsome. There is no one sexier than a hot daddy—or less available.

The baby cries and Richard says to Natasha, "He'll be getting hungry soon. Have you been trained on breastfeeding?" I think this is awfully personal stuff to be asking in mixed company. Natasha, no fan of modesty, lifts her top and presses her huge dark nipple into the baby's face. "How hard can it be?"

Richard smiles and gently pulls her back. "Now, you don't want to smother him."

I look the other way and catch Graham looking at Natasha tenderly.

Trevor pops up the stairs with more champagne. "We've gone ahead and put Mr. DuPont in the cold storage."

Kevin wails, then perks up a little. "It that Cristal I hear?"

"You may use a real glass," Trevor says to the grieving Kevin.

"Graham," Mrs. Weinstein says impatiently, "how long until the Coast Guard comes?"

Graham is still in a daze. "I set off the EPIRB. It won't be the US Coast Guard, and I have no idea how long the Bahamian rescue will take."

Mrs. Weinstein looks at the baby. "Who knew she'd have her baby at sea? Who knew she'd have a baby? She looked so slim at the dog ball."

"That was the other one," Irene says.

"Who can keep them straight?"

"Clearly not Graham," Trevor says.

Richard helps Natasha down the stairs to a cabin, with Irene carrying the new baby.

The moon has moved and is glistening on the quiet sea. We're drifting in the dark. We hear Ernesto pounding on his door.

When Richard returns, Graham points out, "If Ernesto had my gun, he would have shot the lock off by now."

Mrs. Weinstein joins in defense. "Let the poor dear out; the air-conditioning is off."

"Alright, someone let him out," Richard concedes.

Graham heads down and releases Ernesto, who runs to the top deck.

"There are ten other people," he blurts out. "Why would you suspect me?"

"I'm sorry Ernesto," Richard apologizes. "You are the only one I don't know very well. I had to protect my family."

Ernesto grabs a bottled water and pours it down his face and body. "Are we toasting to the new baby?"

Mrs. Weinstein winks. "Yes, something like that."

I wonder what the authorities will make of this.

Richard keeps a wary eye on Ernesto, probably still wondering if he shot Hudson. He looks at me and says he has to get some antiseptic for Natasha below deck. When I don't catch his drift, Richard takes my arm and says he needs my help.

I follow him down two spiral staircases to the lower deck.

He pulls me into his mother's cabin with a look of concern. "We have a dangerous person on the boat, but we don't know who it is."

"It's like a Humphrey Bogart movie. *Key Largo*."

"We've got fumes in the aft cabins and will have to shift people to forward cabins. You stay in my mother's cabin. I don't know who to trust anymore."

"Well, the one person that we know didn't kill Hudson was Natasha. And she was a little too busy to wreck the computer."

"Emma, just how well do you know Kevin?" Richard verbally tiptoes.

Without hesitation, not that I ever hesitate or filter, I defend my buddy. "Kevin wouldn't hurt anyone. One time he swatted at a spider with his flip-flop and a hundred baby spiders came running out in every direction. He was so upset he'd killed their mother that he couldn't drink for a week."

Richard smirks. "Thank you for that." He taps my hand and adds, "He could be going off the deep end. He could have used Graham's gun from the wheelhouse."

I keep my mouth shut about Kevin finding the gun.

"No one is really safe until we're off this boat," Richard says as he gets up to leave.

Locking the cabin door from inside, I find my way blindly to the bathroom to wash my face, but find there is no water. Apparently, you need power to have water pressure. What a day. I wonder who shot Hudson. I wonder who ruined the boat system. I wonder if I'll have sex with Richard.

When I open the porthole window to catch some breeze, I hear voices on the back deck, and can tell it's Kevin and Ernesto. I hear Kevin saying there aren't enough cabins and they have to sleep out there. What if Kevin *has* gone bad? I'm sure he would never shoot anyone on purpose, but I can see him accidently shooting someone. Or accidently doing anything—like accidently getting the computer system wet.

Now I hear Pudge's voice in the hallway saying to Irene. "I think I should stay with Richard and you should stay with Emma."

There's pounding the door—it's Mrs. Weinstein. "Emma, we're moving you to Richard's cabin."

Following the new plan, I find Richard's cabin and climb into his bed. A nightgown would have been handy, I think. Oh well, it's hard to predict the dress code for an event in a stifling cabin with a handsome doctor after a baby delivery and a random shooting. This is going to be a long night.

I see Ping's shoes walk by the porthole. What if he's the murderer, of everyone? He's always got knives in his hands and he's pretty volatile. Maybe he killed Bunny; maybe that little baby is his; maybe he sabotaged the computer; and maybe he shot Hudson! There! It's just easier to blame everything on one person—and neater. I wonder if we'll get that cute detective again.

Richards uses his key and lets himself in. I hear my dog scratching and snorting outside the door, or else it's Ernest Borgnine. Mystery solved, as my baby leaps on the bed and starts licking my ears. Richard seems startled. "Emma? What are you doing in my bed?"

"Your mother told me to sleep here."

Richard chuckles. "And you just blindly take orders to climb in a man's bed?"

Well, yes.

There's a little light coming through the porthole, just enough to spotlight the weariness on Richard's face. He pulls a knife out of his belt and sets it down on the dresser. I feel safer knowing he will protect me, although it's no match for a gun. Richard doesn't say a word and takes his pants off; his belt buckle jangle as it lands on the chair. Boy, he's had a long day. I can't believe he had to deliver a baby, treat a murder victim, and guard his family from a murderer—all the while having to entertain guests. The light glimmers on the bit of hair on his chest. He locks the door and slips under the white sheets and kisses me on the forehead. When I kiss him back on the lips, he whispers, "Don't worry; you're safe now."

"Thanks for finding Ursula."

He laughs. "Oh, that's why you feel safe? Not a man defending you with a knife, but a pug?

He holds my hand, but doesn't try to touch my naked body. I secretly wish he would run his hands all over my body, even if by accident. Then he turns to spoon me, and kisses the back of my neck.

He has me in his arms and rocks me gently with his legs pulling me closer.

60

Before we can get into any mischief, Kevin inquires in a stage whisper, "Emma, is that you in there?"

Richard motions for me to stay quiet.

"Emma, I know you're in there. I can hear your dog. Open the door!"

Richard is gesturing no. I pretend I'm asleep, by letting out an exaggerated snore. Richard tries to contain a laugh, and Kevin seems to go away. Later, when I look out the porthole, I see Mrs. Weinstein walk by. I can tell it is her by her blue veined legs and her Ferragamo flats. What is she doing up? I alert Richard. He whispers out the porthole. "Mother, get back in your room."

She bends down to look in the porthole. "Oh, hello, Emma. Hi, Richard."

I pull the white sheets up over my head.

Mrs. Weinstein smiles at me and says, "Emma, it's okay, everyone knows you're in there with Richard."

"Mother, get back in your cabin!"

Mrs. Weinstein verbally pats his head. "Don't worry. Relax you two and have some fun."

Richard closes the curtains and climbs back under the sheets, staying neatly on his side. Apparently, there is too much life and death going on to have any sort of intimacy.

When I open my eyes in the morning, I see Richard is holding my head on his lap watching me sleep. "You slept like a baby, despite all the noise."

"What noise?"

"Pudge and Irene got into a small altercation, resulting in scratches and iodine. I think Irene won. The baby cried all night; Natasha and Kevin got into a fight over paper towels."

"Oh, I'll bet he cried his eyes out."

"No, he got drunk and spilled champagne all over the main salon. Then Trevor resigned and is now officially a guest. Oh, and we have no idea what's taking the Bahamas Coast Guard so long."

Richard puts on a new shirt and gets up to leave. "I'm taking your dog out; don't let anyone in."

He's very thoughtful—or maybe he's worried about the carpeting. A few minutes later, Richard comes back into the room and I catch him staring at me from the doorway. He opens the porthole and says to sleep a little longer if I want. He fills me in the latest news before he leaves again: the U.S. Coast Guard is having a jurisdictional issue and neither the U.S. nor the Bahamas will tow us, though both are curious about the shooting. My foggy brain starts to replay the events of last night.

I lie back in bed. Richard was very gentlemanly last night. That probably won't happen the next time, nor do I want it to. I hear footsteps on the outer walk, and see the blue veins. I suppose it's time to get up—or be nominated as number one murder suspect.

After a little splash of bottled water, I head up the stairs. From inside, I see the back deck, where Mrs. Weinstein and Richard are talking with Graham. Kevin is sleeping on lounge chairs with a piece of canvas boat cover over his head. I slide open the door and Graham turns around in his seat. He's holding the baby on his lap with a gentle smile on his face.

"The US Coast Guard had another matter to attend to," Graham announces, "but the Bahamas guard is on their way, along with the salvage company."

Graham seems really calm, considering all that has happened. I'm sure he assumes that I had sex with Richard. I can't really go into that now with Mrs. Weinstein here. I look at the baby again in the daylight.

"I know what you're thinking," Mrs. Weinstein says. "We've all studied his face, and damned if we can tell."

Graham says, "Ladies, I'll assume he's mine until we can do the paternity test."

"And if he's not?" Mrs. Weinstein inquires.

"If it's Pierre's baby then she's going to have some 'splaning to do."

"I can see how you and Pierre could get confused in the dark," Richard says.

"The dark? I can't tell them apart in the light."

I find a warm Coke, and start to wake up. "I thought you didn't know she was a twin."

Graham sighs. "That's just it. I'd apparently met this Natasha last year and the other one a few months ago. You can see how I was confused."

"Just be glad you didn't get both of them pregnant," Mrs. Weinstein quips.

Kevin perks up from under the canvas. "How do you know he didn't?"

Mrs. Weinstein laughs. "You men get yourselves into more trouble."

Richard looks at me and Graham catches him. Irene stumbles to the back deck with a bloody Mary. "It's not what you think—I've gone virgin."

"You didn't go into the cold storage for ice did you?" Richard says to Irene.

"Heavens no! There's a dead man in there."

Mrs. Weinstein gets up to go to the galley. "Where's Trevor? I want some breakfast."

"Trevor made me breakfast in bed," Irene says.

"Trevor? Is there something you want to tell us?" Richard asks.

Irene pulls the celery out of her drink. "Well, it just made sense to swap cabins with Ping."

Pudge wanders out to the deck wearing a white negligee, but looking a little hung over. She looks at Irene's drink. "I need one of those, but put some vodka in it."

Graham can't help himself. "So, is that part of your trousseau? For your honeymoon with Ping?"

"You're kidding," Pudge says.

Graham turns to face Pudge and she can finally see the baby. She screams, then says, "Where did that come from?"

"Sometime after you and Ping were walking down the aisle, and after the power went off," I say.

"Didn't you hear the screaming?" Graham asks.

"I thought that was Kevin."

"Do you remember the shooting?" Richard asks.

"Shooting?!"

"Hudson was shot," I say.

"Don't look in the big freezer," Irene adds.

"You are all playing with me."

"I assure you that we are not," Richard says.

"The authorities are coming. Ping's visa was up, so someone thought it would help if he married you," I say.

"Really, don't fool with me."

Mrs. Weinstein comes back out with a bottle of champagne. "Oh, Pudge, is that from your trousseau?"

Kevin manages to stay mum through all of this; that is until he hears a cork pop, and we see a hand and a champagne glass emerge from under his canvas.

Graham hands me the baby. "Will you hold him for a minute? We are about to have company."

I look around. "Somebody better start cleaning."

We see debris and blood and empty champagne bottles. Graham sits back down. "What's the use? They'll just blame me for tampering with evidence."

We all look to see Ernesto get up completely naked; he is unfazed by the audience as he saunters down the outside stairs.

"So that's where he was all night," says Kevin, who's emerged from his canvas bunker.

Pudge takes a puff from her cigarette. "I've got an idea. Let's blame it all on Ernesto. That way we don't have to sit around all day talking to some inept cops in Nassau."

"I'm not one to champion Ernesto," Richard says, "but that would be wrong."

"Okay, but let's at least blame Bunny's murder on Hudson, that way we're halfway off the hook."

"Pudge, we'll all have to cooperate with the authorities. Lying will just get us in more trouble."

"That's Ping," Richard says. "He's at least an octave higher than Kevin."

Ping appears, jumping up and down. "Fat man gone."

Right then Trevor comes up with an announcement: The body is missing.

61

Trevor explains to Richard. "I was retrieving shrimp from cold storage, when it dawned on me that something was missing."

"Do you think he's recovered?" Mrs. Weinstein asks.

"No, Mother. He couldn't have."

"Ok, Trevor and Ping, you search the lower deck. I'll search the mid deck. Ernesto, you search the top deck." Graham says.

The ladies look a little miffed that they are not included in the search for the dead body. "He hadn't turned up at any social events—like the wedding or the birth," Mrs. Weinstein quips.

Ernesto returns and heralds breathlessly, "I've searched the top deck and no luck."

Trevor returns from his quest. "We seem to have lost him," he calmly informs.

Graham comes back. "After enlisting the search pug, it's clear DuPont is not on the boat."

"He must have been thrown overboard during the night," Richard says.

"No need to jump to conclusions," Mrs. Weinstein says. "I'll bet he revived a little, then staggered about, then rolled off. He was kind of pudgy."

Graham shakes his head. "The funny thing is, someone hosed down the blood on the swim deck."

Ping reappears and says, "I clean."

Pudge puffs her cigarette. "Actually, this is tidier than having a gunshot victim onboard."

"What exactly did you tell the authorities?" Richard asks Graham.

"I spoke with the Bahamas Magistrate. The connection was poor, so all I could tell them was that we'd had a shooting."

"Perhaps we should forget he was ever here," Trevor suggests.

Mrs. Weinstein gets a big smile. "Yes, we'll simply say the head count was eleven when we started, and eleven when we ended."

Mrs. Weinstein sneaks up behind me and whispers in my ear. "Meet me in my cabin in five."

Naturally, I wonder what she is up to, but assume it's to tell her latest theory on things. I pass Kevin in the hall, who like his usual busybody self, asks where I'm going. I say Mrs. Weinstein his having a lady issue and that gets him off my trail. When I run into Pudge, I say the same thing, thinking I should remember this. Then I see Richard and say the same thing, and he asks what exactly the issue is. Rats! Sometimes it's bad to have a doctor around. Hmm? Let's see? If it's medical, musical or murder he'll want to know more. "We're meeting Pudge to compare diets tips, want to come?"

"Sorry, I've got to help Graham."

When I make a gentle knock on Mrs. Weinstein's door, I'm surprised to find myself greeted by Ernesto. He's all business, and wearing pants.

Mrs. Weinstein yanks me in the cabin. "Hurry, there's not much time."

She pulls a cocktail napkin and a bejeweled green pen out from her freckled cleavage. "Emma, you do the writing; surely you remember some law from when you stalked that man through your licensing class."

"It wasn't stalking, it was a board requirement."

"Whatever."

"What am I writing? Is someone confessing?"

Mrs. Weinstein lets out a curt, "No, that would be stupid."

"I'm okay with a hundred," Ernesto whispers to Mrs. Weinstein.

She pats his thigh in response. "Oh, Pumpkin, I insist on three hundred. I want it to be enforceable."

My eyes dart from Mrs. Weinstein's face to Ernesto's. "What exactly am I writing?"

"We just need a basic prenup," Mrs. Weinstein explains. "You know, in the event the marriage fails, blah blah blah."

"Prenup? Who's getting married?"

Ernesto points to himself.

"Start with the usual: I, Ernesto...what is your last name, dear?"

"Carvalho."

"That's your last name?" I say. "I thought it was Filo."

349

"It's Filo Rodrigues Carvalho. I use them in different order depending on the situation."

Mrs. Weinstein puts the pen in my hand. "Got that?"

"So, I, Ernesto Filo Rodrigues Carvalho, hereby agree to a prenuptial agreement with a...."

"That's good," Mrs. Weinstein says.

"Total maximum settlement to be...what did you say? Three hundred dollars?"

"No, silly. Three hundred *thousand*."

"Holy moly! Oh, wait. I'd better add Lisa's name."

Mrs. Weinstein's mouth opens wide. "What for?"

"I'm marrying *Esther*," Ernesto says.

"What?" I look at the two of them.

Ernesto makes a fake smile at Mrs. Weinstein. She winks at him.

Mrs. Weinstein snaps her fingers at me. "There's no time for explanation. Let's just say, it's better this way."

"Richard is going to be furious. I thought you were holding out for Lisa?" I whisper to Ernesto.

"How's he going to get her if he's in the pokey?" Mrs. Weinstein says.

"You shot Hudson?"

Ernesto bats his eyes. "Maybe I shot him, maybe Esther did; maybe I pushed him overboard, maybe Esther did."

Mrs. Weinstein puts her hand over his mouth. "Shush, Pumpkin."

Processing the incoming data, I say, "Oh, I get it. One of you shot him and one of you witnessed it; if you get married you can't be required to testify against the other."

Mrs. Weinstein pats my shoulder. "You're a genius! Now keep writing."

"I saw it in a movie," I say to Ernesto. As I'm writing on the tiny cocktail napkin, there's a knock on the door. It's Graham.

Graham seems dazed. "What's going on?"

Mrs. Weinstein closes the door behind him. "No time for chitchat. Did you bring the bible and a glass?"

"Yes, but who's getting married? I'm not marrying Natasha until I find out about the baby."

"That's sweet of you," I say. "But, no, you'll never guess who's getting married!"

"Let's see—Kevin and the late Hudson?"

"Hey, there might be some benefit to that—that is, if he had any real money," Mrs. Weinstein says.

Ernesto must be hot, because he takes his shirt off revealing his toned abs.

Mrs. Weinstein winks. "Oh, that reminds me. Emma, better add a conjugal clause."

Ernesto puts his shirt back on. "You didn't say anything about that. Three fifty if I have to do stuff like that."

"I thought you were keen on Lisa," Graham says.

"He is," I say, "but he's marrying Esther right now before the authorities come. One of them shot Hudson and the other is a witness."

"Not another word, Emma," Mrs. Weinstein says, "or we're going to have to eat him."

"What? And you think getting married fast will get you out of that?" Graham exclaims.

Mrs. Weinstein inserts the wine glass in a sock. "Got any better ideas?"

"We'd better run this past Richard," Graham says.

"He'll just slow it down. Look, I've got a prenup and everything."

Ernesto illuminates it for all. "We stay out of jail, in a year or two I can get a divorce."

Mrs. Weinstein pulls Graham's hand and starts the proceedings. "I, Esther Weinstein, hereby of sound mind and body—well that's debatable—hereby agree to love honor, cherish, all that crap, with Ernesto...what did you say your last name was?"

Graham starts laughing. "This is highly amusing, but you know it will not hold up in court."

Mrs. Weinstein points to me. "Better get Irene down here to notarize it. Besides, it might be just enough to keep them from bothering to indict."

"The 'Why Bother?' defense," I say.

Graham is so tired he can't stop laughing. "Repeat after me. I, Esther Weinstein, hereby agree to marry Ernesto..."

"Filo Rodrigues Carvalho."

"Bring it home, Captain!" Mrs. Weinstein directs.

"I hereby pronounce you man and wife," Graham says in an affected voice.

Mrs. Weinstein runs over and directs "Pumpkin" to stomp on the glass.

"Oh, Ernesto. You forgot to sign the prenup," I say.

Ernesto tells us that he doesn't want any money; his ship is coming in soon.

Really? Why would you be a dog walker?

I can't wait to run upstairs to tell everyone. Everyone but Richard, that is.

A small boat approaches from the back taking in a full tri-deck view of our little sunrise party.

With the recent abandonment of crew, Ernesto has been recruited as first mate to drop the bumpers. It's the Bahamas Coast Guard, escorting another boat labeled *Larman Salvage*.

The salvage company begins the process of hooking up the boat for towing. Richard says for all of us to go below deck and let Graham do the talking. He says I can stay upstairs if I keep my mouth shut. Meanwhile, two Bahamian officials leap on the boat.

Graham hands them the papers for the boat, saying they were on the way to register the boat in Nassau, but things came up.

The officials ask about the shooting. Graham says he's actually not sure there was a shooting, that it could have been a flare being shot. I'm in awe of his coolness.

Richard, in a display of pure honesty, says solemnly, "There was a shooting. There was a death."

When the name Hudson DuPont III is revealed, the officials start laughing.

"Excellent!" one of them says.

"He had no idea we were on to him," the other says. "He thought he could break the law in the Bahamas and that we'd do nothing. Well—it's true, but not for him. We've been trying to extradite him for years."

"Are you sure he's dead?" the first one asks. "We don't want him swimming back to shore."

Richard says, "Yes, I'm sure."

After a lot of paperwork, we are free to go. The tug company begins the process of towing us back to Palm Beach, and the guests return to the mid deck.

62

As we approach Palm Beach, Graham pulls out his binoculars and lets out a, "Bloody hell!" There's a boat approaching. As it gets closer, we see the boat is labeled — *Palm Beach Marine Unit*. Standing on the back of the boat are the last two people on earth we want to see: Detective Perez and Captain Lacey.

Graham, following some sort of nautical protocol, helps them aboard. We're in the Intracoastal; I guess they don't want us to dock for fear we'll all jump ship. Ernesto tosses them a line and assists.

Lacey has a slight grin as he catches us disappearing into various boat orifices. "Hello, Captain Peel, I see we meet again."

Graham throws his weary arm up. "To what do we owe this pleasure?"

"We heard you had a little shooting," Detective Perez says. "The Bahamian government may have no interest in it, but we do."

Graham looks around. "I know it looks bad, but not all of the blood is from the shooting."

Really, is he going to tell them my dog stole the umbilical cord and ran all over the place?

Richard hands me the baby, along a rationed paper towel and tape.

"Hello, Emma. What a coincidence—the gang's all here," Captain Lacey says.

Detective Perez smiles at my Madonna pose, which I hope will garner a glimmer of innocence. "Is that your baby, Emma?"

At first I'm insulted, as I certainly didn't appear pregnant anytime lately. Finally, I say, "No, it's his," pointing to Graham.

Captain Lacey looks confused. "So where is the victim?"

Trevor resurfaces to greet the guests. "Haven't seen him lately."

"It appears he may have fallen overboard during the wee hours," Graham covers.

"Who was it?"

"Hudson DuPont," Richard says. "The last we saw him, he was lingering in the cold storage."

Without missing a beat, Mrs. Weinstein says to Lacey, "Oh, if you're going there, would you be a dear and see if there's any ice left?"

I exchange knowing looks with Richard, who puts a finger up to his mouth to indicate a subtle *shut up*. We all sit and wait for Detective Perez and Captain Lacey to look around.

"We might as well request to wrap this in with the Palm Beach investigation," Perez says to Lacey. "The Coast Guard is occupied with a sinking cruise ship off Ft. Lauderdale."

"But they were in Bahamian waters, so it's their deal." Captain Lacey says to Perez.

"They could have been in U.S. waters for all we know." He looks around. "We don't care where that baby was born, but we care where the shooting happened."

"I'm sure it was the Bahamas," Graham says.

Kevin has gone back under his canvas fort, and Mrs. Weinstein pours more champagne into his outstretched glass. Meanwhile, I occupy myself by gazing down at the tiny baby on my lap. I'd like one of these, except I wouldn't want to go through all that mess and pain. Maybe Natasha won't want the baby if it's Pierre's and she'll give it to me and Graham to raise—or me and Richard. My mind wanders to the movie *Georgy Girl*, where she ends up with the rich, handsome James Mason and her roommate's baby all in one swoop.

Captain Lacey is all business. "Captain Peel, what firearms did you have on board?"

Graham sighs. "I had a .22 in the wheelhouse, but it seems to have been relocated."

I notice he's more formal when he's twisting the truth.

"If you find my fingerprints on it, just ignore them," Kevin calls out.

The Detective and Captain Lacey look at each other like Kevin is crazy.

"I believe after careful investigation you'll conclude you have a classic suicide and a subsequent keeling," Trevor offers.

Pudge lights a cigarette. "Yes, I think Hudson was despondent about killing Bunny."

"And someone tampered with our electronic system, which caused our power to fail," Graham quickly adds.

"Yes," Pudge enthuses, "he was despondent about killing Bunny *and* tampering with our electrical whatever."

"Again? You people sure have a lot of trouble when the power goes off." Captain Lacey says.

Captain Lacey asks, "How old is that baby?"

"He was born yesterday," I say.

"8:21," Richard adds.

"So let me see if I have this straight," Detective Perez says, with more than a little cynicism. "You are the same group of people who found a dead woman in your elevator, and then you all go for a friendly little boat ride out of the country where somebody has a

357

baby on board, the boat gets sabotaged, and a trust-funder gets shot and falls overboard. Is that right?"

"Yup. That pretty much sums it up," Irene says.

Graham throws his hands up. "Bloody hell! Whose brilliant idea was it to have a boating party?"

Err—I hope he thinks it was Kevin's.

"We'll need a full list of who is on the yacht," Captain Lacey says.

"In the meantime, we'll have a look around," Detective Perez says. "And don't anyone think of going for a little swim. It's a long way back to the dock."

Ping emerges from the lower deck; he looks like he was just sleeping, as evidenced by his pillow and Garanimal pajamas. He opens the sliding glass doors to the back deck and reaches up to kiss Pudge. She is sitting and he is standing, and they are the same height.

"You beautiful tai tai," he says.

"Please tell me he's talking about my breasts," Pudge says to no one in particular.

Graham laughs. "No, tai tai means wife."

Pudge pushes Ping off her. "It doesn't count if we were at sea, and a little tipsy."

"Yes, it does. You fall under maritime law," Graham says.

"Plus, I notarized it," Irene says, squeezing her hand to mimic pressing a seal.

"And you and Ping make such a lovely pair," Richard says in an encouraging voice.

"Pudge, you did say you wanted to get married again," Irene interjects.

Captain Lacey descends the outer ladder. "Judging by the blood splatters, it looks like this DuPont character was shot from close range in the aft quarters. A bullet went through this," he says, pointing to Trevor's pudding pot. "So, it looks like, a) this was a practice shot, or b) they were a lousy aim."

"I'd guess b). Can we go home now?" Kevin says.

"That leaves out option c) suicide," Detective Lacey says. "People usually don't shield a bullet with a pot if they are trying to shoot themselves."

"Geez, somebody shoulda thrown the pudding overboard too," Irene says.

"I wonder how the pot got back there?" Trevor says.

Graham waives his hands over his chest. "Don't look at me."

"Dr. Weinstein," Detective Perez says, "refresh my memory. You have an illegal Chinese cook, a dog walker from Peru, a captain with an expired passport and B1/B2 visa, and the Russian stewardess—and you decide to go for a little boat ride."

"I needed to get out of the house. It's sad there without my wife."

"We're making great progress on her case, Captain Lacey jokes. "We've eliminated Kevin."

Kevin jumps up with just his arms. "Yippee. I can leave the country now."

"But now you're a suspect for the murder of DuPont, so don't plan on going far."

"Oh, well. I have no one to travel with anyway," Kevin concedes.

Trying to get an update, I say, "Well, you must have eliminated more than Kevin by now for Bunny's murder."

Detective Perez winks at me. "But not you sweetie. And not Dr. Weinstein."

"Now we have to start all over again," Lacey says to Perez. "Did you hear that Natasha woman has a twin?"

Detective Perez lets out a huge groan. "You're kidding."

"That's why she turns up everywhere. And sometimes has a belly," I add helpfully.

"The perfect alibi," Detective Perez says.

"Does anyone else here have a twin?" Captain Lacey asks.

We all look around.

"I have a twin brother," Trevor says, "but he's a legally blind widower who wouldn't hurt a fly."

Mrs. Weinstein gets a smile on her face. "Really? His wife died? Why didn't you tell me?"

"We haven't spoken for years. Ever since he stole my fiancée."

63

When we tie up to the dock, everyone starts to go their separate ways like ants, only faster. Then we're corralled back to the police station. The police say all on board must remain in town for further questioning, or risk further suspicion. Kevin is a basket case and obsessively pets Ursula's head the entire time before asking for a ride home from Mrs. Weinstein. He says in his best Greta Garbo accent, that 'he vants to be alone.' He takes my dog—so he doesn't have to drink alone.

Richard gives me a ride. He suggests we get a bite of lunch, but he wants to stop at his house first to change. When we get to his house, it's like entering a bank vault—quiet and cold. It feels so different from all the other times I've been here. Usually there's a rustle of activity of butlers, cooks and droppers-by. Now it's only Richard and me. We will just have to warm it up. He says he could use a shower after all the blood, sweat and tears.

He heads to his room, while I am welcomed to take a bath off the green room. The tub is huge, so I put the water on full force and pour in bath salts; I worry the bubbles will end up in a huge, city-block sized blob, like from some Doris Day movie. First, I rinse off in the shower, not wanting to soak in my own filth. What a night. As the water fills, I replay the evening in my head.

I can't believe Hudson is dead. I can't believe Graham is a father. I can't believe Pudge married Ping. I can't believe Ernesto married Mrs. Weinstein. I can't believe I'm still single.

Ahh. Soon I am floating in a pale blue Calgon sea. The sun is beaming into the window, so I close my eyes. When I look up, Richard is standing there.

"Emma, I didn't mean to startle you. But I realized you didn't have any towels." He's just wearing a white towel.

361

I wonder how long he's been standing there watching me. "That looks warm," he says. "And I'm somehow out of hot water."

"Hop in; there's room for two—or maybe four or five." I politely avert my eyes when he takes his towel off and slips in. The water is clear enough to see everything, but I try not to look. He puts his head right under the heavy downpour of the waterfall faucet, which slicks his gray hair back. He turns to face me and I notice he has a slight widow's peak—maybe it's a widower's peak. He closes his eyes and it reminds me of that rainy afternoon spent painting his beautiful eyes.

We just soak there, side-by-side, and let the water fall on us. I duck under a few times and the salty water gets in my mouth. It's like a baptism. Silently, he lifts me from below and holds me flat on his knees. I feel so loved. He takes the shampoo and rubs my temples. Then he gets behind me and straddles my hips with his legs and pulls my knees in close. I feel his face at the back of my neck. He shuts the water off and suddenly it's so quiet, not even a splash. Our souls just soak in silence.

"Emma," he whispers.

That's all. No chatting like Kevin does, where he'd say, "You have a big patch of gray back here." Not Richard, who just utters the word, "Emma." He guides me under the gentle water again and rinses out the shampoo. With my eyes still closed, he washes me with white almond soap, gliding his fleshy hands over my slippery body. With eyes closed, we soak forever, side-by-side.

The water starts to chill and he emerges from the tub. Naked, he embraces me under the shoulders and lifts me out. He dries me off like I'm a child, then takes the same wet towel and dries himself. He doesn't say a word and pulls me by the hand into his bedroom. He lies on the bed and pulls me to him. I decide to go along with his quiet theme and not get too chatty. He unwraps me from the towel and finally says, "You are beautiful." He must not have his contacts in. He kisses my neck and says, "I want you."

It's so warm and relaxing, that I manage not to speak.

362

"I've wanted you ever since the day I saw you in the white dress," he says.

I hear his heart beating rapidly. He was so captivating when he was giving orders and delivering that baby. He puts his mouth on my lips; when I look up, I see he is looking up at me. It just occurs to me that we are about to make love. Is he thinking the same thing? My hand wants to go down there on him to check. Wracking my brain, I can't think of a single reason not to make love. Not one. He's not married; I'm not married. I want to. He seems to want to. Kevin and my dog are not watching.

He leans down and stares into my eyes. Now my heart is really pounding. This is different than with Graham. Graham was hot, red lust. This is warm, white love.

Richard looks right into my eyes and I get a glimpse of his soul. Now, I remember his soul from a thousand years ago. Instead of David Gray singing, I can hear angels singing. He kisses me and says, "I want you, Emma Budnjk."

I don't know what to say. I'm trying to calculate when I last had sex with Graham. Would he find out? Does it matter?

"You're not ready."

I don't know what to say, other than he's right. I was ready all this time, when he wasn't; I was ready until I did it with Graham. There is an unwritten waiting period between lovers—at least for women. Men, I'm not so sure.

My face must flash a worried look, for he takes the white sheets and pulls them up to my neck and kind of tucks me in.

He falls on his back. Thank goodness it's quiet. That is, except for the angels playing in my head. I lay on my side and Richard spoons me from the back. He kisses my ear and says in his mahogany voice, "I've missed this."

"I felt magic."

"I did too." He kisses my shoulders. "Do you want children, Emma?"

I feel the need to clarify. "Do you mean yours, or new ones?"

Richard pats me and laughs. "New ones." He gets up and tucks me back under the sheets. "Why don't you sleep a little longer."

How can I sleep now, when I have so much to process? I see his nakedness in the daylight. He's a runner, so his legs and butt are muscular, but his chest is lean. He looks at my eyes again with his Gulf Stream eyes.

He opens his dresser, searching for fresh clothes. I love to watch a man dress. He silently puts on boxers and a blue and white striped shirt. Men are so sexy in the way they do things silently. I wonder if they are biting their lips to keep from babbling, or is it too hard to juggle a conversation and button a shirt?

"What are you looking at?"

"Nothing, I just love watching you," I say.

He kisses me. "I have loved watching you. I don't know what I loved more, when you got butter all over your mouth eating lobster, or when you painted my portrait."

"So glad my sloppiness is appreciated."

"It's fascinating how you eat and paint with reckless abandon. I remember I felt so sad that rainy day—realizing I was trapped in a marriage with the wrong person."

Thank goodness his wife is not around. Then it all comes back to me. Oh, that's right, she was murdered.

He sits on the bed. "No, now I remember; it was earlier. I think I first fell for you when you sat on my—face."

"Well, don't make that the toast at our wedding." The minute I say it, I regret it. Thankfully, there is a noise downstairs.

"I wonder who that could be." He leaves the bedroom to check.

I climb out of the bed and, like the Weimaraner puppy that I am, silently follow him down the stairs with wet hair and a damp towel.

Richard is at the bottom of the stairs, watching every step of my decent. At the bottom, he pulls the towel in and says, "Do you want to get married?"

"Is that a survey question or a proposal?" I joke.

He pulls me in and kisses me, and before I get an answer, the door opens. It's the impeccably timed Graham. He pauses for moment, then he hurriedly says, "Richard, we need to talk quickly—the police are on their way."

Graham takes a long look at the towel and my dripping wet hair. I'm sure he saw the kiss through the glass. Now he probably thinks that Richard and I have done it. He gets really quiet.

"Nothing happened. I just took a bath," I say.

Richard and Graham disappear into the library.

The doorbell rings. Through the window, I see that it's Detective Perez and Captain Lacey waving at me through the glass. It's too late to run or duck, so I gesture for them to come in.

Detective Perez and Captain Lacey give each other knowing glances, then Captain Lacey says, "Nice outfit."

"We were just looking for you Emma," Detective Perez says, "but we made the mistake of going to your house." He laughs. "Then we thought you might be at the Flagmore, so we stopped there."

I try escaping up the stairs, but they keep talking.

"It was convenient though," Captain Lacey says, "because Pudge Lichtenfelder, Irene Ahr, and Esther Weinstein were all by the pool."

"But, Pudge was tight-lipped," Detective Perez adds.

Captain Lacey laughs. "She probably can't open them."

"Emma," Perez says, "we like asking you questions because you are such a…"

"Blabbermouth?" Graham interjects as he enters the foyer with Richard.

I run up the stairs to quickly change and point to Graham and Richard over my shoulder. "Start with them."

"I've been advised by my attorneys not to make any more statements," Richard says.

"We've discovered that Hudson DuPont's name is really Harvey Djengeleski; he's from Erie, Pennsylvania," Detective Perez says.

Three quarters up the stairs, I'm seduced back by juicy gossip.

"I knew he was a poser," Graham huffs.

"Your mother knew all along, but didn't want to hurt Kevin's feelings," Captain Lacey says to Richard. "She said it was fascinating to watch Hudson's game."

"This town is full of frauds," Richard says.

"He had a thing for wealthy ladies," Captain Lacey says.

"Ladies? I thought he was gay?" I say, pulling my towel up higher.

"He wasn't really gay. He was just posing as a gay man to be cool and get into Palm Beach."

I gasp at the thought, and then his resourcefulness.

"Emma, just out of curiosity, how did you first meet Hudson?" Detective Perez asks.

"At the beach club; Kevin was riding his bike when he rammed into Hudson."

"Oh, yeah," Captain Lacey says. "We almost arrested Kevin for RWI that day. Can you imagine being so hung over you get arrested for riding your bicycle into a car? But the officer couldn't stop laughing enough to get a Breathalyzer."

"That was probably no accident," Perez says. "Hudson set himself up to meet all of you."

"Dr. Weinstein, is that where you first met him?" Lacey asks.

Richard folds his arms. "I'm not answering questions, remember?"

"Dr. Weinstein, you become more suspicious by not answering our questions."

Wanting to hear his voice, I say, "Yes, Richard."

Richard finally says, "All right. I've got nothing to hide. I met him at my mother's apartment, and she knew him from Pudge. That's it."

"We'll have to go back and talk to those three," Detective Perez says.

"And what about this Russian girl?" Captain Lacey says. "Where was she when the gun went off?"

"She's innocent!" Perez blurts out.

Graham and Richard chuckle. "Yes, we can attest that there is no way that she shot Hudson."

"And where was Kevin during the shooting?" Captain Lacey asks.

Richard pauses, then finally says, "He was assisting me."

"So he was on the top deck with you?" Detective Perez says.

"Well, no. He was being such a pest that I made him wait at the bottom of the stairs."

"Kevin is afraid of guns," I say. "Guns, spiders and tapioca. Well I could go on, but you get the idea."

Captain Lacey turns to Graham. "We believe the gun used to shoot Hudson was your gun. We don't have the body, but we know it was a .22 that killed the pudding pot."

"But I was up on the top deck. Emma and Richard can attest to that," Graham says.

Right then we hear someone come in the back door. "Just me," Ping calls out.

He walks to the foyer, sees the detectives and stops short. "I not talk."

"Ping, what were you doing when the gun went off?" Detective Perez says.

Ping looks embarrassed and doesn't answer.

"Do you remember?" Captain Lacey asks.

"I with tai tai," Ping admits.

"Oh, that's right," Graham says. "It was after the ceremony with Pudge."

"Congratulations, Ping. We'll have to have a proper celebration sometime," Richard says.

"What were you doing at the moment that you heard the shot?" Detective Perez asks abruptly.

Ping gets really flushed. "I have say out loud?"

"Detectives, "Richard says, "do you honestly think a man is going to shoot someone in the middle of his honeymoon?"

The captain and the detective look at each other. "It's happened before."

Ping walks away. "I go cook for tai tai. She too shao."

"Okay, should I expect dinner tomorrow night?" Richard says.

"No. I no cook you anymore. I re-quit." Ping continues back to the kitchen and Richard follows him.

Richard comes back shortly with a look of no luck. "Graham, you'll have to speak with him."

Graham smiles. "Not to worry. Pudge will drive him crazy in a few days."

"So you all were on the top deck; Kevin was at the bottom of the stairs, and Pudge and Ping were doing their thing in a cabin?" Detective Perez says.

"And Irene was in a cabin with Trevor," Richard adds.

"That leaves Ernesto and your mother," Detective Perez concludes.

"Your mother," Lacey says, "the fencing spy, who is always up to something."

"She had her hands full acting as Pudge's wedding coordinator," Richard huffs. "Frankly, I prefer not to answer your questions. And I don't think these two should either."

Richard gracefully escorts them to the door.

Detective Perez gets an impish grin. "I'll leave you to your threesome."

After the police leave, Richard asks about Natasha.

"She's gone to her sister's house," Graham answers.

"Wouldn't you love to be the fly on that wall?" I can't help but say.

"What, and get my bloody face punched in by someone? Or watch her sister claw her eyes out?"

"Oh. I can see how you'd prefer to miss that. Come and have something to eat with Emma and me."

I ponder the thought of being part of "Emma and me."

"I know that none of us killed anyone, and I think it's important to stick together," Richard says.

"I agree," Graham responds.

"If we can somehow prove Hudson was responsible, then we'd be off the hook."

"Yes, at least for your wife's murder. Then we just have to figure out who killed Hudson."

"Ahem. What if your mother and Ernesto somehow took care of this messy little Hudson problem?" I say.

"Are you saying my mother was in cahoots with the dog walker?"

"Perhaps," Graham says with a little smile.

Richard exhales. "I can't wait to get him away from my family."

"No one told him?" Graham whispers to me.

Richard turns his head abruptly. "No one told me what?"

Graham is laughing. "Ernesto married your mother."

Thinking Graham is joking, Richard laughs. "Wouldn't that be hilarious."

I press his thigh. "Really! I was there. This way they won't have to testify against each other. I also think your mother did it to keep him away from Lisa."

"That part would be a relief," Richard says, "But seriously."

"Really! Your mother is very crafty."

Richard is falling over laughing. "You're telling me that my mother married the dog walker?"

"She had me write a prenup on a cocktail napkin and Irene notarized it."

Richard gets very sober looking. "Okay, now I am starting to believe you."

"Richard, let's go celebrate your new father-in-law," Graham jokes.

Richard looks to the ceiling. "Dear god."

64

Graham drives his Jaguar as Richard and I sit in the back like royalty. I wonder what Graham thinks. Just because someone is alone with someone wearing nothing but a towel doesn't necessarily mean they had sex.

We decide on Daniel Boulud's restaurant at the Brazilian Court Hotel. When we arrive, we are seated in the courtyard overlooking the garden and fountain. We are the only ones here, but still the maître d' fusses over just where to seat us. I wish Kevin were here. Poor Kevin; he thought he had love and now he has no one.

Right then, Kevin calls my cell phone. I'm dying to tell him about my romantic bath with Richard, but Kevin will surely let out a high-pitched sound that will elicit all the dogs in hearing range. Richard says to invite him.

"Hopefully Lisa's fiancé won't find out about her having a little last minute fling with Ernesto," Richard says.

"Well, she can create doubt by saying he's her grandmother's husband," I say.

Richard winces at the image. "Graham, how could you allow that to happen on the boat?"

Graham imitates Kevin's frequent whine. "What? I'm supposed to sail the boat, keep saboteurs from the electronics, feed babies *and* you expect me to keep Latin men from marrying octogenarians?"

"I suppose you had your hands full," Richard concedes.

"It was definitely sabotage of the electrical system; whomever did it clearly wanted us to be stranded at sea."

"Natasha could have done something before her water broke, or the person who shot Hudson might have wanted it to happen outside the US," I say.

"Natasha wouldn't know to do that; she doesn't even know how to use a toaster. Plus, one needed a Phillips head screwdriver to remove the panel cover," Graham says.

Richard leans back in his chair and folds his arms over his chest. "Who benefited the most from being stuck at sea?"

We all pause for a moment and then shout in unison, "Ping!"

The waiters must think this means come over fast, as three of them descend on our table. Kevin walks in and joins us.

"Kevin, I'm sorry about your friend," Richard says.

Kevin orders two glasses of wine at the same time. "What? I just spent time at the station for questioning. I wore this—I thought a turtleneck and my favorite blazer most appropriate."

"Is that my old jacket? For god's sake, please don't commit any crimes in it."

"Did you find out anything from them?" I ask Kevin.

"The detectives said they found marine cleaning acid when they took the pot to the lab. I wonder who did that?"

We all say, "Hello? Hudson."

Graham sniffs his drink suspiciously. "We all could have wound up bloody dead."

I pat Kevin's arm. "I'll bet you need some cheering up."

Kevin gulps from my wine glass. "Why do you say that, Emma? My boyfriend is dead—oh wait, my killer ex-boyfriend is dead—I'm accused of shooting him, I testify in a church mouse jacket, and my catering business is ruined thanks to all the bad publicity." Kevin takes a big swig of my wine and turns to Graham. "So, how's your baby?"

Graham sighs for a moment, and then punctuating each word, says, "You know for just a few moments when I was pondering your miserable little life, I had forgotten that I'm a murder suspect facing deportation and loss of my captain's license; and with all probability, I impregnated some Russian woman who is a bloody imposter and master deceiver, with whom I will be undoubtedly tied for the rest of my life in some sort of international custody battle spanning the globe—but thanks for bringing it to my attention." Graham laughs a hearty laugh at his absurd situation, and Kevin joins in.

Richard claps his hands. "Let's ponder someone else's life. Take Pudge for example. She got soused and married the Chinese cook, with no prenup. And she's still not off the hook for the Bunny episode. What else?"

Graham clinks his glass with Richard. "And she's bloody ugly."

Richard lets out a laugh usually reserved for the sudden realization of hopelessness. "She's been waiting ten years for me to be single, and now I'm falling for Emma."

Graham suddenly looks furious.

An under-joyed Kevin says, "While I end up all alone."

Graham says to me, "You couldn't wait for me?"

"Nothing happened," I protest.

"I didn't think so until now. And you, Richard, couldn't even wait for your wife to get cold."

Kevin's two drinks arrive and he intertwines them like lovers do. "I'm so glad you guys invited me over."

"Richard, I'm afraid it's not going to look very good for two suspects to be suddenly together." Graham says, as he walks out the door.

Richard looks down, probably thinking he'd better play it cool with me.

"Oh, my god!" Kevin exclaims.

When I look up, I spot an Adonis at the front door. He's tall with dark wavy hair and large blue eyes. Richard stands up and walks over to him and hugs him. As Kevin stares in drooling awe, Richard lures the perfect male specimen over to our table. "This is my son, Mark."

We welcome the Adonis to the table, taking turns to shock him with the events of the past few weeks. Richard's son is a charming and well-bred man, and it's jarring to think of him being related to Lisa. A new theory develops in my head: what if Lisa is not Richard's child? Hmm. I'll have to ponder this at another time when I'm not busy eating lobster rolls and Peekytoe crab salad. I can tell Kevin's spirits are lifted by this new Mark fellow. In front of his son, Richard is a paragon of plutonic behavior towards me. No kisses, winks or spoon-feeding.

65

The minute Kevin and I get home, he cries, "There is a God and his name is Mark!"

I already know that all references to Mark will include an exclamation mark. We climb up to my bedroom and find Ursula snoring away in the sweet spot of the bed, so Kevin and I curl up around her.

"When you marry Richard, and I marry Mark, you will be my stepmother."

Petting Ursula's head, I say, "Kevin, that's nice that you know after having one lobster roll with him. I'm surprised you didn't bring him home with you."

"I don't want him to know I live in the smallest house in Palm Beach."

"Besides, who knows if I'll end up with Richard. I don't know who I love more, Graham or Richard."

"I thought you only knew true love once you've done it with someone. Didn't you do it with Richard today?"

"No, we just took a bath."

"You say you love them both? Go for Richard, not the illegal alien with the illegitimate baby."

"I love them both, but in different ways. I feel like I've known Richard in a past life, but I feel like Graham is my future."

"Your past life sounds better. Anyway, back to me. Do you think Mark liked me?"

"He wouldn't have asked you out for dinner if he didn't. Where are you going?"

"The Breakers. Although it will be kind of creepy to go there."

"I hope the manager doesn't make you pay Hudson's posthumous tab."

"Can they do that?" Kevin gasps.

66

Graham drives me to the Colony Hotel. We ask to dine by the pool—a glorious feature surrounded by lit palm trees. Everything is so peaceful; that is until Graham tells me he thinks the baby is his. And that Richard is on house arrest. Graham is just full of news today.

Not willing to wait for our assigned waiter to come out, I summon a passing middle-aged lady customer over. Pointing to Graham I say, "He got some girl pregnant; can you ask someone to bring me a chardonnay?"

Without hesitation, the heavy-legged lady lopes into the restaurant like she's running a terrier in the Westminster Dog Show. In three minutes flat, she's back with an emergency chardonnay in hand, and one for herself. My new efficient friend parks at the neighboring table to hear more, directing her clueless but obedient husband to sit and be quiet.

I ask Graham if he recalls having been romantic with the "Nice Natasha" on or around August 4th. Oddly, he obliges, admitting he had one of the Natashas as stewardess on the yacht one steamy weekend in Harbour Island. "Steamy" being his code word for "shag" I guess. He adds that she thinks that's when she became pregnant.

"Well, was Pierre on the boat?"

"No, but…."

My mind starts to ponder the state of all things Graham. I didn't even know him then—so how can I be mad that he had sex with both topless Russian secret twins? Despite that realization, I have trouble stifling a glare.

Graham, for some odd reason, decides to escape to the men's room. My chardonnay lady takes this opportunity to float a theory. "She could have had relations with Pierre just before or after the weekend." Graham returns just as she turns back to her husband.

I ask, "What other men were there? I mean on the boat."

"The usual: Trevor, Richard, Ping, Irene—sorry, she's like a man."

"Yup, guy in a girl outfit."

"Funny thing is, looking back, I think both Natashas could have been on the yacht."

"Did you think you were seeing double?"

"No, I never saw them together. I just remember she was really sweet one minute and a complete bitch the next."

The lady at the next table seems to have an inquiry, as she's raising her hand like she's in class. I slip over to her and she whispers in my ear. "Do you think the doctor could have had sex with them?"

Graham hears this, and answers her directly. "Who knows? They aren't terribly selective."

I wonder if that's a dig against Richard, or the twins—or both.

"That's the thing." Graham says. "I suppose I should have noted that one minute she's got a flat tummy and the next she looks like she's having a freaking cow."

"Hello? That's all women!" the lady at the next table says.

"I'm afraid in this case it's actually two different women," Graham says to her.

"Somebody should have labeled them: Good twin and Evil twin," the lady says helpfully.

Graham tips his head to her. "Yes, excellent idea. Perhaps a magic marker would have worked."

Gulping my nerve tonic, I interview Graham. "What are you going to do if it's your baby?"

Right then, the charming Irish Maître d' begins to recite a litany of dinner specials. This causes the chardonnay lady to actually cry out, "Not now!" She then makes her husband go and fetch menus for us.

"I suppose I should do the right thing if the child is mine."

That's sweet of him.

"Naturally she doesn't want her sister to know it could be Pierre's baby, so mums the word."

The lady at the next table looks over and we both put our fingers on our mouths.

I can't help but wonder, what if it's Richard's baby?

Graham orders the Dover sole for two and a bottle of 1996 Montrachet, as recommended by the Maître d'. The lady at the next table spends the evening shushing her husband when he makes any attempt to talk. Graham says he feels awful about the Natasha thing, but now he has other problems with the police questioning him and the INS on his back. Apparently he failed to file some recent forms and lingered in the country too long and is "in a bit of a pickle."

Then, out of the blue, he says, "If it's not my baby, and I don't get deported, will you marry me?"

"What kind of proposal was that?" the lady's confused husband asks her.

"Shush! I want to hear her answer. Although, I think she'd be better off with the doctor."

I guess she knows Richard, or keeps up with the Palm Beach Post. Graham, of course, hears this. He turns to her. "Yes, she'd be better off with Richard —assuming he doesn't end up in jail."

"And assuming it's not *his* baby," she says.

"Margaret, who *are* these people?" the lady's husband finally cries.

After we finish, the waiter comes with the bill. I'm grateful for the interruption, as it gives me time to think; I'm starting to come to my senses. Finally, I say, "I guess we'll have to wait and see."

The lady nods her head. When Graham is preoccupied with the bill, she says to me, "Psst! Hopefully that Dr. Weinstein has had a vasectomy and it's not his baby."

This never occurred to me. Thank you, nosy stranger.

Graham drives me home and opens the periwinkle wooden door to Larry—maybe for the last time.

67

After a few days of eating and drinking in our little hideaway, Kevin and I venture to the beach. "On the bright side, if it's Graham's baby then you know it's not Richard's baby," Kevin deduces. "And you can probably talk *him* into getting married. Hopefully, before Pudge or the skinny Natasha steals him." Kevin tries, but his attempts to cheer people up usually backfire. It's good that he's not any sort of therapist.

I watch the waves. "I wonder where we'll all end up."

"Jail, probably."

"Well, at least by then we'll know whose baby it is, and maybe who killed Hudson and Bunny."

"Okay, so best case you end up married to someone and living happily ever after painting cakes and naked men. But what's to become of me?"

"Why don't you become a catering detective?"

Kevin laughs. "You can be realtor spy."

There is a knock on the door. It is Graham with his head down, like when I first spied him tuning his guitar at the hotel.

"It looks like someone has some bad news," Kevin greets him.

"Kevin," Graham says over-politely, "will you excuse us while Emma and I go for a short walk."

"I should probably come along, that way I don't have to wait for Emma to tell me; besides, she always mixes up the details."

Graham takes my hand as we walk down the lane. "I got the test results and he's my baby all right."

I notice Kevin is behind us, walking Ursula. "Wait, but which Natasha?"

"The one not married to Pierre," Graham calls back to Kevin.

We both let out a lamented, "Oh."

Kevin lets Ursula off her leash, which causes her to run to me and for Kevin to have to follow more closely.

Graham's forehead is a grid of worries lines as he elaborates. "I suppose I should marry her. I'd hate to think of a stranger raising my child, if she marries someone else. Made that mistake before."

"Especially when she gets her husbands by mail order," Kevin quips.

Graham looks annoyed. "Of course she can't pretend to be Pierre's wife anymore, and the police have contacted the INS about both of us. We'll both have to leave the country when this is all over."

"Where will you go? And will you need a dog?" Kevin asks.

"I can get us both positions on a yacht in Mallorca. And if you're talking about Ursula, No."

"What makes you so sure she's not a murderer?"

"Ursula I'm not so sure about, but this Natasha was at a prenatal seminar in Ft. Lauderdale; they have it all on record."

"Kevin, do you mind?"

Kevin and Ursula stop following us, looking dejected.

Motivated to pin this on Natasha, I say, "But Natasha left the ball early, she could have done it. Who knows where she went afterward?"

"I didn't want to tell you—she went to the boat that night."

I flash him a not so friendly look. With the high tide approaching, a huge wave surprises us. The legs of his pants are now soaked, so he stops to roll them up. Finally, he adds, "Nothing happened that night. I wouldn't have been with you if I'd just been with her."

"So, your alibi is that you left the ball to get Bunny, stopped at the house and somehow forgot to get Bunny, then went to the boat with the skinny mean one."

"Well, sort of. The marina has timed surveillance tapes that have been thoroughly reviewed."

"I'll bet. So both Natashas are off the hook?"

"Yes, the police are mostly focusing on Richard now. He was missing during much of the ball, so he could have gone back to whack her. Plus, they think he may have given Bunny a shot to cause an allergic reaction."

"Oh no! Say, I've really got to get going now."

Graham kisses me goodbye. "I'm sorry I didn't tell you about Natasha. I wish it had turned out differently."

"You don't have to marry her."

"It's hard not to love the mother of your child."

I look down. "You love her?"

"Emma—I'm so sorry."

As the clouds roll in, I watch as Graham walks down the shore, his silhouette getting smaller and smaller. I feel like crying, mostly for him.

68

Kevin runs up. "I heard most of it."

"He's marrying her and they're moving to Mallorca."

"Oh, too bad it wasn't your baby; I could have moved there with Hudson and we could have lived happily ever after."

"Yes, if only my boyfriend didn't get another woman pregnant and if only your boyfriend wasn't murdered."

"And if only you weren't a prime suspect."

I tell him we can now eliminate Graham, and both Natashas.

"That's a relief. Well, sort of."

"We should be able to process some of the clues."

We walk back to our houses. "Where should we start?"

Kevin looks next door. "I think we should snoop around Ernesto's place. I just saw him leave."

Following Kevin, who is halfway to Ernesto's door, I say, "Are you kidding? What if we get caught?"

"Hello? We'll use the pug defense."

"You are not using my dog to break and enter."

"Of course not, she's already on probation. She'll just be the cover. You be the lookout and I'll do the B&Eing."

"Take your phone and make a quick video, that way we can analyze it later for anything out of the ordinary. And for heaven's sake, don't leave Ursula inside."

Kevin grabs Ursula; I can hear the screen door squeak open and slam. Biting my nails off, I watch from the front step for signs of Ernesto. The only thing that's reassuring is to hear consistent snooping noises and humming from Kevin. That is, until I hear a scream, and realize he must have encountered a small insect. After what seems like an hour, but is really only four minutes, I see Ernesto ambling down the lane. I call out to him in an overly loud voice. "Hello, Ernesto! How are you, Ernesto?"

I look back and see Kevin lowering my dog out the side window; he sees Ernesto coming and runs out the back door. *Yikes!*

Ernesto's face is all question marks. "Did your dog get into my house again?"

"Sorry. Let me know if she got into your fridge."

"I'm moving back to Brazil," Ernesto informs me. "Maybe your dog should take over my lease."

I hesitate to ask, but want to know. "Are you going with one of the Weinstein ladies?"

He nods his head. "Yes, and guess which one?"

"Well, I'd guess Lisa, if she was not previously engaged."

He gleefully says her engagement to the sausage man is over; he goes into his house without another word.

That's interesting.

Then I see Kevin miming a crazy person. "Let's get in the cone of silence. Grab your laptop."

The cone of silence is my car with the radio on. Once safely in the car, I ask what he's found out.

He rolls up the windows in our spy-mobile. "I found an expired Brazilian police ID with Ernesto's photo, and then I found a framed picture of what is probably his mother. It looks like her name was Marina, because she is holding up a gigantic check for $7 million dollars that says Marina Carvalho on it.

"Kevin, you really should work for the CIA. Did you get anything good on the video?"

"Oh, I forgot."

We drive down to the marina and pick up a Wi-Fi signal from one of the yachts. Kevin types in Marina Carvalho and Sao Paulo. A newspaper article in the Folha de Sao Paulo from four years ago pops up. It appears to be in Spanish, but when we do an online translation, we discover it's in Portuguese.

"I forgot they speak Portuguese in Brazil, not Spanish."

"I wanted to go to Brazil with Hudson. Now you made me sad."

I read out loud: *The police have concluded Marina Carvalho Filho Fuentes, 57, died from an accidental poisoning on September 4, 2009. Someone mistakenly put roach tablets in her mint tin.*

"What? And she didn't notice?" Kevin says.

I read on: *Roach tablets resemble Asteroid mints, and anyone could have made the mistake. The case was never brought to trial for lack of evidence and lack of a suspect. Her husband at the time had been out of the country for three weeks and never charged; he subsequently died from a heart attack. Due to the recent surge in shootings, the case was considered minor and dismissed. Her only son, Ernesto, who was a police officer with the Sao Paulo police, launched his own investigation, which resulted in his dismissal from the force due to his vigilante tactics. There was no will, and the entire lottery winnings went to the surviving husband. When he died, his will left the fortune to his children from a previous marriage. Ernesto, the son of Carvalho Filho Fuentes, inherited only the mother's cat.*

"Wow!" Kevin exclaims. "That explains the cat food. Cat probably ran away looking for the mother."

"Kevin, isn't it curious that Hudson had an aversion to Asteroids?"

"Well, it couldn't have been an aversion to me."

"Remember when we thought Hudson was speaking Spanish at the hotel? Graham told me later he heard Hudson speaking fluent Portuguese."

"He *was* a world traveler."

"Remember when he ate the hot guacamole? He said he'd never been to Brazil, yet he speaks Portuguese. What if he was there four years ago?"

"Where, Portugal?"

"No, Brazil! Let's see…Hudson lied about his name, he dyes his hair from blonde to brown, and seems to have an aversion to Asteroids—or else he just doesn't want to kiss you. I think Hudson is a traveling poisoner!"

"There is no such occupation."

"What if Hudson killed Ernesto's mother?"

Kevin dismisses this theory. "Just because someone dyes their hair, hates Asteroids and speaks Portuguese doesn't mean they poison people. I can't believe you think my Hudson is a mother killer. Come on…I have to take a whiz and I think it's a crime in Palm Beach to do that outside."

"Okay, but let's think about this Hudson theory some more. Let's go to a restaurant so you can pee indoors."

"Yeah, like your dog does."

69

We walk to the leafy via off Worth Avenue. Passing pricey little shops, we take the courtyard entrance to Bice restaurant, where I had my blind date with Graham.

As we enter, Kevin violently points to a man at the bar. It's Detective Perez. I'm dragged into the empty dining room by the frantic Kevin. Once in the other room, he lets out a muffled scream. "Oh no! I'm being stalked!"

The next thing I know, we're hiding under the white tablecloth of the banquette in the closed-off back section of the dining room. Then we hear the Maître d' escort someone to the adjoining dining area. We can't see, but we hear two voices…voices that sound just like Detective Perez and Big Red! Her smoky voice is unmistakable, along with her tendency to cause a chair to creak.

Big Red lights up another cigarette, and we hear the waiter tell her it's prohibited.

"I'm an assistant DA, what are you gonna do about it buddy?"

Kevin and I look at each other and, for once, do not say a word. The waiter asks for their drink orders. I hear Perez say, "Jack Daniels on the rocks for the lady, and Bacardi and Diet Coke for me."

Big Red chortles at being called a lady, which prompts her to change her drink to a Manhattan. "I'm glad they're giving me this case to try. I'm so sick of prosecuting jaywalking."

"Don't forget that big case you had about the lady who cut off pillow tags."

She laughs. "I'm so glad we'll get to work together."

Kevin and I look at each other, shocked about a romance between Perez and Big Red. We wait for Detective Perez's reply. Finally, he clears his throat and changes the subject, indicating his disinterest.

"Let's see, the victim suffered from blunt force trauma, petechial hemorrhage due to minor suffocation, burns on her forearms, and anaphylactic shock."

Big Red quips, "Is that all?"

"Yeah, Lacey said the duct tape was not fully adhered, so she could still breathe, and the burns could have been due to minor electrocution, or looked accidental, so we can't run with that."

"Do you think several people tried to kill her?"

"Who knows. We pretty much had to charge the husband to get the ball rolling. He's got the best lawyer in the world, who will help us point the finger at other suspects."

"Why don't you arrest some of the others?"

"If I do, they will run and get lawyers and then clam up." Perez adds, "I have no problem charging the rest of them if you want me to, but how are you ever going to get a jury to convict?"

"I'm not sure about winning a conviction at trial, but the grand jury indictments will be easy."

"Are we talking ham sandwiches?"

"Oh, I forgot," Big Red says. "All of them except for Kevin."

"I always liked her," Kevin whispers.

"Did you ever find out who was playing the piano? That could be an issue in getting 'beyond a reasonable doubt.'"

"I don't even know where to start with that."

Kevin starts to giggle and indicates to me that he really has to go to the bathroom. Well, he's just going to have to wait.

"We're getting close to the end of the season. We'll have to charge a few of the others, or they'll all leave and well just be stuck with the doctor."

Big Red groans. "Drag. I was all set to indict Harvey Djingeleski."

"I keep forgetting that's DuPont's real name. What for tax evasion? Worse case, a jewel thief. He had no motive to kill Bunny Weinstein, so he would have had to be a setup or hit…or blackmail."

"What did you find in his room that was so exciting?" Big Red asks.

"See, I took a picture of them; I can't pronounce the name."

"Someone has good taste: Debauve & Gallais Chocolates."

"I sent him those," Kevin mouths.

"Why is that a clue?" Big Red says.

Perez must scroll to the next picture. "See what's inside? An earring. In fact, an emerald earring belonging to one Bunny Weinstein."

"So, Harvey what's his name DuPont either stole the emerald earring and hid it in the chocolate, or else someone planted it there."

Kevin shakes his head and mouths, "Not me."

"Too bad it's too late to get him to talk," Big Red says.

"That was pretty clever of someone to get rid of him."

"Okay, so let's go through the list one more time."

I can hear Perez flip through his notebook. "I'll start with the ones with the most motive."

"Yeah, like that Emma girl."

I gasp and Kevin puts a napkin in my mouth.

"I don't think she did it," Perez says.

Big Red's laugh turns into a cough. "Where do I start? She can now have Richard Weinstein; she had access to the house; she had access to the emerald earrings in Bunny's dressing room; she could have planted them in the fancy chocolates; she found the body; she was there at the house that night; she was on the boat when Hudson was shot. Need I continue?"

Kevin looks at me like I'm the killer.

Detective Perez tries to cut her off. "But she's so sweet."

Big Red scoffs. "Puhlease."

"Really, I think it was the old lady; Esther-the-spy Weinstein. She's got nothing to lose, had access, is capable of the whack—she takes fencing lessons for Christ's sake—and her son Richard was miserable."

Big Red exhales what must be a huge cigarette drag. "What about him? I know you arrested him just to get some leverage, but think about it. All of his assets were in his wife's name; he loves the silly realtor girl, whom he was about to lose to his lothario yacht captain if he didn't hurry up and do something; he had access to the earrings; he could have smacked Bunny, or hired Hudson or Ernesto or pretty much anyone to do it; he was there at the house that night sleeping with the girl; he was on the yacht and could have shot Hudson and fed him to the sharks."

Perez sips his drink loudly. "He never should have mentioned the shooting. We'd never have known."

Besides being forthright, I wonder if Richard told because he thought Ernesto must of have done it. This would keep Ernesto away from his daughter.

"Let's consider Dr. Weinstein as a murderer for a minute," Big Red says.

"I doubt it was Dr. Weinstein," Perez says dismissively. "He plays freakin' "Clair de Lune" on the piano. People like that don't kill people. If he wanted his wife dead, he wouldn't have taken all the time and trouble to hire a hit man to strike her on the head after a party, shut off the power, plant an earring in some chocolate, invite the hit man on his yacht, and then shoot him and disguise the noise with a crying freaking baby!"

I hear Big Red slap the table. "But he has time on his hands."

"Why not just give her a shot of pentafluoroethyl?"

I wonder what that is, and suddenly remember the spent hypodermic needle I found in his trash. Maybe he did it that way? Rats! I hate it when I fall in love with murderers.

We hear the melted ice cubes in Big Red's Manhattan as she tips it back. "That makes it look like a heart attack, but is there a drug that looks like anaphylaxis?"

"I'll have to check, but I really don't think he's our guy."

I'm relieved that the detective thinks Richard is innocent.

"Well, I still think it's the husband," Big Red says. "But what about Lisa, Ping, Irene, Graham and Pudge?"

I hear a pen click. "Let's see, Bunny stole Richard from Pudge, and Pudge stole someone from Irene, and Irene stole someone from someone. I'm going to have to get the flow chart from Esther Weinstein. Not sure about Pudge Lichenfelder, but I don't think Irene Ahr did it."

"Hello? Duct tape? Suffocation? Bunny caused the flood in her house, and got her fired from Petco for eating the Christmas dog biscuits."

"Okay, I give you that, so we'll keep her on the list. Now, Graham would have no interest, even though Bunny turned him into Immigration. By making Richard single again, he had no chance at Emma."

I look at Kevin and nod.

"What about a conspiracy between everyone with a motive?"

"Should we indict the Girl Scouts too?" Perez jokes.

I never realized how hard it is to laugh quietly. Kevin probably never realized how hard it is to laugh and not pee.

Big Red says, "So where does that leave us?"

"I'm stumped. Until we get Dr. Weinstein's lawyers to come up with a good case on one of the others, we're stuck."

Big Red chugs the last of her liquor. "I can tie a knot in my cherry stem…want to see?"

"I've got to run; I'll pay at the bar."

Kevin lets out a nearly audible sigh as they get up to leave. I see Big Red try to catch up. She doesn't seem as fat as I recall. Perhaps I'll call her Medium Red. We wait an excruciating amount of extra safety time, then run to our car by the marina. Kevin pees on a historical banyan tree and gets yelled at by an old lady walking her dog.

I ponder the situation Richard is in. "I've got to tell my poor Richard they're just using him to find the killer. That can't be legal!"

"But if you get Richard off on a technicality, they may arrest you or Graham…or me for god's sake!"

70

I call Richard, saying I need to have a chat with him. He calmly says to stop by the house, adding that he's all alone. Kevin, learning that Mark has gone to Lisa's house, decides to go home. When I get there, I tell Richard what we overheard at the restaurant. He seems grateful for the intelligence and says he'll talk to his lawyer about it all tomorrow. We hold hands and chat about Graham and his situation. Richard pats me and asks if I'm upset. My heart is pounding and I say, "I never thought it would turn out that he'd be tied up and you would end up free."

He gives me a nice long kiss and asks how I feel about that. I say, "This is how I had dreamed it would turn out. Well, I'm sorry, not with all the drama."

Richard kisses me tenderly and says, "The first time I saw you, I had hoped for this."

He plays the piano, and I fall in love with Ludovico Einaudi's "Tracee." I bask in the beauty and simplicity of the evening.

As darkness falls, Richard silently leads me up the stairs. I think of the time he led me up the stairs that night, when I thought his wife was sleeping nearby. This feels very different. That night, I remembered thinking I want to be next to his heart. Now, I want to be inside his soul.

I see his hand on the knob to his bedroom door, as he pensively turns it and I follow him in. It is all so slow and quiet. No music is playing, well only in my heart. There is a gentle rain pelting the glass like a million little tears of joy.

He disappears into the bath, which gives me time to think. I sit on the bed, then decide to take all of my clothes off and climb under the covers. I put his pillow over my face and can smell his scent of butter.

This is the last moment of "before." After this I'll know what it is like to be with him. Will he have forgotten what to do? Will he be as gentle as a butterfly landing on a flower petal? Well, not that gentle. Will I fall into deep hopeless love? The kind you can't see your way out of?

I see the light from the bath go off. My heart pounds like the pelting of the rain. He laughs when he sees me hiding under the covers. He lights a candle which illuminates his face; it is not his usual bemused look; it's wistful.

He's naked as he slides under the covers. He's warm and soft. Well, make that warm and hard as my thigh confronts his firmness.

He kisses me on the forehead, then the lips. Then he sits up and crosses his arms over his chest. "Emma, you are so quiet. Are you sure you want to do this? Or do you want to work up to it by doing one of your little vegetable acts that you and Kevin are always talking about?"

I laugh, then I begin to process that thought.

He says, "I'm not Graham."

I look right into his now worried looking eyes and know that I want to make love to him now. I want to know him.

I say, "You're the one I always wanted."

He lets out a sigh.

I put my mouth on his lips and let him know it's time.

****

Afterwards, I know what it feels like to wait for angels and to have them land inside me.

71

The next morning I awake to find Richard lying next to me still sleeping. I think I'd better get out of there before everyone returns. He drives me home and the scenery looks completely different. The sky looks bluer, the grass greener. I can hear the flute in the song playing on the radio. I turn and look at Richard's face and he looks calm—like a lake instead of an ocean tide.

When I walk in the house, Kevin is waiting for me out back tapping his foot. "Well, Missy! That was some chat."

"It was beautiful."

"Glad you didn't waste a lot of time getting over Graham."

Kevin sips his coffee and tells me all that he's processed over the night. "Even though the police are really smart – well, excluding Rusty – they'll never be able to pin this on any one person."

"What if it's a conspiracy that they know will never be proven?"

Ursula escapes out the back door and I'm worried she'll run to Ernesto's. I lure her back with an old Snausage.

Kevin looks at the Snausage. "Eww, are those for dogs? I've been eating them for weeks; I thought they were Combos pretzels."

"You said you lost four pounds, so don't complain."

Kevin grabs more coffee. "Great, I'll write a diet book."

"Meanwhile, that was a fascinating episode listening to Perez and Big Red!"

"What's ana-phallic shock? Is that when someone is so, you know…small, that you are shocked to death?"

"No, I think it's a deadly allergic reaction."

"Maybe it was Pudge. She has been known to be cavalier in the bacteria department."

"You know who we are completely forgetting about? Pierre."

"He could have put hair dye on her, sometimes people react to that."

"But, I suppose if he wanted to kill her, he would have shaved her head and had her die of mortification."

"Besides being redundant," Kevin says, "can people really die from that?"

"I'm sure."

"You know who you are conveniently forgetting about? Graham!"

"No, I'm not. I've already concluded he would have thrown her off the back of the boat and hit the throttle."

"Maybe he threw my Hudson off."

"He would have just done that with Bunny. That would have been so easy. And the sharks make everything so neat and tidy. So I'd say he's safe."

"It's not looking so good for Richard."

I think of the syringe and let out a leading, "Oh dear."

"What?"

"I found a hypodermic needle in his bathroom trash that morning."

"Did the police find it?"

"No, I threw it out the window; it's probably still on the roof."

"You'd better climb out there and get it."

"I know. Will you help me?"

Ursula gets caught on a table leg which causes a chain reaction of catastrophe.

"Yes, but if you and Richard end up in the pokey, I'm not watching Ursula."

I look around. "We'd better start thinking of someone to frame."

Kevin sweeps the broken glass under the table. "Oh great, tampering with evidence, framing, or whatever the legal term is." Then, in a gangsta accent, he says, "You are goin down, sista!"

It's hard not to laugh when he accidently eats another Snausage. "Back on your diet? Say, what about Pudge? Surely her cooking would cause a deadly reaction."

"Hmm. Let's not go there. She's my only client. Let's go with that crazy little Lisa girl. She could have electrocuted her, and probably has a good swing. Maybe her black lipstick caused the phallic shock."

"No, I don't think she did it. Richard would have hired a lawyer for her by now."

"How about Ping? I'd like to get him off me. Follows me around like a lost puppy."

"I think he has a crush on you. But, he wouldn't have done it. If he did, he would have used one of his Henckel knives."

"Great, I've got a stalker with knives."

Kevin walks in and locks the front door, then he pulls out duct tape to seal our windows and doors shut. "What about Irene?"

"Yes, there was duct tape on her mouth, but Bunny Weinstein didn't die from suffocation. And Irene says she was merely helping Bunny remove the ugly black hair, and Ping cut a slit so she could drink her iced tea with a straw."

"Oh, yeah, she ordered that right in the middle of the party; like I had time to serve people. I made Hudson take it up."

"He could have put poison in it, but we'll never know because I put the glass in the dishwasher. Rats! I wish I wasn't so neat; the cops could have tested it in the lab."

"Yes, the *one* time you are neat."

"I can't believe Big Red thinks it could be Richard."

"That would be terrible, because he's your only hope for love. I suppose you could get conjugal visits."

I must look really sad, because Kevin suddenly shuts up.

"I know it might look bad," I say, "but I also know he wouldn't kill anyone."

"Who's left on your list to frame?"

"If we figure out who really did it, we won't need to frame anyone. Okay, that leaves Ernesto, Trevor and Esther Weinstein."

"Ernesto has always seemed like a murderer to me—a hot murderer—but why would he kill Bunny?"

"They were lovers. Remember he didn't want to do something with her that day? She said she knew what he was up to. Maybe she was blackmailing him into sex."

"That's pitiful; even I wouldn't do that."

We both get lost in our thoughts for a moment.

Finally, Kevin says, "I think it's Trevor. He was swinging the wooden golf club before you got to the party. He could have caused the blunt force trauma."

"But her head had a greasy residue."

"What? She was hit by a flying cheeseburger?"

"Or a frozen lamb leg."

"You think Trevor whacked Bunny with a frozen lamb leg?

"No, I think Hudson did. Remember he pretended there was an intruder? Then he retracted it when you said you were going to call the police."

"But she didn't die from it," Kevin defends Hudson.

"Well, it sounds like a combination of things, but I think the anaphylactic shock ultimately did her in."

"That's the thing that Richard gave her a shot for?"

"We don't know that."

Kevin, trying to be practical, says, "Esther probably gave her the shot. She should just take the fall for Richard. She's so old, she'll be dead before anything goes to trial."

"I keep forgetting...we've got to get that needle!"

72

Kevin and I hop in the car to drive to Richard's house. No doubt detecting our sense of urgency, Ursula insists on coming along as our accomplice. Trevor answers the door and barely flinches as the pug runs past. Dr. Phil, dressed as a ballerina, flees the room.

Mrs. Weinstein, Irene, Richard and his son, Mark, are sitting quietly. I don't see any signs of drinking or killing; in fact, they're sitting and having tea. Something must be up.

Mrs. Weinstein fills us in. "In case you are wondering, the police were just here. That's why we're not drinking booze. They were called out on a breaking and entering, but are coming right back."

"They've narrowed it down to four suspects," Trevor says.

Richard points to his ankle bracelet, and says, "I'm on it, naturally, plus you, Emma, Mother and Ernesto."

I say, "What about the Hudson as hit man theory?"

Kevin tries to get off the Hudson subject by saying, "Emma, very nice, but didn't we come here for a reason?"

I pull Kevin down the hall on the pretext of looking for his missing chef's hat. We sneak upstairs to Richard's bathroom, with Kevin acting as my lookout. I climb out the window and dangle from the ledge in a desperate attempt to reach for the incriminating syringe. Meanwhile, Kevin makes himself busy sniffing Richard's cologne bottles. I'm out on a roof with no railings. What if I fall? I have a fear of heights, among other things. Whew, I carefully grab the syringe and start climbing back in the window then I hear a car pull up.

Rats! It's our buddies. My lookout is sitting on the toilet lid reading *Architectural Digest*.

"Emma? Whatcha doin?" Perez calls up to me.

"Umm. Nothing."

I run and hide the used syringe where no one will find it—under Lisa's messy bed. Leaving the dawdling Kevin, I walk slowly down the stairs, like nothing happened.

Richard gathers us around and advises us not to answer any questions. Then he looks directly at me and adds, "Or launch any theories."

Detective Perez and Captain Lacey are at the door, peering in.
Trevor shuffles to the door muttering, "Remind me to order drapes."

When our navy blue friends enter the living room, we see they have someone standing behind them. It's my mother.

73

Detective Perez is clearly having trouble containing his laughter. "Emma, we got a call for a break-in and found this lady climbing in your window."

"Mom! Oh no! I completely forgot to pick you up at the airport."

I feel really awful now, especially when I think of the nine million times mom picked me up from school.

Mom shuffles in. "It's all right, honey, Mr. Ambercrombie knocked my cell phone in the fish tank—I think he was trying to electrocute them—so I couldn't call you. I found a nice taxi driver and told him to take me to Larry."

I'm glad he didn't drive her to my ex-fiance's house.

Richard and Trevor are smirking.

"At first we thought it was Kevin's mother," Captain Lacey says, "because he's always climbing in windows and that stuff is hereditary, but then we heard the laugh."

"Your mother laughs just like you Emma," Perez says.

"What were you laughing at, Mom?"

"Well, the taxi driver got confused between Larry, Curly and Moe, making me climb into the wrong window. So I'm sitting waiting for you to remember your poor old widowed mother, when this Spanish man comes downstairs." Mom takes a moment to blush. "He wasn't wearing any pants."

"Really, mother!"

"Do tell!" says Mrs. Weinstein from the edge of the sofa.

"Anyway, he sent me on my way to the next house. So I'm climbing in the window when my derriere gets stuck. Some idiot put duct tape all over it—the window, not me. And then these nice men came and suggested we go for a little ride. I should thought of this earlier. I could have had them pick me up at the airport and saved $25 bucks."

"Emma, we figured you had to be here," Perez says.

Mom points and says, "Is that Pouilly-Fuissé?"

Irene comes in and hugs my mother; I wonder how long it's been since they've seen each other. Hopefully it wasn't kindergarten. Irene thanks her for the get-well cards and letters, but I can see that Mom is distracted by the surroundings.

As I introduce my mother to the rest of the gang, Kevin comes down and gives her a big hug and asks if she brought any cookies. She pulls out a smooshed package of Butter Scotch Krimpets. "I sat on them on the plane, but I'm sure they'll taste the same."

Richard gets caught laughing, and finally recovers with, "Emma, now I see where you get it from."

"You must be Dr. Weinstein," Mom burbles.

Richard gives her a hug. "Yes, but call me Richard. I can't tell you what a pleasure it is to finally meet you."

Mom looks at Mark. "So, Emma, is this your new boyfriend?"

"No, that's Richard's son."

"Well, where is this English yacht captain I keep hearing about?"

Mrs. Weinstein flicks her hand. "Oy, where do we start?"

Richard comes over and takes my hand in a subtle show of affection.

Mom looks on warily and gulps her wine.

"We have gathered some more information," Captain Lacey begins.

"We would have had it sooner if we had all of Ernesto's last names in the right order," Detective Perez says. "Did you guys know he was with the police force in Brazil?"

"Grandma, your new husband is a dog walker, a masseuse and a cop?" Mark says.

"Those were just his covers. My husband is quite a renaissance man."

Captain Lacey is reeling. "Wait a minute, what do you mean?"

"You know, the era when everyone painted and had banquets all the time."

"No," Lacey says, "are you saying you're married to the dog walker?"

Mrs. Weinstein does a little bow, pirouette and curtsy in reply.

Detective Perez shakes his head. "Well, your husband is quite a sharp shooter, and we're thinking he's the one who shot and killed Hudson."

"What if I say I did it? That would create enough doubt to keep him free."

"Esther, can I have him when you're in the slammer?" Irene jokes.

At this point, I guess Mom has figured out Graham is out of the picture and seems to be warming up to Richard. "So, I heard you're single now. Emma, you should bring him to my house for Easter."

Captain Lacey points. "He's not going far with that ankle bracelet."

Mom practically falls off the sofa when she sees the monitoring device.

"Dr. Weinstein, we don't think you shot Hudson, but you're still not off the hook for killing—or ordering the killing of—your wife."

Now mom begins what can only be described as a not so subtle scowl at Richard.

Detective Perez takes over. "We have some new information, adding back the fifth suspect."

"I hope I'm not back on the list," Trevor mutters.

"No," Perez says, "it's possible Bunny Weinstein was killed by DuPont."

"And it's so neat and tidy that he's dead. No need to continue with a bothersome trial. Did you bring the key for Babka's ankle?" Mrs. Weinstein says.

"The trouble is, DuPont had little motive, so we believe someone hired him to kill your wife. The question is, who?" Detective Lacey says.

Mom stares at Richard, who is forced to say, "Don't look at me. And as much as I'd love to elaborate, I've been advised not to speak."

He slides down to Mom but she recoils so quickly she spills her wine.

"Any ideas who would have hired him?" Mark asks to get things back on track.

"We searched his hotel room and found a four-carat emerald in a box of chocolates," Detective Perez says.

Captain Lacey adds, "And it's exactly like the ones your wife wore to the 2009 Paget's Phalange Ball, Dr. Weinstein."

I pretend to be surprised. "Wow! You guys are good! Hudson must have stolen it during the party."

"Then he would have stolen both earrings. We found the other one in her jewelry box. We believe the first one was sent as a down payment for killing her."

Richard breaks his silence. "Well, don't look at me. I wouldn't have been that clever. I probably would have written a monogramed check."

"What kind of chocolates have emeralds in them?" Mom ekes out.

Detective Perez scrolls through his phone to show us a photo of a dark box with light blue writing that looks like it says D&G, and a lime green sticky note.

"We're checking to see the list of everyone who bought that kind of chocolate. They sell them at that fancy Amici Market on County road. It's right by Cat's Trail," Captain Lacey says.

"Ernesto likes to use green sticky notes, I say. "I'll bet he put them on the chocolate box. He was in Bunny's closet that day. He could have taken the earring and put it in the box as down payment on a hit." I know at this moment to put my hand over my mouth.

"We have found a pair of Stubbs and Wootton slippers," Captain Lacey says to Richard.

"They didn't happen to be navy bespoke slippers with tan piping?"

"Why, are they yours?"

"Never mind; I was just wondering."

"I was wondering who would pay a thousand bucks for custom slippers then donate them," Kevin says to Richard. "They didn't fit me, so I gave them to Hudson."

Mom is starting to inch back toward Richard.

"That's what is making this investigation so difficult; everyone's DNA is everywhere," Captain Lacey says.

"Hudson probably knew the gig was up on the yacht. We think he tried to kill all of you, or at least some of you," Detective Perez adds. "The pudding pot that was shot through contained Ospho acid."

"What's that?" Mark asks.

"Acid-based boat cleaner," Trevor answers without missing a beat.

Richard laughs. "Is that the same pot your dog fell into?"

I slap my head. "That's why Ursula's feet were red."

"He takes my favorite slippers and puts acid in our pudding," Richard grumbles.

Mom whispers in my ear. "Emma, I don't know who he's talking about, but don't invite him to my house."

"Whoever ate it would have died. Not right away, but a slow burning death," Captain Lacey says.

"Lovely," Richard says.

Mark laughs. "Dog Saves 10 Lives. I can see it in the paper."

"I think Hudson was trying to kill us all because most of us wagered on him," Trevor says.

Just when the gossip is getting juicy, Kevin suggests we take Ursula out.

We go out back and see Mrs. Weinstein making frantic phone calls in the side yard. As we head to the pool house, Kevin says, "I had to get out of there. I get kind of upset when they blame everything on Hudson and he's not here to defend himself."

He looks like he's going to cry, so I pull out a coconut lime square, like we had on that hammock day.

He sits on the bench. "Remember that day? We were so happy and carefree."

Ursula sneaks a bite. Kevin takes it from her mouth, and puts it in his.

"Don't worry, we'll figure this out. One thing is, Hudson wouldn't know to give Bunny a shot because he was probably unaware of her allergies to shellfish."

"So you think Esther forced a lobster tail down Bunny's throat?" Kevin says.

"Well, how else would shellfish get in her body? Through osmosis?"

Ursula is licking Kevin's face. "Yuck! I'm getting slimed with chocolate. Ack! I'm going to break out."

I look at Kevin for a moment. "Wait a minute! I think I know how Bunny could have died!" I jump up, then stop suddenly. "They wouldn't send a pug to jail, would they?"

"They would have to prove intent," Kevin quips.

"How could you tell with a dog? With a cat I can see."

"That means seven to fourteen years. I wonder if they do it in dog years?" Kevin laughs. "It's still worth it to get your man out of jail."

"We could visit her on weekends."

74

Kevin and I run back in the house with the culprit, Ursula, in tow. I look around. "Where'd the police go?"

"There was a sudden break in at the Flagmore and they took off," Mrs. Weinstein says.

Excited about my latest theory, I ask, "Richard, you're a doctor. Let's say hypothetically a dog—just a random dog—ate someone's leftover 4½ pound lobster dinner then licked a person all over their body to try to revive them, and that person was allergic to shellfish—would it cause them to go into anaphylactic shock?"

Richard knows where I'm going with this and starts laughing.

Trevor breaks our humor. "Does this hypothetical dog also have a good back swing?"

My glee comes to a screeching halt. "Oh. Suppose Hudson tried to poison Bunny, but she never drank the tea that night because someone put real sugar in it. But Hudson doesn't know this until he comes back to check his handy work, only to find her still alive."

Mrs. Weinstein looks at her shoes. "It's so hard to poison someone who's always on a diet."

Mom looks at her warily.

I continue with my theory. "So, Hudson had to quickly find a new method, something faster, like hitting her with a blunt object. The nearest thing is the frozen lamb leg. He hits her over the head, hoping he's killed her, but discovers she's down, but not out. So, he lingers at the house, keeping track of all of the other people dropping by, so he can finish her off—and have someone else to blame."

"So far that makes sense," Irene says. "He'd have to finish the job so she doesn't revive and start staggering around like Quasimodo. It's just like the time I tried to kill a cricket in my bedroom; I only broke one leg off and it made the most pitiful sound all night."

I go on. "So, Bunny is unconscious in the elevator and my trusty pug, not knowing of Bunny's food allergy, tries to revive her."

Richard wraps it up. "And that is what ultimately kills her."

"Great. Only the pug goes to jail," Trevor deadpans as he leaves the room.

"What a relief," Richard says.

"I'll say, I thought I'd get stuck with her," my mother says.

"But isn't hiring a hit pug a crime?" Kevin jokes.

"But, they hired Hudson," I say.

"But *who* initially hired him to kill her?" Mark says.

Mrs. Weinstein looks around. "What if no one in particular did? What if he saw the global demand for her death?"

"What if the Girl Scouts hired him?" Irene jokes. "They make so much off those cookies they could easily hire a hit pug."

"I seriously doubt my Hudson was a hit man for the Girl Scouts," Kevin says in a huff.

Trevor returns with a tray of shrimp and more Pouilly-Fuissé. "I debated what to serve at a homicide hypothesis party."

Mrs. Weinstein grabs a glass and leans in. "Just between us girls, suppose hypothetically some of the ladies played a little game to figure out the most creative way to eliminate someone. Now is that a crime?"

"Mother!" Richard snaps.

413

"I'm sorry, Babka. We were just having a few martinis on my terrace one day."

Irene helps her. "Remember Hudson stayed at Pudge's place? He could have heard from the terrace."

"How was I to know we had a professional killer in our midst?" Mrs. Weinstein defends herself.

"Maybe he thought he was hired," Trevor imparts calmly.

"Mother, you really didn't suggest someone kill my wife?"

Irene, munching on a cookie, mumbles, "Even if Hudson was a professional murderer, he wouldn't kill someone on spec."

I concur. "Yes, usually someone orders the hit, and then makes some sort of payment arrangement."

Richard looks at me. "Is that so?"

I reply, "Someone clearly set Hudson up to kill Bunny. I think it was Ernesto."

I'm starting to think Trevor missed his calling as a defense attorney when he asks, "But why would Ernesto care to have Bunny murdered?"

"What if she was blackmailing him into having sex?"

Mrs. Weinstein slaps her thigh. "I believe it. How else could she get any action."

Richard looks a little embarrassed about that last comment, but goes on with, "But Hudson looks like an unlikely hit man."

"Oh, news flash!" I say, with more than a little zest. "We think Hudson killed Ernesto's mother!"

Kevin is standing in the doorway. "Emma, you are the only one who thinks that; all because he speaks Portuguese and hates Asteroids."

"You lost me," Mark says.

"Someone put rat poison in a tin of mints, causing Ernesto's mother to die right after she won the Brazilian lottery. All the money went to her new husband, who was out of the country at the time, but who could have hired Hudson to poison her. I think Hudson did it because he is a big fat liar and he dyes his hair."

"That's why I've gone gray," Mrs. Weinstein says.

Richard gets up to pace out the theory. "You believe Ernesto set up Hudson for my wife's death so Hudson would go to jail as punishment for killing Ernesto's mother?"

Irene smacks her leg. "Didn't see that coming."

Trevor plays devil's advocate. "But how could Ernesto hire Hudson for a hit without Hudson knowing it was he?"

"Yeah," Mrs. Weinstein agrees, "it's not like he could leave a note; he has the worst grammar and penmanship. I don't think he could even spell out a ransom note if he cut the letters from a magazine."

"Esther, did you know Ernesto stood to inherit a lot of money?" I ask.

Mrs. Weinstein cleans her glasses. "Of course. Do you think I just marry people without doing a little research?"

"He just had to somehow prove that his stepdad hired Hudson," Irene says.

"So why didn't Ernesto just kill his stepdad?" Irene asks.

"It's probably against the law...even in Brazil." Mark says.

"The stepdad died and the money went to his estate," Kevin says.

"By having Hudson on trial for Bunny's murder, that other murder could be investigated. Then his mother's will would be voided and the money would go to Ernesto," Mrs. Weinstein says.

"That's another reason not to kill Hudson straightaway; he might have been the only one to have known," Richard says.

Mrs. Weinstein looks around. "I wonder if that is a good enough defense for my Pumpkin?"

"But we still didn't figure out how Ernesto hired Hudson. He couldn't exactly call from his cell phone," Trevor says, in a display of keen skills.

"What if he used other people's phones," I propose. "Bunny left hers sitting around that night."

"Very clever on his part," Mark says.

"But someone would have recognized his accent," Irene says.

"He could have disguised his voice somehow. You know, with a slow tape recorder," Richard says.

I jump up. "I know! With helium."

Irene cackles. "Someone takes a hit assignment from Pee Wee Herman?"

Trevor sends me to pour everyone more wine, like I'm his assistant.

"As I understand your theory," Trevor says, "by setting up Hudson go to jail for killing Bunny, he was killing two birds with one stone: Hudson goes to jail and Bunny is out of the picture."

"My Pumpkin is pretty smart," Mrs. Weinstein says.

Richard seems frustrated with his mother. "I'm sure Ernesto's actions were still against the law."

I try to stay in good graces with the sparring Weinsteins. "He might not have intended to shoot Hudson."

"Who says he did? It could have been an accident," Mrs. Weinstein argues.

"A trained police officer misses his target at close range?" Richard says doubtfully.

"Let's see...who's a lousy shot?" Mrs. Weinstein says.

"Ping!" Everyone says.

"Maybe Ping shot Hudson so he could have Kevin," Mark says.

Mrs. Weinstein pats her grandson. "Good alibi. You were always were my favorite."

"I doubt anyone would kill for Kevin. Sorry, Kevin," Trevor says.

I float a theory. "Hudson must have figured out while on the yacht that Ernesto set him up, and so Hudson tried to kill him on the yacht by putting boat acid in the pudding. But the dog fell in, so Ernesto didn't eat it. So Ernesto, or Ping—or someone who looks a lot like Esther—had to shoot Hudson to keep him from killing Ernesto, and it also made for retribution for killing Ernesto's mother."

Mother says her head is swimming.

There's a fervent knock on the door, which Trevor goes to answer. He returns with the cops in tow.

"False alarm," Captain Lacey says. "It was strange; we received a call from Ms. Lichtenfelder saying someone was climbing over her balcony. When we got there she said she never called."

"Then she yelled at us, saying we ruined her facial," Perez says.

Captain Lacey winks at Perez. "Let's put her back on the list."

"That's the safest building in town; someone must have made a prank call," Irene says.

I look at Mrs. Weinstein.

"Well, you can never be too sure, what with all the murders going on," she says, eyes darting sideways. She tries to change the subject. "It's not a crime to shoot someone who tried to kill you with sticky pudding is it?"

"Not if you're in a Mrs. Marple novel," Captain Lacey says.

"So, where did we leave off?" Detective Perez says.

Irene fills them in rapidly. "Here's the latest Emma theory: she thinks Hudson was the hit man on Ernesto's mother. Ernesto comes to town to find him, but doesn't want to kill Hudson or he'll end up in jail, so he gets Hudson to kill Bunny, who was blackmailing him for, um, services. But Hudson didn't kill Bunny because she didn't drink her poisoned iced tea. He thought he killed her but didn't—kind of like the cricket in my bedroom—he just knocked her unconscious; so he wasn't going to earn the other emerald earring. Ursula ate Lisa's lobster and tried to revive Bunny, but the lobster gave her anaphylactic shock, and that's what ultimately killed her. And maybe Ping shot Hudson so he could have Kevin."

"I believed everything until the Kevin part," Detective Perez says.

"Do you guys have a way of finding out if Hudson, or Harvey whatever his name was, happened to be in Sao Paulo on or about March 14, 2010?" I ask the cops.

Detective Perez and Lacey excuse themselves to go outside. We can see through the thick green glass as they kick imaginary stones, that they find plausibility.

Mom peers out the window. "I've got my Miracle-Ear back in."

I alert the others. "If she turns it up, she can hear through walls."

"What are they saying?" Irene asks.

Mom repeats verbatim: " 'Shit, that makes sense. Doctor is off the hook. So, we arrest the dog walker, the cook and the old lady. Did you know the old lady's fingerprints were on the Phillips head screwdriver we found?'"

Richard looks at his mother, realizing she was the one to wreck the boat system.

Mom, relishing her new role, goes on: "Now the police officer who looks like the Skipper on Gilligan's Island is talking. 'The cook is a lousy aim. I think he shot the pudding, but not DuPont. And that's not against the law.'"

Mom changes her voice to quote Perez. "'That leaves the old lady and the dog walker. But then the old lady goes and marries him. Damn it!'"

Mrs. Weinstein makes a dash for the front door, but the cops are there waiting outside. She's brought back inside with her tail between her legs.

Mrs. Weinstein clears her throat and makes an announcement. "It sounds like two different people may have shot Hudson. Yeah, should have known Ping was a lousy shot.

So, that leaves me and Pumpkin and good luck getting us to point fingers, or testify."

We're all on the edges of our seats as Trevor refills our glasses.

Mrs. Weinstein continues. "So, boys, you've got no body. Just a dead pan of poison pudding. Oh, and it probably happened in the Bahamas. Do you really want to waste resources on this?"

Right then we hear someone awkwardly playing the piano in Bunny's study.

It's the killer!

No one makes a move to go investigate— until the fearless Irene goes to the "other side."

We cautiously follow…and see her dog, Dr. Phil, tickling the ivories. Well, more like pouncing on the ivories. Richard and Trevor die laughing. Detective Perez and Lacey come running in with their guns drawn.

"You can come out now, Kevin," Perez says.

Captain Lacey is laughing. "Anyone have a knife? We can cut the device off Dr. Weinstein."

"I can do it. I think I left my carving knife here," Kevin says.

"No thank you, Kevin," Richard says. "I'll wait for the key."

"Richard, we need you to keep an eye on your mother. Make sure she doesn't go around shooting hit men," Perez says. "And I suppose we should round up Ernesto, the dog walker," he says to Lacey.

"For what?" Mark says. "Arranging a hit, stealing earrings, and pushing a dead body overboard?"

Perez laughs. "They are crimes."

Mrs. Weinstein is standing in the doorway with her arms crossed. "Good luck finding him, or his passport."

"Do we really want to put a fellow cop in jail?" Captain Lacey says.

As the two cops head out the front door, we hear them laughing.

"Well, he *is* married to Esther. That should be punishment enough," Perez says.

Richard pulls me in and says, "Thank you, sweetie."

"Oh, with all the excitement, I almost forgot," Mom says. From her gigantic purse she unearths a present and hands it to Irene, saying, "Sorry, I couldn't find anything with frogs on it."

Irene begins unwrapping it, babbling away about how she can wear whatever it is with Trevor next month, and that Trevor is afraid of frogs anyway.

"Now that Lisa's wedding is off, I flew here for nothing." Mark says.

"Too bad. Her wedding was all set up and ready to go in Nantucket." Trevor says.

"And I was hoping to cater it," Kevin says.

Mrs. Weinstein gets a little smile. "Richard, why don't you and Emma get married there?"

Richard looks at me, pauses for a while, and finally says, "What a great idea."

He takes my hand and gets down on his ankle bracelet. "Emma, will you be my wife?"

Do I really want to marry into this crazy family?

Mrs. Weinstein quips, "Oye, she has to think about it—after all I went through?"

Irene has finally opened the gift; she holds up a sweater covered with blue butterflies and cries out, "Blue butterflies. It's a sign!"

Richard looks into my eyes.

"Yes," I say.

"Hallelujah!" Mrs. Weinstein shouts.

The End.

Epilogue

June 26, 2014 — Nantucket, MA

The White Elephant hotel has an unusual amount of activity for an early season Saturday. A beautiful, eastern light falls on the marina, where Graham is playing the guitar on the stern of Trevor's boat. Natasha sits next to him, holding mini Graham. They're getting married today at 1:00 on the dock; I'm invited and will be in charge of diapers.

Irene is standing on the bow, her white caftan billowing like a jib in the slight breeze. At 2:00 she is having a ceremony on the boat to formalize marriage with Trevor. Irene is beaming. Who wouldn't? She ended up with Trevor, her daughter has come back from Australia, and she has been declared cancer free.

I'm sharing a room with Kevin, and we're getting ready for the weddings. Actually, I'm waiting for him to finish his bath. When will I learn not to share a room with him? He has been called off service on any catering events, and is to accompany Mark to Lisa's marriage to Ernesto. This was to be the site of her marriage to the sausage heir, until someone named Esther blabbed about her escapades with Ernesto.

Mrs. Weinstein, never one to lose a deposit, suggested she marry Ernesto instead. He was able to avenge his mother's death and ended up with the lottery winnings. Yes, there was that pesky problem of Ernesto being already married to the elder Mrs. Weinstein, but lawyers can come in really handy at times like this.

There's a knock on the door. It's Mother; she's nervous and wants to come in to have me put her necklace on. At 3:00, her weekend Manhattan time, Mom is marrying Captain Lacey in the garden. During the investigation, they discovered they belonged to the same En-Joie golf course in upstate New York.

He remembered an incident where she climbed into the clubhouse window to change someone's score, got her fanny stuck, and he had to help her out.

Detective Perez looks so handsome, with a new haircut revealing his sexy hairline. He's wearing a morning suit. I see the back of a woman in a red dress walking toward him. It's hard to believe it's Big Red. She got some sort of tropical disease and lost forty more pounds. They're getting married in the bar at 4:00. I'm hoping to attend, if I can get in the bathroom in time.

Now I see Ping running across the green lawn. He's wearing a little white tuxedo. It seems love can run faster, as there is Pudge, catching up. His cooking has caused her to gain forty pounds, and now she thinks she's too fat to ever attract a normal man. She's going to re-marry Ping in a ceremony at the church on Centre Street at 5:00.

I haven't had a drink yet, but I think I'm seeing double. I swear I just saw Trevor on the boat, yet I see him far in the distance holding hands with Richard.

My heart drops. I knew this day would come. I had a feeling that day when Trevor turned Richard's piano pages. How am I going to break this to Irene? Might as well have a little something from the mini-bar. Oh, look…a little half bottle of Veuve Clicquot. Won't even look at the price list.

When I look out at the marina again, I burst into laughter. It's not Richard with Trevor—it's his mother, wearing a hat and no glasses, walking with Trevor's blind identical twin from England. They're getting married today at 6:00 on Richard's yacht.

Now I see Richard. He's walking toward the sea. He keeps walking. I hope it's not like James Mason in *A Star Is Born*, where he just walks into the ocean and dies. I mean, I *really* don't, considering he's supposed to get married at the Nantucket Yacht Club at 7:00. To me.

Made in the USA
Charleston, SC
03 January 2015